A Fox Song

Written by Avi Albert

Illustrated by Stefanus B.

RPSS Publishing - Buffalo, New York

I dedicate this book to the special people who stood by me, unwavering and steadfast, even in the darkest of times. Your support, love, and belief in me never faltered, and you were my strength when I could find none. You carried me through my turmoil, never giving up on me, even when I struggled to believe in myself. This work is for you- your kindness, your patience, and your unwavering faith have made all the difference. Thank you for being my constant, my anchor, and my light when the world seemed hollow.

publisher@rockpapersafetyscissors.com

A Fox Song - Perfect Bound

ISBN: 978-1-956688-42-9

Printed in the United States of America

10 9 8 7 6 5 4 3 2 1

RPSS Publishing - Buffalo, New York

CONTENTS

THE COPPER FOXES

Late, it was midnight's glee. In winter's finest gloom,

Thou poor brother foxes, are they off so swift, Far from their bunker of twisted roots, Hopelessly adrift...

Scour for ye father and mother in dour unknown— Gone...

They are gone,

Drifting, drifting as if alone...

O' what had befallen Thee, hapless kits?

Tread lightly over the newly slick cotton snow. No light...

No light...

They call and call, No answer...

No answer yet replies.

But the cruel, taunting moans From the whipping wind beside.

Keep to your strength, young, fearless foxes,

Keep to your spirit and tread on through the gloomy,

Bloodstained soil—Too deep, Too deep,

In unlit pits and trenches, toiling steep. O' poor brother foxes!

Your copper coat with frozen stain Cannot stop the freezing pain.

No sight again you find,

No sight at all to ease your troubled minds—

Blinded by the heavy, twirling snowfall,

A family divided...

Divided... abandoned.

List they do to the weary moan

Of hunger, cold, and biting breath.

They strain against their path of death.

Be wary, junior foxes, There are dangers abound... Make not a sound...

Hither and thither,

Eyes may glance a' thee And send thee to eternity!

On yonder frightful fen, Thinks thee hear voices again.

Hither and thither,

Unknown as from a devil den,

Hear the ghoulish howl of hounds marked ten,

Prowling, growling, out hunting then.

Cursed foul fiends starve for bitter blood—

Silent ye wait for thine own good!

Yet above it all, within the storm, A shadow looms—a dreadful form.

O tyrant who grins behind the swarm.

Your malice reigns, your hate still warm.

The master of hounds, who laughs at their cries,

Feeds on despair as another soul dies.

If together bound, might ye strive— Together ye may alive stay.

If together yet ye might give,

Each another's life may last the day

Chapter One

Strange Contraption

On one drowsy, misty late spring afternoon that felt around four o'clock or so but was only a quarter past two, to be precise. The day slowly droned on, where a second felt like a minute, and a minute felt like an hour. A Hare with a fine cinnamon-brown coat named Wally was dressed in blue jean overalls and a straw hat that hung closely above his lazily closing eyes. As the cool breeze stroked through his soft, wispy fur, he chewed on a long stem of sweet grass. He was comfortably resting beneath a large maple tree whose green leaves were just beginning to show. He found himself half-asleep on top of a small hill in a nestled, hidden highland valley where grass felt as smooth as velvet. The blowing leaves of the bending tree covered the ever-so- glittering sun that gleamed brightly from above. The sounds of this gorgeous, sleeping meadow blooming with tranquility were of no one sound, but all of nature's pleasant, alluring sounds.

Lightheartedly, the birds flew high and above, chirping gaily. The buzzing and whirring of swarming insects, which pollinated and flitted about, could be distinguished amidst the general ambiance. The insects were headed towards the nearby flower groves scattered throughout the valley's meadows.

The harmonizing sound of the rushing brook named the Bromby River softly filled the afternoon hours. The river sparkled and glistened like a dark blue emerald illuminated by the sun. It curved through the valley's center, splitting it into two halves. Bromby River ran with small rippling waterfalls gently sloping across the spaces where the rocks and reeds formed ponds well- nigh full of the late spring spawn of bluegills and black bass. Sweet, pink rainbow trout swam quietly by the stream and jumped and sprung above the Crestwick Bridge, which arched over the stream. Within the tiny cottages of the warm-hearted river creatures, inhabitants with good-natured faces and pleasant demeanors were the ones who spent the long day daydreaming, working, and happily singing. By night, there were often songs and celebrations of each season, and other songs were played at different times for joyous reasons, for each creature had their song to sing.

The cottages were nestled into hillsides in little burrows spread about in small clusters throughout the valley. In secluded little neighborhoods, there were small plots of land with hedgerows, walls of rough fieldstones, and welcoming archways before each entry path to each home. The houses that sat on higher ground were carefully edged by small sections of timbers that retained tamped earth, making a charming stairway, which was intriguing to behold; it gave one a feeling of quaintness hinged by an inevitable curiosity of what and who might be within each domicile. Wooden lampposts that lit the valley by night could be found in every street.

Minor hand-painted and rough marking signs displayed the name of each street through this valley that genuinely had the softest and most fertile ground on this side of the world, which has never been known to only the fortunate ones who live there. Low green mountains could be seen in a distant view. On chilly autumn days, these same hills burst forth in a glory of red, orange, and yellow as little chimneys in the distance released pale, wispy smoke, belying the warm hearths within each home. Such was a familiar scene for as long as anyone could remember and seemed to have existed long before written history. Thus, the name given to this alluring and elegant valley is called by a name that completely describes a rare and rustic beauty, Ambrodale.

Wally, the Hare, was also highly regarded by his friend Sampson, the sleepy-headed grump of a Moose. Sampson was a very soft-spoken, gentle creature. Despite his colossal size, he was friends with all the creatures of the wood because of his kind and mild temperament. Sampson was also slow-moving, very thoughtful, and warmhearted. He often laughed with deep-throaty laughs. He also had a quiet side to his personality, pondering and asking himself, with his deep, husky voice, odd questions he could never figure out. Sampson would engage in a philosophical monologue as he thudded around the valley, which shook it in a series of rumbling aftershocks. He considered all the creatures of the meadow his friends. A philosopher by nature, he disliked causing pain to any being and carefully avoided situations that might disrupt others. If it could be said that way, his only foe was the blistering winter season that seemed to roll in from the far-off hills quickly. When such a time came, he always muttered, "Oh, how much I hate the cold!" All the dreary day long. With the falling of snow, Sampson would retreat into his cave, rarely to be seen in the winter days; he would only appear to gather food and afterward spend his days in his cave until the snow melted away. Sampson was highly thought of by the creatures as an authority figure with very clever thinking and a kind heart to go along. His other friend, Booney, the speckled Frog, was quite the opposite of old' "Sampso" Moose. Unlike Sampson, Booney was spontaneous, energetic, opinionated, and inappropriate at times (he spoke what he carelessly thought). He was always seeking an adventure or two. Stopping daily at "Pheniggan's Pub" or, as most locals called it, "Phenny's." Almost all the creatures of Ambrodale went there to see what news was happening, if any. But most went to get together and have celebrations for whatever reason. The creatures always had celebrations for any lovable and, by now, a frequent occurrence. However, Booney could be a very egotistical, self-centered, eccentric, whiny, small- minded fellow. But he was mostly a boor.

The egotistical Frog always slowly strutted into the bar (casually appearing). He wore a red suit uniquely tailored to his liking. A boater hat with a red ribbon was always slightly tilted to the right, covering his small head as he waved his black walking cane (though he rarely ever used and carried it. Really, he only used it when he felt like it! It was never ever necessary for him to use or own it as everyone knew). He strutted around and hopped along in a high fashion way. But he was not even remotely high-fashioned whatsoever. After making his big entrance, boasting about his appearance, he would abruptly and invariably say, "How do ye do today, fine gents?" He would then follow with a cheeky grin as he commented on his "dashing" appearance. However, after such a display, the river creatures would usually not respond for the sake of becoming much too formidable, as they already were to the Frog. He was not such a lovable, charming character as he highly thought he was. Indeed, he was misled by his overt self pride, thinking of how the other creatures valued him. In truth, the creatures felt the exact opposite of what he thought of himself. His foolish impressions were to be held accountable if anything went wrong. The creatures of the wood turned their heads away, despising such a show. It could feel as if no one was there at all, coldly leaving the Frog to only talk and ramble to himself. After a while of Booney's gin drinking and his made-up tales, he would bombard the listener (if any) with more stories. It was certainly not the stories he told that was the problem. No, not at all! Most were quite amusing. But how loud and obnoxious he babbled in his unintelligible knack that would drive the listener off without saying toodle-oo!

Thanks to his big mouth and general lack of sense, he usually got in a few scuffles or two. He usually began by insulting someone with rude comments and remarks out of his sheer drunkenness and belligerence. Nor would he halt his sarcasm. He was quite stubborn and bullheaded (and how Wally or Sampson had ever put up with it, no one knew or bothered to know). Sampson and Wally would eventually have to break up the scuffle to save their friend.

Those in conflict would retreat without hesitation when they saw big ol' Sampson rumbling in, asking, "What's going on here?" Though too large to get into the small bar stationed in a toppled and hollowed-out, mature, red oak log (Sadly, though in a way, not large enough to accommodate the colossal Moose), Phenny's Pub was where the weasels, water rats, and other small rodents often gathered in the evening, carrying on conversations of their own. They were invariably waited on by a bartender named Murry, who was to be a gossip-loving yet kind badger. The giant Moose often jammed his head through the round window, but only his jellied nose and droopy maw could fit due to his antlers. With his space, he would take a deep hissing inhalation, puff out his cheeks, and let fly the loudest bellow ever heard in those parts. Such a bellow would shake the interior of the crowded bar, thus stopping the assault or bickering involving Booney as the many patron's jaws dropped. Inevitably, the uninitiated would cower away and scurry out the door.

Even though Sampson was Booney's friend, he did not quite appreciate Booney's immaturity and did not get along with him as well (as some, like Wally, wished) as he did with others. Always being very strict as a teacher with Booney and never tolerating any negligent behavior, he often tried to teach Booney right from wrong. Though with no such luck to prevail. Booney's wit and mischievous cunning always outsmarted the old temperate-natured Moose. Booney would simply ignore Sampson's daily teachings and instructions, either covering his Froggy ears or making a quite annoying loud humming sound to drown it out. This tactic often did the trick to stop Sampson's sermon, but it usually led to them arguing about Boone's childlike behavior.

Sampson would frequently advise Booney regarding his careless actions. "Booney, when will you ever learn? Whatever you give, you shall receive." The Moose could not help but strictly scold him when Booney appeared again in trouble.

However, Booney needed to understand that advice: "Oh, sure thing, Sampso!

An' what does that mean?" The speckled Frog would ask, turning to Wally, who was also at a loss to solve the problem of Booney's recalcitrant troublemaking!

Anyway, that describes his friends, but not Wally. Wally could not be described like Sampson nor Booney. Wally was shrewd yet an optimist who always believed in the better part of things and that everything would eventually work out for the better. The jumpy brown Hare with lop black-tipped ears (that were so long and dangly that it was to be seen as though they were hovering as he bounced merrily through the wood and looked rather silly. It was much of a burden than a joy for the Hare to see his ears so long and floppy that he had to sometimes bundle his ears and tuck them into his hat so they wouldn't get in the way). Like Booney, he was adventurous, though unlike Booney, he was very cheerful and never sarcastic. He was whimsical, but just like his Frog friend, he was always on the road for no apparent reason but to suit his taste of the moment (though the rest of the inhabitants of the wood thought the Hare and surely his Froggy friend were absurd and most strange for their restless habits of seeking an adventure or two.) Stranger still to them were the intriguing tales both told upon returning to their cozy woodland homes. The creatures did not want nor yearn for such wild adventures; life within Ambrodale was entirely satisfying. Such was their way; there was no need to know or bother to know the happenings of the broader world beyond where they saw the peaks of the mountains. Their daily lives kept them well occupied, and, what's more, they were mostly happy.

Meanwhile, the Moose, Sampson, like the other creatures, would never be on the road for more than a day. An adventure in Ambrodale was plenty for him. Like Sampson, Wally knew the difference between right or wrong actions and the consequences involving both. Wally loved to have fun and tell jokes. Everyone was aware of that side of Wally. Wally was also a rather forgetful Hare, and if something special wasn't on his daily calendar, he was sure to forget his plans if not reminded.

Once, during Wally's annual day of lounging about until suppertime, nothing was exactly on his mind. He stared endlessly with a blank mind, which showed in his dulled expression at the shape-shifting clouds drifting on this long day. After a couple of hours of relaxation, a deep voice called his name, mindlessly gawking at the bright blue sky since noon and a quarter past. Wally jumped up in excitement, wondering who it might be!

"Sampson!" He yelled, thrillingly waving his paws to greet the Moose who slowly sauntered on the dirt path that strays far and beyond below the hill. It went along and past the maple planted on top of the hill, standing next to the bubbling brook. Quickly dashing down to meet his friend, he pronounced the same old greetings. "How are ya taday me friend?" And so on.

"Just on my afternoon stroll. There's nowhere to go," was the soft reply, spoken through a sleepy yawn.

"Ohhh, how most delightful!" Wally remarked, hopping from one spot to another as he excitedly circled Sampson. "May I join you?" He asked briefly with a delightful smile that brightly lighted his face. Sampson replied with a shake of his furry head and a raise of his massive hoof pointing to his back. Wally quickly jumped onto the giant Moose's colossal back with contentment as Sampson bent down low so Wally could sit on him without displeasure or concern. However, the giant Moose's back was too big to spring onto. Wally jumped and jumped with no such luck as he stumbled, fumbled, and staggered down countless times. Wally kept trying until, at last, he succeeded as he gripped Sampson's fur for support and slowly climbed up for the third time.

"Third time is a charm!" Wally chuckled as he got ideally situated on Sampson's back. Sampson nodded in agreement.

"It is for sure."

With Wally comfortably seated on Sampson now, the old Moose looked back, stomped his legs for good measure, and then marched slowly. He dawdled along with the spare time, which they both had plenty of to spare. He had dawdled since spring cleaning had ended not long ago, and they both merrily laughed as they talked and joked about their cleaning. "No more brooms, dusters, or spring tools!" Wally said with a chuckle.

"And no more aches and pains of the back or weary and tiresome arms and feet to complain about!" Sampson added.

They walked down the dirt path with nothing to talk about, just small talk, because there was nothing really to talk about. Nothing exciting or new had taken place in the glen, so they just roamed aimlessly.

"I've never seen such a pleasant day like this before in my long life!" Sampson stated as he looked astonished at the change of seasons that flew by as fast as they rolled in.

The trees danced and shook with endless motion as the soft breeze passed through the young green canopy of leaves. Endlessly, they talked and talked and talked about this and that, asking each other about their past week's experience. Had anything new recently come up? "No" was the usual answer, with nothing new to say. It was the same old stories and tales they passed to each other. For nothing unique and eccentric ever visited. They slowly strolled along the riverbank, nodding and greeting the fellow neighborhood creatures who passed by for their own business. Schedules for nut collecting, burrowing, or something else of that nature had to be completed. Wally, who loved to sing and dance all and all, always to have a good time, had a song in his heart. He started to sing and sang it only when there was bound to be an adventure or two nearby.

"Foot by foot Tail by tail

Each to his own upon the trail Crossing hill and trickling stream Till we meet upon the Dale."

Moments later, a very unusual contraption painted the deepest red they had ever witnessed before flew and spiraled above. A strange, thick, greyish-white cloud seemed to trail from behind the flying contraption in a series of irregular puffs. This peculiar contraption stretched with a long round beak, exposing its inner functioning mechanical gears in front and a strange three- sided tail, stroking up and down from behind. A white propeller spun rapidly that seemed to keep it aloft. It was tightly clamped onto the circular beak. This machine had a funny-looking pair of wings, or should I say one long, divided, extended wing; bolted struts attached it to the fuselage. Flaps of the wing would rise, and fall based on the pitch of its chosen direction. The sound issuing from its smoke-belching motor was that of a thousand beehives filled with angry buzzing bees. The contraption was driven by the most unusual-looking creature they had ever seen before. It was wearing a brown leather pilot helmet. This creature had a long snout. His strange furry paws gripped the "Wooden Bird's" (is how they called it) control as if in some unknowable hurry in quick haste.

"How very odd!" Sampson declared as he suddenly stopped and stood in the middle of a meadow. He was looking at the contraption with big, open eyes.

Wally said in excitement, "Hmm… I have never, ever, ever seen anything like it! I reckon to believe it's something wild, like a wooden bird or something! Yet, what is that funny-looking creature that rides it?!"

He also stared at the aerodynamics and the tricks the wooden bird proudly showed and displayed as it spiraled in circles, up and down, left and right. Like a corkscrew, it zoomed and zigzagged above. The two were astonished and bewildered by it all. Then, after a couple of good long minutes that felt like hours of gawking, the strange doohickey zoomed so fast that it had sparks flying from behind it. Posthaste, it immediately vanished in the sky, beyond a thicket of tall trees, near the end of where the river seemed to stop flowing! That was a bleak place, a curse among the fine Riverfolk where nobody went or would bother to. It was a deserted, muggy, insect- ridden fen named Gorse-End.

An old Owl by the name of Ben, who was the eldest and wisest of the creatures, never strayed too long but only for a short while. He too often traveled alone into other valleys. Ben stood stiffly on a tree branch above, watching without so much as a blink as the two animals conversed back and forth with one another. They suddenly noticed the quiet, staring Owl and approached him, introducing themselves naturally as one might do with friendly tidings.

"Pardon, Ol' Ben." Wally happily remarked, standing on Sampson's back.

Sampson also stared at the Owl, who kept rotating his fluffed head in circles, fluffing his ruffled feathers and picking them afterward.

"Ye…s?" He gasped, tilting his head. "Did you glimpse that flying contraption that flew by?" Wally hurriedly asked.

"Aye… indeed…I… did!"

"Well! Can you please tell us what that is exactly?!" Wally asked. "I… can!" Old Ben slowly responded with a big, exhausting sigh.

Waiting for an answer, they cried, "Well, go on, please tell us!" Wally jumped peevishly, awaiting a direct reply. Wally was not a patient Hare!

"Hold on, their young one… I'm not as young… as I used to be!" Old Ben interrupted.

In his exhaustion and catching his breath, He was disturbed by how impatient Wally was. Old Ben was by far the slowest-speaking animal ever encountered around Ambrodale.

"Why… it's an… auroplane!" Old Ben slowly answered, his giant eyes wincing as he shook his head in grief.

"Why this auroplane you speak of…what is it?" Sampson asked in confusion, standing on his hind legs while looking up at Ben.

Wally quickly jumped off the moving Moose's hump and stood next to him.

"The sight… of an auroplane …means danger… and nothing more… Be wary, my young curious friends… Be wary of the danger awaiting," he cautiously whispered.

The warning Owl hooted as if he had seen it before, spreading out his long, feathered wings, which seemed ready to take flight. He repeated the words of danger louder this time and flew now, flapping his wings between the trees of the distant wood. He disappeared through the thicket of bristly branches, which were tangled upon each of their twisted and knotted ends.

Chapter Two
Floating Down the River

The glaring sunshine struck hot on Sampson's and Wally's backs. The soft breeze whisked through their fur and brows. They silently stood beneath the tree from where the Owl hooted the warning, shaded now from the sun. They were still at a loss to understand what an auroplane exactly was.

"Maybe Booney saw it! Let's go ask him!" Wally sprung up, shouting with pleasure, wanting to see his friend. His flopping ears stood up and pointed like two straight arrows, and his open arms raised high.

"Oh, bother. Must we? Why t'at frug is too selfish to look at anything other t'an his own reflection!" Sampson moaned and groaned, huffed and puffed.

"Oh, come now, Sampson, Boone's not all that bad!" Wally strongly encouraged the grouchy, mumbling Moose.

"Very well, my young friend… very well." Sampson sighed, rolling his deep brown eyes and kneeling on the ground once more so Wally could leap onto the large hump on Sampson's back. Regretting the decision made, he tramped on forward.

"Oh, joyous day, how splendid!"

After moments of lumbering through the meadow, they both heard humming, a very familiar hum, in fact. It was none other than Ralph, the Hedgehog! Nibbling on a cracked apple by the side of an apple tree in the corner of the dirt path, hidden by a bush.

"Hello, 'ere Ralph!" They both greeted simultaneously.

The nervous Hedgehog jumped and yelped. He scoured to his left and peeked to the right, quickly covering his grubby apple with twigs and leaves so no one would come upon it and steal it when his back was turned. Then, with one hop out of the bush, "Oh, oh my!" Ralph nervously replied shakily. His breath became even more chopped and quick, not that it already wasn't.

"How are you on this fine day, Ralph?" Sampson slowly asked, twisting his contorted body as he tried to peek behind the skittish Hedgehog (who was much more skittish than intended, I assure you), wondering what he was hiding

"G-Good… good… nothing behind me or anything n-nope not one thing! Ya could check if you would like!!" He promptly offered as he stuttered, falling upon each and every word. His double personality would scold him for saying the rest, "O, stupid, stupid, stupid… how stupid!" Ralph said agitatedly, himself in disarray and hitting the top of his head. He craned back to where he buried his apple with concerned eyes.

"Very good, very good." Sampson quickly answered, "Well, we should probably be on our way now!" He looked back at Wally, who nodded in agreement.

"That's a great idea. A very great idea! Be on your way now! Oh, I do mean with kindest regards!" Ralph jittered, stomping his foot in a fast-paced, skittish beat and quietly muttering. Ralph was still looking back as he waved goodbye waggishly at the same time, shooing them away as quickly as they had come. Then, as Sampson and Wally continued, Ralph, being fearful as he was, promptly dashed back to his apple, making sure no one had thieved it and munched on it. In a scrambled, persistent, self-doubting voice, he simply nervously laughed, "Oh, my. Oh my, oh my!"

"What a very odd fella that Hedgehog is!" Wally cheerfully remarked, chuckling, looking back at Ralph. He snarled and hissed defensively at any sniffing oncomer who might have accidentally gotten much too close for comfort to his intended meal. A few steps of strolling, chatting, and viewing went by. Before long, an interruption of a whistle whipped through the air, carried by the softly blowing breeze. The whistle was shrill and familiar and seemed to come floating down the river. Both animals observed a small raft gliding across and over the calming river as if bound by a peculiar spell. Coming near this drifting raft, Wally quickly darted off Sampson's back and ran towards it. Sampson charged on behind. A song, clearly out of key, could be heard dreamily sung.

Hee hee hee, and ho ho ho,

To the Rainbow Valley, off I go! Ha ha ha, deedle dee dee,

What a fine, fine day it is to me. With a hey-ho-hee and a fin-fin-fee, Down the stream, I wander free.

I ponder here, I ponder there,

With naught but time and the open air.

With a hey hum holly and a skiddle dum dee, A picnic basket rests under my knee.

Stuffed with muffins and brimming with tea, What a fine, fine feast it's going to be!

"Booney!" Wally shouted in joyous laughter. He was happy to see his Froggy friend.

There was no reply from the whistling speckled Frog resting on the raft. Booney continued to sing lazily, lying on his side. Entranced by his reflection, at which he mindlessly gawked, hypnotized. The chattering river almost replied for him in a rhythmic melody.

He held a long fishing pole, gripped by his webbed toes tied tightly around a red handkerchief. The line was strung and cast into the river while its bait swayed afloat atop the waters. Though rather strangely, the bait was already long ago swallowed by Booney, considering it was an insect, after all. The daydreaming Frog caught each buzzing fly that zoomed and dashed busily around him. Each catch ended with a sizeable smiling smirk of satisfaction on his face. "Ah, I love flies so delectable and fine, yes sir 'e!" Booney croaked, smacking his lips with much delight as he loudly gulped the last of the flies. He patiently counted each fly he had eaten.

"Ah, fourteen, what a delicious number." He declared, patting and rubbing his pot belly that slumped over his unbuttoned red jacket in a sag.

"See what did I tell you!" Sampson retorted in a groan, shaking his head in shame. Booney looked up. "Why hullo t'ere fellas! My compadres! Come! See the world! Travel!

Explore!!!" The grinning Frog cheekily answered, waving hello with his little flimsy paddle. He

started to row towards them. Wally waved back with a smile, but Sampson was not impressed nor excited by him.

"Hello, 'ere friend! We will be right there! Come, Sampson!"

Sampson paced ponderously along the riverbank, then clambered into the old rowboat with a gruff sigh of relaxation. The Moose's massive weight caused the boat to dip dangerously low into the water, but with an immense splash, Sampson settled himself in. He gripped the oars and began to row with slow, steady strokes, the boat cutting through the cold water.

Wally perched on the boat's edge, holding on tight as Sampson rowed them toward Booney's floating raft anchored in the middle of the river.

Once they reached it, Wally quickly transferred from the rowboat onto the raft and sat beside Booney, who made room for him. Their hanging feet rested, carried by the soft current of the rippling river. Cattails shot straight up nearby, and a cluster of surrounding wildflowers dropped their petals and hung low on both sides of the Bromby River. The river tickled their dragging feet as water spiders quickly skittered by, along with the rest of the dashing river insects.

"How are ya today, Booney?" Wally asked, leaning back.

"Not too shabby, my compadre, not too shabby, I must admit!" Booney replied, twiddling his thumbs and gazing at his reflection in the water with high hubris. It was no surprise to see him romantically glaring at his distorted, watery image, love-struck by his own appearance.

"By the way, Boone, did ya happen ta' see a strange bird flying above you earlier today?" Wally asked, curious.

Booney thought and thought some more, unable to recall, and simply replied, "Not that I was aware of or can recall… I was much too busy, much so!"

"With what?!" Sampson interrupted, his voice booming.

"Hmm… well… I forgot!" Booney shrugged, still staring at his watery reflection.

Sampson sighed a great big sigh, closing his great big eyes. In moments, he began to snore noisily, his deep snores reverberating across the river. The bright midday sun hung overhead, casting warm golden rays that sparkled on the calm water. The rowboat, small and weathered, rocked gently beneath him, its oars resting idly in the locks as the breeze pushed it slowly along.

The day was still, save for the occasional splash of a fish breaking the surface or the soft rustle of leaves from the distant shore. The sunlight bathed Sampson in a warm glow, highlighting the rough lines of his face as he lay sprawled out, his massive form almost too large for the narrow boat. His head lolled to the side, one hoof draped over the edge of the boat, trailing lazily in the cool water.

A dragonfly buzzed past, briefly landing on the tip of his nose before darting away again. Sampson snorted, deep in his slumber. The boat drifted onward, the sunlight glinting off the water and creating a dappled reflection that danced across Sampson's broad chest as he snored on, oblivious to the world around him.

Agitated, Booney scowled at the tremendous old sleeping Moose. Leaning toward the river, he scooped up some water with his paddle and splashed it onto Sampson's face. Startled, Sampson jerked awake. "I was having a brilliant dream. Why did you wake me?" The Moose demanded fiercely, glaring at Booney, who just smiled innocently and quickly hid the wet paddle behind his back. The Frog whistled nonchalantly, pretending nothing had happened.

Wally chuckled in amusement and slapped Booney on the shoulder.

The Crestwick bridge slowly came into sight as they drifted beneath its stone-walled arch.

After the stone bridge was past them, it was followed by a peculiar cottage. The ramshackle look of it made it appear to be abandoned. An odd smoldering smoke cloud gently wisped from the inside as it arose from the crumbling stone chimney. They had never noticed the house until now as it stood by the side of the river. Trimmed bushes and shrubs hid the edges of its threshold.

Wally noticed something that was not to be easily seen, and it was not seen at all by the sleepy Moose nor by the self-indulgent Booney. Wally glimpsed a pair of sly-looking, color- mismatched eyes peering at him. The left eye happened to be green, but the right eye was blue as ice, glimmering at him. The eyes gradually grew into an outline of a funny-looking head. It stiffly observed Wally from within the rustling, tangled green bushes near the house. Both eyes intensely stalked the movement of the three friends unblinkingly. The staring eyes gave Wally a painful, dreadful chill from behind like a stabbing knife's sharp, jagged pain. A feeling of uneasiness transpired, and a specific unexplainable worry ensued. Enthralled by curiosity, Wally was incapable of ignoring their situation. Still hidden yet, then suddenly, two twitching red ears popped up.

The tips of those ears had patches and streaks of black. By the sound of a silent whimper, the strange creature retreated into an unseen tuft of the Sullen Fields (Boulder Fields). The Sullen Fields was an abandoned dreary wood that crept southwards on the opposite side of the river to

Ambrodale. Below the rustling meadows and the green fairgrounds after that, as large as an eye could see, its rocky borders were strewn along the sides of Gorse-End. It was dreadfully bleak, unexplored, and uncharted by the likes of anyone. The river animals lived in fear of such a frightening place so close to their cozy homes. They lived in fear of the unknown sickness and an unexplainable foreboding that was said to dwell in the physically disfigured miasmic landscape. Strangely, after the creature had fled, so too did his enchantment, and Wally could not recollect anything from his now-drained thoughts. He could say nothing of what he had just observed. "It was just my imagination playing tricks with me!" He said, lifting himself up and reflexively wiping away the memory of the dizzying gaze witnessed by his watery eyes.

After the bridge and the mysterious cottage were past them, it was inevitable at that drifting time that the all-unknown territory of the Sullen Fields became a frightening reality. The glimmering light of the countryside dimmed and slowly faded. The decrepit trees were taller and more horrific than the ones the three were well used to. The trees now seemed to have many hidden, abhorrent expressions twisted amongst the bark. The golden light of day turned into the grim darkness of nightfall.

"We should probably be turning 'round about now!" Sampson announced in a deep and nervous tone, looking back from where they had started. He began slowly and steadily paddling backward from where they had drifted to.

"Come now... ye deadbeat Moose! Where is yer fearless spirit? Ye ol' senile baggy codger!" Booney nastily remarked, calling him every dirty name in the book of dirty names.

"Oooooh! Your impertinence... watch your tongue... you... you!!" Sampson bellowed, struggling to come up with an insult to hurl at Booney, who stood on the shore with a smirk of self-satisfied pride.

Booney waited for Sampson's unspoken retort, but instead, the Moose let out a loud grunt of frustration. Just then, the rowboat, with Sampson still inside, struck a submerged boulder with a jarring crash. The impact sent the boat lurching violently, and water surged in, soaking Sampson and causing the boat to start breaking apart.

Sampson flailed his massive hooves, trying to stabilize the rowboat as it began to splinter and sink. The Moose's attempts to keep the boat afloat only made matters worse, sending more water gushing in.

"Come, come, fellas... we're all friends here. There's no need for a fight floating right out here in the middle of the stream!" Wally called out from the shore, trying to diffuse the situation amid the chaos. The bickering was momentarily forgotten as Sampson grappled with the rapidly disintegrating boat.

Chapter Three
A Marshland Adventure

The river soon dried up, its water seeping into the cracks of the dirt, forming muddy puddles in the uneven ground. Marshlands surrounded the gloomy; the humidity was unbearable. Dark,withering trees carried the cold wind and the displeasing vapors of the swampland. Black ravens cawed as they sat above, clutching the twisted branches overlooking the three; their eerie shadows hid the cackling ravens.

Embarked on the dry shore, the two friends Sampson and Wally gathered in the circle as Booney parked his raft on the side of the plateau and then joined them after doing so.

"Oooooh! I knew it would be a wretched mistake to take advice from an immoral giant nematode like yourself, Booney! I just knew something bad would happen if, for once, I made the wrong decision to tag along! And now, we are lost! You never get things right...you do NOT...LOOK AT THIS GLOOMY, DOOMY, WRETCHED PLACE". Sampson dramatically declared in a resentful growl, for he most hated being lost. Sampson Moose abruptly heard a strange screeching sonance hammering in his head, so acutely excruciating it felt like his crying ears would start to bleed, beyond straining to endure; it seemed to control his wavering emotions that were conserved, well-ordered, somehow manipulate them into a particular beguilement of his most undesirable motives, during such a brainwashing state his unreasoning anger he held erupted, bursting into a beast he charged Booney. In a panic, the Frog scrambled up a nearby tree, perching himself on a low-hanging branch. From his new vantage point, Booney began to taunt the Moose—hardly the brightest idea, but being Booney, he didn't know any better. He grabbed a handful of large, spiky pinecones, aiming them at Sampson and pelting him one after another, laughing all the while. To Booney, it was all in good fun, but the already enraged Moose only grew more furious.

Sampson, eyes wild, lowered his head and began ramming the tree with immense force. Booney, clinging desperately to the branch, lost his grip and tumbled to the ground with a thud. For a brief moment, he tried to calm the beast, realizing too late the danger he was truly in.

But Sampson, unable to control his growing rage, let out a guttural bellow and pinned the helpless Frog to the wet, muddy earth with a swift thrust of his antlers. Booney gasped as Sampson's massive hoof pressed down on his chest, his once playful taunts now a distant memory as he struggled beneath the crushing weight.

"Lumme go ye biggie, ol' galoot!" The squirming Frog yelled. Tightly clutched, Booney wiggled and wobbled. His jiggling legs jerked violently, but his lack of strength, especially to Sampson's unmatched power, was his undoing.

Booney trembled as Wally tried to intervene and quell the ongoing quarrel from behind the two creatures. He was utterly flabbergasted by Sampson's sudden violent outburst; he had never witnessed anything like it. It was as if something mysteriously changed, as if a bewitching spell empowered Sampson's brute, unknown action.

Booney pleaded with the Moose to spare him, with no such luck. Then, with a sharp look of Booney's weeping expression, suddenly, the transcendental screeching sound ceased its torment, and Sampson was brought back to his usual self. His angry, narrowed eyes showed great tension and then suddenly became relaxed, glazed, and comfortable once again. He immediately let go of the speckled Frog that immediately ran behind Wally. In a quavering voice, the Frog exclaimed, "Next time, I'm bringing me fishie knife to defend meself!"

Sampson himself was dumbstruck by his recent actions. "I 'ave never felt t'at way before; I do not know what just came over meself... Boone, I deeply... I deeply apologize for my disturbing and quite frightening conduct." Sampson clumsily sat in a stupor from where he stood and hung his head low with the most profound remorse from this incomprehensible, dishonorable act that had seemed to cloud his current state of mind. While the two quickly made up as Booney had also apologized, Wally investigated the bizarre environment they were lost within.

"The trees..." he murmured, scrutinizing the mangled, crevassed trunks. Their twisted forms seemed to radiate an ominous force still unknown to him. He wasn't sure where he'd heard the unsettling rumors, but an uneasy feeling gnawed at him, refusing to be quelled. A shiver ran down his spine each time he examined the withered bark.

"It's the trees!" Wally shouted back, drawing Sampson and Booney's attention. "Come again?" Sampson asked, frowning.

"I reckon the trees are behind your violent outburst, Sampson!" Wally said, his voice tinged with urgency.

"And what makes you say that?" Sampson demanded, pacing back and forth. Just then, a shadowy figure flitted across the marshland, briefly glimpsed from the corner of an eye.

"Some books I've read mentioned that certain trees can provoke hysteria when one is alone in a forest, being closed in and all that," Wally explained. "I never believed it until now. Besides, we've never seen a place like this; just heard tales of such a wicked wood!"

"All in all, this spot seems too dangerous to explain here. I can feel something is listening to us, and it's bothering me; let's keep moving!" Quavered Wally, transfixed rather frightened as he gazed around the wickedly demented surroundings that embodied an unshakable and unearthly guise. "How can an unsavory climate exist so close to our dear tranquil Ambrodale!? From now on, I think we should avoid this mucky pit!" Asked Sampson Moose observantly, "It's downright repulsive! How utterly unbelievable!" and that Gorse End was made of everything melancholy. Hungry for fear, this acrid-fumed swamp could engender tenacious phobias and metamorphose them into a mirrored reality! Such was the ghoulish power of this grim marsh! The trio trekked deeper into Gorse End, unaware of the many future dangers.

Traveling further in the uncharted marsh, they soon became groggy and disoriented. Each of them began thinking strange thoughts while feeling the spleen of strong emotions as the predatory Gorse End seemed to bedevil and warp their fragile senses. Fostered by its preternatural sorcery, Booney was its second target. The ethers of the swamp ruthlessly lashed out with wicked supremacy while he nervously shuffled along with his friends. They quickly noticed something not quite right about him. Booney seemed to be significantly disturbed, as if the poor Frog's being was being subjected to such terrors. He desperately tried to contain what he heard, felt, and saw. Still, the power of the wasteland had such an overwhelming intensity that it multiplied the natural nervous temperament of the Frog, making him jittery. Like a ragdoll in a windstorm, it manipulated him against his will.

Quivering and pleading for protection, the airs of Gorse End began draining his willpower. Suddenly, in an all-out eruption, Booney began hyperventilating, making a bellows-type wheezing sound. With shattered nerves, a strong feeling of affliction harried the Frog. He shambled, falling onto the mucky, stony ground in a mangled mess. Through his streaming tears, he saw the monstrous mass of distorted trees. Their swaying, shiny, moist, and twisted limbs pinned him like a sacrificial lamb. Their spiky bark reflected the dull light of the forest like colorful scales greased with venom. The towering, gnarled trees started to make a ghastly hiss.

His very own fear had turned him into a raving lunatic. When he shrieked out loud, Wally and Sampson could not help the poor Frog, for they could neither see nor hear anything. As they watched Booney's breakdown at the imaginary downpour of serpents strangling him, they felt a helpless sort of pity. Neither of them had seen Booney like this, nor anyone they had ever known. Not even Wally's kind but bold strength could temper such agony for Booney. Even those who are kind and tenderhearted may have dark impressions they subdue, but with Gorse- End's influence, such wicked impressions were revealed, unlocked as they might be. That baleful influence could turn those compassionate ones into ones tormented by monsters of normally hidden fears. Such fears became the servants of an everlasting delirium to the unfortunate ones so affected! While the poor Frog suffered in his insanity, the mists of the fevered marsh had sensed the deepest fear of Wally as well, and without any mercy, its strike was predictably heartless.

In the fear of being unable to assist his dear friend in need, Wally began to feel powerless. That feeling was unusual in him. He lived to help others, but such sentiments were useless here. He felt a kind of isolation uncommon for him. He simply did not feel the power to connect to someone he dearly cared for. At first, the feeling was an annoyance. It started to intensify quickly and rose to a pitch with the helpless screams of the poor tortured Frog. His feelings of helplessness began to rise higher. He began to feel alone in the growing dark. He could yet see and sense the presence of his beloved friends, but he could not feel them there anymore. It was a sense of growing void, a vast gap in his thinking that was even devoid of fear. It was a feeling of nothingness. For the first time in his life, he did not; he could not care about the fates of those he loved. It was an alien presence in him. To be swallowed whole. "I am to be swallowed whole," he seemed to hear himself say. But it wasn't him. It was, but it was not him. It was the part of Wally that Wally always denied existed. It was the part of him that did not care about anything. "Anything," he whispered to himself. He began to realize he spent so much time caring for others because he could not face the idea that he did not care. 'Anything..' he said again. 'Anytiiing,' he said again. 'ANYYYY…. TIIING'… 'aaaanyy!' He stopped.

'AAAANYYYEEEEE…' Something in him seemed to break the trance. 'Anytiiing..' he seemed to catch a stray thought. It was about fishing on the pond with Booney. "AAAANNNNYYYTIIING!" He screamed. He could cancel the thought invading his mind by remembering… "AAAANYYYYTTIIIINGGG!!!!" He cried in triumph. "AAANNYYTHIIINGGGG!" He saw Sampson teaching a few of the children.

"AAAAnnnyyythhiiiinggggg!!!!" He became calmer. He saw the rolling of the river that swept his tension and relieved him of the encroaching, disorienting, ugly thoughts; these frightening returning emotions were replaced by a sense of being reborn with passion and the comfort of knowing he existed at peace with others. He became calm again. Wally, seeing these traumatic events take hold of his friends, started to cheer for Booney and Sampson Moose; in a desperate act of rescuing his friends, the brown Hare had begun to sing a song attempting to inspire and uplift them, a motive of empowerment, to spurn such despairing strife, he adjured them to sing along and in a weary strain, so they did:

Though three were one, No need to run

Or cower.

In all good deed,

We'll face this time together. Can one be three?

Can all be freed?

We'll soon see the light together. One for all,

Two for luck, Three for cheer.

We must be brave together. Here we go, marching in haste To where we chase,

Until, at last, we shall see the brightening, In fair and stormy weather.

Through the perilous trials of their insanity caused by this devilish power the marsh possessed and inundated its victims to breaking point, the three friends, each dealing with their personalized traumatic onslaught, had to band together and support each other in great effort to wake from their terrible distinct misery, the vicious power of which held them as hostages soon had no control over them as they encouraged themselves through its nightmares with enough courage they rallied to resist such horrid displays and in vain the sickly force of the marsh had been successfully stalled for now.

Strangely echoing footsteps ran from behind. The trio turned to look back but only to see a black shadow watching them in return. The shadowy figure jumped and hid in the surrounding marshland environment. The shadowy figure sprung once more at a consistently fast speed, keeping a close eye on the wandering friends.

Suddenly, without warning, A group of shrieking, ugly bats dive-bombed through slim openings from twisted branches of the diseased trees; the three friends, startled by the barrage, quickly ducked low to evade them. The vicious bats swooped up once more and dived again.

"Getta outta 'ere ye nasta, stinka moffis bloodsuckas!!!!!" Cried Booney, jumping and flailing his boater hat around the flitting swarm hovering above them like a screeching, clawing billow. The bats clicking, bony wings flapped in unrelenting flurries. Yet in their continued assault of clawing and nipping, they were to be miraculously disbanded by something hidden within the rustling bushes. The figure pelted the once assailing rabble of bats with several small sharp pebbles, and with each screeching bat's plop, once struck by the whizzing pebbles, the other would flee, bat by brainless bat. They would fall or retreat, and soon, there were no bats to defend against, only the remains of the struggle. Wounded, the squealing, crumpled bats helplessly flopped around the huddled trio. The group was in tremendous relief but also in disbelief, still considering the mysterious aid they had received, "Ain't so toughy ay!?" Booney exclaimed mockingly, kicking the dirt as the drifting specks covered the bats. Upon further investigation and to thank their unexpected rescuer, whatever or whomever it might have been, Booney charged into the bushes where the stones were to be seen flung.

Along with the bats, their rescuer had also absconded without a trace of their presence. "Nasty little cratur t'e battsy be. I don't like'm, Notta bit!" Booney pats out. They all laughed, considering Booney hated being caught off guard by anything; Sampson chuckled. "Come Booney wit' all your bragging 'bout ye loving adventure, a few batties shouldn't make you go, shall I say BATTY?!!!" All laughed and continued talking somewhat more cautiously, especially now aware their "friend" might still be around watching and following them.

The walking friends soon approached a circular, straightforward platform similar to where and how they entered the marsh; the only exception was that fewer wicked trees were around than before. Wherein such an unpredictable moment, something quite strange and unusual slowly came into view; parked in the center of the wet plateau was a peculiar contraption, cleanly painted red; certainly was it not recognizable to Booney, who was puzzled by its strange look, on the other hand, it seemed very much familiar to Sampson and Wally. The trio neared the contraption. It was the red auroplane they had seen flying earlier. The auroplane was neatly polished compared to the grubby environment surrounding it. Resting on the hood of the plane was a brown leather helmet. Its long leather straps dangled by the edge of the red cylinder shape front, and cooling vents crevassed the sides of the plane. Excitedly, Booney swiped the hat and tried it on. It was too big for the Frog, and it swallowed his small head whole! The large clear goggles that were attached (though the shining transparency the glasses gave was the color of light yellow) tightly fastened above the leather helmet. Wobbling, he teetered back and forth, trying to catch his fall; he took the helmet off, seeing his lost breath instability, and left it where it was, making a flumping sound upon letting go of it. He swapped back to his boater.

A pair of light brown gloves loosely hung on the black lever tightly bolted in the center of the mainframe from where the user sits to control the contraption. Examining the plane, it seemed to be hot; the warm steaming motor was still running and only stopped shortly after approaching it, appearing it had been recently flown. Their judgment came more valid when they saw and touched the soft, wet mud splatters on the wheels on the bottom corners of the auroplane and its treading landing marks dragging from behind. The plane had one cockpit to fit only one, with its single black padded seat. Naturally curious, of course, Booney hopped right on in as if he was the proud owner and started playing and jiggling the many blinking switches and rapidly joggling the levers it contained. "Whadda fine an' fun tinga ma jigga this is! I need to get un of t'ese!" Booney unreservedly boggled excitedly announced as he kept randomly pulling, twisting, and flicking the countless doodads and doohickeys; however, his frisky enthusiasm was terminated by Sampson's quick preach, "DO NOT POKE AROUND BOONEY WIGGINS WHAT DOES NOT BELONG TO YOU!" Booney objected to the Moose's criticism, but it was forcefully resolved when Sampson gently lifted Boone and dropped him on the ground. "Lemme go, ye ol' crabby grump! I'm just havin' sum funs whuts the harm in t'at!?" Booney cried, ranting. "Plenty! if ye do not take proper precaution, moreover it isn't yours to play with, without permission!" Sampson logically explained.

Again, as they kept scanning and looking for an answer or clue to the answer, a strange yelp interrupted their proceeding research of the auroplane; by another glimpse, a shadow quickly darted in front of the investigation, peering through a bush, Wally once again saw the same old mismatched eyes that gave him the same shivering chill from before. The unknown creature suddenly fled behind a bush where, in a short time, there seemed to be a hidden, secretive path; it appeared the retreating creature covered his tracks with twigs and leaves led astray from the abandoned plane. Oddly, there was relatively more than one pair of muddy feet imprints; there were several! All were leading in the same direction. So, from the perspective of the three friends, they burned with curiosity following the trail of footprints. In growth, the plateau turned into a woodland tunnel, and then, in their advance, the tunnel slowly dipped into a steep hill.

Slowly sauntering down the slope, they cautiously avoided any thorny bush that suddenly popped up on the sides and might be prickly enough to be punctured when unexpected.

Hence, the name given to this thorny bush-invested fen, Gorse-End. Watching where they were placing their feet was rather slippery due to the wet mud (not as slick as one might think; some coverage was dry by moss and such); nonetheless, it was reasonable to manage. The steep hill became a flat and murky plain once more. However, the trio lost the tracks they were following, no doubt from their over-cautious trudge.

In their ongoing confusion deciding upon a clear direction to take, in an aimlessly bumbling tizzy, they stumbled upon a vast, indeterminately lengthy, and barren copse marked by thorns and brambles and burdened by fog! They had no idea where they were now, for this fog had layered everything, making the landscape intangible. They could not see even one step ahead. Parts of themselves had become invisible, clinging to dampness. By then, the putrid and suffocating stench of this mysterious section of the shrouded plain had become intoxicatingly noxious. Their eyes started to tear up. The smothering smell was awful, like rotten eggs' stench and foul sewage ripe with fetid fumes and circulating like gas around them. The putrid odor was inescapable even as they tried to block out the wretched smell by pinching their noses. It was extremely difficult to breathe, now even worse than before. Every time they tried to draw air, it felt dry and sour. They had all started to choke from its unsettling and permeating scent. In the flush of a hurried decision, they stopped in their tracks until they indeed knew where they were headed. While they had waited for the fog to become apparent, a strong gust of wind fulfilled their wish and pushed back the heavy fog. When they finally realized where they had been, they found that they were standing in the middle of the flat plain. This knowledge had completely terrified and traumatized them for the moment. They all froze involuntarily and unblinkingly. A disgusting and ghastly sight in a fiendish visage greeted them where they now stood! The image before them made them want never to step outdoors again. In plain sight, a profane and terrifying sight loomed before them now. It appeared to be a sunken and cratered burial or soiled battleground, which embodied a dauntingly bleak ambiance. It was a life-draining monument of some past desolation. The slimy pits they beheld were filled with scattered, crumpled bone shards. Above the pits were flags dangling from splintered staffs, rooted high and waving like the fingers of destitute witches on some black night. Below the flying standards of some unknown tribes were large blackened and leathery carcasses. The bodies shimmered in the mist, pig-like and grotesque, as if some abominable ruin had surfaced from the depths, unseen by daylight. Their skin, tight and stretched across poles, hung like ruptured sacks, decomposing. It was a haunting display of death, a silent testament to lives lost in a battle whose scale the three onlookers could only guess at, as the wreckage fanned out before them like thick, spreading ink over the moss-strewn, broken field.

As they looked past the remnants of the battle before them, a line of spiny bushes guarded what seemed to be an encampment further down the road; there was no way to bypass this burial site in any way possible. Henceforth, they all mustered their courage and delved into this foreboding realm of the dead. They were determined to cross it. They pushed themselves onward with long strides, though Booney's were more like double hops. Ignoring their common sense and their natural objections that bullied them in disdain for being stuck in such an abdominal place as this. Everything was alright, though, aside from being trapped in a death zone until one cocky Frog, who claimed he had no fear, charged ahead, eyes closed and accidentally tumbled into a pit, then screamed aloud, flailing, at first contact, with the rattling bones that danced on top of him. He begged to be pulled up. They all cheered when they finally got past the stinking burial ground.

All of them felt pride in surviving the unexpected ordeal. Exuberantly, they exited the dismal mud, mist, and bones tomb... Walking on, having paused to cheer one another along, they examined the line of bushes, noticing a slight gap between some of the dark, blistered thorns. Booney was quite the risk-taker, so he self-volunteered to venture beyond the spreading ruins. The big blowhard, egotistical Frog overconfidently strutted to the bush from where the gap was; he tightly tucked below from where the small gap began, roughly crawling underneath. Thriving in the present moment, he thought highly of himself and surely thought he deserved a marvelous reward for his courage. Little did the daydreaming Frog know, who was too caught up with himself of the future rewarding dreams, that his jacket was suddenly grasped by an extended and twisted thorn branch. Instantly, it punctured his red coat.

The Frog tripped and stumbled, becoming tangled and trapped. The bush held him hostage, and he could not get loose! Like a cobweb, the bush would not release him. He tried to move and wiggle out. "Yoooow!" He cried. Again, he tried to yank and wiggle loose. He wiggled, twisted, and jiggled with no luck. He was still caught and now was even more tightly grasped with even more shouts of pain. Reaching out for support, Wally grabbed Booney's extended hand, the tips of his fingers. In an extreme and heaving effort, Wally pulled the helpless Frog out; they pulled, tugged, and heaved. Finally, the bush and branch seemed to spit him out. Released by the force of the pull, the Frog was ejected outwards, toppling the Moose and Hare all at once. But only he had escaped such a fate. His red tailored jacket, now thoroughly torn, was still imprisoned in the thorn bush. "No, I will simply not leave without my jacket... that is simply not done for me," Booney insisted as he went about protesting in a harsh demand on trying to get ahold of the draped and skewered jacket; now he did feel very naked and indeed looked uproarious without it. Leaning on his tiptoes toward the edge of the thorny bush, Booney successfully wrestled the jacket from the thorns. Fortunately, he was unharmed, though a few tiny needles jabbed at him like splinters and were quickly plucked out moments after they were found. However, that wasn't to be said about his red jacket. Needless to say, the coat was now pierced, tattered, and utterly ruined by holes and rip marks.

"Look at my jacket; it's completely ruined and ravaged." The downhearted Frog said glumly. He held the jacket above him, putting his two wriggling fingers in and out of each of its holes.

"Wull, none had asked you to do it! Maybe if-"

"Pipe down, ya's ol' codger you, with no help frum you, I am in, terribibble, terribibble torment presently as ye may be'a witnessing an' I do not need your foolish mentorin' right now s'usual!" Booney quickly snapped back, pouting with a glare as he held up the jacket in front of the unamused, mumbling, mocking Moose.

Ever the voice of reason, Wally interjected once again to quell the rising tension. "Oh, come now, Boone, a few patches shall rectify the matter entirely! Indeed, it may turn out even better than before! Let us not squabble over such trifling concerns; there's no need to be glum. Let us all come together amicably, shall we?"

Booney, begrudgingly, slipped on his tattered jacket and offered a rough grunt. "Now that we've settled the matter, shall we find a way across?" Wally suggested.

The trio scanned their surroundings, and Sampson's keen eyes soon spotted a dilapidated plank bridge half-buried in the swamp's mire. It was barely visible from the broken planks jutting out of the muddy sludge, nestled at the end of the line of bushes on their right. Sampson pointed it out with a flourish of his mighty antlers.

"Excellent work, Sampson!" Wally exclaimed, his eyes twinkling with optimism. "My dear friends, we shall overcome any obstacle with teamwork!" His buoyant spirit lifted their morale.

"Yes, yes, let's get moving then!" Booney said, waving his friends forward with a somewhat dismissive air. He stepped gingerly onto the rickety bridge first.

The bridge creaked and groaned under Booney's weight, its every wobble threatening to send it crashing into the bog below. Booney made it across safely, and then Wally took his turn. The bridge trembled under the Hare's light frame, but he crossed without incident.

Next was Sampson, the massive Moose. The bridge, already on the verge of collapse, gave way under the Moose's considerable weight. With a sudden, alarming screech, the planks splintered and fell apart. Sampson plunged into the swamp with a resounding splash, the jagged remains of the bridge scattering around him.

Wally's heart raced as he saw his friend struggling in the mire. He dashed towards the edge, where the swamp plants and grasses grew thick, but he found himself stuck, unable to move.

"Hold on, Sampson!" Wally shouted in a panic. "Booney and I will find something for you ta grab onto!"

Booney, however, merely observed the unfolding disaster with a detached interest. His own safety was his only concern. Seeing Wally's distress, he chuckled, "It's not just amusing—it's downright HYSTERICAL!" Desperate, Wally spotted a vine hanging from a willow tree nearby. He attempted to climb the tree, but his efforts were in vain. Turning to Booney, he pleaded, "Booney, please, grab the vine and throw it down!"

With a disdainful roll of his eyes, Booney initially refused. "I have no wish to make a fool of myself!" Despite his protestations, he could not conceal his deep-seated desire to assist.

Reluctantly, he approached the tree, seized the vine, and tossed it to Wally.

With a determined look, Wally lassoed the vine around Sampson's antlers. He then turned to Booney with gratitude. "Thank you, Booney!"

Booney, with a forced smile, replied, "What is this thanks for? Swamp's no trouble for me... not really, never was!"

Wally nodded, and he and Booney began pulling with all their might. The

Moose remained stuck, and despite their best efforts, they could make little progress. Their arms grew weary, and it appeared all hope was lost.

Suddenly, Wally had an idea. He wrapped the vine around a sturdy swamp cherry bush and instructed Booney to assist him in pulling. They counted to three and pulled with renewed vigor. Sampson slowly began to inch his way out of the mire, the gunk around him gurgling and releasing bubbles as he emerged.

With one final heave, Sampson was pulled from the swamp. He landed heavily on the bog's edge, shaking himself with such force that mud and swamp water splattered over both Wally and Booney. Covered in the foul muck, Booney's frustration was evident, while Wally reveled in their victory.

The Moose emitted a low, disgruntled murmur as he surveyed the unsightly blemishes defacing the fine weave of his cherished sweater vest, his expression, a study in indignation and dismay.

Sampson, now liberated, rejoined his companions, the shattered remnants of the bridge fading into the distance. Booney, his red velvet jacket reduced to tatters and smeared with foul grime, maintained a sullen silence, though the quiet turmoil within hinted at the steadfast loyalty and rare kindness buried beneath his gruff exterior.

Unfortunately, now, the way they came was destroyed and could not be the way to return home if and when they should decide to return the same way. Sampson shook the icky gunk from where it remained to stick, though some of its patches stained his tan sweater.

"Nice goin' you, ol' dolt; now we can't go back." Booney snickered sarcastically. "If anyone is a dolt here, it's you! We wouldn't be here after all if not for you!" Sampson, offended by his attitude, snapped back. After looking at the destruction of the small bridge behind them, they were on the trail again and found the footprints in front of them to follow and lead them onward. "I do wish we won't 'ave 'eny more' trouble," Wally said despairingly.

Little to no time at all after following the trail, they noticed that the footprints had dispersed. They soon approached segments of broken fences sunk deep into the seeping ground they were standing on. Giant, abandoned, ramshackle watchtowers kept guard above, standing on four lookout posts under the dark, withering sky. A series of burning torches were placed in sequence on all sides, and in the center of the torch-lighted encampment was a relatively small and mangled hillock. The hillock had deep holes that were drilled into a largish mound, driven in, apparently, at an angle. The mound seemed to conceal what must have been an underground cavern or sub-grade enclosure. Strange sounds emanated from the most significant hole in the middle of the mound, flanked on either side by smaller holes that all could have been connected, considering the proximity of holes to one another. It sounded like many dwellers lived below, scuttling and jostling beneath the surface where the trio stood before the mound. The cacophonies of screams, insane laughter, yells, hoots and hollers, clattering and crashing, and noises of general mayhem gave off a muffled yet eerie presence. The noises reverberated around the encampment, lending a threatening air to the mysterious site, radiating menace to all outsiders. The scent of the murky encampment was a rancid stench of plaguing disease, though this rancid stench did not only haunt the encampment but the whole marsh itself. Then, almost immediately, their noisy surroundings had turned dead quiet.

"Well, well, well what do e' 'ave 'ere boyz? Three's los' tressie' passers. A moos, rasbit, n' a froogsie?!"

Suddenly ambushed, a pack of snarling, ravaged, wild-eyed Hounds dashed before the startled trio. Recent rumors had spread across many of the valley towns that groups of Hounds had viciously mauled their owners unexpectedly, only to be seen and reported as runaways from their farms afterward. Based on their rough and threatening appearances, these were the same Hounds. Mysteriously, they had appeared from the tall, gnarled, twisted tree woodland ahead with its bordering sidelines encampment and savagely leaped out from the mound.

"Why' it'd be dinner time already, oy hows timesies fies!!!"

Surrounded and trapped, the gathered fellowship shrank before the circling, growling, feral dogs. Defensively, Sampson safeguarded Wally and Booney as he boldly stood in front, having them both safely behind him, keeping them away from harm.

"Aren't you e' runaway Hounds tha' we 'eard 'bout?" Wally had asked.

"Whut's t'it te yer's!?" They replied in a threatening snarl. One of the circling Hounds snapped and lunged at their skittering feet, laughing insanely.

The growling, raggedly hunched Hounds presented a gaunt and emaciated visage, yet their presence was undeniably fearsome. They were clad in oversized, battered wool jackets that draped loosely over their wiry frames, frayed at the hems, and stitched together with rough, makeshift repairs—each patch a testament to countless brawls and shadowy haunts. The sleeves, ragged and rolled back, unveiled scarred and sinewy arms, each suggesting a readiness for mischief. Paid caps, askew and precarious, sat on their heads. Beneath the brims, their eyes gleamed with a brutish cunning, ever watchful and scanning their surroundings with a predatory focus, betraying the keen intelligence lurking within their rugged exteriors.

Their long, ragged ears drooped beneath such caps, adding to their feral appearance. When they spoke, their voices were low and guttural, marked by a country drawl that hinted at fields and farmyards left far behind. Their speech was slurred and unrefined, holding a coarse simplicity; yet, within their blunt words, there lay an unmistakable menace as if each utterance carried a quiet, unspoken threat.

"This is restricted premesee, absolutely no 'un e'llowed!" "No 'un!" The others copied.

Just then, a Wolf's wavering and angry howl in the near distance broke through the fearful silence. The howl continued into an ostensibly hideous laugh, or so Wally thought. The circling Dogs slowly backed away into separate rows. The resulting middle row was left transparent and open. In a brief moment or two, a rangy grey Wolf with muscular legs and swelling calves proudly strode through the empty line toward where the disturbance had started.

"Gentlemen, gentlemen, what seems to be the problem here… hmm? We are reasonable fellows, aren't we?"

The Wolf stood before the trio, his demeanor exuding a blend of sophistication and cunning wit. His attire spoke of a well-traveled aristocrat: a sharp, hunter-green tweed sports jacket, though well-worn, was adorned with brown elbow patches and brass buttons that, despite their age, gleamed with polish. A small golden chain draped from the jacket's hip pocket to a buttonhole on his rich, purple plaid vest beneath. A red ace of spades was tucked into his chest pocket.

A black bowler hat was perched at a rakish angle secured a single auburn braid, drawn taut and hanging to his shoulders with a polished gloss, a striking contrast against the drab, dim sunlight. A long, ornate belcher handkerchief monogrammed "K.C." in gold thread was draped around his neck, carrying a heavy scent of red wine as if the cloth had been carelessly stained and left to dry. His breeches dyed a fancy copper and embroidered with arabesque patterns, completed the ensemble.

The Wolf held a dark-stained walking cane, its brass knob twisted with regal bearing, which he brandished with an elaborate motion as he spoke. His smile, both debonair and devious, revealed teeth that were perfectly aligned yet marred by a single chipped incisor. His long, sharp fangs, glistening in the light, unnerved Wally. Despite his severe and noble demeanor, his charm and warm courtesy were laced with a sense of magniloquence.

He peppered his speech with convoluted Latin phrases, a testament to his highborn upbringing and fondness for his bilingual prowess, even if the phrases were often untranslatable. When he spoke, he occasionally cupped his right paw over a noticeable scar on the left side of his long snout, a minor but distinct flaw he seemed almost embarrassed by. An oversized mole on the right corner of his snout added to his complex appearance, suggesting a being who was both spoiled and prone to fits of rage if his demands were not met.

The Wolf's gaze was fixed expectantly, waiting for a response that had yet to come. "Some intrudees, Kaliber!" One of the Hounds announced.

"Oh, that's non-Bonum... oh, not one bit!" The Wolf in false sympathy as he caught a pair of red dice, tossing them up and catching them.

"What should 'e do with 'em, Kaliber?" The captain of the Hounds asked. His left eye was covered by a black, tattered eyepatch. He was the most beaten and ragged of the threatening Hounds that stood near Kaliber.

"Well'a I say we'a strin' em up by er's tendar's feet, roast t 'em a 'live an 'a commence with is delicious feas,' we shud!" One of the scruffy Hounds suggested. The gang was going berserk from starvation. Frenzied, one of the Hounds licked his slobbering lips, tilting his brown Brixton-brood cap in front of his concealed wild crossed-eyes.

The others, drooling, enthusiastically agreed and cheered, "Whatta marvelous ideer!" They all shouted and hollered with zealous merriment. But another Hound suggested to cut them up into small 'ittle pieces and boil them into a stew, and so an argument began and soon broke out in an all-out vicious brawl, quarreling between themselves on which way was the best way to cook the strangers as they frantically yelled out their ideas.

"Est satis, that's enough!" The Wolf sharply added as he rolled his eyes, in an alarming interruption ceasing the ongoing bickering. Sneering, Lord Kaliber concluded with reverential politeness, "Alea, loquantur simul ad iudicium! Let them speak, let them breathe!" He instantly rolled the red dice grasped by his right paw onto the bare ground below. His yellow searing eyes widened, then hideously bulged, his nostrils flared, feverishly chewing on his lip as he rubbed his sweaty palms together. Kaliber cravingly awaited the result of the roll. The others watched with anticipation; the three friends were puzzled by it as they watched the silent reaction; they did not know what to think.

Slowly, the pair of dies stopped spinning, showing their numbers.

"Ah, seveeeeen! Denique perfecto numero notaretur!" Kaliber declared with a dramatic clap. He returned the pair of dice to his side pocket, a dainty grin playing on his lips. He polished his signet ring against his coat as he continued. "Well, since this is their first offendiculo… let them relinquo. Of course, they must not speak of this to anyone… conpectus?!" The pack of craven Dogs, still stunned by the verdict, groaned in disappointment.

"I must excuso for my coetus. They do have terrible and heinous inclinations! Tell me what your names are, good fellows! Fine friends, Amicis, are you? Come tell me, though we look a bit rude, we all are friends here in this wood after all... aren't we?" He could hardly contain his grin from breaking out into demeaning laughter.

The three didn't speak in cold fear of the raving Hounds surrounding them until Kaliber reassured their safety and shooed them off. They took a short step back, but they still intensely stared them down into a petrified quietude.

"Come, come now, no need to be conterriti! We're not malus, bad blokes once you get to know us!" Kaliber said lightly with a pretentious smirk. Upon hearing Kaliber's words, the Hounds chortled quietly amongst themselves. Kaliber turned at his Hounds and glared at them with a deadly presence. "Well, I'm Wallis... an' this is Sampson n' Booney," said Wally in an uplifted mood, though he was still cautious and on edge. Yet how hard did Kaliber carefully keep trying every which way to get Wally to lower his defenses.

"Ah voluptatem, a pleasure! As you are already well known by my cretini tuuuuurbaaa." Kaliber turned, facing the gang of Hounds with a dirty scowl; the Hounds whimpered, and then he bid his attention again to the strangers with a warm smile. "I am Kaliber, Lord Kaliber Marcellus Coveton the Seventh! At your servitium." The Wolf bowed with gracious suave decorum.

"For you have, as such, the greatest and quite rare privilege to be acquainted with someone as phenomenally prosperous as I! It would be best if you were wholly grateful to be in my presence. Let alone have the highest honor to speak to me; much too few have that magnificent casus." Booney shrank back into his torn jacket collar by much of his envy rapt by the Wolf's formal aspect.

The boastful Wolf continued:

"Should you know, I come from a long family line of Reguim imperatouri residing in AltaRotha." The braggart Wolf recommenced to proclaim. (Little to their knowledge, the three had known absolutely nothing of such a town called AltaRotha and had not even known such a place existed. It seemed quite a fabled, wonderful town, as he bragged about it and the great extent of its feudal society's conduct. Proudly and haughtily, he leaned on his cane and continued to speak. He began blowing on his golden ring, encrusted by tiny shining jewels resembling rare gems and luminous diamonds. Reminiscing about his glorious past, in a flashback-inspired reverie, he greatly triumphantly exclaimed, "A marvelous Coveton Arche estate ... In truth! It is so grand and imposing that any lowering eye dropped to the ground out of sheer shame at its grand elegance. Soooo powerful and incredibly wealthy are mea magmorum populi, so much so that whole rooms are completely dedicated to seventy-four treasures. Still, of course, that's not all the rooms our mighty castle holds, all with their stunning luxury of ma.j.estas regia and filled with treasures and great piles of purest gold. With such splendid and obedient servants at my disposal, to serve at all requests, at any whim, and with such fine and rich cuisines for my pleasure at any time I wish. Such dishes are brought to us in our candle-lighted, spectacular dining room trimmed with gilded tapestries of the finest silk, where my large family gathers on occasions for the most opulent of all the royal banquets, I being the youngest of the adults; naturally, have the greatest amount of attention of the elders at all times and unlimited access to the family treasury. With the finest décor and objects of wonder... aaah and such, such, such... magnificent golden afternoons after delightful tea time out on our terrace occupied by several of marble water fountains, stone statues, and large banquet tables and rococo chairs, on such perfect days golden archways which can be seen by the four-way corners of the castle, lead us to our private gorgeous and enormous walled garden of the freshest blooming flowers of enchanting multitudes to where we take our wonderful strolls among ourselves of beautiful paradise when wanted. Leisurely games of bocce ball and tennis, as well as my family's favorite game of all time, croquet, played on our freshly cut and sweet-smelling green playing field, do we live. We look over the sparkling sea surrounding our castle as its high-reaching towers overlook the columns that set the breathtaking horizon. Iridescent waves breaching over the rocky boulders of the sandy shore below!" Though as the Wolf was reminiscing, it seemed to be from his sharp, harsh, and hoarse tone that he was choking back on the bitterness of some distant memory unrevealed to the others. He sometimes seemed to become agitated when he spoke. He would also tightly clench his fist, grinding his teeth like he held a grudge against something or someone. Though he often caught himself and apologized for his daydreaming.

"Well, if it's so beautiful, what are you doing here, if ye don't mind my asking?" Wally asked genuinely. When he asked a most simple question, he received an unusually piqued answer that startled the Hare from the brash delivery.

"You could say, I'm on vacation! A luxurious life does get ever so tiring every so often! The Wolf snapped.

"But that's beside the point, and I must say, gents, you took us all by surprise with such an unexpected visit. What might you be doing here, might I ask!? No one has ever been here except for my co-workers and me! Surely, there cannot be residential neighborhoods around here, could there!!!?" Kaliber expressed excitement, though it seemed a bit overdone, as he swung his cane at specific points of emphasis during his eccentric speech.

"Ooh, but there is a wonderful valley called Ambrodale. You see, it's up the river, yet. Unfortunately, we got lost when we explored a bit too far down this way," replied Wally. Now relaxed, he began to feel the way before they entered the mysterious wood. He let his guard down with an easing comfort.

Kaliber glared with a crafty gaze, and a strange smirk lifted his face. It was as if he planned to take each one apart right where they stood. He retracted his head backward, though it wasn't to be taken under any consideration of anything suspicious to the three friends who had never had such encounters or strange conversations before.

"In oppidum? Vos doesn't say... Hmm, how delightful! How interesting! Praeclarum!" Said Kaliber, clapping as if he hid something he had already known before his speech and his fabrications.

"By any chance, would you happen to know how we can go back!?" Wally asked in a pure, innocent simper that seemed to be awkward and queer to the Hounds and the Wolf, given that they were not familiar with the simple-hearted personalities of the Riverfolk.

Kaliber paced, thinking. He thought and thought and thought some more and came to a simple conclusion. Interlocking and quickly releasing his grasping paws in anticipation, he replied: "Follow this trail north, and you should reach wherever you came from!" He pointed to a hidden murky winding trail that was hard to spot, for weeds and scrub bushes covered most of it. Wally noticed that the twisted path led crookedly out of the encampment.

"But please do make yourself domi. We rarely ever get guests, so you must stay! Oporetet, oportet! Let's play a game of billiards!" Kaliber cried in mock anguish.

As soon as Kaliber gave the commanding word, the surrounding pack of Dogs retreated into the mound behind them, only to appear suddenly again. They brought the table, sticks, balls, and chalk to play with. Now also appearing dressed for the game, they looked eager to begin.

The three kindly refused the game. With the snap of Kaliber's finger, his gang retreated again and returned empty-handed.

"Ah yes, what was I thinking? Adeo stolida! Billiards is such a complicated and hokey lusus, how about a friendly round of Blackjack? It's a fine game indeed! With a side of delicious treats of orange marmalade, Stilton cheese crumbles, and some tasty crisps to go along. Now, doesn't that sound suavis? Etiam, etiam, it simply must be sooo."

Again refused, Kaliber grew upset, and in an unsettled effort, he growled a wicked staccato growl; he calmed himself in a few restless moments, slicking back his grey, wild, entangled hair, which stood dry and frizzled, like quills, from his blustering fluster. He stroked his hair over his right paw while twisting his long whiskers with his other paw. He bore a sharp and edgy frown.

"Well, I don't think so... we should be off by now before it gets much too dark to see!" Wally said.

"Oh no, please don't go, oro, oro!" Kaliber insisted ingratiatingly, stepping right in front of them while stopping their advancement. He extended his arms in his persistent mockery of wounded feelings.

"Or maybe Bluffers Roll, better yet!" His frown gleamed into a facetious smile upon the pronouncement of his great idea. "Doesn't that sound like a nice game for friends like us? I am very sure you'll like it quite a lot! Oh yes, splendid! How perfect. A nice way to bid farewell between friends, yeees, yeeeesssss!!" Showing his genuine love for the game in a thrilling enthusiasm, his breath quickened, and his heart raced with eagerness. In a shrill voice, he yelped incoherently. "My specialty…" He whispered to himself with a shady grin as he pulled a couple of dice from the hidden interior pocket of his jacket in an offering. He had a couple of spares he had now shown to the three mystified travelers.

Bluffers Roll, or Bluffer, was a game of mischief and cheating. The only way to win was to cheat. The game is comprised of dice, boards, and rolling blinds. According to the rules, each player would get three dice and a board to accompany them. The square board is bordered by bolted planks of wood called "rolling blinds" or "blind visors," with a sliding slot carved in the middle of the blind wall. This wall formed a square barrier that hid the opposite side of the board from each player or roller. The bordered edges were placed so that whatever each opponent rolled would be unseen by the other, hence keeping the other players guessing each other's roll. In a fair match, two judges would stand on each player's side to ensure they were playing by the rules.

There are three rounds per match, and three matches make up a game. One turn of each player makes one round. A total of 9 rolls made a complete game. Both players would roll off to see who goes first, and then, with a friendly and hardy handshake, they would begin the game.

During each player's turn, they must roll three dice individually. They automatically lose the round if all the dice numbers are one or six. To win the round, the player must get their roll result as close to seventeen as possible and not over, the rolls being combined at the end of their turn. If their roll was lower than seventeen or near to it but in no way over it, they can roll one extra die if they would prefer. It was this roll that often undid the hopeful player. The fourth roll is intended to make the other anxious and fooled, risking the fourth roll themselves and thus possibly losing the game. They must first declare if venturing upon a fourth roll. If the fourth roll was higher than the third roll they made, they must keep it, discarding the third roll if lower, and thus possibly tipping the point balance against themselves by scoring above. When the fourth roll is made, they must announce the result. But it could also be a trick to fool their opponent! The other player is now allowed to strike back if they do not believe it is the result;

perhaps by reading the facial expression or any other hints to provide their outlook, the offender could proclaim a "Bluff" in which, after the declaration, the defendant must show their roll giving the dice to the judge on their corner to show to the other player who called on it. If the player who called "bluff" were correct, they would win the round, but if they guessed wrongly, they would lose the round! Those were the rules of the game.

Nevertheless, it was indeed a gambling game (though it was outlawed, it was quite common to see it played for money), in which you could spend your earnings for a fortune you were swindled by, leaving you with empty pockets afterward. Star-crossed by bad fortune, Bluffer's has a nasty reputation from the many swindlers and ruffians that are found who play it in pubs and similar, smoky, lowlighted dwellings.

With a polite denial, they kindly refused his "generous" offer.

"Perbene, perbene!" Dissatisfied, Kaliber sighed brusquely in disappointment. "Si sic necesse est…"

"But please do not speak of this base of operation sworn to secrecy! Tandem silentio auratum," Kaliber suddenly said abruptly, catching them off guard, which he was certainly intending to do. When the trio asked why, Kaliber ignored the request as if it had never been said and smiled with false pretense. He continued buffing his ring with his green jacket sleeve in an uncanny leer, examining it from afar. Seeing his lack of response, yet with Kaliber's request in mind, they promised and quietly and uneasily agreed amongst themselves to an unusual request addressed to them.

"Oh, you do look quite worried, don't you… Non amicus, non. We are, aren't we? And friends, we'll stay? Isn't that nice now? Of course, there will be things we must all agree upon. Yes, it's true," Kaliber said in a cloying voice, flashing a tattered paper for them to witness. He held a quill pen already dipped in murky black ink. An extensive black splotch line was on the document for their consented signature.

"What does it say?" Sampson said, rather suspicious by now.

"It's just a contract," Kaliber said with a dismissive wave. "Noli commoveri!" He quickly read through the document in a jumbled mix of Latin and English. "Obsecro, mihi fiducia sicut signum! I assure you, I would never do anything harmful. Habeo codice honorem. I'd be most grateful if you signed." His tone was syrupy and sweet, and his eager grin only added to the discomfort.

The three friends were taking their time deciding what they should do.

"Noli patientia mea, rude eius nimis, I am a patient Wolf very much so, but not for this regard. These are matters which we should decide in all conscience. It will be oh so helpful to sooo many to see us form an agreement like this. Yes, why this will go down in history! I ASSURE it!" Ever the lover of all things historical, Wally wondered what that might mean. Yet somehow, the idea intrigued him.

"Do we perhaps have any choice?!" Asked Sampson. He was awfully concerned about the contract and what it entailed. Never had any of them been asked to sign a document for which no reason was given to them to sign.

"Im afraid not; im valde!" Replied the pompous Wolf.

After a moment's further consideration and rather shortsightedly, Wally signed, rushed by Kaliber. However, the orotund print of the document itself was tiny and practically unreadable as the Hare signed. He was quickly interfered with by Sampson, who was very skeptical. He thought differently from Wally of the strange dealings taking place, as anyone could tell.

Suddenly, Kaliber's demeanor shifted. "Stultus es?" He snatched the signed document from Wally's writing paws, smearing the ink across the tattered document in the process. Before Sampson could clarify his suspicions, Kaliber stuffed the document into his jacket with a shady grin.

"Oh, thank you, thank you! Gratias tibi! You're so kind. Sic genus! And don't worry about the fine print—it's just legalese. I wouldn't even harm a June bug—'Ne June bug quidem nocet.' Now you all are much very free to badisso. I promise you won't hear from us again!"

He then displayed a warm-looking but counterfeit smile while showing his long, sharp fangs.

The three friends jointly begged their leave and followed his expedient directions through the winding dirt trail.

Waving goodbye until there was no sign of the trekking trio, "bene valet amicis meis explorer!" The Wolf called out. Kaliber's warm smile became a grotesque and depraved grimace. Turning toward his jaw-gnashing Hound dog gang behind him, he snarled with aggressive malice. "Why did you let 'em get away, Kaliber? We could have had 'em!"

"Witout goin' hungry eaver!" Said one of the other Hounds, now exhausted due to their starvation. They started to doubt and secretly desired to challenge Kaliber's confusing leadership.

"Don't you amentis mentis inops understand? As your powers of retention are quite undeveloped and sickly wet and as unspeakably crude and dense as you all are, I am sure you will grasp the marvelous vision we all truly share! If there is another settlement, as they say, there is." Kaliber suddenly stopped. "All in good time... there will be plenty for you in the end," He muttered gruffly as the others glanced around at each other with jittery suspense

"Follow them! We shall take their precious little valley from right under their unsuspecting noses, such poor, pitiful fools! It's facile and simply easy! "Kaliber gloated with a demeaning laugh, clutching his right fist-shaking rabidly for his future success as he twirled his cane almost in a slashing motion.

Suddenly, a shadow of a slinking figure in a shrouding cloak popped up near where the Wolf defiantly stood. It moved swiftly with fearful silence in the direction where the three friends had just departed.

"Silas, velox veniet, I need a word." Kaliber whispered, "The rest of you, regredior!" Upon hearing the harsh command, the Hounds dispersed into the dark maw of the mound behind them. Silas, the Hounds' commanding captain, strode forward to meet the Wolf standing alone. Once again, he began tossing the pair of red dice up in the air, but he was suddenly interrupted by a fly landing on his shoulder. Kaliber looked with a disgusted scowl and quickly swatted the resting insect, flicking it away. "Ooh grotesque insects... vile nuisances are they... simply despise such repulsive, worthless little pests!" groused the Wolf.

"Yes, Lord Kaliber, sir?" Silas said as he stood beside the Wolf, awaiting what Kaliber might say.

"Make sure your Hounds will be paratus paratus; I shall not tolerate critical missteps during the execution of this plan. Do you understand me?"

"Certainly Kaliber, I can give ya's e full-fledge's guarantees everythin' will'a go as yer planned, is that all me, Lord?!" Replied Silas in a salute.

"If not, your hide will make such an excellent trophy and a marvelous coat to add to my collection...' Of disappointments, that is,' Kaliber thought to himself.

Silas grunted with uneasy acknowledgment. Signaled by the Wolf, the gang of

Hounds ambled out from the mound, gathering around where Kaliber stood.

Silas started to shout, "Long Live, Lord Kaliber!"

"Long Live Lord Kaliber!!!" The wild Hounds cried out loud, taking off their hats and holding them in front of their chests. Unnoticed by the self-gleaming Kaliber, some did not do so. The Hounds circled the Wolf, repeatedly chanting while saluting and praising the noble Wolf. Rather arrogantly, proudly holding his chest pocket flap, he closed his eyes and lifted his head.

With a sharp and degrading grimace, Kaliber howled a long, wicked howl. Through the dark, blistered wood, what became a scream of victory rent the night air. The bleakness of the wasteland seemed to glow in an unfortunate shade of grey death under the slowly rising moon.

"FOVE! FOVE! FOVE!!!! My dear militibus! Follow me, and none of you shall ever be famelicus again! We shall be prosperous and wealthy beyond your wildest dreams! As it was always intended to be! Be paratus! Be fortis, my like-minded friends. A glorious new era awaits all of us! Nothing can prevent the reign of I, REX Kaliber Marcellus Coveton the Seventh! At last, we shall all be given our dues!" Kaliber shouted in more sickening and atrocious laughter over the incessant chanting he had longed to hear (which fed his starving mind.)

Chapter Four
An Unexpected Visitor

"O', what a merry sight to behold… home at last!"

Nightfall soon approached Ambrodale. Small dabs of twinkling stars were dotted across the clear, dark sky, with only a few fluffy clouds that slowly drifted on by. The yellow-shining moon yawned widely, and it winked its sunken eyes in a warmly welcomed greeting. The chirping crickets harmonized in a melody with the rushing of the Bromby River. Flitting about at night and mirroring the stars above were many fireflies hovering like sparks of a well-tended fire.

As the trio arrived, weary from their adventure, the soft glow of a flickering lamppost guided them home. Most nearby cottages had already gone dark, but the pub was still alive with echoes of laughter and merry singing. Slowly, they made their way to Wally's cozy cottage at the end of Whittler's Ave.

They followed the cobbled stone path toward his little red plank door, its brass latch adorned with intertwining symbols—rosy apples nestled beside ponderous grape leaves. Above, the conical roof, sheathed in weatherworn green shingles, rose steeply, crowned by a small brick chimney softened by the passage of time. Round windows, set deep into thick walls, had protruding sills overflowing with lush greenery. Flowers in shades of violet, blue, and crimson— Gentians, Sweet William, Nasturtiums, and other rare blooms—tumbled freely, filling the night air with their fragrance. These vibrant blossoms reflected the care Wally had poured into his home, a legacy passed down from his kin.

Groves and patches of vegetable gardens were planted on the sides of the Hare's cottage. As Booney and Sampson went in, Wally quickly gathered some of his vegetables from the many growing patches, grabbing ahold of the willow basket hanging from a wooden peg of his home to pick the vegetables. He went on plucking and placing them into the basket. Wally then joined his friends inside. Who scanned and scavenged for food. Wally's cutesy cottage had smoke- marked, darkened oak walls, rows of cabinetry, shelves, and closets for freshly laundered linen in every room. There were five in total, and all were on the same floor. Each room was immaculately clean and tidy, polished to an illustrious shine, and smelled of fresh meadow breezes. Nothing was left as if carelessly dropped throughout the entire house. Everything was neatly kept the way it should be. There was a small entry vestibule with dark cherry, wood floor, and a small knotted wool burgundy carpet. It was a short entry hall shaped like a tube, which tunneled into the warm interior of his home, lighted by small reading lamps on the side. It seemed several small, hand-carved green bookshelves occupied the hall; their side paneling was custom-designed with engraved wood markings of waves, curls, and streaks that bordered smooth green edges. There were signatures and symbols with curlicues and wooden shelves filled with books. Flanked on either side of each of the bookshelves were tiny little reading nooks, with handcrafted desks and chairs made from some indistinguishable knotty old wood.

Years of varnish had effectively hidden any sign of wood grain, giving the little sets of furniture the appearance of what one might find in a dollhouse. The desks had a red quilled writing pen, a half-empty inkpot, a stack of blank papers, and a small ceramic cookie jar that was always full. The jar was there in case of a craving for something sweet while Wally wrote one of his by-now famous greetings or perhaps some shred of his early memoirs, which he could never quite bring himself to finish (perhaps one of these days it might just happen). The narrow entryway grew narrower and narrower, only to end with a round archway that opened to the main living quarters of his house. The entryway led to his living room, the largest room he had. Unlike most living rooms, his living room was combined with a small kitchen by the corner, separated by sturdy maple counters. The room was brightly lit by a chandelier hanging above. There were lots and lots of pegs for hats and coats, slightly left of the center of the room. When one stood in the entryway, there was a charming, well-made, and cozy fireplace with a hearth. The fireplace was made from the rounded stones of the riverbank, which Wally's grandfather had carefully gathered and constructed into what became the main gathering spot of the house. Above the oaken mantle of the fireplace hung many portraitures, a long line of his kin (it seemed, for what else could a large family of hares represent). Encased in hand-carved wooden frames, each likeness captured the rustic and humble ancestors of the current owner, dear Wallis H. Tunnelly of Ambrodale. Between the portraits, small speroids of polished glass dangled from brass hooks, catching the flicker of the firelight and casting soft, dancing reflections upon the walls—a curious embellishment that added a hint of whimsical charm to the otherwise traditional display.

Below Wally's priceless family portraits was a hearth of a dark flagstone upon which sat Wally's beloved and most useful cast iron stovetop. As if an actual resident of his home stood on four legs, the stove was always boiling and whistling with pots of tea, bubbling with vegetable stew, and baking with freshest, crispiest wheaten flatbread, which were usually crackers, and plump biscuits. Daily before teatime, the stove gave off the scent of sweet baking, filling the room and the spaces around his home. The living room had several cozy chairs, comfortably fluffed cushions, and rich damask fabric with floral patterns. They were all close to one another, so loneliness within the dwelling might never happen as the chairs faced one another whilst company sat together within. The room contained a small dining room table with spindly legs and a thick wood plank, the table being top-dressed with light brown woven river rush placemats. The matching chairs that went along were also spindly and delicate, but for the seat, which was a thick wooden board. Like much the other furniture, this dining set was also carefully hand-carved in a somewhat rustic fashion. The appearance of Wally's home was earthy, to say the least, yet somehow thoughtful and dignified, Sampson, who towered over the house, had to maneuver carefully, crouching and sidestepping to avoid bumping into things with his grand antlers. Despite his imposing size, he made a concerted effort to avoid causing any damage, choosing to sit politely on a braided rug crafted by Wally's great-grandmother. At the same time, the flickering light of the fireplace bathed the room in a warm glow.

A large grandfather clock stood sentinel in the center of the house, its steady ticking a reassuring backdrop to the daily rhythms of life. Every hour, the clock's chime would resonate through the rooms, marking time with a familiar cadence. The archways leading from the living area to the pantry and the hallways provided a seamless flow, though they also hinted at the home's compact nature. There was no cellar in his home, but there was a loft for storage in case of any emergency, which was rare but still happened occasionally. Each room was adorned with flowerpots, their vibrant plants adding a touch of life and familiar color. The home, though humble, was filled with warmth and a sense of belonging, embodying the spirit of its kind- hearted owner.

Booney hopped from cupboard to cupboard, opening them to find dried carrots and similar items. "You wouldn't find anytin' there, Booney; that's why I brought some more," Wally said with a chuckle, carrying the basket along. "Well, hurry it up 'en, I'm starving!" The Frog exclaimed, checking what the basket contained, he rummaged through groupings of beets, onions, new potatoes, ripe pears, full heads of tiny cabbages, and long stems of bean sprouts, all wrapped and bundled by a soft, patterned white cloth. The Frog made a sour face at what Wally had brought, quite disappointed, "To be quite frank, it isn't good for a Frog to eat such!" With a quick dart out the door, Booney returned smiling with a jar of flies for his scrumptious supper to be gobbled.

"It is not wise to call one early for dinner, after all!" The Moose added with a deep throaty laugh.

Sampson then found a small cluster of grapes still hanging from the vine in one of the cupboards, unseen by the searching Frog, who was now happily chewing the dried crunchy flies with smacking lips. The Moose started to nibble and munch down the bunch of grapes, contented soon to sit with a loud thud that shook the interior of the Hare's home, rattling the pans and dishes hanging from their holders and cabinets. The boiling, steaming kettle whistled and shrieked; Wally quickly raced towards the pot, pouring the hot water from the kettle to the heating pot, where the steaming water sizzled on the impact. The Hare then dropped all the vegetables from his basket into the pot, mixing them and adding the many spices from his spice rack that leaned above the pot as he went along, stirring.

"What a fine stew will it be!" Wally chuckled, thinking about how much he loved hosting his friends while tapping the pot with a wooden spoon three times. The remaining boiled water he had in his whistling hot kettle was lightly poured into several teacups with golden trim, delicately placed at their accorded spots on the platter, with the cups now filled to the very top. The changing of colors happened right before their eyes; the hot, clear water had turned into a fair jasmine tea. Its smell was strong yet compellingly sweet.

The tea bags in which the flavor evaporated into the water stayed afloat. Wally continued to stir every cup, swirling the bags so the strong flavor would be present. Then, with the last few drabs, he placed the soaking tea bags next to the platter.

He rushed towards the pantry room, rummaging through the sliding racks. He grabbed a loaf of bread and seed cakes. He then laid the loaf onto the counter with a chopping board beneath. He served the seed cakes first to his guests, then quickly sliced the loaf, also grabbing some sweet treats of small strawberry tarts, toffee puddings, and shortbread biscuits. Wally began spreading them around a circular silver tray. He brought the tea and snacks, placing them on the table for their enjoyment. A loud knock interrupted their ongoing discussion as they discussed the strange day and the unusual experience they shared.

"It's a bit late for visitors, isn't it?" Sampson added, surprised; he looked at the clock that rang a quarter past nine. Booney ignored the knock and what Sampson said, taking no notice nor care, and enjoyed his scrumptious meal. Wally agreed with Sampson and scuttled through the passage towards the door to greet the knocker as Sampson followed. The loud knocks continued several more times, more rapid and maybe even frantically impatient. Wally opened the door as Sampson stood behind. In shock, Wally shivered, absolutely bewildered at whom he saw on the other side of his door! Those mismatched green and ice-cold blue eyes now haunted his anxious mind as if hypnotized. The Fox stood before them, small and unsettlingly scraggy, along with a bushy, long, dark orange tail. He resembled an ordinary fox that one might see running about; with a short snout and fangs, he looked harmless; nothing unusual about him except his bizarrely daunting eyes. His squat-shaped, scruffy head was covered by a well-worn tin pot, slightly tilted. His manner of presentation was draped in a bright yellow raincoat, perhaps one that a child would wear on a rainy day. His throat was looped by a ratty red tie. The gangly Fox mumbled nervously, almost skittishly with a high-strung whiffing and with actions that displayed his twitching anxiety.

"Hello...? But do we know you? Surely, we have never seen you here in Ambrodale before. Are you new?" Wally managed to ask, though not to be rude, even though it may have sounded that way, but the Fox's unchancy leer lost the Hare's intended politeness. I assure you; Wally was as fond of visitors as in Ambrodale, and I bet even more so. Still, he preferred to know the visitor beforehand for an invitation, just to be sure he did see the Fox. He would undoubtedly rush an apology if the Fox were indeed recognizable.

"Dear me, oh gracious no, no, no, I'm really quite sorry, truly am! Do not mean to intrude." The Fox shakily replied, glancing behind the Hare and Moose to see the interior of the warm, cozy cottage.

"Me oh my, I must say ye 'ave such a charming 'ittle hum." Said the Fox with an endearing snicker.

Wally thanked him and, just like that, offered him to come in; the Fox hopped right on in, and from his blistered, grody feet, tracks of mud that were adhesively clumped on the bottom of his grimy heels trailed in behind which smudged the Hare's ornate carpet. Though this was noticed by Sampson and Wally, and the greasy trail was detested equally, by both, Wally thought it best not to begrudge the visitor. Still, Sampson thought it best to call it to attention, but Wally calmingly urged the Moose not to say anything. The strange Fox, aware of the tracks and his Host's displeasure, frenetically apologized, took a stick he saw from the corner, and scraped off the last of the gooey residue from his well-travelled drifter feet.

Wally felt quite sorry for the odd, shaking stranger for an unknown reason. By the innocence in his heart, he was glad to welcome such company. Maybe too trusting, but nevertheless, he thought it was the right thing to do! After all, Ambrodale does get quite chilly at nightfall.

"No need to catch a cold, my friend. Please come along in and make yourself right at home! We do have some tea and treats if you would like it! I'm Wallis, but friends call me Wally!" The Hare happily said, closing the door behind them, soon to walk back to where Sampson was slowly lumbering through and with a close watchful eye on the Fox who swayed in front ahead of them both. In amazement, the stranger gawked at all the unique items he had never seen.

The Fox's eyes, alight with curiosity, scanned the room with unrestrained delight. "Whyles is me name. A little pint of rum wud do nicely if'n ye p'ease! An' some cakes if ye 'ave 'em!" He chimed in, his voice bubbling with enthusiasm.

Without a moment's hesitation, Whyles began his tour with vigorous excitement. His hands flew from shelf to shelf, casting aside books with an almost childlike abandon. The globe on its stand was spun with a great flourish, its colorful continents blurring in his whirl of discovery. He peered into every cabinet, flung open each door, and rummaged through every drawer, his movements a whirlwind of energetic exploration. The room soon bore the marks of his enthusiasm, a charming chaos of overturned books and scattered curiosities that spoke of his boundless fascination with the new and unknown.

"Plenty!" The Hare found himself answering with a deep sighing and quiet recovering breath as he dashed across the room. Quickly pulling the hot steaming biscuits from the oven with his red and white laced oven mitts, he hopped to the corner and filled a tankard with rum from a barrel. He made it two tankards after the Frog had called for some as well. Still flabbergasted by the stranger, Wally called the Fox to come to sit and join them for the meal. Whyles quickly

scurried, did as he was told, and sat on a comfy red seat. He seemed to have never sat on one before from his excitement squishing and wiggling on the chair with such unusual joy. He jumped on the springing seat for a moment, but then he soon stopped when Wally handed him a bowl of stew, his cup of rum, and a biscuit. Now warmed by the lighted fire, gazing at the sparks that flew as little flames danced 'round the firebox illuminating the dark stone hearth. Such was the lively power of Wally's fireplace before a new visitor.

"Booney, this is our new friend, Mr. Whyles..." Wally introduced the Frog to the skittish Fox.

"Hella t'er', I'm Booney! Put it here. I bet ye are much honored to meet me; why 'ave you heard of me!?" The speckled Frog introduced himself rather boastfully, reaching his hand out for a hardy shake. Still, it was left to be empty as Whyles, with a greedy air, tipped back his tankard and poured the rum down his throat in great gulps. The frothy liquid, not all of it finding its way within, splashed untidily across the floor. As he set the tankard aside, he seized a crumbling biscuit and took a hefty bite! As crumbs fell onto the now dirty floor beneath him. One could not help but feel a wee bit of sympathy for Whyles. He bowed his head in acknowledgment of the Frog. "If I may ask, where are you from, Whyles?" Wally asked, now finished with his meal. As he started to collect all the used plates and silverware from the table, he balanced one on top of another, stacking it up on the counter to be washed whenever he could (certainly not now.) He sat once more on the stool in the center of the room, and while crossing his legs, he clenched his whittled corn cob pipe. Fitted with a river reed stem, the pipe dangled between his buck teeth. He grabbed ahold of a tobacco jar from where it sat on the hanging cabinet above, stuffing tobacco into the very top of the bowl, he briskly lit the bowl. He then started slowly drawing and releasing in relaxing repetition. The escaping smoke he lightly blew changed into a series of small and large smoke rings just before they sailed away. The smoke rings lofted by the soft breeze that swiftly came by from an open window. (No doubt he acquired the trait from long years of practice, one might think.)

"No whar in particular, just here and there, most everywhar!"

"Well, surely, you must have a home? Somewhere with yer family an' friends?" The Moose asked.

"Got none!" The irenic Fox boasted with a shrug. He didn't seem to care much, either. The Fox seemed to be quite nonchalant with this gloomy matter.

"The fact is, having a family is much too troublesome. I have not the slightest desire to be a part of one netta!" He happily confessed.

With short-winded gasps of surprise, the trio of friends looked at each other, thinking they were in the presence of some fateful tragedy. What might have happened to the Fox's family? In such a case as this, they did not know what to say other than sorry.

"Surry? Surry for what? Certainly, it ain't a concern! I do manage. Not anyone's fault anyhow, me own." The Fox announced, looking at the many pictures of relatives the Hare scattered throughout the room. With each picture, Whyles came up with many inquiries on who each family member was, pointing to each as Wally chuckled and gave the Fox an answer: "That's me Great Grandmother, that is, Gamma Ann Tunnelly! A sweet creature was she, and there she is with my Great Granddaddy Charles Tunnelly, who, believe it or not, built this cottage with his own two paws. Me bein' in the family an' all, I now rightfully inherited this haven! My kin was one of the first families of this Wood. True story!" Wally replied when the Fox asked who was in the frame in the center of the hearth. Whyles was quite intrigued by such a large family as he continued to examine the umpteen portraits.

"May I?" The Fox had politely asked, looking at the lighted pipe he had pointed to.

"Well, I'll gladly share a bowl of tobacco with you, friend; such a fine blend is it!" Wally smiled, handing it over to the eager Fox, who started to puff it as fast as he could. "Do be careful; my pipe has some kick to it, I must say. Slow and steady!" Warned Wally, but alas, before too long, the fast-puffing Fox he was talking to disappeared into a heavy and thick smoke, and through the midst of clouds from the billow, they could see a green, sickly face. Joyous laughter filled the room, seeing the Fox as green as one could be on Saint Patty's Day and as vile as a sea tossing ship taking a series of breeching waves of seasickness. After a while of talking and talking and more talking, it was getting very late in the night. In fact, just before Sampson and Dooney went home, the night was about to be soon over, Whyles had started a little game of telling riddles, He highly enjoyed telling them, he seemed to be quite the expert in telling them too! And if one could only know how much the three quaint friends were fond of good puzzles. Unfortunately, they weren't very good at them…

Riddles of Whyles.

"Thirty men, but only two women, yet these two hold the most power. Dressed in black and white, they could fight forever. Who are they?" asked the eager Fox, though the others did not have a clue. They had guessed as well as they could, though each guess they shouted was incorrect, not once, but four tries.

"Chess pieces!" Whyles answered with a proud laugh.

And so, as the Fox was about to ask the next riddle, the three friends thought for sure they were to get the next one correct. They were very confident they would indeed manage.

"On we go!" Whyles said.

The fire slowly died down, and only the many shadows cast upon the dying light outgrew the four sitting friends.

"Aura cadaver, in graveyards we gather. In the living, we exist; in your closet, we persist. What are we?"

It was now Sampson's turn to answer. He tried to think, repeating the riddle to himself and comparing it to what an actual graveyard was associated with. Sampson brightly gleamed when he neared his answer, Whyles started to silently hiss. He seemed to not fancy anyone solving his puzzles. "Well, come on then! What is it?" Whyles rudely rushed the Moose.

"You are skellingtons!" Sampson had enthusiastically jumped with an answer. Whyles groaned as Wally congratulated Sampson, who felt wholly proud of himself!

"Oh, clam up, you ol' naffy. That was an easy one!" Booney butted in.

"You t'ink so, me friend? Well, let us see!" returned Whyles. "This one is for you!" He pointed.

"I'm easy to get into but hard to get out of. What am I?" The three friends thought, and right away, Sampson and Wally knew the answer: why it was so simple! It was what the Frog always was. But Booney's pride and smartness were nowhere to be found, and he was completely stumped. Stomping his feet, he demanded to know the answer. He looked to Sampson and Wally but was given nothing more than a chortle and that he was one of the biggest causes. The festering riddle bugged him, so he kept impatiently trying, pestered for the answer he could not figure out!

"TROUBLE!" they all shouted.

Booney's excitement turned to disapproval. With a quip, he responded, "Ha! Me? Trouble? Why, what an absolute joke! It's not funny, no, no, no, not one bit. I refuse to play such a foolish game!" The conceited Frog pouted.

"Oh, come, Booney. It's just a game. Besides, we were only kidding!" Wally encouraged. With this, the Fox continued.

"I arise when light shines but fade when dark appears; I grow when you are far but shrink when you are near; what am I?"

"Give up?" The Fox asked, giving them no time to answer.

"I am shadow! Shadows is me!" the Fox snapped, his voice cold and biting. There was not a moment's hesitation in his sharp reply, but the harshness of his tone, paired with a low, threatening growl, carried an unmistakable hostility. His eyes, cold and fixed, seemed to cut through the room with a keen, menacing glare. It was clear he had no grasp of how the riddles were meant to be played—or if he cared at all. The others exchanged uneasy glances, having no idea what had caused the Fox's sudden turning. His mood had shifted so violently that it soured the very air of what was meant to be a light-hearted game.

With this strange and unexpected boutade, the game quickly ended from tired yawnings to sleepy eyes.

The fire was now out with only a few lit embers. In the dark, from where they watched the firelight die, Wally turned the lamps on nearest to him. The clock struck eleven.

First, Sampson, who yawned and stretched, begged his leave and thankful for the company, began to lumber home. Then Booney left.

"Well, I think it's been quite a fun and amusing night, but the pub calls; see you chaps later!" "'Ave a good night!" Answered the Hare as the whistling Frog strolled out the door.

Soon, Whyles and the Hare were left alone. But before too long, Whyles slowly slunk away, hinting he had nowhere to stay.

"Don't be silly, friend, why surely, if you haven't a place to stay, why don't ye stay here if ye like!?" Wally kindly offered.

"Just gimme a moment or two so I can prepare!"

"I wouldn't like to be such a burden, me frien', I surely do witout!" Replied the

Fox.

"Come, Whyles, don't be foolish; you are certainly not a burden!" Wally yelled back as he made his last adjustment in the guest room, patting the soft pillow and bed and tucking in the sides of the red blanket. He called the Fox and said it was all ready whenever he wanted to retire. The Fox thanked him and, just like that, turned in for the night, shutting the door.

"What odd company I do invite." Wally thought to himself as he poured a pot of cold water onto the remaining embers, which steamed and sizzled out and were replaced by soaked ash. Little did the Hare know he was carefully being watched by the Fox from the door's crack. Wally closed the door of his room and grabbed a stack of blank sheets of paper. Sitting on the chair, he held a quill ink pen; in the dead still silence of the night, the Hare started to write; after a while of jotting, he took a small break, wiping his watery eyes. He briefly glared through the window by his side. With only a few cottage lights flickering in the distance. Mere faint music played in the background and could be heard as Wally wrote. The wavering music, which slowly became more fluttering, sounded like those flittering colorful wings of a floating butterfly. The strange music had come from Whyles's room and echoed around the ghostly quiet home. Indeed, the Fox seemed to be playing the fife with its soft high and deep low ranges comprising a wispy melody, an enchanting whisper rising and falling, as Wally kept writing page by blank page throughout the night…

Chapter Five

A Day in Ambrodale

The morning dawned bright and busy. Wally, ever prompt in his habits, scurried about to prepare a hearty breakfast. Toast with jam, a bowl of oats and grains topped with slices of ripe banana, succulent pears, and berries freshly picked from the market, all neatly arranged. A dash of salt sprinkled over the bowl and a fresh bottle of milk to complete the spread. He called out to the Fox for the morning meal, but no answer came.

Perplexed, the Hare made his way to the guest room only to find it empty. Whyles was gone. Yet, the state of the room made it seem as though some wild revel had taken place in the night. Drawers hung open, papers torn and scattered upon the dark-stained cherry floor, and the bed was a scene of utter disarray. Wally stood in the doorway, quite taken aback at first, but then his surprise gave way to a soft smile. A mess like this was no burden to him—cleaning, after all, was just another task in a well-ordered life.

"Certainly, if he did leave, it would have been most polite to leave a note to say it! How odd, I surely didn't hear him." He thought to himself after walking to his cooling meal once more, for he had a whole day planned of showing Ambrodale to the stranger. However, as he watched from his window, whence he sat and ate, he saw the Fox lingering about, seeming to strangely observe his fellow Riverfolks' daily lives. After Wally was finished eating, he stepped out onto his porch, still watching Whyles quickly chase after some of the folk who tried to do their work of farming. The Hare called the Fox, but he was much too far away to be heard. After several attempts to call Whyles, Wally ran after him, catching up to the Fox (he wasn't mad but more surprised when Whyles snapped back with a harsh growl after Wally had asked when and why he had left so soon.) With this, the matter was dropped, and Wally started to take the skittish Fox around the wood. He had introduced Whyles to many of his friends who passed their way, including a rather bizarre pair who waddled through, carelessly bumping into one another while stepping on each other's feet. They chatted away until they saw the new stranger and Wally coming along the trail.

"Hullo 'ere Wally! A fine day, isn't it?" "Good day, sisters, very fine!"

"And who is this dashing new stranger with you? Oh my, a very charmin' fellow!" The two asked with excitement. They were sisters, the Quaddling sisters, to be precise, and they were quite the pair of twins those two Ducks were. Adelia was the oldest, and Miriam was the youngest. The only way to tell them apart was the different kinds of colored ribbons they were wearing on their otherwise matching Mobcaps they garbed. Both were in a very decorative style, wrapped with a floral wreath. They had also fashioned themselves with identical homespun gingham dresses with frilled collars. They both lived upstream in Sunberry Pond, where the Bromby River seemed to start flowing and small waterfalls rippled.

The sisters were both sometimes quite irrational, obnoxious, and always loquacious. They never carried on a dull conversation, though Miriam was more obnoxious and talkative than Adelia. It was clear that both were very hard to understand. Still, there was something quite charming about their misunderstandings of how they illogically communicated, waiting for the other to finish the endings of each sentence. They always seem to bicker amongst themselves about how this or that should be appropriately placed and how this should happen and not that in their ongoing dispute.

The two sisters spent most of the long day fussing over their looks while waddling around the wood. They spent undue amounts of time gossiping to one another about this and that, that, and this. Although, the most compelling thing about them was how they innocently tried to be so perfect. They often spent hours in the sunshine by the glistening river, preening their feathers to nearly refined perfection. The diligence with which they tended their bodies and manner of dressing made them quite unusual for the inhabitants of Ambrodale. Whilst others in the wood spent their hours pursuing spontaneous and somewhat lazy pleasures, the sisters felt these pursuits were beneath them. Each sister thought it was her duty to look her best in all circumstances and present herself to the world as a beautiful and desirable member of the community in which they lived. The care each took in preparing and presenting their tea time meals and the delectable tarts they baked had a certain grace felt by each guest they entertained. As stated before, squabbles did occur between them; even on such occasions, their guests, other than Wally, would often feel embarrassed and awkward by their strange bickering behavior.

Despite their sometimes-conflicted demonstrations and disagreements, their guests often felt gratified by the sisters' devoted attentions. Both sisters also had the same infatuation, Wally, who happens to be our hero in this story. They both fondly adored the Hare from afar. Due to their frequently close proximity, it was difficult for them to show their admiration for him. When Wally walked by, they would giggle and blush like giggly schoolgirls. Since the other sister often ended the other's sentence, it was hard to acknowledge what was to be interpreted, so the two sisters constantly bickered over the Hare in this way. This sometimes left poor, confused Wally to decide which was best suited to offer helpful tips and advice. Wally would have to judge the advice given by one lady over the advice given by another while considering their best traits, skills, and personalities. The difficulty came when Wally had to assess them in this way.

The problem was that their traits were almost identical, with a few mild differences. Wally had to carefully consider each of their strengths as he knew they would benefit from their conversations. Their method of talking to the Hare and almost anyone else, including themselves, was incredibly strange. But their little adventure shall be told later...

And so, with this conundrum in mind, Wally answered, "This is my new friend, Mr. Whyles... Whyles, this is Miriam and Adelia."

Whyles didn't speak at first but just nodded in response, his eyes cast down. "How do you do?" Said Adelia.

"Goodness, a bit shy, I would say! Is he mute?" Asked Miriam in oblique concern for him, with a bit of added sass put forth. She was somewhat worried that the poor Fox could not speak or hold a conversation, specifically an intriguing one.

"Oh, do hush up, Miriam, where are your manners? Be civil about it; don't you harass the poor creature for bein' mute. He cannot hulp it!" Adelia scolded her younger sister, flapping her wings.

"But indeed, he is a mute? It seems naturally indubitable!" She, too, asked curiously, a bit too blatantly.

"Naturally, indubitably, it does!" Said Miriam.

"Well, no, certainly not... just not very talkative presently, nothing wrong with that, is 'ere?" Wally answered chivalrously.

Both sisters looked at each other and giggled. Just like that, they begged their leave and awkwardly wobbled away, continuing to talk to one another while looking back and laughing at the stranger.

"Many strange folks!" The Fox finally answered with a heavy sigh of relief, turning to Wally as they both watched the two sisters argue, with the asynchronous honking, like of two crackly nonmusical tooting horns, stepping on each other's feet in the distance.

"What a gabbling pair; one might never know what might come out of their beaks!" Admitted Wally.

They continued onward, only stopping in the center of the wood from where all the creatures gathered on bright early mornings. This would happen, and everyone might greet each other in the large market area where they had bartered for their daily needs. A giant Allen Russell tree that seemed to reach the heavens was rooted in the middle of the market plaza, a most beloved centerpiece of this village. It stood before them, bedazzled with ornaments. The giant, healthy roots twisted their long stems for the tree's stability. Under the twisted and elevated roots, the river folk would merrily laugh and sing as they all gathered in celebrations in the central plaza. If one was not careful, it was much too easy to stumble on its large, noticeable sows surrounding and entwined the colorful market stands and festive banners drooping from above. The banners were tied on wooden supports amidst the roots. The tree itself was a sacred monument.

"Why, this is the first tree ever encountered by the first settlers of Ambrodale, for good reason, too! You see, it's an extraordinary tree, we do reckon. It shines a bright blue light at the darkest of nights; no one can explain it; it's very odd, but all we can truly agree on is that it was always here and will always be here!" Wally casually answered with a friendly, perky hop.

Wally told Whyles that it was called Miracle Tree or Father Tree, depending who you asked. It indeed was a sacred tree that guarded this wood, a particular myth was recorded in connection with this bizarre phenomenon. It was spoken of in ages past when Ambrodale was first discovered. Ambrodale's first settlers, not yet equipped for the harsh environment, fell severely ill from the disease. By a desperate act of rogation, they turned toward the most fabulous marveling sight they had ever seen. They thought it was a glowing tree smoldering with a bejeweled fire. They beseeched the luminescent tree for the cure for their illnesses brought by their harsh travels, offering plenty of the gifts they had carried to appease whatever saintly presence the tree possessed. With its extraordinarily anomalous presence, the gifts they offered seemed to significantly please the tree itself. It had begun to blossom with many colored blooms, and through the final stages of its blossoming, it ejected many tiny flecks within a shining mist that spread through the sickly settlement. As the floating specks whirled across the highland, miraculously, it had begun to cure any lingering infections and other diseases the settlers had been blighted with. From then on, the shining tree had been a sacred spot, the very heart of Ambrodale. It soon became a gathering place for those devoted to nature. Even those who sought remission of stubborn, sometimes crippling illnesses were granted blessings and attained good health; by each season's beginning, Miracle Tree was always highly celebrated for its selfless marvels. Like the first celebration of the foundling travelers, it would always be an ongoing tradition to toast the tree with salutations and vespers for health and good fortune.

The Fox was not interested in this tree and was not impressed by it. For he has seen many trees, all the same, all of them quite ordinary, he never believed in such fairy tales, but again, he seemed not to have much to believe in anything. He quickly turned to see Wally at a corner stand picking some sweet apples freshly picked this early morning. Soon afterward, Wally had returned with plump, sweet apples in a basket and offered one to the Fox, who had brashly snatched it from the Hare's paw. Just then, the two noticed an elderly turtle waving a stick in the direction of a small, clustered group of children standing in a row with quiet and fervent attention.

"Children are much tha same almost everywhar, always being scolded fir such foolish little games." The Fox belittlingly snickered, but as he thought of what scolding they must rightfully have deserved, the Fox's thoughts were interrupted and, must I say, silenced by soft, lovely voices that gently broke into a song. The vesper, once faint, grew louder and louder. Each singing adorable child was not being scolded but rather conducted by the kindly old turtle. He called out slight changes in their performance, such as, 'Leo, switch positions with Mary' and 'Harold, a little louder, please,' 'Jane dear, please no slouching stand straight and tall, sing with passion, ah, that's it!' Such, it seemed, was the right way to the children, they amiably obliged what the teacher had corrected. Now, with heartfelt passion and three taps of the stick, they began to sing from their hearts instead of their heads. The many Riverfolk who were on their way for their farming were soon to stop and huddle around the choir in a crowd of delighted faces.

Merrie May

Ah! Hey, ho!

O'what a day!

Indeed, it must be Merrie May.

Glistening leaves a-whirling 'round, Ol' Maypole crowned,

High from the ground,

Through bushes, trees, and muddied knolls, On and on the festival rolls.

Out we come to see it all,

The freshest of things that e'er there be,

Dancing flowers, purest hues, the blooming of trees.

With a hey-ho-ho And a fiddle-dee-dee,

O' day before us, bright and free!

O' night we leave behind,

Brings warmth to the hearts of every kind, And songs so merrie and fine.

Oh, my May, let us tarry 'Neath the blue sky,

Till evening's twinkling stars on high. Bring our voices here, both far and near,

O' month of joyous hours,

We sing, we dance in the bloom of Merrie May!

Once the song was softly finished with cute giggles and whispers, it ended with a loud happy cheer and cries of an encore, the deafening applause from the ever-heartening crowd. The little fidgety children with rosy, plump smiling faces took a bow. They scurried their way down to the gathered crowd as the children huddled around them. "Oh, such lovely children, indeed are!

Such a wonderful song was it! Bravo, children, very marvelous, all of you did very splendidly!" Cheered along the laughing Hare as he gave each child a swinging toss of a hug.

"How did I do, Uncle Wally?" A little bunny asked, tugging Wally's overalls.

"Absolutely marvelous, Clarence!" Wally said with a slap of a knee and a tickle of Clarence's stomach. He was Wally's unique little buddy, and Wally took it for granted that any of little Clarence's needs were mostly well met. Clarence was the smallest of the children and certainly the most rascally of the bunch. He was timid but often rather excitable. He was a little whirlwind. Clarence had a naughty reputation for being a sweet snatcher, earning the title on the count of stealing scrumptious tarts and other delectable pastries when no one was looking. He poked his little head around, making sure everything was clear, then swung his arms and snatched whatever was left cooling on the windowsills. Whenever little Clarence was caught, the giggling bunny, unaware that his face was smeared with jam and pasted crust flakes, would deny such accusations, hiding the empty tin pot behind his back.

The mercurial Fox, not wanting to draw any attention or be involved in this blundering gala, cautiously slinked away from the crowd and frankly refused to join in any such convivial palaver. The Fox, suspicious of this mysteriously joyous occasion, merely desired to be left alone, While crouching alone in the shade, he bequeathed bone-chilling stares while throwing unseen arrows into the vulnerable backs of the celebratory congregation. The Fox began mumbling to himself in some incomprehensible way. It did not matter what untasteful cusses he was muttering; no one was there to hear him as he lurched behind a few good feet away from the cheering group. Whyles found it altogether detestable, everyone but Whyles was quite impressed and amused. The Fox felt anything but joy: with spite, embarrassment and discomfiture, a surreal anger met this spontaneous adulation dotted with such strange and rather unusual company chattering before him. It was a disturbing shock for such a newcomer who had never participated in the odd-seeming experience he was now spitefully witnessing. (For example, say one would wake to find they were living with a different family that morning, talking in a foreign and rather strange language that was unclear and untranslatable. One might sit and go on pretending to know what they're saying, dumbly.) That was precisely how the Fox was feeling, alone in the crowd, as it were. With all this randomness, strangely enough, part of the astringent Fox could not reflect back the warm feeling the community was sharing. To him, the very thought of it caused him to scorn and loathe the idea of being so confined with joyful strangers who seemed to mock his misery. Both sides of his mind were clashing as he stood there alone, unfavorably observing this boisterous shindig, racking his addled brain over this outlandish intimacy. It was beyond aggravating to have any understanding of this incomprehensible gathering.

At the top of his pique, the disturbed Fox could no longer stand such unbearable oddity. The huddled children, now shying away from the tremendous amount of loving attention they were receiving, speedily ran off to an empty green field a ways yonder. It was just a perfect little spot to be played within. The little troupe began romping and laughing during their games while screaming aloud,

"Catch me if you can, you can't catch me!" And on, they chased and dodged. Some children stayed put, cavorting nearer to the Fox than he preferred.

One of these rambunctious children ran behind the unsure Fox, hiding behind him. The nervous Fox was feeling several teeny fingers fidgeting beneath his coat. The Fox let out a surprised chortle and then realized that the hapless child was indeed tickling him with a gleam of pure innocence. Tantalized and surprised by the tender child's peculiar ebullience, the charmless Fox bit back a raving impulse to strike at the youngster. He alternatively curled his scarred lips while proudly unveiling his fangs. This gave the Fox such a menacing glower, just as if he spat out a wordless chiding. "Get away from me, BRAT!" The giggling child, bolstered by untapped beatitude, quivered with the mute Fox's smoldering comportment. Their lively spirits were instantly sucked away, and breaking into blubbering tears, they ran off in terror. Thankfully, soon forgetting the whole ordeal, whence he caught up to the rest of the small band of children playing tag or, how they say it, 'Catch me if you can,' he was surrounded by his little friends again. Each child stepped into proper formation, skedaddling off, playing on the lush green fields again.

Shortly afterward, the many creatures who happened to see the new stranger, called him down and greeted him with open arms and smiling faces. 'Very strange, why so many folks are happy...very witless,' he thought. He did not respond to any of the welcoming creatures. He also felt quite odd dealing with these folk. He never wanted or desired to know, as such, the warm feeling of having or being a friend. He concluded it was too much of a hassle to keep a friendship going and too much of a burden to make it last. He answered with not a word but responded to their well-intentioned inquiries with an unfriendly snicker, shooing them off. He seemed obnoxious, bothered when approached with a friendly greeting, and was not the kindest one to meet, so it looked. With sneers and hisses from the Fox, the creatures did not say a word but quickly left in fright and bewilderment.

Even though they might accept this stranger with open arms, the Fox would never understand that. What would have been most disturbing to the riverfolk was not the Fox's stubborn taciturn and off-putting refusal to acknowledge their friendly gestures toward him. Instead, they would have been horrified to see the shadowy hooded figure beneath the moon, his skipping feet twirling along the twisted path of Sullen Fields. He lured them away by the mysterious call of his piping. His strangely ecstatic, solitary dancing with a bewitching call might be leading them right to their doom. Unbeknownst to the dancing figure, he would sadly regret this in his moments of conscience, later to emerge. Despite his best efforts to kill that same voice of spirit that longed to live within him.

Chapter Six

Resentment of Whyles

Prejudice, it appeared, was a matter of established pattern. The Fox had grown increasingly bitter toward the Riverfolk, as he had made abundantly clear on numerous occasions. Their presence unsettled him, like a discordant note in a symphony, and he found their lightheartedness maddening. They, in turn, regarded him with suspicion, wary of his sharp tongue and erratic moods, which suited Whyles' temperament just fine. But Wally, who prided himself on fairness, had always taken to Whyles like an older brother—though even he couldn't ignore the Fox's deeply ingrained prejudice.

One such instance found Whyles prowling through the market as if searching for prey in a henhouse. The stench of fish guts and damp fur filled the air, mingling with the clamor of voices, setting Whyles' teeth on edge.

An Otter approached, balancing a basket of fresh fish. His whiskers twitched as he smiled. "Morning, stranger! Care for some of the river's finest catch? Fresh as can be."

Whyles stopped, his eyes narrowing as he took in the otter. His lips curled into a sneer. "Finest? Looks more like yer dredged up garbage from the bottom of the river. Ye lot would eat anything, wouldn't ye?"

The Otter's smile faltered. "That's uncalled for," he said, his voice tight

"Work hard?" Whyles cut in with a derisive laugh. "If splashin' about like drunken tadpoles and selling scraps counts as work, then perhaps I've been giving ye too much credit."

A hush fell over the market. Riverfolk paused to watch, their eyes narrowing. The Otter's grip on his basket tightened. "You've got a sharp tongue for someone who doesn't belong here."

Whyles leaned in, his grin sharp as a knife. "And you've got a short temper for someone who's knee-deep in filth. What's tha matter? Not used to hearing the troot?

The Otter lunged, shoving Whyles backward. Fish scattered across the ground as Whyles stumbled but quickly regained his footing. Without hesitation, he swiped a claw across the otter's shoulder.

"You think you're better than us?" the Otter snarled, struggling to push the Fox back.

"Better?" Whyles laughed bitterly. "That's not even a question. I wouldn't trade places with one of ye filthy creatures for all the gold in the kingdom!"

Before the altercation could escalate, Wally appeared, squeezing through the crowd. His ears flicked with irritation. "Whyles, what are you doing? This is the third time this week you've caused trouble!"

Whyles scoffed, brushing off his coat. "Trouble? I'm doing them a favor. Someone needs to teach these muck-dwellers their place."

The Otter growled, but Wally stepped between them, holding up a paw to stop him. "You're not helping anyone, Whyles. You're just stirring up trouble."

The Fox's eyes flickered with something darker. "You, too? What's the matter with you, Wally? You feel right at home with these… these bottom-feeders?" His voice was low and clipped, as if the words pained him.

The crowd grew tense, but Wally remained calm. "You can't keep pushing everyone away. You'll end up alone."

For a moment, Whyles stood still, his eyes betraying a flicker of uncertainty. But it vanished quickly, replaced by the familiar scorn. "I've wasted enough time here. Let the rats have their scraps," he muttered, turning on his heel and stalking off.

The otter muttered something under his breath, but Wally held up a paw, calming the situation. "Let him go," he said. "He's not worth it."

As the Riverfolk returned to their business, Wally lingered, his gaze following Whyles' retreating form.

"You keep this up, Whyles," Wally whispered to himself, "and one day, you're going to find when you most need someone there none will appear."

Wally's mind wandered, pondering the roots of the Fox's bitterness. Whyles' behavior seemed erratic, some days distant, others volatile—but one thing was certain: he wasn't merely the product of prejudice. Something deeper was at play, and Wally had an inkling it had to do with the ghosts of Whyles' past. The Fox never spoke of it, of course. But it was there, hidden behind his sharp retorts and cutting remarks. There was something about Whyles—a sharpness that went beyond mere disdain. A part of him seemed always at war with himself, like a mind that couldn't quite hold onto the threads of its own thoughts.

And yet, Wally persisted. No matter how many times the Fox lashed out, the Hare couldn't quite bring himself to abandon him. Perhaps, in time, Whyles would let his guard down. Or perhaps not. It wasn't for Wally to know, only to stand by as best he could.

Trouble In Teacups

As a long afternoon went on, Wally had spent the entire bloom of his early morning rise in a decorous preparation. However, being a forgetful Hare, he managed a get-together that never went according to his scheduled plan. The parties he threw were either too late or too early, and as frequently happened, he had completely forgotten some of the details. He would fail to remember such occasions when he did invite his friends. On the day of the event, he sometimes saw his guests show up when he did not recall scheduling any such party or event himself. It could really make him quite addled, alarmed, and embarrassed when they approached with a smile and with an expectation of being fed and entertained. When he somewhat reluctantly invited them in, though, it was all in his good nature for him to keep to his promise. It was already a quarter past four that day, and he was still preparing. "Oh, darn it all." He said sharply and exasperatedly as he poured the tea into the cups. He hastily hung the party banners above the tea set. "Quarter past and still have lots and lots n' even more lots to do…"

Now did he start to rush, paying no attention or heed to the time. Quickly, he scavenged anything he could and messily rustled up a fine stew. He then ran to his pantry and grabbed plump blueberry muffins, which he laid on the wooden tabletop.

As Wally readied himself for their surprise afternoon gathering, Whyles fidgeted restlessly in his room, his impatience barely contained. The Hare, typically adept at keeping secrets, was rendered nearly speechless with excitement. Meanwhile, in the confines of Whyles's room, the Fox's agitation was manifesting in a torrent of frantic mutterings and vexed curses.

Without warning, just as Wally completed his preparations, a series of thunderous crashes erupted from Whyles's chamber, jolting the unsuspecting Hare into action. Rushing to the source of the clamor, Wally was met with a scene of utter chaos. The Fox, consumed by an uncontrollable fury, had laid waste to the room. Furniture lay scattered, quilted blankets were shredded, and the walls bore the marks of Whyles's claws, tearing through the striped wallpaper as if it were mere paper. Plaster dust swirled in the air like a storm, covering everything in a fine, ghostly layer.

The sound of destruction was unrelenting—a harsh, drawn-out screech akin to metal scraping against a chalkboard. The room was enveloped in dust and debris, a stark attestation to Whyles's unrestrained rage.

As Whyles turned to the distressed Hare, his voice was a mix of despair and bewilderment. "Oh, my poor walls! My dear room!" He moaned, gesturing to the wreckage strewn about. Wally, deeply concerned, surveyed the damage. Much of what was ruined were irreplaceable relics, cherished heirlooms passed down through generations. "What on earth has happened?" Wally asked, his voice thick with worry and disbelief.

"What's it taking so looooong!!!?" The Fox aggressively snapped, "Ye t'ink I've got nuttin' better to do than WAIT, WAIT, WAIT.WAAAIIIIIIIIIITT!!!!!!"

"OOOOH, weeeell, pardon me! It does take some time…yes of course, as well it should. You must have PATIENCE…patience is how balancing works, after all, without pati-"

"Patience is for fools who shrink away like cowards!" Whyles snarled as Wally calmly interrupted his tirade.

"Patience is quite a virtue; it can make things happen well when needed!"

The Fox grunted in disagreement. He did not want to agree, but Wally's calm tone began to still his agitated mind.

"Why, can you imagine a world without patience? Horrible! Why, if there was no patience, where would there be compassion and care for others? When a muhther holds her screaming child, can she not feel something of patience for it? Does she not love it even though it screams and screams? She wants the child to be happy at any cost, even if it doesn't please her much at the time... but it's so easy to judge rashly and so easy to fall hard."

Whyles stood motionless, half angry and half about to cry out loud. He could not believe that Wally could see so deeply into him, even though Whyles had tried hard not to reveal anything about his past.

"I did nae mean nuthin' by it." Whyles whispered under his breath unconsciously. They both stood aghast, though Wally had not heard him at all.

In the awkward silence, Wally lovingly added, "Oh well, no need to make a fuss for such a silly thing. It's quite an easy job to fix, and before you know it, it'll be like new. Come, it is ready now!" The Hare happily remarked, trying to lead the Fox. But Whyles only hunched and glared now with a transfixed harshness. It was a kind of standoff-like staring into the mouth of a coldhearted shark that had no feelings for the world.

Whyles' black pupils reflected the soul of such a creature. Some may have kicked such an unkind bother out of their home. Wally had not the slightest thought of doing it himself; he could not help but feel very sorry for a despairing being such as Whyles, who was unaware that he had called for aid, to Whyles though it seemed it wasn't a cry for help, nor was the Fox grateful for Wally's understanding and kind attention. It was as if some strange mixed signals interfered with his misconceived, even myopic thoughts. Once some incident or memory triggered his emotions, Whyles could become almost invaded by a buried mental crisis brought on by his unsettled past. He could not yet conceive that anything might even be entirely wrong, though he still seemed to grieve from time to time for reasons unknown to him. He would prefer to keep his history a secret, which is hard to maintain. In it all, he felt so very ALONE.

The Hare, who sat alone under the festive banners, tapping his cup of tea with a spoon as he gingerly plopped three small cubes of sugar, was soon greeted by the heavyhearted Fox. Whyles did not make eye contact, but with a quick look of guilt, he quickly cast down his eyes; with no word, he joined the Hare sipping his tea; deciding it was too hot, Wally started to blow to make it more relaxed. "Funny thin's are 'ose muhther's." Wally began slowly to make small talk.

Whyles continued quietly murmuring to himself, not wanting to be heard, just hoping… Whyles cynically stared into his cup of tea and saw his watery reflection. As the Hare continued to speak, Whyles listened.

"So much do they love their child that they would comfort them ceaselessly an' 'ey would through all the nights. They would nay but sleep until their child is merry! Protecting 'em n' all, at any cost… what sacrifices they choose for the safety of their little lads and lassies! Dare I says, what strength 'ey must carry all o' a' days! Life is what you make it, friend; the world, as you see it, can affect all your relations… those who are lucky can see what exemplary life can genuinely possess. If not, they won't mix into a lousy crowd somewhere. It better not having to deal with such ruffians who play upon innocen-"

With this said, Whyles could no longer bear his inner grief. Whatever Wally had mentioned made the already wounded Fox rashly hurl his cup of tea at the wall on the other side of the room! I HAD NE'ER A MUTHER! I GOT NOTHING…. NOT A FAMILY… I WASN'T ONE OF THOSE LUUUUUCKY ONES, PLUCKING CHRISTMAS PREASUNTS WITH JOLLY,

WHOOOOLESOME PLEEEEASURES! The Fox hissed. His pain was evident with each gasping breath. "I've had the worst of times NONE has ever has; im da only one to feel the torment of having.. nothin'.. no one understands an' never they will."

"My friend, everyone has had the worst of times at some point. Why I'll bet most half of folk outside are havin' troubles of 'ere owns…They might also be afraid of what might happen if they don't go on and give in to 'ose fears. Why, no one has ever had the best of days all o' the time.

An' why maybe they do know the pains you're goin' throughs. After all, you'd nevah know. Some of my plants in the garden are green all year, and some turn brown in a week or so. By and by, the brown ones sometimes show a green in 'er time. And from the witherin' of the stalks an' stems grows a flower or two where all 'as a dead. Things have seasons. Things need to grow a' the time. Things change; they must do so." Wally continued in a slightly jovial tone:

"It's a fine life, and it will be only fine if you make it fine!"

Wally had finished his counsel with a last calm slurp of his tea (and for you readers to know, the Hare was found to be very down to earth and starkly contrasted to the emotionally distracted and overwhelmingly uncollected Fox. Every acquaintance Whyles had met generally regarded the Fox as ungrounded and spacey. The look of his shallow, cold eyes seemed not to be holding any real focused awareness. It had seemed, indicated by the Fox's impassive face, that he had no hope for his future, and no hope was to be considered.

Whyles continued, this time in a low voice:

"I was raised in neither home nor safe place, with not a roof over me head but a cold, mossed stump, full'a buggies and en' wormies sliming en nipping me skins n' boney's bein' wit' no such a welcoming family, straining ever.. dead while alive, going 'ungray day after day. Still, a friend who took me in not long ago saved me from ruin. When they found me half-a'tumbleydowned, I only remember I 'uz all but gone. They offered a place to stay, warm meals, AND… for thanks, I am indebted for their efforts. Now I must runnin' n' go. I work for what I get, and they give me more! Traets me well, traets me fair 'ey do." He added in a barely audible sigh. "An' give me more they do than I even wants, it is." Whyles looked suddenly glum after he spoke those words. Wally noticed the change in Whyles and could not guess that such a good deal could make someone sad.

However, did it take a while, maybe a month, he suddenly remembered. In a way, during those four weeks, he had hinted, with small riddles and murmurs, that his past was not to be remembered without a shred of a tear but a truly deadening and upsetting expression. But for concealed and saddening reasons… hideous events of former abuse, did he quietly confess his hidden grief, which he had until now, little showed to his company of Wally when they both were alone. During the times when those quite chilled evenings came, Wally did not answer right away to the sudden news from Whyles about his troubled past, but he listened to what the Fox had to say.

He heard stories of abuse not by such strangers but by those close of blood, and so by each year's passing of his mistreatment, his trust in those around him had become string thin then, to almost no trust or love at all, to anyone he met. He did not feel any such comfort in trusting anyone nor showing any compassion to any but to himself in fear of such unspoken trauma, which had seemed to place a heavy, overwhelming burden on his behavior. Though he did not know why, he felt it right to say what was on his mind to a stranger whom he so utterly disliked; perhaps he was nuts, he thought. As surely as distrustful as Whyles was, he had soon felt an odd, different kind of bonding between such lovable characters as Wally indeed was and himself. He had thought he could have said anything to him without being snickered upon like some type of laughable joke (like the speckled Frog would surely do.) Complex as Whyles was, where one minute he was joyful, which would follow with an unexplainable instance of instability, he would unconsciously switch attitudes as if expressing another personality displayed with an irritated, angry stupor.

Wally was different, different from the rest from whom he met. By the acts of kindness he had so lovingly offered and his not being of critical judgment, did Whyles first realize how ungrateful he had been to those who had cared for him like the Hare, just plain ungrateful. Despite this, he would have only trusted the Hare to keep his secrets, definitely not anyone else. Somehow, did he know it was for the right reason to be suddenly so open with his, dare we say, "friend"?

Somehow, as he opened his heart, it was once closed hard to those who were loving of a loving nature. When I do say those, I mean Wally; his wretched past slowly faded from his mind, never to haunt nor torment as if awakening from a dark, chilling nightmare only to see those of his loved ones by your side the following day. The more the Fox had talked about his inner fears with the guidance of the Hare, the more those inner fears had ceased to manically overshadow how he had seen the world and its inhabitants. He had so been frightened for all these years past, not from wariness or intimidation, but by lack of compassion from those who could never be called friends.

Unfortunately, Wally was the only creature Whyles had befriended since the long month of his arrival. From their nightly intriguing discussions of exploration and travels, with no sense of ridicule, did Wally earned the trust of the Fox. The rest of the Riverfolk Whyles had paid no attention to and still showed no compassion nor acceptance the way he did with Wally.

▷ɔ

A Burden Unknown

The day began early for Whyles in a quiet, low-spirited way. It was the way it always started for him, but something in the Fox today was odd—maybe much more than usual. As if nervous, he was more neurotic than he usually was. When breakfast consisted of oats and grains, Whyles, who usually ate five bowls full, had a measly half of a bowl. He seemed to dread this coming day, anticipating a specific future moment that dug into his mind. When asked by the Hare what was wrong, the Fox did not say but jumped up. When approached by his friend, Whyles' paws unwillingly trembled, and his knees clacked together. The strange Fox was found by the Hare who, lighting his pipe, observed Whyles from inside his home. Wally grew concerned as he witnessed the Fox muttering to himself and hunched by the corner of the porch outside. Whyles was fearfully viewing the distant borders of the Sullen Fields that hauntingly loomed near quaint Ambrodale in a hideous mockery of Ambrodale's quiet serenity. Whyles said something or other about a summit.

When Wally asked the Fox about this meeting that he had not heard of, Wally shuddered at the thoughts of Whyles' obsession. It seemed altogether unhealthy and repugnant to Wally that his friend could not free himself from a fear that visibly consumed Whyles. The burdened Fox had not directly responded to Wally but unexpectedly begged his leave to stroll freely through Ambrodale. Willingly, Wally did not intend to force Whyles to bide, and he was more anxious than usual by asking overwhelming questions that did not seem very appropriate for this time. The Fox's doleful mood expressed his annoyance at Wally asking those nosey questions. His questions did not make this situation any better but somewhat worse. Though, to be sure, Wally did ever so want to accompany Whyles, he now thought it would be for the best if Whyles were to be alone and for Whyles to solve his apparently hard-reaching problem for himself. Whatever it was, indeed, it left a rigorous, burdening conflict in resolving Whyles' emotional casualties.

In the rousing conclusion, Wally realized that the situation traumatized Whyles greatly. Because of the anticipated request from Wally to accompany him, Whyles quietly thanked him. The only way he knew how was to walk away. He continued until he suddenly stopped to think in front of Father Tree. Walking around the trunk, he made sure not to trip over the large roots of the tree. Many creatures saw him blathering to himself, and they quickly tried to avoid being caught.

"Why, t'ese Rivafulks huve nothings to offers, this'eh seems fooldish tah me's... thy friend will not be pleased by what I shall tell 'em all 'bout 'ere folk! 'Em good persons, howeva; happily odd. They may not like me and I the same, but truth is truth. Ne'er, they did me so much as a wrong deed. Can I not be somehow dismissed from it all?! E'er it is wi' myself. E'er there's naught but any choices." He continued to mutter and ponder, unaware of the crowd he was drawing in. When the Fox did look about, he saw the creatures looking at him. The onlooking creatures stood alone or in small groups, sometimes far from where he shuffled forward. They stared as if the small, lean Fox was unapproachable and crazy.

Whyles hissed at the watching rude strangers, but they did not leave; the Fox then scampered from where he stood, getting away from the bystanders. He ran as fast as he could, attempting in vain to escape from his agitated thoughts, which Hounded and confused him so with their many different and opposing voices. The voices told him what to do and not to do simultaneously without him being able to come to a single meaningful decision or conclusion. This time, he ran to find himself; he ran to forget, he ran to forget what he was meant to do. He somehow felt that by physically running, he might quell the voices in his suffering consciousness by the effort of sheer exhaustion. He had hoped that the voices would have died long ago, but the same voices seemed to be still observing him, poking and prodding into his moments of peace. It was all just the same to him as before. He could not loosen the grasp of the conflicting thoughts upon his restless mind. Everywhere he turned for peace, creatures were watching... nowhere was quiet, nowhere was there a secret place to hide from the creatures and even more from himself. Though he could name and describe what he desired, peace of mind and clarity were always out of reach; he could not attain it for any length of time. Still shambling, walking forward, he then saw a peaceful little spot in the wood. He hurried, in distress, towards that little spot on a hill where a giant maple tree stood. The tree's shade cooled him off as he rested beneath its broad trunk. He felt that the trunk supported him as he stood above the valley. As he began to enjoy that solitude, the thoughts of Sullen Fields were an invisible, stalking presence in his exhausted mind. Could there be a sanctuary from these invading thoughts that seemed to revolve around and around, leading nowhere but to a simmering confusion? With his indecision, he did not know whom to trust nor where to turn. 'But again, why can I nae repay for what they did for me?' he stammered. 'Clovis, what will they do to me… Clovis Kaine!! Why must I ta' face such cruelty for not obeying? But I am no criminal. Why must…? Why must I so?? Whyles asked himself while throwing clumps of grass and crusty leaves downhill to see them swept aloft by the cool breeze. Whyles started to twitch, unsure of his dark future. The truth for the Fox was unbearable. What was the unwanted truth to him? Why hold his fear? Why not throw his fears away? This, he wondered. This he wanted.

Clovis Kaine

That night, Wally slept peacefully in the room beside the restless Fox. Whyles could hardly get a wink of sleep as he mindlessly stared at Sullen Fields with terrified, widened eyes. It was the same story the whole day. With the dimming candlelight that soon went out, this was the time. This was the time when Whyles could no longer get away with stalling for time. The Fox quietly slipped out of the dark house, lit only by porchlight in the darkened wood. The birthstone blue stars brighter than ever illuminated the dense, inky, and ghastly hallucination that Sullen Fields had appeared to be. From where the Fox sneakily prowled through Ambrodale, passing cottages, fields, hedgerows, and dirt paths alike, the cottages in which he came across sneaking by were not wholly lighted. Each cottage had but one fading light of a waxen candle melting in silence at the front window.

Each path led in the same direction, and Whyles followed with quick, anxious steps. He stopped at Father Tree, its ethereal blue glow catching his eye. For a moment, wonder softened his otherwise wary expression, but he pressed on, knowing he couldn't linger.

Inside Phenny's Pub, the air buzzed with lively chatter, mugs clinking, and the rich smell of ale thick in the atmosphere. Booney the Frog sat at the bar, his red velvet jacket slightly askew, eyes half-lidded as he drained another swig. He leaned back, elbows propped against the counter, and launched into his usual rant—this time, about Whyles, the Fox.

"I tell ya, that Fox is one strange critter. Always skulkin' about like he's up to no good. I see him whisperin' to himself, eyes dartin' like he's seen the end o' days!" Booney's voice boomed, drawing the attention of the pub's patrons.

Nibber the vole, who had been quietly sipping his drink, piped up. "Saw him near the ol' mill last night, actin' all secretive, y'know."

"Aye, he's been around the burrows too," squeaked a mouse from a nearby table. "Sniffin' around, makin' my whiskers twitch!"

Booney gave a dramatic shudder, finishing off his drink with a satisfied gulp. "Mark me words, summypin off about t'at Fox. Wouldn't trust him near a chicken coop, let alone anywhere near us decent folk. Always schemin', I reckon, with sumptin' cookin' in t'at mangy head o' his."

Murry, the badger behind the bar, leaned in, his gruff voice low and conspiratorial. "Word's spreadin' 'round here, Booney. They say he's been sneakin' off at night, disappearin' into the fields. Some say he's meetin' with strangers, dealin' in all sorts of things." The gathered crowd murmured in agreement, nodding their heads.

"Aye, aye," Murry continued, voice dripping with intrigue. "Just last week, Old Fenna swore she saw him near the market after hours. Said he was talkin' to shadows."

Booney slapped the counter, grinning. "See! What'd I tell ya? He's a crafty one, alright. But I reckon I'll get to the bottom of it; just ye wait." As the night wore on and the crowd thinned, Booney drained his last mug and rose from his stool. He waved a crooked finger at Murry.

"Keep an eye peeled, Murry. I'll be the one to catch him in the act."

The crisp night air hit Booney as he stepped out, clearing the haze of the evening's drink. He staggered slightly, but his gaze remained sharp, his mind alert. The mist swirled around Father Tree, its branches glowing with a soft, mystic light.

Then, out of the corner of his eye, Booney spotted a figure moving through the mist. His heart gave a jolt. It was Whyles—the very Fox he'd been ranting about— slinking toward Gorse End with a furtive urgency.

Booney's instincts flared, suspicion gnawing at him. "Now, what's he up to?" He muttered, narrowing his eyes. Without a second thought, he straightened his jacket and slipped into the shadows, following the Fox.

As Booney drew closer, he noticed Whyles was lost in thought, his eyes darting nervously as he trotted through the mist. Without hesitation, Booney stepped forward and blurted out, "What's got you sneakin' about this hour, eh? Ye got sumptin' to hide, Fox?"

Whyles stiffened at the sudden voice and tried to brush off the question. "Just out for a stroll," he muttered, though his voice lacked conviction, and his eyes betrayed the anxiousness he tried to mask.

"A stroll, eh? In the middle o' the night?" Booney wasn't buying it. He squinted, inching closer. "What's really goin' on? Yer up to sumptin', and I can smell it."

Whyles shifted uncomfortably, his tail twitching. "Nuttin' important. Just needed some fresh air."

"Fresh air, is it?" Booney's eyes narrowed to slits. "Don't t'ink I'm fooled by yer fancy dribble. Why all the secrecy?"

"Secrecy? What secrets?" Whyles' voice wavered, clearly flustered. "No secrets, none at all." Booney crossed his arms, staring at Whyles with unabated suspicion. "I've got me eye on you, Fox. Whatever you're hidin', I'll figure it out, mark me words."

With that, Booney turned and staggered back into the mist, his footsteps fading into the night. Whyles stood frozen, watching the Frog disappear into the gloom, his dread deepening. He hesitated momentarily, then resumed his anxious journey toward Gorse-End, the cold light of the stars above indifferent to his plight.

He crossed the Crestwick bridge, then, suspiciously looking back, making sure none had followed, he continued to venture to the edge of Ambrodale (the luscious smell of the sweet grass dew was to be suppressed by the heavy stench of Gorse-End's grotesque swamp gas), and to the hideous entryway of Sullen Fields. This daunting region was haunted by nightmares of ghoulish shapes and deep cackling noises, a constant creaking of withered wood, and it embodied the desolation of forlorn and avoided landscapes. The last place and vividly nightmarish realm he wanted to travel through was, unfortunately, this broken land of despair. In his need to abandon such places forever, he now uncharacteristically began to hope for a way to conquer his lifelong fears and obtain the elusive serenity of mind that he sought. Indeed, rather than give into fear, this desolate waste made him realize that he never would seek contact with such a revolting site again. He felt a twinge of disgust at himself for his situation.

With a nervous twitch, he continued through the deepest and most treacherous heart of Sullen Fields. His reason for going the far distance on his journey was entirely his own. Firstly, it was cold, a deep cold that chilled the marrow in his bones. He did not chatter his jaws due to the cold but rather due to residual fear that had previously welled inside him.

A fine, bluish, phosphorescent mist hung about the twisted trees, and the sawtooth, silhouetted grasses cut at him as he walked slowly and cautiously forward. The black twisted trees seemed to stalk the Fox's every move. The cold, moist ground, so slippery that one may be swallowed whole, dogged his every sloshing step. Soon, as he kept to the strangely marked path and did not stray as they specifically said, he could hear faint whispers and ring of growls about him that he could hear but not see from whence they issued.

"Come out, Clovis, your attempts to frightenin' me off will not work! Come n' out an' show yourself.... I do have tha news!"

"Yer's are braves for's a dumbfounded idiot t'at ye BE!" Said a gruff voice in a quiet tone.

"Enough of yer absurd mockery, come out! I will go, and ye will never hear the news I have gathered! What say ye?"

With a loud guffaw came heavy treading steps, and out swaggered Clovis Kaine, tall, lean, and abominable. Clovis Kaine, a fiend, a grotesque tapestry of menace and distortion, was the sadistic embodiment of wild brutality. His long, saber-like fangs hung downward from a snarling maw, the sharp edges glinting faintly in the dim light as though eager to taste blood. His lips curled back in a sneer, exposing not just his fangs but jagged, uneven teeth, each one a shard of menace in itself. The rest of his face seemed to be carved from nightmares. His eyes were perhaps the most unnerving feature. Twin pools of blazing red, they burned with a malevolent, almost otherworldly fire, staring out from beneath heavy brows that shadowed them slightly adding to their eerie glow. They darted about, alive with malicious glee and an insatiable hunger for chaos.

His fodder always seemed to be those innocent beings that he desired to corrupt for his own barbarous advantage. A being with little strength or will could not withstand the onslaught of one like Clovis. Clubfooted he was, but it did not impede nor alter his petrifying demeanor. Clovis was always ghastily entertained when he preyed upon and caused havoc to the innocent. The brutal events he staged for his own pleasure often spiraled into bloody scuffles that seemed to erupt without warning, throwing those involved into a frenzy of violence. The confusion was tangible, as though something unseen were guiding the chaos— yet no one could put their finger on what it was. Victims would lash out at one another, their minds twisted by fear, each one feeling as though they were fighting an invisible enemy but seeing only the madness of the others around them.

Clovis reveled in this, watching with twisted satisfaction as the bloodshed unfolded. The scuffles, the desperate cries, the frantic attempts to control the uncontrollable—it all played out according to his design. And when the carnage reached its peak, he would stand at its center, surveying the wreckage, his cruel enjoyment only deepening as he realized how easily he had made fools of them all.

His origin was obscure and attended upon rumors of some primal past, never understood or assimilated by the hearer of such tales. Standing before Whyles, he could see Clovis' torn-apart ears in shadowed outlines. They were long, ragged, and looked as if something had taken large bloody chunks out of them. Also, such ears were pointed inward, adding a sense of profound deformity to his overcast appearance this wicked evening. In the darkness, Whyles could see his small golden earring glinting in the moonlight. It hung limply from a widened puncture in his left ear, dangling as if a useless trinket. His frizzled, oversized head was covered by a rusty brown, elongated, tattered tricorne hat. A long, dark scarlet feather seemed to pin the hatband. A giant, cumbersome, maroon frock coat hung on his lean, robust frame that curved and split into tails at the bottom. The coat was made of ancient velvet and had straying seams. Hanging like a veil, it was buttoned with black obsidian, four-holed buttons.

The coat hid Clovis' famished body, taut from constant roaming and predation. He buttoned the coat but for the two top buttons, which were to be left open plainly, exposing a bare chest with dirty, infected scars appearing to be some form of burn marks. (To those who had the most unfortunate curse to know such a cruel monster, it was to be obvious those scars were indeed burn marks.) Mottled across his scorched thick neck, meeting in a large hairless but bubbly spot on his blighted chest, searing by some internally abiding chthonic smoldering flame. Lashed along his waist was an old, raggedy white sash. Clovis wore dark brown pantaloons on his lanky calves and thighs below.

Beneath the coat, where the fabric twisted and swayed with his movements, a monstrous tail emerged. It was a great, coiling appendage, long and sinuous like the tail of a dragon—gleaming with iridescent scales that seemed to flicker in the dim light. The tail was lined with jagged ridges, its end tapering into a barbed, serpentine tip, glistening as if it could pierce through armor or bone. It flicked and swayed with a menacing rhythm, its every movement betraying a terrifying sense of control, and its scale-covered surface reflected a shimmer of malice.

His tail was just as twisted and nightmarish as himself, a physical embodiment of the chaos and destruction he so craved.

Whyles knew the fiend's bloodlust all too well, for it wasn't the first time he had spoken to such a dismal creature, and he had seen Clovis often whispering to his Lord at private council when needed. As he neared, the Fox dwarfed in comparison, who was trembling again in fear from being in the presence of the one whom he had significantly attempted to avoid in the past. His resolve to quit the world of the darkened forests of the Sullen Fields was forgotten in the terror he saw before him. The breath of Clovis had the grotesque reeking stench of stale blood and rotted flesh that trailed this monster and made poor Whyles almost tear up with its pungent and stinking odor.

"What's says I?" Clovis repeated in a belittling snarl. In an instant, his great paws shot forth, clasping the Fox's neck in an iron grip. Whyles gasped and writhed, his breath stolen by the brute force of Clovis's clutch and the sickly reek of death that clung to him like a fog, oppressive and unrelenting. The Fox's struggles seemed but a feeble sport to his captor, whose ferocity bore no hint of relenting.

"You's took'ee you're merry own times to get back ta' me. Why is t'at? The Lord in waitin' doesn't tolerate any sorts of stupidly wastage like'n yerself! What is the manner of this Ambrodale that e' Lord is so enthralled with? SPAKE NOW, CRETIN," he roared in the night and continued:

"For I yearn the sight of blood right about now if I don't get an answer!" Clovis thundered, the claws of his monstrous paw biting cruelly into the Fox's neck. Whyles flinched as the sharp nails pierced his skin, a thin trickle of blood tracing its way down to stain the fur beneath. The brute's eyes gleamed with a savage light, his thirst for violence barely held in check.

Whyles was still and quiet. He could barely breathe, let alone speak, at this moment. He was soon to turn sickly purple. "SAY IT!!!" Clovis bellowed, his voice splitting the air with the force of his fury. "OR BY HEAVEN AND HELL, YE

SHALL NOT DRAW BREATH COME

THE MORROW!" His wrath boiled over, a tempest barely contained, his savage shriek echoing like the cry of a beast unhinged.

If I could only be so luckay. The Fox found himself thinking.

The Fox slowly and deliberately spoke, measuring each word, he wheezily half-pleaded. "Tell me, Kaine, if you kill me now, who else would resemble one of 'ose Riverfulks as close as I do at best? All o' the rests o' the others are much too beastly looking for that world and could nevah work IT THROUGH. You know it well… admit it or not, you KNOW IT VERY 'ELL! I'm the sole one you can depend on that for… Isn't t'at right? …. So by killing me now, ye will learn nuttin about the wood or tha fulks. If'n yer want me to talk, t'en put me down, and I shall tell everything I observed!"

Clovis, baffled by the Fox's answer, violently threw him onto the ground, looking down on such a crestfallen, outcast creature. He gave a hideous smirk and exclaimed mockingly.

"THERE! Now tell me, what does this wood and folk have to offer, anything of value?" Asked Clovis, smiling and rolling his enormous ink-stained tongue.

The Fox dusted himself off, discovering he had a bleeding gash on the side of his cheek and neck. "T'ey have nuttin', nuttin' at all… t'ey is simple fulk, an' t'ey don't have much but themselves, an' as much as I wis-"

"LIAR!!!!!!!" Screamed Clovis in reply. "YOU HAVE FALLEN FOR THEM! PITIED THEM, THEY HAVE TRICKED YOU INTO THINKING THEY DON'T HAVE ANYTHING, THEY HIDING THEIR OFFERINGS FROM YOU AND ALL OF IT! …ALL OF IT!!!!!!"

"Tey have nuttin ta offer ta us!" The Fox shouted back. Just then, Kaine reached inside his coat pocket and brandished a little shining object that he had grabbed from within the deep velvet folds of his jacket. The object had caught the wandering eye of the nervous Fox. He pointed to the object that turned out to be a loaded silvered-cylinder revolver with a dark oak handle.

Clovis steadily grasped the weapon in his right paw and deadlocked it on poor Whyles, who wanted to scramble for cover. He did not have such courage, though, and he was stiff as any would be with a gun in their face.

"ALL LIES!!! YOUR TRYIN'A PROTECT 'EM THOSA 'A WORTHLESS RABBLERS!

FOR REASON, I DO NAE KNOW NOR HAVE ANY CARE TO! TELL ME! TELL ME NOW

IF YOU WANT TO LIVE!" He slowly cocked back the hammer. "I suggest you tell me the truth before anything horrific happens!" Clovis snarled in a threatening whisper.

"But sir, all t'ey got is fish! It's the trooth… Ive told you everything I observed… I'm not hidin' anytin'; I swears it! I neee'; I need mors' time!"

"MORE TIME…MOOOORE TIIME? Ya' LIMEY!!! HA…. Your time was already up long ago, cretin FOX!! Time is not on our side, as you well know! TICK TOCK GOES OUR CLOCK. You BLAGGAAAARD!!!!" Clovis screamed, his veins bulging.

"I'm the only one-" As if reading his mind, Clovis had replied, "We can find others! You mean nothing ta' us unymore, yer were just enova mouth feedin' burden tae us aul!" Clovis laughed hysterically, still pointing the deadly revolver at Whyles.

Without warning, the Fox felt the icy bite of steel as the pistol struck the side of his head with a brutal, resounding crack. The blow left its cruel mark immediately—a gash that spilled warm blood in a steady stream down over his brow. Dazed and reeling, Whyles clutched at the wound,

his thoughts a frantic whirl as he swayed on unsteady feet, paralyzed by pain yet poised for a desperate flight should the chance arise.

Clovis Kaine, his frown curling into a wicked grin, watched the battered Fox with a pitiless gaze. The once-defiant creature now stood shrunken and wretched before him, every inch the coward Clovis had willed him to become. Raising his pistol, Kaine aimed it just above the Fox's bloody head, his squinting eyes narrowing as he reveled in the terror painted across Whyles' face.

Whyles closed his eyes tight, his heart pounding an unrelenting rhythm of dread. He waited for the shot, every nerve screaming in expectation of the end. The agony of waiting—miserably anticipating, hopelessly preparing—consumed him.

His mind rambled in despair, and, unable to bear the torment, he fell to his knees, babbling a desperate plea for his life. But Clovis was unmoved, his countenance as unyielding as iron. He pulled the trigger. The gun roared, a deafening blast that tore through the air and sent echoes rattling like sinister laughter through the empty space around them.

Whyles froze, his mind certain the end had come. Believing himself struck dead, he staggered, clutching at his chest with a gasping wail. Then, as the silence crept back in, the Fox began an extravagant display of his "death"—his voice quavering in prayer, his legs buckling with dramatic flourishes, his every gesture a last-ditch entreaty for mercy from the reaper. Trembling and tearful, Whyles twisted and howled in the damp moss, writhing in desperate agony before collapsing in a heap, motionless—as though death had finally claimed him.

The silence stretched on, thick and oppressive. With each passing second, his frantic panic began to ebb, only for the grim realization to settle in: no finality had come. No death had claimed him. It was only after an awkwardly long moment that the Fox dared to inspect his body. His paws fumbled over his fur, searching for the telltale signs of a wound—a bullet's burn or a tear—but found nothing. Only the blood from his head, a souvenir of the initial blow, marked him.

Whyles blinked and cautiously opened one eye, testing the truth of it. Slowly, with mounting disbelief, he patted himself over and over, gasping in shock as no further injury appeared. He could find no bullet wound, no sign of harm.

He looked up at the towering Clovis, whose grin had never faltered, and then, groveling with unrestrained humility, the Fox, in a fit of raw relief, crawled forward and kissed the brute's feet, thanking him for his mercy—an action demanded by the cruel force of Clovis's will.

Clovis, with a devilish smile, balanced his revolver once more, the steel muzzle now grazing Whyles's chin. The Fox winced, his heart leaping in his chest, but Clovis was far from done. With a swift, mechanical motion, the hammer of the revolver was cocked back, and in a low growl, he bellowed:

"Next time yer won't be as LUCKY, ye NUMPTY!"

Whyles flinched in terror as Clovis pulled the trigger. The hammer struck the barrel with a hollow click, but no shot rang out. There was only the silence, broken by the psychotic mockery of Clovis's laughter. "BANG!" he snarled, a gleam of madness lighting his eyes as he continued his twisted charade. Each time he cocked the revolver and pulled the trigger, the same staccato click filled the air, and Whyles jumped with each one, his body wracked with spasms of fear.

The dread of the unseen bullet weighed heavily on him, and with every click, his pulse raced faster, each moment dragging him deeper into madness.

Night To Remember

"FOX!" A voice called in the distance. The Fox and Clovis Kaine both turned to look simultaneously to see who had called. A smoldering torch was all they could see. As the torch came closer, it was to be seen that one of the ruffian Hounds was coming towards them while angrily gripping the torch in the oppressive darkness.

"Who goes 'er!?" Clovis Kaine called back.

"It's I, Quinn! The noble Lord demands yer presence immediately. I am here to lead ye back at once!" Clovis drew back his weapon. They met the waiting herald and followed him through the dark, murky pits of Sullen Fields. Clovis slipped past Quinn; his form wreathed in a shimmer of pale light that no mortal eye could perceive. A curse bound him to the in-between, where only those attuned to shadow could ever glimpse him. They knew their way to get across was safely lighted by the burning torch that led the way. "If I can't make yer tells us the truth, 'en 'sure's the Lord n' waiting for WILL!" Clovis grunted at the Fox, his swarthy face lit by a diabolical, predator smile that had haunted Whyles day and night. His presence gave Whyles sickening chills as he saw Clovis's malign leer. Clovis began forcefully hauling the Fox by his raincoat collar.

Soon, the large mound where the Hounds dwelled emerged from the fading swamp mist, its monstrous silhouette looming against the veiled horizon. The fog clung thickly to the damp, moldering hillock, suffocating the encampment in heavy vapors. Echoes of hideous laughter and clattering sounds spilled from the gaping black maw of the mound, its wide entrance framed by bruise-colored stalagmites that dripped like the sharp teeth of a snarling beast. A repugnant odor—mold, sweat, and swamp gas—permeated the air.

They leaped inside, where blazing torches cast flickering shadows across a cavernous room consumed by riotous pandemonium. It was called a pub, though the label hardly suited this den of depravity. The walls were a macabre mess of rough pelts, crooked antlers, tarnished weapons, and battered shields, all bearing the scars of violence and excess. Dank pool tables served as battlegrounds for drunken scuffles, the crash of cue sticks splintering against wood drowned out by guttural laughter and enraged roars. At card tables, ruffians threw down hands of blackjack and poker with wild abandon, profane accusations of cheating sparking sudden brawls that sent chairs flying.

Elsewhere, brute strength was tested with arm wrestling contests, the participants roaring with exertion as onlookers jeered and laid bets. At the dartboards, blades, and darts were hurled with reckless precision, with wagers as bizarre as the Hounds themselves. In a darkened corner, a grotesque spitting competition was in full swing, the contestants expelling thick, black streams of tobacco-stained saliva into overflowing jugs, accompanied by raucous cheers and ghastly cackles.

Throughout the room, the barrels of rum stood as chaotic altars, besieged by frenzied mobs who tore at one another for a turn at the overflowing taps. The stench of sweat spilled liquor, and acrid smoke hung thick in the air, clinging to every surface and every breath. It was an infernal symphony of clamor and chaos, the kind of place where time dissolved, and madness reigned supreme.

Quinn thrust his torch into an iron holder bolted to the rough-hewn wall, the flickering flame casting jagged shadows that flitted across the tumultuous scene. With a beckoning gesture, he led Whyles and Clovis through the storm of chaos, where uproarious laughter and drunken brawls collided like warring elements. The stench of sour spirits clung to the air, thick and unrelenting, as the trio navigated the frenzied throng.

They pressed toward a dark passageway, where the cacophony faded into a sinister quiet. The walls, slick with damp earth, gave way to rows of bunk beds carved into the very stone, stacked precariously like the forgotten shelves of some morbid crypt. Each earthen hollow seemed more of a grave than a resting place, and from within came the guttural snores and restless growls of slumbering Hounds.

The sound was a rumble, low and menacing, like the murmur of a gathering storm deep beneath the ground. Whyles kept his eyes forward, his every instinct urging him not to linger. To meet the gaze of one of these grotesque sleepers, even by accident, was to court a peril he dared not imagine. Their purpose in Kaliber's gang was veiled in shadows, their roles as enigmatic as the depths of this cavernous den. The Fox felt a chill crawl down his spine as they passed, each snort and bark in the fitful slumber of these creatures seeming more like a warning than an idle noise. The oppressive air seemed heavier here, the silence between snores more dangerous than the clamor they had left behind. Whyles tightened his pace, his steps careful but swift, as the tunnel yawned ahead like the maw of some ancient beast. Whatever lay at its end, he thought, could hardly feel more foreboding than the uneasy company of Kaliber's slumbering monsters.

Deeper still, the tunnel's silence seemed to press in on all sides, suffocating the air, until a faint sound—a trembling, almost imperceptible note—shattered the stillness. It was the sound of a harpsichord, but not one that played of mere mortal joy or sorrow. This melody was a thing of vile horrors, wailing from someplace beyond the grasp of the living. The notes fluttered like the whisper of a phantom, each one pulling the very soul towards it, as though the instrument itself wept for something lost, forever beyond reach.

The sound was soft at first, but it grew, its mournful strains weaving through the oppressive air like a banshee's cry. It held a power that was not of this world, resonating with an ancient grief, a sorrow that made Whyles's chest tighten and his heart tremble. The music itself seemed to call to him, its wailing notes wrapping around him like cold fingers. It was not just the harpsichord he heard now, but the wail of a phantasmal banshee—an ethereal, mournful voice that rose from the abyss, calling those who dared listen into the shadows.

The air grew heavy, as if the very walls of the tunnel were listening, waiting. Quinn and Clovis moved ahead, their presence feeding the darkness, but it was Whyles who felt the pull of the wail most keenly. It struck at his fragile spirit, draining his resolve, each note piercing his mind like a whisper from the grave. The sound was an unearthly thing, not of this world, and as it wound its way around him, Whyles could feel it in his bones, a lament for the lost, for the forsaken.

He pressed on, though his body felt as though it were being pulled backward by invisible hands. A banshee's wail seemed to cling to him, seeping into his very soul. It was as though it did not merely call to him—it claimed him, offering neither escape nor peace. With each step, the mournful sound wrapped tighter around him, and the path before him seemed to stretch into eternity, a dark, suffocating march toward some unknown, inevitable end.

They stopped abruptly at the large, blood-red, blistered, leather-covered, oaken door where two enormous brass bolts and latches gleamed in the dim torchlight. Large, especially- carved, triangular-shaped, rough-hewn panels were spiked to the outsized door's top and bottom. The door and panels were sculpted with unusual markings. They seemed rather arcane and deeply set. Carved into the middle of this door was a diamond shape with a Wolf's head in the middle.

Quinn stepped in front of the Fox and knocked on the door. There came no reply, but the clandestine music continued even louder and more surreal bemoan than before; several knocks followed without answer until the ongoing music ceased to play; all was strangely ghostly quiet, and all was dead still. And with the sudden stopping of the music came the slow tapping of perhaps a cane striding toward the door to greet them. The slot slid open from the top as two yellow piercing eyes peered. "What is it?"

"Lord, I brought ye te Fox yer wanted to speak to," Quinn confidently replied.

"How excellent! Yes, very much a grand job, Quinn," Kaliber hissed in a voice as heavy as the door that swung open. "Please do come in, of course!" Greeted the familiar voice to the three. Whyles was ambivalently hesitant and did not immediately follow Quinn further but stayed at the edge of the opened door. "Get'a movin's!" Clovis barked from behind, viciously shoving Whyles into the room.

The room they now entered was Lord Kaliber's chamber. The bedroom chamber of their Lord was nothing hideously gruesome like that of the pub, nor was it dark and murky like that of the Hound's sleeping quarters. Indeed, Kaliber's Chamber was never remodeled to such a plebian degree. Instead, it was to be seen as fit and proper for the master. If it was not designed and detailed to Kaliber's exact liking or perhaps perfect by the Lord's standards, then Kaliber would not hesitate to punish such impunity and lash out in his angering vexation and rancor. Those of the Coveton habits and traits followed this noble ma.j.esty almost everywhere and had an affection for those who had the special marks of acolytes. His large room seemed well-lit by a hanging chandelier of gold. Suspended from the mural-painted ceiling, the mural itself was an elegant, ma.j.estic view of the lofty heavens. There were swirling clouds, winged angels and cherubs holding bugles cavorting in the depicted ethers, and the orange-golden glow of some hour of the day shone behind them. The mural was painted across a vaulted dome above where they now stood. In the center of the deep dome was a radial gilded medallion shaped like a beaming sun. At the center of this medallion, a golden chain supported an elaborately decorated chandelier. Arabesque curves, bedecked in crystal pendants, held burning red taper candles that flicked with intensity at all hours. The large, smoldering hearth kept Kaliber's chamber warm and free of the dampness that plagued the other rooms of the cave mound.

The intricate woodwork mantel was itself a masterpiece. The mantel was once a large ash log, caved in situ after the dark earthen walls had been dug out and the mantel lifted into place above the shining obsidian hearth. The room contained a variety of delicate handworks, the likes of which were rarely seen in a museum or a collector's reserve. The Hounds who had been in the chamber would dare not speak of or even more show such treasures to the others in danger of such objets d'artes being stolen and the wrath of Kaliber being invoked at such an occurrence.

In this chamber, the Wolf had dressed in his nightwear of a red velvet cap and gown, still wearing his belcher handkerchief. Kaliber sat intimidatingly and modishly on the little, black- cushioned bench, trimmed with golden-braided thread. An intensely grand and mammoth harpsichord of ornate design was its captivating companion, an opulent and monumental sight to behold. Its elegantly ravishing appearance was enhanced by a dark ebony shellacked frame. It had two deep sets of red keyboards, the sharp and flat keys colored in white. Its decoratively golden music rack was arched and matched the filigree carving of its golden pedals. Its exquisite open lid could be sold alone for the price of an unimaginable fortune, as it was finely and ornately painted a beautiful, prepossessing scenery of such you would not be able to locate the spot, for most of the serenity spots it had gorgeously depicted are long gone and terribly forgotten. Kaliber had a chamber not only to be enthrallingly studied. One could be subdued and held captive by magnificent artworks such as these splendors. A ma.j.estic trompe l'oeil it was, it captured not only the lustering divine spectral essence we all may come to see when we go to dream, but the chamber also captured the gloaming threat of perdition we all fear sooner or later.

Kaliber faced the fire and poked and jolted the logs to intensify the flames; thus, the room's heat slowly rose. He turned to face the three standing before him and commanded Quinn to leave immediately. As the Hound left to join the rest of the crew in the main pub revelries, Whyles could hear the muffled screams of their regular debauchery. Kaliber called upon Clovis, who stepped next to the Wolf to listen to what Kaliber had to say privately. They huddled together and faced away from Whyles, who, in curiosity, tried to peek quietly from behind. Kaliber whispered to Clovis as he kept tinkling with some of the eerie harpsichord keys:

"Is our Fox friend cracking, Mr. Kaine?"

"My Lord, I do not trust this filthy cretin. He seems all too fragile. All too distracted, I despise him. If granted, I can make him spill all he knows with a good bashing! Why should that skimpy Weasel Fox keep with us? He's useless, and we must look out for his wretched self every moment; it's all the better if he'd die soon."

"Calm yourself, Kaine. Perhaps a softer touch may necessitate answers, not gruff threats. It's obscene to think that. What he needs is an altruistic charm, which only I possess. I have faith that he is still helpful to us and has not become completely worthless, no, not yet. Remember, Mr. Kaine, everything has a purpose until it is disposable."

"But by all means and any methods... keep up your ways, and eventually, he will surely break. Like any weak-minded fool, he shall come to me for guidance! That is our goal: continue to break his will until he has surrendered it to ME. Then, it will be easy for us ALL TO PREVAIL! Nunc suus ' tempus meum loqui vulpes." Kaliber snickered in his ear as they separated on their own; Clovis then strutted to the door, shoving Whyles.

"Move RUNT!" Kaine shouted in reply to a hasty shove. He looked at the Wolf, who now had a malicious smirk on his face, giving, in turn, a quick nod of satisfaction to Clovis Kaine, who sneered back.

"If you may be off now, I would like to chat with our mooost delightful friend, Mr. Whyles. Oh, how brilliantly charming it is to see you!!!"

Kaine left as Whyles, submissive as he was, joined Kaliber. Kaliber then put his arm around the Fox's shoulder, who quivered at the first touch.

"Dear me, Whyles, where did you receive such an appalling blow to your poor head? You're bringing blood in! How dreadfully awful!" Said Kaliber, inspecting the grisly wound."

"Oh, it really doesn't matter anyhow! Here, just wrap it up with this and dress it properly, I insist; it isn't very orderly to keep a wound untended; it should never be done; it could bring disastrous side effects! Now, we wouldn't want that, would we!?" Kaliber continued.

He handed the trembling Fox a cloth, and Whyles dabbed it. The fabric began soaking up the blood, and then the Fox tied it around his head. Whyles thanked Kaliber, "O', not a problem, my friend. I am most happy to help when most wanted, but what seems to be the downhearted problem? You seem far more troubled than usual. Come tell me your aching burdens, and I shall give you the greatest benefit of my support! Some rest is due to you." He continued to speak in a kind whisper to Whyles. "After all, we are a true family; we are the only family, just the two of us--"

Whyles soon interrupted in a shake of refusal, "But sir, the Hounds are yer family; I am honored to be looked upon like ye own blood, but I am merely a guest; I have no need for a family. It is such a waste of searching. No, no, the Hounds should rightfully be considered yer family."

Kaliber frowned with hurt theatrical feelings. "Hooounds, the hooooounds? Come come, Whyles, this is not a time to have jokes, is it?! Absolutely not, how amusing! Ney, my friend. Simple dimwitted carbonieri!" he hissed in feigned disgust. "Carbonieri are used, my friend, as a diversion. They are indeed great in number, BUT THAT'S IT! Juuuust numbers and high numbers can cause confusion in the ranks. Where I step in is to maintain such order. If not, why will the numbers fall? Bah! The Hounds, simple pawns." He snickered. "True without them, we shall not get anywhere… I feel for you, Whyles. No, my friend, you are my only family. Alas, being banished by one's own kind when everything was for the right! Kicked to the canalis!

FLUUUUNG OOUUTT!" Kaliber's pain was evident.

"Eiectus! We both are outcasts; we are both without our kin!" Kaliber seemed somehow lost at his pronouncement. He almost sympathized with the crestfallen Fox in his spoken misery.

"I thank you, Lord, for your kind thoughts and worries, but I assu-"

"The care I have given you… WHO was the one that found you as a stripling and rescued you from that miserable pit?" Announced the Wolf, emphasizing the miserable pit in an exaggerated lilting whine. "Who fed you HOT SIMMERING MEALS THESE PAST YEARS… until you couldn't eat? Kaliber trailed off in mock sympathy. Kaliber continued in a jolted phrase, "Which gave you shelter from such wretched weather-beaten conditions when you were found 'ere half dead?"

Whlyes whispered the correct answer under his breath, but Kaliber, in reply, asked the Fox to repeat himself louder.

"YOU DID!"

"Presse! My utmost concern has alwaaays been for you, of course. Look at how freely you move amongst the ranks and in Ambrodale. Without you, how might WE succeed? Take heart, my lad, you and I are destined to win this one AT ANY COST. Now, don't I know Clovis has been exceptionally harsh on you? Whyles, a brute he is, but you must remember it is all just for the sake of our progress. Without Clovis, who would be strong enough and brave enough to take control of our plan?"

Whyles did not respond but sat cross-legged on one of the Rococo chairs and stared at the dying flames.

Kaliber pulled up a chair and sat next to him, looking at the exquisite artwork. The pictures hung on the hand-gilded floral and vine motif on the red-flocked velvet wallpapered walls in his chamber.

"You still seem incredibly absentminded, friend; come, there is no need to have any second thoughts! What more do you ask? Let's put aside your confusion and your current métier. Rest easy for now, but do not forget your task! You can have assurance that I am looking out for you. You need not worry! After all, we have the HEART for this." Kaliber leaned forward onto a small table. Rummaging through the boxed shelf, he soon found what he sought. It was a cherry wood chess board with all the unique hand-made pieces.

Setting up the board, with the help of Whyles, the game began. Whyles knew Kaliber would immediately become upset if he could not go first. Whyles had no preference either way, so he volunteered to go second when he saw Kaliber's distress brewing. Kaliber moved one pawn, and Whyles did the same. Pieces fell one by one; as the game continued, Kaliber mocked and teased the Fox about his moves and the decisions Whyles made during the game. When it was Kaliber's turn, Kaliber decried that it was all in 'friendly sportsmanship' and 'not to be taken in a serious manner.' But as the match slowly progressed to a deadlock draw, there were no pieces except for the two chess kings in the same row. The Wolf, dissatisfied with the game's outcome, growled.

"PUUUUURE LUCK! IMPOSSIBLE, I, LORD COVETON, NEVER LOSE! I REFUSE TO

GIVE UP! I COME FROM A STOCK OF CHAAAAMPIONSSSS!'" Came his unintended hiss. Gradually, Kaliber moved his king to the center of the board, meeting the enemy king face to face. By now, Kaliber felt quite agitated and grew even more disturbed when he saw the enemy king lunge toward his own. It was a sore spot to be so dominated, and now it was even more evident to Whyles that Kaliber's hidden tragedy was being played right before the Wolf's own teary eyes. Kaliber could not conceive of a downfall of any kind. Not even in chess. He started to hear voices long ago, during the days and nights of his luxurious life. Strangely to him, it seemed that he lived such a life no more. Now, he was to be subjected and victimized by self-doubt, rancorous thoughts and judgments regarding his past failures.

The Wolf once again choked on a bitter memory as he grasped the king from the chess board and viscously threw it at the dying hearth; as it collided, the dying flames hellishly ignited, and with ignition came the ghoulish wail of Kaliber's unexpressed exasperation. His combed, slick back hair was now rumpled and grew raggedy by such rage as he hurled his cap. His mouth started to froth, and his wild eyes blazed with inner hatred and grief. For the Fox who was watching such an event taking place, Whyles could scarcely comprehend the sight before him. To see one so highly placed, so grandly fashioned, unravel in such a way— it struck him as both perplexing and inevitable. The Wolf, who had long cloaked himself in the airs of a gentleman, with all the trappings of cultivated grace born from royal blood, had spent his life concealing the flaws that now, in a cruel twist, tore through his facade. It was no surprise, then, that a being who built his life upon pretense should so easily falter when the truth, long suppressed, burst forth.

He glanced at the fire, its flames licking hungrily at the hearth, while his fingers toyed absentmindedly with the harpsichord keys, producing a thin, tentative melody. Then, in a sudden fit of revulsion, he brought his paws down with force, striking the keys with terrible violence.

The sound that erupted was a cacophony, a screeching, discordant wail—like the very cry of a soul in torment.

Still trembling, the Wolf's fingers traced the keys in a soft, gliding motion, from the deep resonance of the lowest A to the sharp peak of the highest C. The sound flowed, smooth and eerie, before breaking into an unsettling disarray of notes— at once ethereal and grotesque. The melody faltered, lurching into a tense, crashing forte, each note hammering with fierce intensity, only to fall back into the same haunting, fragile cadence with which it had begun

"I, A COVETON BANISHED, RENOUNCED, EXILED!!!!??? BAH, HOW DARE THEY TOSS ME OUT LIKE... LIKE GAAAAARABAGE AND RUUUUUBISH, I AM AS EQUAL AS THE REST OF THEM! I AM NOOOOOO REJECT; I Kaliber HUMILIATED from my

VERY OWN bloodline!? Am I so low and crass to have to smuggle my belongings AWAY!?" demoralized, Kaliber hamming as he waved at all the décor in the room. The mysterious revelation of Kaliber's past was now perceived by the Fox, who was still at a loss. Though the Wolf did try to keep his secret from all, he could not contain the apoplectic, disconsolate sentiments of discounting obligation any longer.

"ME A DISGRACE? I CAN HARDLY BEAR IT!!!! They'll all see, they shall RUE the very DAY when I return triumphant, THEIR'LL BE CRAWLING, BEGGING, PLEADING FOR

FORGIVENESS!!!! AND I SHALL GIVE THEM NONE! RETRIBUTION SHALL BE FINAAAAALLY MINE!"

Whyles jumped in fear. He had heard of these emotional attacks and abrupt blathering Kaliber so often had before but never was a witness. It was to be Kaine who witnessed them and sometimes caused them. Whyles had known little of Kaliber's past, whatever was gossiped through the ears of the Hounds. Just then, there was a series of knocks on Kaliber's door. The repetition of knocks was starting to sound like some Morse Code.

"WHAT IS IT!? Cease the BOOOOTHERSOME noise!" Screamed the Lord in reply to the knocks, which stopped upon harsh request. One of the scruffy Hounds entered wearing a tattered white and red striped tee-shirt, approaching the Wolf and the Fox.

"Excuse me, Lord; I apologize for 'e barge ins, but e' banquet is prepared; we are awaiting yer presence the start; we have been waiting for quite some time!"

"WAIT LONGER! I SHALL COME WHEN I FEEL LIKE IT! Tell me, is there any silverware for me to use? Using paws is outright wretched and FIIIILHTY!!" Kaliber was bombastic in his arrogance.

"Just for you, sir."

"Is there any rich, fine red wine or, better yet, SPAAAAARKLING champagne? No rum, if you please, simply horrible heavy stuff that does nasty things to the likes of me, makes my stomach churn!"

"Certainly do, just for you, Great Lord!"

"Then I shall come shortly; I must change!" He turned to the Fox with now a cool head. "Whyles, you may go and have as much as you like! Why, I insist you do! You look altogether malnourished and mangled. Have those silly simpletons been feeding you at all? I cannot EVEN remotely imagine what kind of poor meals they give you. So, I naturally do assume you haven't been eating anything decent!"

"I do not mean to impose on you, Kaliber, but I assure you that I am well off, and nothing can ever compare to YOUR excellent cuisine, I must add! I did eat very well, considering, but since you did mention it, I am a wee bit famished… but please don't go out of your way and trouble yourself to be feeding me 'n all! I'll do just fine wit'out." politely replied the dubious Fox.

"Go out of my way? COMPLETE BILGE! Don't be foolish, and trust me, friend, we have much more food than we can eat! Go with Burke here; eat merrily, Whyles, and have as much as you sooooo desire!" Urged the Wolf, who convinced the unsure Fox to dine.

By this act, Kaliber had earned yet another instance of admiration from Whyles, who was again fed as a favor. Burke and Whyles walked out of the door of the Wolf's palatial chamber. Kaliber, now alone, turned toward his luxurious king-sized bed. The bed had towering ebony bedposts adding a sense of royal flare to its façade, with the grand, violet damask canopy suspended above the oversized feather mattress.

The frame was decorated with a painted marble motif, showing a design of celestial bodies swirling within the aethers of some forgotten universe. Above the frame, the curved and polished headboard and bench endboard were carved into rustic wooden tablet-shaped monoliths with filigrees of leaves, wings, and vines. Several large, crimson velvet pillows of dark and thick color and texture matched the high-seated upholstery, which hung with gilded tassels.

Kaliber stood at the foot of the bed, brushing his tousled fur. He stared at the long tapestry banner of burgundy color, draping from the dark wall behind his bed. It was a powerful presentation, somewhat overwhelming for one who might prefer to sleep over the pleasures of the overly wealthy. In short, as everything was in his palatial bedchamber, the whole ensemble was simply grand. With its black trim, the banner above was the one and only jewel-encrusted Coveton family emblem. The regal flag was woven by cautious hand as if a moment's inattention in its making might ruin the supreme icon.

The unfortunate workers in such a circumstance would be left with no hand after such an incident. The banner was marked by a strange golden, circular wave pattern design. The banner had an almost Renaissance-like appeal. These unusual markings looked more like golden leaves, forming a perfect circle within the center of the banner. The frontal view of a black Wolf's head was in the middle of this circle. The image of the head was made of an embroidered fabric.

Which type of cloth could not be determined by viewing, though it had the natural sheen of a new papyrus scroll. The head of the image sported a golden crown, like the leaves around it.

Kaliber stood motionless as if challenging and mocking such a flag that he now felt had only brought him harm and disaster. He had scorned the thought of the 'Significance Category' to which he once belonged. It was a category he could not live up to with its high merit put upon the holders of such a station. The expectations of every member could be so onerous to one who might prefer a simpler life as to induce unrelenting despair. Kaliber now felt that perhaps he was just such a one as that. The feeling the banner now gave him reminded him of such an abysmal grudge against those he had lived with since birth. Jaundiced by the sight of it, he scrutinized its flawless execution as he blew on his family crest signet ring. A deadly glint showed in his wild eyes, which now held such a horrifying presence of animus and spite. Spite towards those who turned their backs on him and the fiendish remembrance of his flaunting heritage holders' betrayal of him.

These ideas all crossed his perturbed mind. For what reason did they give to Kaliber his unceremonious exile? No reason was good enough to hear now, for the Wolf's vigorous compulsion for revenge upon them all, strong indeed, grew as he stood there.

Indignant enough, he was for the craven recrimination given to him by his family, and he desired to avenge himself against all who got in his way. This desire did now subsequently blind him from knowing the reason for the shameful humiliation he had unintentionally brought into the unforgiving judgment of his treacherous kin. Had he really caused this disgrace on his own?

Was it some oversight he had incurred by carelessness in dealing with the rapacious family he had unfortunately inherited? The idea that he was to blame for it all he had carefully hidden from thought.

Were his present feelings merely the manifestations of a deep trauma he refused to confront? A wound he had suffered for too long? And what had provoked this unbearable urge?

"By what divinum ius do they dare deport me?" Kaliber snarled, pacing like a caged animal. "I am not some base-born commoner like these incompetent fools and filthy swine I'm cursed to deal with! Deus avertat! What tiresome, wretched company I'm forced to endure. I am a Coveton—by birth, by nature, by pure sanguis. Not by their falsa acceptio or meager pity."

His voice rose with venomous fervor. "I should be among their distinguished ranks! But no... I, Lord Kaliber, am reduced to cleaning up the messes of these grimy, unwashed louts in this forsaken mudhole I must now call... home! All for the absurdum of earning their respect!"

He spat the last word, cursing his family under his breath as he yanked on his purple vest and buttoned the four golden buttons of his green coat. His paws moved with swift precision, but the motions felt hollow. His dignity had become a costume, a mockery of what he once was. He adjusted his bowler hat, staring at his reflection, lips curling with disgust.

"Proba te dignum nostrae gloriosae hereditati," he mimicked in a mocking tone. "Bah! What a pack of blaggards!"Screamed the Wolf against the sudden realization of its condemnatory meaning... he once again sat on the little black bench and had again began like he had started, pitifully playing a sad melody on his grand and opulent harpsichord with the heavy and despairing emotion of the extreme longing for redemption and retribution amongst his own kin. Yet somehow, it had uncannily seemed Kaliber was just a helpless puppet, and the harpsichord he played deftly on was his master.

Meanwhile, Whyles found himself once again in the haze-filled den with Burke, surrounded by grizzled Hounds gulping down thick, dark ale. The Fox's jittery movements drew the attention of the Hounds, their growls intensifying as they noticed his presence. Clovis, seated at a table, had been playing a dangerous game of finger fillet, his jagged knives clinking rhythmically against the wood. With a sudden shift in focus, Clovis started tossing the knives at Whyles' feet, each one landing closer and closer. Whyles' heart raced as he scrambled to avoid the blades, his feet slipping on the blood-stained floor, nearly tripping over knives already embedded in the ground. The Hounds roared with laughter, reveling in his near misses. As he stumbled, Whyles' eyes widened in horror. Strewn across the tables were the mangled carcasses of recently hunted boars, their bellies slashed open, entrails spilling out in a gruesome display. The stench of rotting flesh hung heavy in the air, a sickening reminder of the Hounds' brutality.

Amidst the uproar, Captain Silas sat beside Clovis, his attention seemingly riveted on the grotesque scene before him. However, an eerie chill began to settle over him, a sensation that made the hair on the back of his neck stand on end. It wasn't the scene of carnage or the foul stench that unsettled him—it was the cold, unsettling presence of Clovis himself.

Silas could feel the chill radiating from Clovis, who, despite his outward show of enjoyment, exuded an icy, oppressive air. The contrast between Clovis's rough exterior and the steely calm beneath was unsettling. As Clovis took a monstrous bite from a lamb's leg, his grim satisfaction evident, Silas couldn't shake the feeling that something was deeply wrong. Clovis's demeanor was disconcerting, a veneer of joviality masking a deeper, more sinister undercurrent.

This underlying coldness seeped into Silas's bones, making him uncomfortable despite the chaos around them. Clovis's eyes, cold and calculating, never seemed to fully engage with the revelry but remained watchful and detached. The more Silas tried to ignore the creeping chill, the more it seemed to intensify, leaving him with a gnawing sense of unease.

Whyles, his mind racing, backed away from the revolting scene, trying to keep a low profile. The Hounds, however, were still eager to torment him, hurling insults and threats his way as they indulged in their feeding frenzy. Some of them began chasing him around the den, their jeers echoing through the chaos, while Clovis and Silas paid them no mind, lost in their own revelry. Kaliber, still unseen and unheard, remained perfectly still, watching the disorder unfold with cold detachment. Even as Clovis bellowed a coarse laugh and raised his revolver in a crude celebration, Kaliber stayed hidden in plain sight, waiting. The Hounds, unaware of his presence, continued their rampage, oblivious to the silent wrath that hung just beyond their grasp.

Hound Pub Song

Petty jokes 'round the goin', And bumbling blunders, Thine fangs are showin',

Too grand for us and our wonders. Kick the lowly ones down,

Drag 'em all wild, 'E ones too mild,

To find the hounds away, To beat the beasts away! Beat 'em till none are left,

Brawlin' till they're bruised and sore,

Grovelin' ain't enough; there's still more to score! Oh, send 'em out the door!

Into the hall, weaklings stagger and fall, Then we'll give 'em moooore!

OH, then we'll give 'em moooore! Plenty of games to be had,

Drink up, ye hearty,

In yer belly, the ale's gonna flow! Oh, drink and drink again!

Roll out the sticks And the golden mix,

The finest of tobaccos here, To smoke away tomorrows, To smoke all tomorrows,

Awayyy

These endless nights to steal away!

Chompin' on jagged bones,

Tearin' strips o' flesh and moooore, OH! WHAT WE CRAVE IS MOORE!

Aaaaaaahhh, Games of gamble,

Cards and coins stacked high, What fun to be had,

If cheats get caught,

A thrashing they'll earn,

And 'neath the table, bleedin', The rogue shall be beaten!

Come one, come all, to the feast, To carouse and drink and cheer, 'Ere this grand gathering,

Set before ye down, Down, down, Down and down,

So far away, outlying, So underground,

In our ancient grotto's bowels, 'Neath this raggedy, tumble town, Doooooown,

In this raggedy, tumbely town. For yer crimes, they're a-playin', The innocent slayin',

Their bodies a-layin' All o'er our Den,

Be ye wolves of men! And send 'em to their end!

Aaaaaay, away, away again!

My friends... Oh, send 'em to their end!!

The song's deafening and obnoxious rambles and the Fox's chasing and scaring went on until echoing tramping sounds could be heard coming from the Hound's sleeping quarters. Muffled at first, it grew louder as it neared, thumping like a faint heartbeat. Soon, the sound was recognized as a cane striking and beating on a hard surface. Some of the Hounds paid no attention to the sound and kept singing as drunk and snockered as one can be, perhaps even more for a ruffian type of Hound.

"SILENCE!!!!! What tasteless CLAMOR am I to hear?! UNEDUCATED, BLUDGER, nothing I hate more than Low-Class PUB SONGS, ABSOLUTE VULGAR! I WILL NOT TOLERATE

ANY OF THIS RUBBISH AS LONG AS I AM IN CHARGE!" Screamed the Wolf in his annoyance. "Haven't you brainless imbeciles ever had the wonderful pleasure to hear REAL and SOPHISTICATED music of CLASSICAL SYMPHONIES composed by men of brilliance who aren't the ordinary, mortal men but gods and mighty heroes of melodies. Have any of you ever experienced the great philharmonics that I have? I have many fond memories of private performances and magnificent concertos played right before my family and me in our large extravagant concert hall for our solitary enjoyment, the Covetons, to hear! For the performers, performing for us must be a great privilege! The mighty, triumphant, low brass section blared with sonorous glory like the sounding of an oncoming battle! The strings softly embellished the roar, quietly at first, with their bright plucks and the light touch of swiping and fiddling timbre selling to a crescendo, then the rolling and rumbling intensifying percussion section soon to thunder louder and louder, beating the same as the gusto of the heart with a clash of the cymbals! Then and only then do all the sections unify to create a masterpiece of incomparable magnitude!" Said the Wolf, strolling freely through the crowded, hazy pub.

With stares, the niminy-piminy Wolf fixed anything misplaced in his displeasure at seeing such a disorganized mess; he had soon noticed that a section of a wall in the middle of the pub was partially covered by a dirty white muslin sheet hiding what seemed to be an elongated object, a golden cord swaying next to it. He asked the Hounds what the hidden object was. Still, he was given no clear answer other than, "It's 'er surprise!"

"Oh, how I despise surprises." Replied the upset Wolf in a grumbling tone. Kaliber continued to talk about the fine art of classical concerto, expressing his genuine love for the arts. He spoke of the grand nightly soirées and gatherings, though once again a bitter memory had slipped into his thoughts as he choked on his words, expecting the Hounds to listen; they did not, most loudly sang amongst themselves intelligibly still harassing the Fox, Whence Kaliber had seen such the display he rushed to the Fox's aid, harshly striking the group with his cane.

"Drop him, drop him immediately, you DULLARD BRUTES! Can't you see that he is not fond of all these dastardly deeds and mistreating he is to be subjected to? YOU INSOLENT IMBELICILES…" With a strike of his smacking cane, the Hounds yipped and yapped in pain, instantly dropping the Fox to the ground where he was on his paws and knees, looking up at the five Hounds surrounding him.

"Wit aull due 'espect, we were onla havins funs with 'ere nutter!" One of the drunken Hounds stoutly bellowed.

Kaliber smirked, holding out his paw in an intimate gesture to boost the scrambled Fox to his feet. Then, the intimidating Wolf slowly strutted toward the pool table. "Billiards is such insignificant animosity, hardly worthy of any consideration at all! Polo is the premier occupation in the sporting culture, and my kin has ever played it in our glorious centuries of polo champions!" Gloated Kaliber, the Wolf gathered all the pool balls and set them into the pool triangle, racking them up; he dug the end of his cane into the green felt of the table.

"Besides, this Fox ain't one of us! Ha! Look how gawky he is, what a dunce…" laughed a group of Hounds. Kaliber once again smirked now heinously and shot the white cue ball over the table. As it flew through the murky, stagnant air, knocking the head of one of the laughing Hounds, (shutting him up, he rubbing his ball-struck head and looking at the cue ball lying below him on the ground!) the Hound turned towards the Wolf who stared back. "Oh, I'm terribly sorry, my paw must have slipped! Oh, does it hurt? I bet it does…."

Kaliber apologetically mocked. The Hound growled and brushed his swelling head, where there seemed to be a significant red welt. However, ignoring it, the Hound went back to drinking his fill. "Where is the banquet that I am sooooo looking forward to? I am simply ravenous!" Asked Kaliber.

"Yer lookin' at it!" replied a Hound, paying attention to the pile of carcasses on the table. Kaliber's eagerness turned sour-faced.

"Oh, how utterly revolting! I refuse to eat such slop as this; what am I, a savage? Come, come, must you all be taught the proper way of delicacy cuisine? This is not remotely of that class. It's hardly edible in any manner; this uncooked sewage will likely kill me by some venomous disease if I so choose to eat, which I will intend not!" The Hounds grumbled and groused at the comment, "And how on earth shall Whyles eat this!? This does not fit him! He is much more righteous than I; hard to believe, yes, but it is true, very true!" Kaliber boasted about Whyles.

Upon hearing such words, the Fox standing next to the tall Wolf, who seemed like a giant from the Fox's slumped perspective; felt awkward and uncomfortable by the flattering unwanted attention the Wolf spouted.

"He's a nut! Hardly worth a blooming thought nor concern." One of the Hounds replied,

"INCORRECT YET AGAIN! Must you all be reminded? WE WOULD NOT BE AS FAR AS WE ARE WITHOUT HIM!"

The Hounds grumbled again as they threw darts, spat tobacco, and played cards. Kaliber looked on at the slayed carcasses in putrid repugnance.

"I demand you saute' these meats at once just for me and my good friend Whyles here, and will you kindly add some edible decorations to make the plate more appetizing?!" Suggested the Wolf.

"Ay' Lord, as yer wish it!" Replied a Hound. The Hound rushed toward the small kitchen with a handful of meat. The others were silent, muttering to one another in small gossiping groups.

Most of the ruffian Hounds were mistrusted and Janus-faced to the Wolf, wanting a leader other than Kaliber, but they did not dare to speak their mind in fear of what would happen if Captain Silas had heard any plan to overthrow the youngest Coveton. Of course, the numerous kills that Kaliber had brought kept morale high, and the ma.j.ority favored the bumptious Wolf and his dealings. Still, the Hounds were naturally suspicious and awfully dangerous; they were allies but mendacious, and they did not tolerate many of the belittling comments the Wolf would deliver to them.

They were also much irritated by his obsessive, pedantic demeanor. Kaliber, as cunningly and shrewdly vigilant as he believed himself to be, was frankly blindly conceited and unaware of his ineptitude and inability to consider that he knew nothing about these cutthroat Hounds. In fact, he hardly knew anything of their predilections or proclivities before any of the criminal activities, which they had all been drawn to before they met Kaliber.

Long before they met Kaliber, the arranged summit of their agreeable allegiance to him was desired. Kaliber assisted them in their barbarous escape from inevitable punishment for their prolific crimes in their former habitations. Never had Kaliber dealt with any stranger outside of his own castle. The Wolf was callow, callow in decision, in observations about others, and naïve not by desire but by his pampered laziness. He was raised with an uncharitable degree of unwarranted, luxurious, and dependency-provoking life based on opportunistic freeloading. He had everything he always wanted placed right in front of him by the grant of others. Never did he not get what he wanted, and if his craving were not fulfilled right away, the young Coveton would shriek, shout, and throw a tantrum in an ungrateful paroxysm. This was a tragic oversight in his upbringing, for his empty, short-sighted, ungrateful, and childish judgments were filled with bitter negativity.

This became worse over time, as even more hateful habits grew during his angry adolescence. The situation collapsed when he was exiled from his family. Most of his frustrated tantrums came not from the unfortunate timing of his banishment but the reluctant reality that he would not be cosseted from now on. Kaliber's lack of self-reliance was aggravated by his own dearth of life experience as he was left to making his way alone in the world. The problem of his expulsion from the protection of his family's castle made it seem as if insanity would soon be his next visitor. He feared this most of all, as he had never bothered to consider who he really might be inside without the trappings of his former life. For what he indeed was, he never knew (He really knew nothing more than the self-centered, unjust Coveton modus operandi and didn't bother to step outside the comfort of a life which had been preordained from him and only then to be iniquitously shattered in a relative moment. Like most families where the children are taught to follow the family rules for their own safety, the rules Kaliber was forced to follow were often unreasonable and intentionally cruel. Unmindful of his crude company, he did not care to cease in his narcissistic and maladjusted behavior under any circumstance, for in truth, the Coveton way was all he knew!

"YOOU THERE!" The Wolf shouted, pointing at one of the Hounds playing darts. The chosen Hound turned with a snicker and faced the haughty Wolf. The Hound fretfully waited to hear what the Wolf wanted now.

"Bring my red throne, FORTHWITH!" Kaliber snarled, directing the Hound's attention to an oversized chair looming in the corner of the room. The seat, draped in faded crimson and adorned with spikes at each corner, stood as a grotesque mockery of royalty. The first Hound, brow furrowed and muscles straining, tugged at the throne. It was weighty and solid, fashioned from dark cherry wood, as stubborn and unyielding as the Wolf who claimed it.

Kaliber's thin lips curled into a sneer as the Hound toiled. "Fool! You'll need help with that." Another Hound was summoned with a glance—a reluctant participant, muttering under his breath as he approached. With both Hounds grunting and sweating, the chair grudgingly shifted across the floor.

Kaliber's voice rang out, sharp and cold as iron: "Mark this—if there's but a scratch or reckless mar upon my throne, you'll pay dearly for your carelessness!"

The two Hounds pressed on, ignoring their master's threats, until, at last, the throne stood before him. Kaliber's laugh was soft and cruel. "Ah, see now? It wasn't so difficult after all, was it?"

"FOR YER AY', HARDLY LIFTED A FINGAH!!!! WE AIN'T YER DRUDGIES. Pick it up

yourself if yer needs it so bad. Yer is an indolent louse, working back and forth all day long for what!? To PLEASE YER MAJESTY! D'EY OTHAS MAY PUT'E UP WITH 'ERE RULES

BUT IMMA FED' UP!" The indignant Hound screamed in reply to the Wolf's sinister sarcasm, letting go of the throne as it crashed down onto the floor, making a loud, unexpectedly jarring noise as it did so. As the throne dropped, startling even the most intractably disinterested of the Hounds, the room became quieter.

The crowd became much more interested and eagerly awaited any corollary, for this occurrence rarely happened, but it wasn't the first time. It became apparent that enough was enough for the Hound. As his veins bulged, his chin jutted out, and their eyes deadlocked in a standoff. The hoary Hound held his ground against the young Coveton, who was now quietly aghast and sneered at the apprehensive Hound, who, seeing the others appalled, regretted saying anything.

Now, he was alone (to defend himself.) Whyles spasmodically took cover behind the throne, peering from behind it, for he knew of Kaliber's choleric orientation toward any who impertinently transgressed his mandate. He knew of Kaliber's inevitable reaction firsthand. Kaliber stood motionless, shooting a baleful stare, bearing a crocodile smile upon hearing the pleas of the Hound for forgiveness. "AN INDOLENT LOUSE AAAAAAM IIIIIIII?

APPARENTLY, I AM! OH, HOW TIMELY FOR YOU!!! Begging is such a worthless attempt at an apology; after all, you DO KNOW who you are addressing, don't YOU? But do not fear; as you know, I am an honorable gentleman. Implausibly, to the likes of you, I CAN be merciful…." Kaliber gently remarked with a curdling smile. The Hound sighed with relief, thanking the nobly intoning Kaliber and kneeling with respect before the menacing Wolf. Above the aged Hound's bowing head, Kaliber's pseudo-sympathetic crocodile smile grew wider and wider.

Momentarily, they were both silent, but the Hound was unrelentingly knocked down with a sudden malicious strike of the Wolf's cane.

Then, after the unending bludgeoning, with one quick twist of the Wolf's brass-knobbed cane, Kaliber drew out a long, gleaming sword previously concealed in the cane's wooden hollow. The broken Hound, half-conscious, realizing the imminent danger before him, hastily dragged himself in floundering retreat as Kaliber pointed the sharp weapon toward him. The sword's long, thin, fuller blade was shaped like a rapier. It was noticeably engraved and bronzed with Renaissance-styled designs and symbols

With light feet and flawless agility, the Wolf capered around the frightened Hound, looking for aid amongst his kind, reaching out for a friendly paw; he received kicks and smacks. The surrounding cavorting gang started to cheer in their raving bloodlust. "And oh look, your fellow brethren are highly enjoying such a stellar performance; YOU KNOW WHAT THEY SAY?

THE SHOW MUST GO ON! How MARVELOUS! I am never one to disappoint!" Kaliber declared in high-spirited zest.

"It's a dreadful shame I don't feel merciful today. What a pity. My utmost condolences for this, you poor, unfortunate, TREACHEROUS fool! It's nothing personal; why no, not in the slightest, it's simply ME! You see, absolutely no one shall EVER CROSS ME! Say a prayer or TWO miserable ingrate!" The wrathful Wolf advised the tearful Hound as he continued to circle him. In the hope of clemency, the Hound kept pleading with his master for forgiveness, and Kaliber only cackled. Slowly, the Wolf swiped the sword's tip across the Hound's grey shoulder. At first, it seemed like a kind of jesting game, but then the point began to thrust deeper as it moved laterally toward the Hound's chest. The sword started to draw blood, thus causing the slow-burning and stinging pain. The Hound's sliced vest was stained from the blood flowing beneath the tattered garment. As the blade pierced more, plunging into the spurting wound, Kaliber's smile, which was already grotesquely wide, grew more expansive and even more hideously demented. His unforgettably deranged, reddening, and bulging eyes made him appear as a hideous and murderous specter of some forgotten lore. It was clear to the Hounds present that Kaliber had begun to lose his mind, for the bleeding gash was no joke, but their savage cheer grew even louder by the first sight of the trickling pool of scarlet blood. The Hound, silent at first, began to bay in terror. His eyes were deadlocked in fear of Kaliber's demented visage. "Aw, how terrible of me, how I hope it's not too painful… After all, it could have been GRAVELY WORSE! Kaliber's crackling voice ended in a deranged hiss as he continued to slice the grisly chest of the Hound with the edge of his sharp blade in endless succession. Then, with a suddenness that struck like lightning, the Wolf seized the Hound's bloodied shoulder, his cruel claws sinking deep, tightening with a force that seemed bent on snapping the very bone. The poor beast's body writhed under the savage grip, as the Wolf's trembling paw quivered with a terrible, unyielding strength, born of a fury that could no longer be contained.

The Hound gasped, trapped in a torment so intense, so relentless, that what began as a dull ache soon twisted into an excruciating aftershock—an agony that gnawed at him with a cruel, unyielding bite. The wound blossomed into a nightmare, each pulse a sting more vicious than a thousand blisters pricking the skin, each sharper than the last. Kaliber pressed on, his voice growing deeper, more thunderous as it bore down upon the shrinking Hound.

"YOU DARE TO CHALLENGE!? DISRESPECT!? I LORD KALIBER M. COVETON THE SEEEEEEEEVENNNNNTH!!!!???? MISERABLE UNGRATEFUL, INSIGNIFICANT SWIIIIIIIIINE!!!! I AM ROYALTY; I AM ALLLLLLL THAAAAAAAATS

MIIIIIIIGHTY!!!!" Kaliber shrieked in abhorrence, horrifically scornful as he was and most remorseless.

He could not have cared the slightest if the Hound was to be permanently crippled afterward and for such a paltry outburst as this. The Wolf continued vigorously clinging to the gruesome wound in retaliation for the Hound's rebellious confrontation against the Coveton.

"Ple-please lo-lo-lord s-sir, I am 'very shamed, ne- nev- nevar ag- again 'ease sir 'have mercy on me-" The Wolf, hearing the plea of mercy, only squeezed it tighter. "What was that?"

"I su- I –su- I- sub- I SUBMMIIIIIIIIIIT!!!!!!!!" "WHO IS THE GREATEST!?"

"Yu- yur ar's…."

"WHO IS ELEGANTLY SUPERIOR AND CULTURED?!" The Wolf demanded to know, squeezing the Hound's shoulder even more tightly.

"YOU! M- m- m-ME LORD, PL- PLEASE, IM BEGGIN YE'R…. LE- LE- LET ME G-G-G-

Oo-O-o GO I- SU- I SUB- I SUBMIT!" The Hound tearfully wept as the Wolf slowly released his grip. "Save You're laughable plead! Redeeming the decrepit is such a foul convention ignominy of Coveton kindred!" Kaliber hawked and expectorated upon the disgraced Hound now lying on the ground. The Hound was mournfully tending to his ripped contusion as he pitifully continued to whimper.

"EXACTLY YOU SORDID GOON, AND NEVER FORGET IT!" Kaliber announced with sibilated emphasis. "ALL OF YOU, I AM YOUR SUZERAIN! I AM YOUR MASTER;

NEVER FORGET IT!" Kaliber said, turning to the other Hounds. Silent and stimulated, they willingly concurred. "NOW GET UP!"

But the Hound could not physically get himself up. Though he did try, he fell instantly into a tumbling heap. Kaliber then dipped one of his fingers into the pool of blood which had splotched the tip of his sinking finger. Kaliber stood briefly transfixed. He apathetically stared (and examined) the blood dripping from it. Suddenly in a flourish, he grotesquely sucked the blood off from his paw and devilishly grinned, smacking his maroon lips and licking around his mouth which still dribbled. His eyes went cold as if to sample the refined savoring of the fallen Hound's blood. It now seemed that the terrible disease of Gorse-End had already started to take an overwhelming domination over the young Coveton. He was oblivious to the seizing change in himself, as such did overtake all who had dwelt here for very long. A sickening malady of the mind wherein such a dankly dismal and forlornly bleak region did its bogey magic not only mysteriously change one's thoughts but also lead one onto a demented and forevermore accursed enchantment. The place had the power to turn even those mighty in will and sturdy in temperament into blood-lusting savages. Such a one might resemble Clovis Kaine, the fiend, at one's own looming and untimely end.

"Oh, how extraordinarily fascinating! Bitter... yet delectably SAAAAAAAVORY!" He horrifically said at last with the most psychotically vile and downright ghastly damnable simper and with a particular strange ill-omened bearing.

"I SAID GET UP!" The Wolf again snarled. Incapacitated, the vulnerable Hound, was sprawled upon the ground, crippled and mangled as he yet cried out in agony. Clovis widely smiled as he walked right next to the fuming Wolf, happily enjoying seeing the impaired Hound whine and hysterically convulse.

"One less mongrel to deal with!" Clovis whispered to the Wolf. Kaliber, enraged by the grueling sight screamed "Get him out of my sight! Hurry, propero, finish what I've started! I am much too pura to execute this stultus fracto!!" Kaliber cynically belittled, while demanding two other Hounds to accomplish the horrendous task. Without a single hesitation of resistance and with the

fearful and vindictive presence of the rancorous Wolf possessed by verbose obscenities, they rushed toward the beaten Hound. With a slow process, the mangled Hound, who could barely walk was hoisted up grudgingly by the two Hounds. They made their way to the Hounds' main sleeping quarters where suddenly the quiet den burst into a blood-curdling shriek that rang through the dark chambers. Kaliber was now pleased but still fiery, secretly craving more bloodletting.

"ANYONE ELSE DARE TO IMBUE ANARCHARCHY!!!!?" Kaliber shrieked in a desultory and insincere question, flailing and slashing his sword. The group of Hounds was utterly amazed by the Wolf who just showed them his proper monstrous form and had utterly forgotten any past meetings sworn to dethrone the Coveton. Now in recognition of his forcible dominion, they rejected such a dreadful possibility, if any rare opportunity ever came to be. The Wolf was nonsensically crude and self-seeking. He was very unsubtle in the pronouncement of his demands and loyalties. To be in the presence of such high authority, a monarch in conviction of his own ideas and beliefs, was only to be constrained and apprehended by the young Wolf. The Hounds were decidedly absent of ideas in their fear that their ideas might have been significantly in conflict with the Wolf's own. Indeed, his adolescent ethics and tyrannical repression of all things made him an unquestioned and bigoted totem of misused power. The Wolf was not to be taken lightly as they now knew. The thought of him as an effeminate braggart quickly left the Hounds in general. Kaliber sat on his throne with the twin lion heads of the Toscano mahogany armrest glared at the dumbfounded gang standing beneath Kaliber's clenching paws.

"THEN SHALL I ASK, ARE ALL OF YOU IN OR OUT!?" He turned to the hiding Fox and offered him a seat next to him. He pointed at the empty chair with his saber, so the skittish Fox quickly scooted right in. The Hounds were awfully quiet and broke into a cold sweat. "GO ON, TAKE YOUR TIME! THINK WISELY…I'LL ONLY OFFER THIS ONCE!!! Just a kind reminder." The Wolf blissfully remarked in a cackle.

From behind Kaliber's groomed head, each Hound could visibly see the richness of a crimson, burgundy cushion pinned by brass fittings, which glittered in the low light of the cold and damp dwelling. Still awaiting an answer, he grew restless, impatient, and incredibly agitated by the exasperating respite. At Kaliber's tapping, fidgety feet were the scrollwork-clawed feet of some mythological creature, lion-like yet strangely anthropomorphized as a kind of angelic or dark angelic being. Above Kaliber's head was a carved coat of arms holding a miniature scroll below the gilded family crown. This family emblem gained the most praise and attention when presented with the elaborate heirloom throne passed by on by each successive generation. The daunted group had yet to speak any answer to Kaliber's shrieking invitation.

"Be warned, all double-crossers shall be severely punished!" Kaliber snarled; his teeth bared in a menacing grin. "Take my advice: I am the one you all need! Follow me, and glory and fortune are yours for the taking!" He promised, his voice laced with high hopes that they would all fall in line. "But to reach that pinnacle, you must unconditionally obey my every command without a single pathetic, wretched complaint!"

As Kaliber's words echoed through the den, Clovis and Captain Silas slowly stepped to his side, clearly signaling their allegiance. One by one, the Hounds fell in line, their fear of Kaliber's wrath evident in their cautious movements. The room was filled with tension, with some Hounds visibly nervous about the choices laid before them.

The intense, scrutinizing gaze from the other side of the den left them with little choice. They faced the grim reality of either serving under Kaliber or facing savage execution for any hint of treason. This fear was heightened by the harsh punishment they had already witnessed, a stark warning of Kaliber's mercilessness.

With the threat of death looming large, the decision became clear. Under the weight of Kaliber's relentless and authoritative presence, they, too, joined the ranks, falling in behind him like timid sheep flocking to their shepherd. As they did, Kaliber's smile widened in satisfaction. Seated on his grand throne, he saw that no dissenters remained; all had rallied to his cause. Any further resistance was now futile and non-existent.

"Oh, how EXCELLENT!" Kaliber exclaimed, his voice dripping with arrogance. "Put your faith in me, my companions; I promise we shall not falter! After all, ego sum dominus largitatis!" he bragged.

As he heard the Hound preparing the feast announce that the meal was ready, Kaliber called for assistance. "Assiste mihi, amici! Bring forth the feast!" He commanded.

Noticing some of the Hounds moving to where the food needed to be brought, Kaliber ordered the rest to pull the large table to where he sat waiting. He watched as a quartet of Hounds struggled to drag the enormous, polished table from beneath his throne. His gaze shifted to a covered object on the wall across from him, and he wondered what they might be hiding. "Certus aliquid mirabile," he mused to himself. "Surely something marvelous."

"Bring forth some ravishing ornaments at once, if you will," Kaliber scorned, seeing the plain table before him. "A meal fit for a Coveton shall never be served on such a modest table!" The Hounds scrambled in all directions, searching for decorations to please the Coveton Lord. Two raggedy Hounds, Butch and Hutch, discovered a richly colored red lace tablecloth. They proudly showed it to Kaliber, who gave a stiff nod of approval. The two Hounds began to unroll and spread the cloth over the long rectangular table, but their usual bickering resumed as they fought over the placement. They started to slug each other until Kaliber intervened with a growl, directing them on how to properly arrange the cloth. In truth, it didn't matter much, but they double-checked to ensure the cloth was neatly pressed and free of creases.

Satisfied with their work, Kaliber saw his gratitude reflected in their hurried departure as they helped find more decorations. A separate group of three Hounds clumsily arranged three burning candles on separate copper candlesticks at the center of the table. The candles were tipped over, dripping wax onto the cloth and almost setting it on fire before Kaliber adjusted them with a scowl of annoyance

"What do I expect from blithering imbeciles?" Kaliber muttered. The table was soon adorned as the Hounds scurried about, finding and rearranging various items. Exhausted from their labor, the Hounds panted heavily, tongues hanging out and eyes half-drowsy. Kaliber, pleased with the result, congratulated each Hound and handed out copper coins as a reward. However, the Hounds, unaware of the true value of the coins, gushed with pride and eagerly sought more. They approached Kaliber, who gave each five coins. When they clamored for additional coins, Kaliber waved them off with a sneer. "Non rewardo tales abiectos vagabundos et lumox mendicos, minimus!" he growled. "I do not reward such abject vagabonds and lummox beggars, not in the least!"

Kaliber snatched the coins from their outstretched paws and slapped them away, leaving the Hounds with nothing but irritation. "O, quam errore, dilecti mei! You shall be either satisfied with what you have or have nothing at all! Intellegisne, aut opus est pluris clarificatione?" He chortled. "Dear me, how terribly mistaken you are! Do you understand, or do you need more clarification?"

Kaliber's moment of satisfaction quickly turned to vexation as he grew impatient with the delay of his ceremonial banquet. "Velim citius! Will you hurry it up in there?!" he barked in frustration. The Hounds, desperate to placate their irate Lord, did their best to hasten the preparations. They drew his attention to the covered object on the wall, which he had noticed earlier. Two Hounds approached it at a brisk pace, one on each side, with the cord still swaying.

"If you would be so gracious as to direct your attention to our presentation," began one of the Hounds. However, Kaliber's eagerness turned to irritation at the hesitation in the Hound's voice. The second Hound quickly corrected the slip. "To your distinguished attention!"

"Yes, yes, yes, I am the most renowned! Please, GO ON!" the Wolf declared; his impatience evident. He detested waiting, and the Hounds' delay had begun to fray his nerves. But what they revealed was worth the wait. It was a magnificent portrait of Kaliber, a sight he had never seen before. Though he had seen many portraits of his family and distant relatives in the grand halls of Coveton Castle, this was the first private portrait of himself.

The Hounds sighed in relief, watching Kaliber's reaction with a mix of anticipation and amusement. They nearly witnessed him burst into tears of joy. The painting was large and exquisite, depicting the young Coveton in his prime—dressed as usual, standing with dignified grace, cane tucked under his arm, with the ma.j.estic Coveton Castle as the backdrop.

"Oh, how absolutely tremendous!" Kaliber exclaimed; his voice filled with rapture. "Where did you find this masterpiece? It's simply brilliant! Look at how distinguished I am! Oh, the unmatched cleverness of myself is a marvel. How did I ever manage such a heavenly portrait?"

The cutthroat marauders cheered along, chanting, "LONG LIVE LORD COVETON! May his dice never stop rolling!" They seemed more delighted by Kaliber's enthusiasm than by the portrait itself, enjoying the rare sight of the Wolf's broad, genuine smile rather than his usual scowl. In contrast, Whyles stared at the painting with growing terror. The portrait included a long red fox pelt draped over Kaliber's shoulder, making poor Whyles tremble with dread.

The gruesome depiction of the dead fox, coiled like a trophy around Kaliber's shoulder, was a haunting sight. It intensified Whyles's fear, making him wonder if this might be his own fate. The Hounds, however, remained oblivious to the unsettling detail. Their insensitivity to the gruesome image was typical, as they were accustomed to such displays.

Kaliber, despite his initial delight, was soon overwhelmed by a wave of anguish. The portrait triggered painful memories of his family's fall from grace. "THE LAUGHTER, THE DISRESPECT THEY SHOWED! CURSE THOSE MISERABLE BOURCHIERS!" he wailed n agony, his grief morphing into a vengeful rage.

The Hounds were aware of the Bourchiers' role in Kaliber's life—they had taken over Coveton Castle when he was a child, leading to his family's downfall. The Covetons had lost everything to the Bourchiers in a game of Bluffer's Roll, including their son, young Kaliber. Though the Covetons had been allowed to remain as guests, their nobility had diminished, and they had become mere shadows of their former selves.

Kaliber, despite being loved by his own, had been mistreated by the Bourchiers, especially by his cousin Tyrus Byron Bourchier the 5th, who was two years older and notoriously arrogant. Tyrus had often belittled Kaliber, exacerbating their rivalry. Their conflict had culminated in a bitter duel, and it was rumored that the scar on Kaliber's lip was a saber cut from that fight. The name "Lucrecia Van Kloss" also seemed to provoke Kaliber's rage, revealing the depth of his unresolved bitterness.

"How dare they all TOSS ME OUT!" (And by "they," the Wolf had meant the Bourchier's and his Coveton kin as well, for he was too spiteful of them for being a losing wager than to be handed over like one would do when they grow tired of the useless object they wish to trade.)

By this time, Clovis had reached his paw to the Wolf's shoulder, clutching it tight, he started to whisper in Coveton's ear, which had been thought of as advice but was seen by many to make the Wolf even more enraged by his bygone era. The Wolf was yet to become even more agitated than before Clovis began to whisper, as the violent flails of Kaliber's yielding sword and the unrestrainable profanity he rashly ranted had terrifyingly paraded as some may never believe it to be accurate if explained and not shown. The Hounds watching dared not to intervene to calm or agitate the Wolf, screaming and crying (similar to what you might hear outside the walls of an asylum), collapsed on his throne, crying out loud and blowing out of proportion. It was only too subdued when the food was sizzling and hot, and it was quickly brought rushing to serve him in front. The grieving Wolf made his face suitably decent for the company and not of a crybaby fool, sheathing back his weapon into his cane and giving it one tight twist; he then had imminently apologized for a sorrowful performance.

"I must be hungry; that must be why I had a moment! I have such a terrible time when it comes to malnutrition whenever food is untimely late!" Kaliber said in half-truth reasoning of his embarrassing outburst, but this reason was to be doubted by the Hound in their own; these events had happened so often they figured him to be more insane than genuinely stable in thought, but again, who were they to judge from being crazy lunatics themselves.

The Wolf began his meal with gusto, savoring the tender cutlets braised in a rich dark wine sauce accompanied by potatoes and green vegetables. A sweet, plump bun soaked in cinnamon glaze sat in a side bowl. Kaliber, content for the moment, ate heartily with his silverware while Whyles, seated beside him, picked at his meal with a visible lack of appetite. Whyles was visibly shaken by Kaliber's presence, his stomach too unsettled to enjoy the feast.

As Kaliber enjoyed his meal, a Hound approached carrying a velvet cushion with a golden chalice. The chalice, adorned with sparkling jewels and engraved with Kaliber's initials, was presented with great ceremony. Kaliber took a delicate sip, savoring the fine beverage and patting his lips with a handkerchief. His sharp eyes darted toward Whyles, narrowing as he noticed the Fox hadn't taken more than a tentative bite of his food.

"You're lacking spirit tonight," Kaliber remarked, pouring a dark crimson wine into a goblet. He slid it toward Whyles with a deliberate motion. "Bibere et fruere," he said smoothly, his tone brooking no argument.

Whyles hesitated, his paw brushing the goblet's stem. "I appreciate yer generosity," he began cautiously, "but I'm not in the mood to drink—"

Kaliber's snarl interrupted him. "Not in the mood?" The Wolf's claws rapped against the table before he suddenly snatched the goblet. "You will drink," he growled, standing and leaning toward Whyles.

Before the Fox could react, Kaliber grabbed his muzzle with a firm, crushing grip, forcing it open. "Open wide, little fox," he sneered, his voice low and mocking. He upended the goblet ruthlessly, the dark wine surging into Whyles' mouth.

The sharp liquid flooded his throat, the acrid taste stinging his tongue. Whyles gagged and sputtered, his paws clawing at Kaliber's arm in a feeble attempt to break free. The Wolf's grip remained unyielding as he tipped the goblet higher, his claws digging slightly into Whyles' fur.

"Swallow," Kaliber commanded, his tone as unrelenting as his hold. The Fox had no choice but to comply, choking down the bitter mouthfuls as the wine spilled down his throat and dribbled from the corners of his mouth.

Finally, Kaliber released him with a harsh shove, watching with smug satisfaction as Whyles slumped back in his chair, coughing and wiping at the wine that stained his fur. "See?" Kaliber said with a smirk. "That wasn't so difficult. A bit of spirit might even suit you. Now, entertain us with one of your clever riddles, Whyles. My Hounds and I always enjoy your wit."

The Fox, familiar with his role as the jester, stood and cleared his throat, though his hands trembled slightly. "Very well, Lord Kaliber. Here's a riddle for you:

'Every night, I'm told what to do, and each morning, I do what I'm told, yet never do I escape your scold. What am I?'" Kaliber, eager to show off, answered with a laugh. "A careless buffoon!"

Whyles shook his head. "Incorrect. The answer is 'Your timekeeper.'"

Kaliber's face darkened. "Time? What nonsense! I have no use for such trivialities. Change it to something more fitting, or I might have to make a new rule!"

Whyles, stuttering and bowing, replied, "With all respect, it's my riddle, and I like it!"

Kaliber's temper flared, but he barely controlled it. "Fine, fine. Continue, but make them more challenging."

The Fox, still nervous, continued. "Alright, here's another: 'When you need me, you throw me away. But when you're done, you bring me back. What am I?'"

Kaliber and his Hounds were stumped. After a long pause, Kaliber, visibly frustrated, shouted, "Enough! What is it?"

Whyles answered quietly, "An anchor."

Kaliber, either mishearing or ignoring the answer, puffed up with false pride. "Ah, of course! I knew it all along. Now, something truly challenging."

He raised his chalice for a toast, and his Hounds cheered loudly, though their enthusiasm was exaggerated. After the noise settled, Kaliber fixed his gaze back on Whyles, his patience thinning. "One more riddle, fox. Make it worthwhile."

Whyles, deeply anxious, took a breath and asked, "I'm like a child, a lamb, and a fool at once. All are born with me, yet few possess me at their death. What am I?"

Kaliber, losing his composure, snarled, "I can't tolerate this! Just tell me!" Whyles, exasperated but resigned, answered, "Innocence."

Kaliber's eyes gleamed with sinister delight. "Innocence? How fitting. It reminds me of something else entirely." He snapped his fingers, and Clovis, grinning maliciously, produced a signed document and a quill.

Kaliber scrutinized the document, his laugh turning darker. "This will seal their fate. Trust is indeed a disease. I can feel it."

As Kaliber scribbled on the parchment, Whyles watched in growing fear, uncertain of his own future. Meanwhile, the Hounds, tired of their games, left Kaliber alone with his dark plans, and the Fox stood uneasily, contemplating the Wolf's cryptic words and chilling laughter.

"And soon," Kaliber continued, almost to himself, "I shall possess the power I am rightfully entitled to! Take this, Kaine!" Clovis swiftly tucked the document into his coat pocket.

"My family shall fall at the sight of Lord Kaliber Marcellus Coveton the Seventh! They'll live in infamy, as will the Bourchiers!" Kaliber's voice grew louder with each word, and his eyes blazed with a crazed passion. "And that wretched swine, Tyrus, that bane of my existence—he'll swing from the gallows where he belongs! And Lucrecia... my sweet Lucrecia, she'll be mine again." Kaliber sighed, lost in his delusion of love. Suddenly, with a burst of energy, he cried, "Sing a song! Come, you fools, sing!" He leaped up, twirling and dancing, but no music accompanied him. The Hounds stood aghast, confused by the unusual command.

When the silence stretched too long, Kaliber shrieked, "SING! You mangy curs!"

The Hounds, still bewildered, exchanged glances until Kaine broke the awkward moment with a loud guffaw and began to sing:

"Who is greater than our exalted? Who is wiser than his ma.j.esty? Trickier than the noble Lord? Who is more intimidating? None can compare to Kaliber the Mighty! Bold is he, Riches bloom in his garden, Let us toast! To our revered host! Hail, oh hail! To the young Lord of Coveton.

Hail, hail, prodigy!"

Kaliber joined in with a triumphant solo, "Who is more fearlessly great than meeee?" His operatic voice echoed through the hall.

At last, the Hounds joined in, singing loudly, "Tra-da-da-da!" They danced with their Lord in wild abandon, their voices growing more raucous with each verse. The chaos went on for quite some time until Kaliber, out of breath, called for Whyles. The Fox, weaving through the tumult, made his way to the corner where Kaliber awaited him.

Kaliber draped an arm around the Fox's shoulder, speaking in a low voice. "In a month's time, Whyles, we will arrive. Whether you're ready or not, we will arrive by summer's end." "When exactly should I expect your coming?" Whyles asked, his voice trembling.

"You don't need to know!" Kaliber snapped, his patience wearing thin. The Fox persisted, pleading for more time, but Kaliber cut him off. "Five weeks is more than enough to do your task. I will not stand idly by while time slips away!"

"TICK, TOCK! Time is running short, and I won't wait any longer. Make friends in Ambrodale if you like—it will be all the more bitter when the truth comes out." Kaliber smiled grimly. "You don't need them. You have me. I provide everything: shelter, company, food!" He waved at the Hounds, now brawling after their dance had turned into roughhousing.

"All I ask is one small favor, and in return, you shall earn…" Kaliber paused, reaching into his coat and pulling out a die. He rolled it onto the floor, his eyes widening with manic anticipation as it spun endlessly. Losing patience, he stamped his cane, and the die stopped, showing a "3." With a grin, Kaliber leaned close to Whyles' ear. "Freedom," he whispered. "That's your reward for loyalty to me."

Whyles, pale and shaken, stammered his thanks, though a part of him doubted the Wolf's promise.

Kaliber, sensing his hesitation, raised a paw and swore, "On my Coveton honor, Whyles, you shall have your freedom when my reign begins."

But as the Fox bowed and thanked him, Kaliber's fingers, hidden behind his back, were crossed, betraying the vow as false.

"Now be gone," Kaliber commanded. "Return at the end of each week to check-in. And bring gifts—don't forget. You wouldn't want to make me angry, would you?"

Whyles, startled by the sudden slap on his back, hurried away, slipping into the night and heading toward Ambrodale. The journey back was haunted by the Wolf's threats, and though exhausted, Whyles could not sleep when he returned to Wally's home. The dread of what awaited him in three weeks weighed heavily on his mind.

Soon, time would run out.

Days passed, and during this time, Whyles kept his solemn promise to Lord Kaliber, surreptitiously pilfering Wally's most treasured belongings. The unsuspecting Hare, unaware of the Fox's deceit, believed he had lost or misplaced these cherished items himself. Little did he know that his prized possessions now lay in the hands of the wicked Lord Kaliber Coveton the Seventh, who adored these trinkets.

Whyles had stealthily taken Wally's grandmother's pocket watch. The silver locket, which held a miniature portrait of Wally's late father, now adorned Kaliber's collection. Wally's favorite book of fairy tales, filled with personal notes and bookmarks, was now a curious trophy in Kaliber's library.

The handcrafted wooden pipe, a symbol of Wally's pride and skill, was displayed prominently in Kaliber's study. Wally's lucky charm, a miniature bell, had found its place among Kaliber's prized curios. The hand-stitched quilt, lovingly made by Wally's mother, now provided comfort in Kaliber's quarters.

Kaliber marveled at the collection of rare coins Wally had amassed over the years, each coin a symbol of the Hare's adventures and trades. The music box, which played a soothing melody, was a new favorite distraction for Kaliber. Wally's family portrait, once a cherished reminder of his loved ones, now hung in Kaliber's private gallery. Finally, the gardening tools Wally had meticulously customized were displayed as trophies of Kaliber's new 'artisan' collection.

In return for his thievery, Whyles was awarded the title "Sir Whyles the Crafty." Fearful of Kaliber's wrath and the lashings he might receive, he mindlessly obeyed. The guilt gnawed at him, haunting his every thought, but his cowardice kept him chained to Kaliber's demands.

Worse still, as the Fox carried out these wicked deeds, he unknowingly stole something far more valuable—Wally's joyous reputation among the Riverfolk. The same creatures who once admired the Hare now held him in contempt, blaming him for introducing the Fox into their midst. Unaware of the growing rumors, Wally faced the cold shoulders of his once-friendly neighbors, and the weight of their scorn settled heavily upon him.

The late afternoon air hung dense with the sweet fragrance of ripening grapes, and the Riverfolk busied themselves with the vineyard, planting and fertilizing beneath the golden sun. But each passing day brought Whyles a more profound sorrow as the burden of his crimes weighed heavily upon him. Alone with his conscience, he feared the inevitable downfall of this peaceful town, now under the cruel eye of Lord Kaliber.

Once welcomed by the Riverfolk, the Fox was now met with suspicion and distrust. Whyles' strange and insolent behavior had driven a wedge between him and the community, and silent complaints about the rude stranger traveled fast. Ever the trusting soul, Wally knew little of this animosity, continuing to roam the woods with Sampson and Booney. Yet, his companions harbored their own suspicions.

"I do not trust 'tat Whyles as Wall does… somethin' seems quite dangerous about him. I do not like it… nope, not one bit," groaned Booney, not out of jealousy but caution, though envy did play a part in his feelings. Since Whyles arrived, the Frog disliked not being the center of attention. As he strolled alongside Sampson one warm afternoon, even the Moose had to agree, though it was rare for him to see eye to eye with the stubborn Frog.

"If you ask me, Wally is asking for a lot of trubble bringin' that uncivil Fox here… He's much too trusting for his own good. Why, that fella might be anything but good," Sampson said, recalling a recent quarrel with the Fox over some trivial matter. The Fox had insulted the Moose with crude remarks about his philosophy, mocking Sampson's love of quiet contemplation. The Moose had lost all tolerance for the Fox's rough language and exploitative behavior.

"Come on, Sampson, let's head to Phenny's. I dreadfully desire a drink of some good mead… to put this aside. Oh, me poor head is a achin' for one, and be golly, I haven't had a taste of it for so long, I utterly forgot the flavor!" Fussed the Frog, clutching his head as he hurried toward the crossroads that led to the bar, Sampson stomping slowly behind.

That evening, Wally hosted another celebration, eager to toast the newcomer. As dusk settled over Ambrodale, Wally and Whyles stood outside the Hare's home, marveling at the bright orange sun dipping below the horizon. The sky was awash with pomegranate pinks and other vibrant hues as the distant mountains were slowly swallowed by a rising fog. Wally waved kindly to the Riverfolk passing by, but instead of returning his greeting, they glanced nervously at Whyles, who glared back with flickering blue eyes. Even the Quaddlings, who always stopped for a chat, painfully ignored the Hare's desperate call as they shuffled past his home. Baffled, Wally turned to Whyles, who guiltily looked away, struggling with an unfamiliar emotion—one of guilt and shame for the harm he had caused.

"Oh, never mind them, me friend! They must have a great deal to do!" Wally said with a lighthearted smile, unconcerned by the cold reception. He believed in the goodness of everyone he met, no matter their flaws or misdeeds.

"Come, let's step inside now. It's getting much too chilly out here! Let us wait for our friends inside, and I shall start a cozy fire!" Remarked the Hare, opening the door for Whyles, who walked in with a heavy heart.

"They ain't me, friends," muttered the Fox gravely as he watched the last light of the setting sun disappear behind the door. Inside, Wally busied himself by lighting a fire and arranging logs to create the perfect warmth. The Fox, meanwhile, sat in silence, consumed by dark thoughts of Kaliber's scheme—a day closer than yesterday. All he could imagine was his head mounted above a mantel or his skin laid out as a rug before a burning fire, a prized trophy for the cruel Lord. His mind spiraled into paranoia, and he felt himself losing grip on reality, haunted by visions of his inevitable fate.

As the fire crackled warmly, Wally settled into his chair, pipe in paw, and began to write. No one could say what he wrote, for Wally often penned his thoughts at random, crafting stories or recording his travels. That evening, he worked on a map of Ambrodale, carefully tracing the routes he walked each day, like an explorer mapping out a treasure hunt. But as the hours ticked by and the clock struck ten, and just as he was about to retire for the night, a knock came at the door.

Wally greeted his visitors warmly, his surprise evident—guests had become a rarity since Whyles' arrival. At the door stood Sampson and Booney, their expressions a mix of curiosity and unease.

"Has the Fox turned in for the night?" Sampson asked after a moment's hesitation.

"I believe so," Wally replied, puzzled. "His door's locked." He stepped aside, motioning them in. Once inside, Wally couldn't hold back his curiosity. "What's everyone so uppity about Mr.

Whyles anyway?"

Booney answered before Sampson could intervene, his voice sharp and unapologetic. "Because he's a no-good bugger, that's why!"

Sampson sighed, but the Frog pressed on, his indignation growing with every word. "He's a rull loonie and a danger, I tell ya! Not fit for our wood—not a bit of it. Look at him! Always skulkin' about, always actin' all superstitious. His look is somehow terrifying, and it sends frighties up me spine whenever he gives me a shiverin' glare! And I tell ya, it ain't just that either! Lemme tell ya, he ain't the perkiest fella—no sir!"

Booney leaned closer, his voice dropping to a conspiratorial whisper. "He's no good for nothin'—a rottin', no-good SPUNGLER!"

Sampson, though hesitant, reluctantly agreed. "O' how I utterly despise admitting that I must agree with Mr. Wiggins, but dear Wally, I'm afraid he's right! This Fox seems somehow twisted and almost distrustful. I know you mean very well, Wally, and I don't mean to offend, but you may be a bit too kind and generous to those unworthy of your time! If you haven't noticed, Wally, Mr. Whyles… if that really is his name, is not the-"

Wally opened his mouth to respond, but his attention was pulled away by a faint, eerie melody drifting in through the open window.

Outside, a cloaked figure, nearly invisible in the darkness, once again, glided through Ambrodale, carrying a slender fife. The haunting melody wove its way through the village, not merely a tune but a lure. Its hypnotic pull reached into the dreams of the Riverfolk.

One by one, the villagers awoke, their movements slow and deliberate, as if summoned. In a trance, they exited their cottages and formed a ghostly procession beneath the moon's glow. Their steps, precise and synchronized, moved with a disturbing, ritualistic precision, as though following some unseen command.

Wally, peering out the window, stiffened. He squinted into the night, unsure of what he was seeing. "What in the world…" he muttered, watching as the villagers moved in eerie, almost ceremonial unison. The strange stillness of the night, broken only by the fife's haunting refrain, sent a shiver through him.

The cloaked figure, hidden in the shadows, observed with satisfaction as the entranced Riverfolk advanced toward the forest. Their steps were silent but deliberate, as though compelled by an unseen force. The figure's fingers twitched slightly, making sure each note was heard, and each dream was touched.

As the last villager disappeared into the trees, the melody faded, leaving an unsettling calm in its wake. The cloaked figure dissolved into the shadows, their task complete.

Wally turned back to his guests, but the sight had unsettled him deeply. The conversation resumed, but the night's eerie events lingered at the edges of his thoughts, a dark omen of what was to come.

Chapter Seven

To Whyles with Love

The early morning sunrise was brisk, yet it was all too colorful from the drizzle of rain from the previous night which created a giant palette of crystal blue that seemed to be dripping color. A translucent and resplendent arc hovered over Ambrodale in ease and grace—a riot of buoyant color, a work beyond art, a promise of bliss. Booney, the Frog, made himself ready for the new day in his mossy log home. To say the house was large would be an overstatement, particularly when Booney began one of his famous monologues for his often bored and distracted visitors. At those times, Booney was in his element, and his voice and gesticulations could grow directly proportional to his confidence in sharing his yarns and tall tales. The place was relatively small and rather snug. The moss that grew through the cracks in the log walls made a rather cozy yet dark, dank space. It was always moist and cool in summer and draft-free and warm in winter.

Winter was when Booney was most likely to launch into an elaborate story. He always felt this would remove the chill from a winter's night; however, most guests refused the morsels he occasionally offered during these times. It was, however, these morsels he sought at the present moment. He began his day scrambling for a breakfast of fresh chirping crickets, slimy slugs, and crunchy snails that he kept in a large clear glass container. Reaching in, he took a handful, gobbled, and munched them up, having a quick, scrumptious meal. After he finished, he went off on his march outdoors. Strutting along whistling a melody to himself, he carried his hand-carved fishing rod that was indeed poorly crafted, for his pole was misshapen and corroded with blistered marks and scars. Booney's destination today was Wally's home for their routine rally of morning fishing. When the right weather came, Boone's elbow went 'bout twitching. "A fishin' twitchin'," he called it. The Frog, knowing the right time, would run off, pole in hand, to fetch Wally for a friendly competition of sorts, vying to see who could catch the most fish; Booney, the Frog, considered himself a champion when it came down to reeling in the bigger fish.

Booney, the Frog, strutted with style down each forest and glade path, greeting everyone he met with whoops of "OOOOOO! It's me lucky day it is! Ye wanna' know why? NOOO? Well, I tells ya anyhow!" And off he would ramble, making definitely sure that they perfectly knew what he was up to whether they so cared or not.

Wally had already finished his breakfast when a loud knock came on the door. Wally, too busy to answer the beckoning call, requested Whyles to answer the ongoing holler. Whyles dashed to the door, slowly opening it with just a crack. He poked his unkempt furry head out to see the caller. Not seeing anyone, he slammed the door shut, and with the shut came a shrill of curses, "YEEEEEEEEEEEEOOOOOWWW M-M-M-MEEEEEEE fooooooottttt!!!!!! Ye closed the door on me poor, poor big toey! Ya' LOUT!!" Puzzled by the scream, Whyles cautiously opened the door and looked at the vast world before him. He felt a sudden, violent tug on his rain jacket.

"Down 'ere ye bovine divvy!"

Whyles looked down, directing his eyes on the Frog in a deadlocked staring match. The Fox seemed agitated by Booney's appearance. "Well, what da ye want?" The Fox coldly asked. Before the Frog could say anything, the Fox bitterly retorted, "If'n nuttin, then be on ye merry way and don't come back!"

The Fox knew that Booney mistrusted him and, likewise, for that night of questionable confessions and what Booney had seen when he trailed the shady Fox in the dead of night. The frantic Fox and opinionated uptight Frog were at each other's throats. Both appeared to be quite convivial and good-humored when their fellows were in their company, except when the time came when each made their separate ways in the village. The good-humored gambit of the two would quickly become hostile. Each one wanted to have a tussle to finish up what they each thought must be done. For reasons rooted in a cautious nature, Booney would patrol the streets of Ambrodale once night had descended and a hush had settled over the village. With everyone adequately tucked away in slumber, Booney ensured nothing untoward would pass unnoticed.

On such nights, curiosity and suspicion drove him to follow the gliding Fox, who carried mysterious bags that hinted at hidden dealings. Under the dim, trembling light of the streetlamps, Booney kept close to the shadows, his unease growing as he witnessed the Fox engage in furtive conversations with figures that emerged from the gloom. The whispered exchanges and veiled gestures laid bare the sinister depths of Whyles' clandestine schemes.

"I am here to see if Wally is up for sum fushins. It's a most lovely day, is it not?!" Booney answered, throwing up his arms to show the world around him.

"Hmm, yes, yes, it is..." Whyles said, not too impressed. "It's like any other. It ain't nuttin' special 'bout it! But I'm terribly surry, but I don't think Wally will be joining ye. Now RUN ALONG!"

"Oh, we'll be seein' 'bout t'at!" Booney replied as he hopped right in, calling the Hare's name. Whyles, agitated by the speckled Frog, suddenly picked him up by his red jacket and fiendishly growled in a deep, scratchy voice, spinning him around like a twirly top.

"RUN ALONG, YE GOON!"

Booney swung hard, but the Fox extended himself, so the speckled Frog was only flailing and missing. Then, realizing he wasn't getting anywhere, Booney whispered, "Don't t'ink ye can fool me, like ye are doin's te, Wally. After all, I am a Wiggins, and we Wigginses are ones to solve mysteries. I know I know what you are. If I sees ye once by t'em swamp, I can bet ye goes t'er more, and it ain't for pickin' no daisies, a bag filled to the top of all our goodies, strange lights flickerin', comes back all sneaky 'ike! Ye are a fine actor! But ye can't fool me! AN' IF IT'S ONE THING I CAN DO PERFEC, IT'S I TELLIN T'EM ALL!"

Whyles started to cackle. "Is t'at t'e bes' ye can do!? Ye an' I both know t'ey wunt believes it now wud t'ey? That bag could be filled wit' anytin', and you wouldn't know what! Face it, Booney, ye are just a little fella in a big wide world tryna play hero. Lumme gives a secret: this world, as dangerous as it is, eats up heroes! You are makin' a dreadful mistake, me frug fella. I wouldn't be poking me nus' in utters affurs, or ye may find yourself on a spike. A very unlucky fate ye will have!" Whyles threatened, shaking Booney roughly. The Frog just laughed, mocking the Fox.

"Oh, me O' my, I'm so teribbibliy scared I'm shuking. Try ye worst, ye GNASHGABBING, LUBBERWORTED, RAGGABRASHING YALDSON!!!!" And just like that, Booney sucked hard, snorting whatever mucus he had, tasting the mass of salty slime from the back of his throat before he projectile spat on the eye of Whyles. "T'ats how I t'ink of ye, silly thruts! An' ye may keep it as yurs, ye rotter fink!" The Frog boldly declared.

Wiping the icky slime off his eye in disgust, Whyles gravely swore with belligerent odium, "I won't forget—"

"Good, I hope ye won't!" Booney mooted. "Now put me down 'ight now!" "As you wish…" the Fox snapped back and dropped Booney on the ground.

Just then, Wally walked in with a journal and an updated map in his paws. Greeting Booney, he noticed his weathered fishing pole and exclaimed, "Ah, well, golly be! It's fishing time already, is it Boone?!"

"Well, of course it is! Why else would I be curryin' this pole 'round, lookin' all silly-like, and a fine day it is to go catch some fushies. A perfec' day in fact, and I know by me twitchy elbow and te cool breeze! Ye can't beat me after all; I'm a natural!" Booney proclaimed in a charming way of boasting.

"Well, we'll just see about that!" The Hare replied, accepting the Frog's challenge of a fishing contest. "Alright, Booney Wiggins, I've got no choice but to take ye on!" However, he noticed the Fox's disgruntled expression and thought it is only necessary to be supportive and cheer him up, so Wally invited the Fox to come along.

Whyles refused instantly, saying he had other business to attend to and could not play hooky. "And what business may that be if I can so ask?!" Booney chimed in, looking at Whyles with evident skepticism.

"None of yours, I hope ye know!"

"Yeah, yeah, I bet!" Booney rolled his eyes with a faint smile.

"Best be careful, Booney!" Wally softly whispered, not to offend the Fox. The Fox did have a biting temper, after all. "Oh, don't worry," Booney replied, "If he keeps out of me business, I'll keep out of his, but if he doesn't, well…"

But just as the Frog's back was turned, Booney heard something snap, and it didn't take long for him to know what it was. It was his fishing rod. "NOOOOOOOOOOOOO!" Booney lamented as he glared at Whyles. The Fox grinned, twirling the half rod he broke. The Frog snatched the broken rod out of his hand. "Ye dirty scum! Ye broke it. Ye will pay for this!"

"Ooopsy! That's too bad! Seems you can't fish today after all!" the Fox mocked, patting the Frog on the head with exaggerated care. But what happened next was so surprising that Wally couldn't believe his eyes. Booney dropped his pole and rammed into the Fox's stomach with full force, headbutting him and swinging his fists wildly, hollering, "ROTTEN SCUM, GOOD FOR NOTHIN'—TAKE THAT! YE PUNK! I'll GET YOU FER T'AT!"

"Booney!" Wally cried out, pulling the Frog off Whyles. "STOP IT RIGHT NOW!" Whyles wiped off his snout, sneering down at the Frog. With that, the Fox stormed out of

Wally's place. Booney, still steaming mad, tried to give chase, but Wally held him back. "He isn't worth it, Boone, let him be. C'mon, now we can fix your pole," Wally reassured him, hoping to calm the upset Frog. They soon headed to Gilly's Trading Post to mend Booney's rod, the sun's warmth on their backs as they tried to put the incident behind them.

Wally and Booney had set up their fishing gear on their favorite spot by the river, the gentle babbling of the stream providing a soothing backdrop to their friendly competition.

Wally was in high spirits, preparing his fishing rod with meticulous care. "Ain't it a perfect day for fishing, Booney? The river's just right, and the fish'll be biting soon, I bet!" he chirped, adjusting his hat and smiling brightly.

Booney, with his weathered fishing pole in hand, responded with equal enthusiasm. "Aye, Wally, it's a fine day indeed! An' I'm ready to show ye how it's done. Just wait and see; I'll have 'em all biting in no time!"

Wally chuckled, oblivious to the tension bubbling just beneath the surface. "Well, let's get to it then! Remember last time? I got that whopper of a trout. Hope you're ready to up your game!"

Booney grinned, casting his line with a practiced flick of his wrist. "Oh, I'm always ready, Wally. Watch and learn, mate!"

As they settled into their fishing spots, the two friends began casting their lines. The peaceful silence was punctuated only by the occasional splash of water or the soft rustling of leaves.

Wally focused entirely on the gentle rhythm of his reel and the excitement of the contest. He was completely absorbed in the sport, happily chatting about their past fishing adventures.

"So, remember that time we caught that gigantic catfish? What a fight that was! I thought my rod was gonna snap right in half," Wally reminisced, pulling in a small nibble with a satisfied grin. "Those were the days!"

Booney, equally absorbed, laughed heartily. "Oh, indeed! We made quite a splash with that one, didn't we? I swear, that fushie was nearly as big as me!"

Wally's eyes twinkled, prodded by the playful challenge. "You know, if we catch something big enough taday, we could feed the whole village! Imagine the look on everyone's faces if we haul in a whopper that could feed everyone. That'd be something to remember!"

Booney's grin widened as he adjusted his hat. "Aye, that'd be quite the catch! They'd be talkin' 'bout it for weeks. And if anyone could land a fish like that, it'd be us!"

Wally nodded, casting his line with renewed vigor. "Here's to hoping we get lucky then! The whole village could use a good feast. What do you say we make it a bit of a friendly wager? Whoever catches the biggest fish gets the first slice of pie at the next village gathering."

Booney's eyes gleamed with excitement. "You're on, Wally! But don't think I'll go easy on ye. I've got my eye on the prize, and I'm not lettin' up until we reel in a real monster!"

Underneath the summer sky, Where the gentle river flows,

I cast my line with dreams awry, Where the tranquil water goes. Oh, the fishing days are fair, With a lure that dances bright,

Watching the river's sparkling sight In the warm and golden glare.

The river's song, so sweet and dear, Sings a melody of old,

Of the countless fish that steer Through the currents bold and cold. With a rod and reel in hand,

I await the silken bite,

On the soft and yielding land, In the sun's embracing light. As the shadows softly lean, And the day begins to wane, I drift into a gentle dream,

Where the river's whispers remain.

Unbeknownst to them, just down the path from their idyllic fishing spot, Whyles the Fox was skulking around. The Fox's expression was one of dark determination as he peered through the underbrush, his gaze locked on Booney. The previous altercations with the Frog had left him simmering with barely restrained animosity, and he was concocting his next move.

As Booney cheerfully bragged about his fishing prowess and Wally continued chatting away, Whyles quietly approached the riverbank. He was careful to stay out of sight but close enough to keep an eye on his rival.

With a subtle rustle, Whyles emerged from the bushes with a mocking grin. "Well, well, if it isn't the famed Booney Wiggins and his trusty fishing pole," Whyles called out mockingly. "Thought I'd come by and see how the frug's doing. Still thinkin' you're the best at everything, eh, Booney?"

Booney's eyes narrowed as he recognized the voice. "Whyles, what're you doin' here? This is a friendly competition, not a place for your shenanigans."

Wally glanced over, noticing Whyles but remaining cheerful. "Hey, Whyles! Fancy seeing you here. Why don't you join us? We're just having a bit of fun."

Whyles feigned interest, stepping closer to the riverbank. "Oh, I'm just here to watch, that's all."

Booney bristled, his frustration from earlier still simmering beneath the surface. "Don't think ye can come 'ere and mess things up. I've got enough to deal with without yer interference."

Whyles's grin widened, clearly enjoying the tension he was creating. "Oh, I wouldn't dream of it. Just thought I'd drop by and see how you're managing with that piece of junk you're callin' a fishing pole."

Booney clenched his jaw, trying to ignore the provocation. "This 'ere pole might be old, but it's still good enough to show ye a thing or two."

Still unaware of the deeper conflict, Wally continued to reel in his line, chatting with Whyles. "So, Whyles, what's been keeping you busy? Any new adventures?"

Whyles shrugged nonchalantly. "Oh, just the usual. Nothing that'd interest you a lot."

As Whyles lingered nearby, he kept a close watch on Booney, his eyes gleaming with mischief. Booney tried to focus on fishing, but Whyles's presence was a constant distraction. When Booney cast his line, he felt an unwelcome irritation fueled by Whyles's taunts.

Meanwhile, Wally remained absorbed in the friendly rivalry, pulling in a decent-sized fish with a cheer. "Looks like I'm winning this round, Booney! How about that?"

Booney managed a strained smile, though his frustration with Whyles was apparent. "Aye, ye got me this time, Wally. But don't get too comfortable; there's plenty of time left!"

As the day wore on, the atmosphere remained deceptively calm. The riverbank was filled with friendly banter and the occasional splash of water. However, the tension between Booney and Whyles was palpable, though Wally remained blissfully unaware of the brewing storm.

Whyles continued to hover near the edge of the river, his dark intent masked by a facade of casual interest. Occasionally, he would throw a taunt or a snide remark, further aggravating Booney while maintaining his outwardly polite demeanor.

By late afternoon, as the sun descended toward the horizon, Wally and Booney continued their fishing contest, with Wally leading slightly. The peaceful scene, filled with the sounds of nature and the occasional friendly challenge, belied the growing animosity below the surface.

The riverbank, once a place of serene relaxation, now harbored a simmering tension as Whyles's scheming presence added an edge to the otherwise idyllic day. Wally's cheerful demeanor and Booney's strained patience starkly contrasted the underlying hostility.

As the afternoon sun dipped lower, casting golden light across the river, Booney's cheerful boasting grated on Whyles like nails against stone. Each word, each chuckle from the Frog, tightened the knot of frustration deep in Whyles' chest.

"Another one for ol' Booney! I reckon I'll be the king o' this river by sundown!" The Frog boasted, reeling in his line with a smug grin.

Whyles' teeth ground together, his irritation boiling over. His eyes locked on Booney, every croak, every word from the Frog like a splinter under his skin, and for a fleeting moment, the sounds around him faded—the gentle trickle of the river, Wally's chatter—everything dulled, except for the Frog's voice.

'If only I could shut him up!' 'I can! I can!'

With sudden, deliberate steps, Whyles moved toward Booney. Neither Wally nor Booney noticed him approaching. His breath came slow and steady as if the world stopped turning and time froze, his senses narrowing in on one thing... Booney.

And then, without so much as a warning, Whyles' paws shot forward like a viper striking its victim. His claws coiled around Booney's throat with terrifying force, squeezing until the Frog's gurgled croak turned to a strangled gasp. The fishing pole slipped from Booney's slackening grip, clattering uselessly into the water as Whyles bore him to the river's edge with ruthless precision.

"Let's see how well you fare beneath the surface, you wretched creature," Whyles hissed, his voice low and venomous.

With a savage pull, Whyles dragged Booney into the river's depths. The water rose in frothing waves, swallowing their forms as Whyles plunged Booney under, his grip ironclad, unyielding. Booney's limbs flailed in panicked spasms, his webbed hands clawing futilely at Whyles' arms, but the Fox's hold was unrelenting, cold as death itself.

Beneath the shadowed surface, Booney's eyes bulged with an unspeakable horror, wide and glazed as the river's murky depths contorted his frantic movements into grotesque distortions. His complexion, once lively, now turned a ghastly shade of purple, a stark manifestation of his terror. His croaks, once bold and defiant, dwindled to pitiful, ghostly bubbles, each one a muted, spectral plea for mercy swallowed by the encroaching darkness.

As Booney struggled, his mind raced in a haze of panicked clarity. Each gasp was a desperate cry for a life that seemed to slip further away with every passing moment. In those fleeting, horrified seconds, he glimpsed a grim, watery vision of his own demise, the cold embrace of the river sealing his fate.

Whyles, standing with a cruel smile of malignant satisfaction, seemed detached from the world around him. His thoughts were consumed by a malevolent pleasure, a twisted satisfaction in watching the life drain from Booney's terrified eyes. The river, now a dark and oppressive shroud, seemed to conspire with him, its icy currents dragging Booney deeper into its cold depths as if feeding off his torment.

Whyles' grip, unyielding and merciless, was a physical extension of his inner cruelty. His gaze, cold and unwavering, observed with a perverse delight as the light of life slowly ebbed from Booney's widening, terror-stricken stare. The Frog's desperate thrashing, once a symbol of his fight for survival, devolved into a feeble, spasmodic dance—a final, macabre performance against the relentless pressure of the water.

As Booney's movements grew weaker and more languid, his thoughts fragmented into a blur of fading hope and growing dread. With a final, shuddering gasp that expelled one last feeble bubble to the surface, his body surrendered to the cold grasp of the river.

His form lay still and lifeless beneath the surface, a ghastly, pallid specter adrift in the darkened depths. Whyles, his cruel grin widening with predatory satisfaction, lingered over the scene, savoring the grim finality of the tableau. The water's surface, once churned by the struggle, now lay eerily calm, a silent witness to the dark deed. In that stillness, Whyles' dark satisfaction mingled with the somber silence, a haunting echo of his cruel triumph.

The river, once serene, swirled with disturbed ripples, its surface reflecting nothing but the last rays of a dying sun.

"Whyles! Whyles!"

The sudden call shattered the illusion.

Whyles blinked, his vision clearing. He stood at the river's edge, the water calm and untouched. His paws were empty, and Booney was there—alive—mere feet away, holding up a wriggling fish with a proud grin.

Wally, oblivious, chuckled as he glanced over. "Whyles, mate, what are ye starin' at? You look as if you've seen a ghost!"

Whyles' breath hitched, the afterimage of Booney's lifeless body still haunting his mind. He swallowed, forcing his lips into a crooked, humorless smile.

"Nothing," he muttered hoarsely, his voice strained. "Just...watchin'."

But in the back of his mind, the vision remained—Booney's limp body sinking into the dark, cold depths.

The day was quiet and peaceful when they returned from their fishing trip. Wally and Whyles had discovered an invitation tucked into the door, and Wally asked Whyles to carry it in his pole. The Hare opened the letter.

It formally stated:

> Please join us for high tea with Miriam and Adelia Quaddling. All the beautiful decorations have been arranged.
>
> The special treats are already in preparation for your arrival. Please come on time, at 4 p.m., not a moment too soon or a moment too late.
>
> We humbly thank and expect you!
>
> Sincerely,
>
> Quaddling Sisters
> SunBerry Pond

With a gleaming smile, he exclaimed, "O' how delightful the Quaddling invited us to come, Whyles! We must not keep them dawdling; it's already past four!"

The Fox coldly rejected the invite with a frown. "I think I'll pass. I must attend sum'tin more wort' me time. An' besides such a malign and crude way for an invitation, 'expecting us' oh please, what a sad excuse for wanting company, if t'er lonely why don't t'ey stop bein's all pompous like an' boter sum'un who cares…"

"Come now, that's no way to be chummy! Certainly, they are a wee bit overbearing and demanding, but it's all for good impressions and isn't harmful in the slightest, but it's fairly amusing. Come, don't show a frown, they most definitely mean well. Think of it as an honor to be called by them hardly anyone does. I'm afraid because of their most high standard routine of hosting, they, from their extremities of pleasing service, often ended up with their guest hightailing as soon as they could get because of their silly engagements of what is appropriately necessary or not! It's actually rather charming to see such effort only to make your guest feel overburdened. I humor them for the sake of keeping peace. I genuinely feel for them in a way a brother would! They don't have much but themselves and a sense of a proper lifestyle. Anyhow, we won't be there for too long. But if we dally any longer, we must make it up."

Whyles begrudgingly agreed to those terms, feeling for what Wally had said of the sisters: "Very well if ye say so! Luts get it over whit' But ony for a quick bite!"

"Then let's be on our way!" Grinned the Hare, glad he had convinced the Fox.

With a hop, skip, and a jump, Whyles and Wally both were off, the sun blazing red traced their way by shadow lines... a good slogging trek away...widened to a hill- bounded passage replete with darting birds that swiftly cut across the Fox and Hare's field of vision. This was the district of the birds or the featheren as those who traversed this rolling dale on good terms would call it. The birds would gather there, hovering and darting above the clearing where the broad pond glistened like a rare diamond in a setting of brilliant green. So peaceful and placid was the surface of that pond that the slightest billowing wind seemed almost gently intrusive upon the sheen of its mirrored surface. It was also well known that the aerial troupe's fastest, if even the best, looked at their own reflections while gliding above the pristine surface, which reflected each one as a mirror does. The faster saw their own speed and, most beautifully, admired their own image as they flew above it. In that sense, it was a gathering space for those endowed with the gift of flight and the yearning to be with others of a similar fascination. SunBerry Pond, luxury guaranteed, was in every way perfect for those two sisters; it was paradise. The quaint little home of the Quaddlings was tucked in the corner of the sparkling pond. Made of grass, this hut was spick and span, just the way the Quaddlings liked! No dust and no mess could ever make it through their door without being brushed away unless they were the ones who made the mess, albeit infrequently...

Approaching their hut, they were soon stopped by an Owl. It was Old Ben, sitting on a garden fence. Wally greeted the Owl, and Old Ben greeted him back, however, with a few questions asked by the curiously mindful Hare about what the outside world might be like. The attentive owl turned to Whyles with a piercing stare. Whyles had not shown his face but cloaked it with the collar of his jacket. He remembered the Owl flying above the gathering of the Hounds, watching ever so leerily. "You shall soon see my friend if any other tricky strangers are comin' around here; not all too friendly!" Old Ben declared in an almost sympathetically low spirit, for he knew that Fox well, too well.

"Anyhoooooooo, I must be off again!" "Where this time?"

"Anywhere the wind takes me." The Owl said with a grin, "And do take care of yourself, Wally; you and your friends have much too pure hearts to see what's really taking place. Mind your company before they mine you!" Before Wally could ask any other questions, Old Ben soared up and away into the distant mountains off for another trip. Another twisted voice rang through Whyles head. 'Knows too much, must go!'

'Too much, GO, GO. But how, how?' Then the answer came, 'Net!'

He was then jarred back into reality with two loud honks coming from who else but the Quaddlings standing out of their quaint home and stamping their feet in disapproval, fanning themselves with their two folding fans. "It is hardly polite to come late unexpectedly, nor is talking with someone whom you are NOT supposed to!"

"I say, it's very, very rude, not to mention unsightly and unpleasant, keeping us waiting like that! Now then, the tea and the muffins have gone cold!" squawked the moralistic sisters, babbling complaints one right after another whilst expecting an explanation. Wally tried to calm them down with charming compliments that alone always did the trick.

"Ah, veeery lovely as ever, my two; I see that the Quaddlings are never the pair to arrive later nor early but precisely at the time expected. Truly admirable! My most humble apology for the delay, but we took a quick detour-"

"Detour? Whatever for? If'n ye knew where to go, why bother? You know, if you try to chart the uncharted, it will only lead to the unexpected, and gosh, the unexpected is quite dangerous, and it isn't the correct way. To be tardy when expected and timely when unexpected is the most serious, yet avoidable, blunder there could eva be!"

"Quite right, detours lead to straying away someplace unexpected and, by golly, it certainly ain't very gentlemen-like now, is it?" Added Miriam.

"Well, all that matters is that we are here now. Again, please forgive us; it won't happen again!" "I most certainly hope not!" Snapped Adelia.

"Oh, I assure you, my two lovelies, it won't! I promise!" Wally laughed with a solemn swear. "We'll take ye word on it!"

"Well, now that's been tuken care of, and now t'at ye are finally here...please do come in!" squawked the two sisters simultaneously. Pushily insisted both guests walk in first, but just before entering the house, they were stopped and importuned, "Wait here for a moment if you please?!" The Quaddlings ran in and came back with a beautiful pitcher.

"Paws!"

Doing what they were told, Adelia poured rosewater, cleaning their grubby paws, Miriam had held a water basin underneath, not wanting any to spill. She then threw the dirty water back into the pond (now less sparkling), raced around her home, and returned, presenting a linen towel in which she had roughly scrubbed their wet paws dry.

"After all, you never do know where paws have been, messy, messy, messy!!" As they graciously curtseyed but being as close together as they were, they were stepping on top of the other's feet. The Hare hoped in and complimented the sisters for such a tidy home; nothing was out of place, and everything was orderly; this is what the Quaddling valued most of all: cleanliness. But before Whyles stepped in himself, the two stopped him at the border, acting like suspicious border guards as they inspected his dirty feet. Not wanting to have mud tracks, they demanded rather obscenely.

"There shull absolutilly be no tracks, no traces and no fraggiment of mud! Wipe before entering!"

Whyles groaned and did what was asked, just wanting to get it over with as fast as he could without delay; he stepped in afterward, and the two Quaddlings followed right behind into their living space, which they were very proud of, and they were eager to show off! Their little home had a weird, distinctive ambiance of a gewgawed grandmother's house. The gabbling henpecking pair seemed to prefer collecting family-owned curios.

There were oversized doilies and puffy knitted chair covers that took up a lot of space, considering their walls were also fully covered with baubles cluttered around. It managed to give an aspect that nothing was too much but rather too little. More strangely, nothing seemed to be misplaced despite their small accommodations; surprisingly, everything was meticulously spotless. In fact, the space was positively cozy. It reeked a bit of old lavender and daisies, but one felt a kind, almost caring presence within those four walls. Though the décor could not be specifically relevant to Whyles himself, he did feel a certain release of tension in the arrangements hung and placed in order before him now.

Miriam had waddled over to the settling Hare and carried a folded sweater as she promptly presented it.

"This is a very special sweater WE made for you, Wallay! We hope you like it!" Adelia butted in, "Try it on! Go on!" putting the befuddled Hare on the spot.

Wally examined the sweater, discovering one half of the wool-striped sweater was oversized and floppy while the other side was far too petite and constrained, an uneven mess! The stitching was misaligned; not trying to be rude, but he couldn't help but laugh.

"We did our best, you know!" Miriam confessed, keeping the tears at bay. "But you didn't have to!"

"Oh, but Dearie! We wanted to!"

"It's most certainly… well…genuine!" "You must try it on! We tried ever so hard!" "I'm very sure you did, I can tell!"

"Even though Miriam couldn't get the proper measurements at all, you made it toooooo smaaaaall!"

"Meeeee? Are you insinuating what I think you are insinuating, Delly?" "Quite!"

"How dare yooooou! You are much as to blame as I am, if not more! You made it toooooooo biiiig!"

"I am not blameworthy! It's all your fault-" "Please, ladies, do not bicker! It's not bad at all!" "Well, try it at once!" they squawked at Wally. "Of course, of course! How can I not?"

Wally slipped it on; the sweater looked like it swallowed him on one side and strangled him on the other like a noose, its wool unbearably itchy against his fur.

"It's nice, very comfy!" He uttered, wanting to please them. "We are most glad you are pleased!" They giggled.

Wally had taken it off, setting it aside with a sense of detachment. The gifts seemed to be churned out like factory products, a constant flood of gestures meant to win him over. Although he accepted their carefully crafted offerings, he grew weary of their strained efforts to "please" him. The constant attention felt awkward and overwhelming, and while he didn't want to hurt their feelings, he went along with it out of politeness.

The Hare made himself right at home, being comfy on a gimcrack caned chair, which resembled the rest of the chairs with woven cloth and all facing the center of the room. There also stood a small knotty table covered with a pink doily that held biscuits and cold tea served on a silver platter.

The Hare gleefully grabbed a handful and started munching, wriggling a bit on the upholstery to adjust the fluff of his tail. Miriam noticed and swiftly brought over a homespun cushion. She asked Wally to stand up briefly while she placed and patted the cushion, making sure it was comfortable. However, she wasn't satisfied and found it a bit lopsided. Insistent on perfection, she had Wally sit in another chair. The Quaddling sisters, ever meticulous, rushed to the new chair, ensuring it met their high standards.

However, still wanting more, they asked Wally to change his seat one after another. Before he could answer, clearly having previously posited that any chair would be just right, they were still finicky. They felt genuinely disgusted with themselves while shaming each other. Around and around, they circled their sitting spot, fussing, switching, and rearranging their furniture and other knickknacks as they did so.

Very often, everything was different when it came to arrangements as they habitually reshuffled each and every piece the house had acquired. The rearranging included the row of mason jars filled with assorted hard candies positioned on the shelves, which proceeded to slip after they attempted to open them. Tottering about in the ruckus, each Quaddling almost falling to the ground, the clumsy sisters tried to save the motley-colored candy jars, but too late, the jars shattered, and the spilling hard candies sailed like projectiles from some candy cannon, skittering across the cracks of the Riverstone floor. The sisters, so frazzled by it all, began to panic.

"Broom… sweep, sweep, sweep!" They cried, their dedication to perfection evident as they cleared away the broken glass and scattered candies until the floor was pristine. Yet, as the mess was tidied, Whyles began to feel the initial comfort of the scene slipping away, fading like a distant dream. The tea, once a comforting brew, had grown almost ice cold.

Out went the cups and tea, and the sisters, engrossed in a lively debate, argued over their tasks. Who should boil the kettle and prepare the victuals, and who should entertain their guests? "Why not both?" They chortled, settling the matter with a laugh.

The tin kettle soon began to steam once more as they turned their attention to their visitors, who were now thoroughly amused. With everything finally in order and the new batch of tea brewing, the Quaddings began to share tales of their family's past before their arrival in Ambrodale.

They gabbled with gusto, even though it seemed most of the information they told was too good to be true. Even with this, though meant to entertain, it was extremely tedious. The only excitement guaranteed to their guests was the many squawking aggravations of the sisters' interjections of their stories. Both had their "correct" opinion, and both spoke their mind rather impertinently. Too busy with telling their own versions of the same basic story, both sisters had completely neglected the tea that was now starting to boil over. A loud hissing sound escaped the jouncing pot. The lid popped off the kettle as bubbling tea sloshed out of its containment. This event went on as the sisters appeared unaware and had to be apprised of the kettle boiling over.

Maybe somewhat sadly, the Hare was hushed down because, as Miriam stated, "it is very indecent to interrupt; you must wait till we are done talking, then you may speak!" But it was far too late to talk over them as they were drowning out the screaming kettle.

As had happened before and to less effect, the gabbling sisters were too caught up in their memories. When they were done and gasping for breath, they promptly smelled a ghastly toxic whiff of heavy smoke, and again, it had caused an uproar. "Oh m -m -m- m -m- m- my myayyyy!" the two Ducks scrambled amok in sheer confusion, "FIRE! FIRE! NO NO NOOOOOOOO!!!! WHAT

SHALL WE DO!!! I AINT 'UN TO BE ROASTED!!!!!!" Miriam

screamed, trying to grab the handle of the smoldering pot. It was much too painful, however, and Miriam cried out at first touch!

"Certainty not, how dreadfully morbid to t'ink it…positively! We don't want our beautiful house to be up in flames!!!!!! DOOOOOOOOOOOO SOMETHING!!!!!!" Adelia frantically ordered her sister, "I'm TRYING!!!!!" Miriam kept repeating.

"Well, try HARDER!!!" Adelia retorted as she unbecomingly tried to keep the guests under her control (though she herself was over the top hysterical.) Wally assured her everything would be alright as he started to dish out some water onto the black steam of the pot. The resulting steam created a foggy atmosphere. A crackle and sizzle replaced the whoosh of overflowing tea. The smell was worse, yet somehow. The kettle itself looked completely ruined. It was covered in a dark brown milk skin, burnt and nauseating to look at.

Yet the smell, the smell, was penetrating. It was the acrid smell of ugly things unmemorable that had now replaced the sweet fragrance of gently bubbling tea within their posh pond home.

Whyles watched the jostling mayhem as a spectator, noisily chomping on crackers and biscuits, but enough was enough; tired of their shenanigans, he marched his way out. However, noticing the scruffy Fox headed out their grassy door, the Quaddlings rushed to block the entry like an unpassable barrier, then contritely hangdog of themselves scolding each other for terrible hostesses and pleading with the Fox to stay a little longer. "Come, you haven't had any tea yet; you simply can't leave wit'out a sip!" Whyles tried to excuse himself, but with one look of the heartbroken sisters he could not refuse, something changed drastically within him; he felt, well, he didn't know how to express it, not even knowing of empathy, but he knew their efforts all too well trying to please those unpleasable was unbearably overwhelming, so he stayed in self- forced deference.

Unfortunately, the tea they had burnt was consequently their last pot of tea; both sisters maintained a sense of dignity by subduing the strong smell by tossing in fresh herbs and spices and other strange mixes, blending them into the charred septic-looking drainage of whatever remained of the tea that was drinkable.

"Drink up!" The black icky tea tasted absolutely wretched; they all gagged at first sip; the ranking flavor was strongly indigestible, and the sisters felt awfully embarrassed that they shuttered in disdain to think of the bitter, tart tea as distastefully unrefined as they always boasted in grand exposé's about how delightfully, full-flavored palatable their fine homebrew tea was "Like no otha's, a family special recipe!" they put it, "It ser' is 'pecial alright!" Whyles dry heaved. But the poor glum sisters felt despondent when things hadn't been predicted faithfully according to their high hopes and obsessed planning. It was all backward and unsuitable, and the coeval pair was at a loss for words, which was incredibly rare. There was no reaction but embarrassment. Nothing could be said at this moment. Nothing right could be said to make things seem better, to fill this certain void of confused reality both sisters felt; it hadn't come out the way it always did; it was below par, and they were left by this unanticipated mistake speechless and miffed in their discomfiture, refraining from crying. The only smart thing to do was extract the fetidly mawkish residue from its current site and start anew. However, the sisters were overconcerned about the unpredicted incident, and to call them apologetic was a severe understatement. It was most undoubtedly over-the-top, and it was an undue appeal.

Wally had to step out a quick breath of air and view the stunning scenery, and the Fox was left to deal with the Quaddlings alone, which was no easy task of calming them down. They were overwrought with guilt, "is t'er anyway to get ye mind off it any'ows?" Asked the Fox. The Ducks scanned the room, and soon, they stopped whining and came up with their idea! Pointing at the wall of books, Adelia excitedly proposed.

"Oooooooo, I know the absolute bestest way to cheer everyone up!" Adelia said. "Miriam, be a dear and grab one of em poetry books if'n ye please!"

"Wellin, I do please! Ye have two legs yeself duncha? Why don't ye do it yeself?!" Miriam huffed in refusal! Unwilling to do what was requested.

"Wellin t'er is no excuses! What I say goes!" "Well, t'at ain't fair! Not in the slightest!"

"It certainly is fair! Because I say so, and what I say, you should listen! After all, I am the oldest!"

Miriam silently got up and skimmed through the books she had asked her sister about. "Out of these many, many books, which is the right one to pick? This is a big collecty'in'"

"AAAAAAAAAANNNNY book will be just daaaaandy Miriam!!!! Just CHOOOOOOOSE! It ain't hard to do!" Miriam was now quite unsettled by her sister's retort. She picked out three and hauled them over for her sister's approval. Adelia scanned through each of them. She finally made her decision and handed the book to her sister, who then promptly directed her to give it to Whyles. And so, Miriam did what she was told and waddled over to the seated Fox.

She heaved it on top of Whyles's lap. The Fox was unsure what to do with it, as the two prudish sisters were watching him. He cautiously opened the thick volume of the poetry, glancing over the many poems it had inscribed within. But to him, it all looked like a bunch of disordered squiggles and scrambled jumbles. In a confused tizzy, he realized the book gave him the chills.

"What am I sooppose to do wit' this?" The Fox blurted out.

"Is you tellin' me these snaky things and squiggles an' all can talks to you? "He stammered on, 'Why would 'uny body want that? I don't think any good could come frum dis!'"

Adelia corrected him gently, "You are a jest, now, ain't ya, but this ain't the occasion for it! Please read it, of course; recite it! Let the beauty of those words flow!"

Whyles, not wanting to disappoint Adelia and Miriam, so desperately tried. Alas, he couldn't. The effort was a muddled ordeal for the Fox, and it gave him a panging headache just by gazing at the small sea of indecipherable figures. The giant book pressed in front of him looked completely foreign. It was an ocean that looked like gibberish; it was all these invisible people's thoughts crammed in an ugly, heavy, square box. In truth, his problem was that he was completely illiterate.

"I-I-I-I can't!" He said, squirming. "Is sompin the matter!? Go on!" "But I tulls ye I can't!"

"O don't be humble. Surely ye can ! Come now! Why don't ye give a try, ye must!" "But I-I-I-I t-t-t tell you, I can't!" Whyles repeated as he started to choke up.

"It's all nonnysense to me. It's painful. What should I care what sum other bodies are thinkin?" The sisters were baffled at such a thought, "Care to explain!?"

"Because no un neva tuht me to 'ead or wite, I neva lurned! I'm as dumb as a board; I am just a useless rottin' mook! I ain't bright, and I ain't smart, I ain't anyting to be proud of, im just a chumper! I never understand meself nor no one elses!"

Pitying the Fox, the Quaddling interjected. "Quite on the contrary! Ye, ain't useless if you haven't tried it! It ain't ya fault if no un taught it to ye!"

"QUITE right, Miriam, quite right, but dear, it ain't right for a proper gentleman to go about not knowing to read and write why it simply will not do! It is all too uncouth!"

"Adelia?"

"Yes, Miriam? What is it!?"

"Well, I have an idea if'n ye like to hear t'at is!?!"

Whyles brightened for just a moment, then quickly sunk back into despair. "Well, what IS the idea, Miriam? Spit it out!"

Well… What if'n weeee teach him how to read an' write!!" "Why, Miriam, thut's tremendously brilliant!"

Miriam beamed with delight at her sister's compliment.

Whyles shrunk back as he began to mumble a kind of sing-song ditty, apparently warding off impending fear.

"Mr. Whyles, for now, we shall call you that. May I beg your kind attention!" Whyles stopped his mumbling and lifted one eye toward her.

"Mr. Whyles, may I beg your indulgence to have you listen to a passage from this book?" "Well, if'n yoe does it, I don't t'ink it could hurt."

"Nonsense, books don't bite, now do listen, sir. The rain that falls,

As diamonds new And wet the ground We call it dew."

"Well, that's just silly; there's never been a dimond up there! Why, I'd be rich!" Said the Fox. "I beg your indulgence, please…"

"Oh, do go on; I do love it!" Giggled Miriam. "Ahem." Adelia cleared her throat and continued:

"The dew upon the ground, we see Does bring us joy

As a gift most heavenly.

For every bird that flying goes,

And all the ones on four and two legs know,

That this gift born from clouds above Does give a life to those we love."

Whyles looked positively perplexed. "Are those pictures in that box?" "Most certainly," said Adelia, projecting the confidence of a born teacher. "Those and many, many others," she said in an almost motherly tone.

"Is they the words of somethin's beautiful…somethin's maybe more?" "Without any doubt," she said in a gentle voice again.

"Maybees, I wants to learn t'em, maybe…"

"Then we should begin. The first step is called the alphabec. Each of those squiggly lines is part of the alphabec family. You see, this letter that looks like this?" Adelia made an "A" shape with her folded wings. On she went with careful patience, explaining to the Fox in a prolonged, systematic, yet curiously entertaining manner.

The class ended just at teatime, so of course, the Fox was treated to cakes and tea that day.

As he left, Miriam noticed that Whyles had a slightly straighter gait. He seemed burdened yet relieved as he disappeared into the evening. Miriam could have sworn she heard him say, 'maybe' again and again as he walked down the trail away from their home. All had yet to learn how much 'maybe' meant 'yes.'

Strangely enough, Whyles felt a deep sense of gratitude for the Quadding sisters' unwavering dedication and their selfless efforts in teaching him. Despite this, he often harbored doubts about the merit of their endeavors, questioning whether all this fuss over learning was truly worth it.

His concerns emerged in the form of plaintive remarks: "I don't wish to cause any poblems." day, the sisters, visibly frustrated by Whyles's reluctance, voiced their exasperation.

"Problems? What problems?" Miriam declared with a hint of impatience. "The problem is you don't know yet how to read or write, and it is simply not right for a future!"

"Surely, you mustn't have all this time to teech me!?" Whyles retorted, his frustration evident. "Beg to differ," Adelia insisted. "We have faaaar too much time, dearie!"

"We are most honored to be your tutors!" Miriam added with enthusiastic affirmation. "Most honored indeedin!" Adelia chimed in.

"It's too late to lurn anytin like t'at!" Whyles exclaimed, his eyes welling with tears. "As I said before, I'm a no-good louse; no hopes at all for me! It's better to dig meself in me own grave rather than failing!"

The sisters, moved by his distress, handed him different handkerchiefs. "Here Dearie, why don't ye use this to dry ye tears!" Miriam said gently.

"It's neva too late; if'n ye don't try, ye never know! N'busides never trying is believing or not failing. Better to try than not at all!" Adelia encouraged.

Choked up by their offer, Whyles agreed. "How could I not? What more is there to say?"

"Then it's settled," Miriam said with a smile. "With our continuin' hulp, you'll be a' reedin and writin as fast as ever, wid us by ye side. Notting cun go wrong!"

"Well, well," Adelia said, "we started with the alphabec weeks ago! Now, how does it go again: a-c—e-b. A? D?"

"No, t'at aint right!" Miriam interrupted. "It's a...e.c.b.?"

"t'at dunty sound right eiter!" Adelia argued, furrowing her brow.

And so, the guessing of the alphabet continued as the Quadding sisters bickered over the correct order, turning their lesson into a comical and chaotic debate.

"But please do not tell Wally what we are up to!" Whyles urged, trying to quell their debate. "Oh, but Dear, we simply can't; we tell Wallay everything!" Miriam quacked playfully. "But please, you mustn't tell him about this!" Whyles implored.

"Well, why not?" Adelia asked, genuinely curious.

"Because it's a secret just between us and a surprise for Wally!" Whyles explained. The Quadding sisters, intrigued by the idea of a surprise, exchanged fascinated looks.

"Ooooooo, how we adore surprises!" Miriam exclaimed. "Will there be a party afterward? We just love parties, especially throwin' 'em!"

"The secret's safe with us," Adelia promised with a nod. "We won't say a word."

"But do be kind enough to come punctual; there will be no dillydallying!" She added, emphasizing the importance of timeliness.

At that moment, Wally, his floppy ears drooping, hopped back in to fetch Whyles. "Alright, Whyles, we must be on our way, I'm afraid!" He said.

The Quaddlings, though disappointed, understood that it was getting late. They reluctantly allowed their leave, but as they headed out, their animated chatter nearly revealed the secret of Whyles's tutoring sessions. The ever-curious Wally inquired about their conversation, but Whyles deftly concealed the truth.

In the TWO weeks that followed, while Wally was engaged with Booney or Sampson, Whyles took the opportunity to slip away for his lessons with the Quaddlings. Despite his initial doubts and the rigorous nature of the learning schedule, the Quaddlings remained steadfastly patient and supportive. They handled his frustrations and struggles with new concepts with unwavering dedication, allowing ample time for him to overcome his difficulties.

As time went on, Whyles found himself increasingly enjoying his time with the Quadding sisters. Their spontaneous and cheerful dispositions began to fill the void of mistrust and emotional confinement he had long felt. The lessons, though challenging, became a source of comfort and growth for him, bridging the gap he had once felt so keenly.

Chapter Eight
Beginning of The End!
Venture of The Quaddling Sisters

I shall now tell you a short adventure the Quaddling sisters had while picking wild berries on the borderland between Sullen Fields and Ambrodale, as I said I would in the beginning when they were first introduced. This story, which I will tell, is quite funny but also desperately tragic, involving both two imprudent sisters, leaving one of them missing in the end. (Let us all do hope that none shalt never make another trip there any time in the future after this.)

The pair had often traveled to the mysterious borderland that exists on the frontier of Gorse-End and Sullen Fields. They would stroll each and every bright early morning, just before the sun had risen above the misty mountains. Carrying their homemade wicker baskets along with them, as I said earlier, to gather berries and other nourishments. Not being the brightest pair, however, they were always getting lost. On they would continue in their rambles, foolishly bumping and stumbling into one another. Often, it was only because they were unaware of how close they were together. When their inevitable collisions occurred, they were invariably startled and frightened, screaming aloud due perhaps to their natural waddling clumsiness and quickly frazzling nerves while out of doors. It was as if their inability to move about freely outside of their cozy little home was too much to consider at times. It seemed to all that they were meant to live their entire lives solely within the cozy comforts of their riverside home. In their short-step waddling, they could never actually tell which way was where, and they could never tell their left from their right. Even somehow knowing this, they bickered which way was where...

"I do believe-" "It-"

"Is."

"Thatta way," they would always say together, concluding that they had found the direction they were seeking. However, they would each typically end up pointing in a different direction than one another. And this day, things were no different.

By the earliest hour, when they had just begun venturing out of the door of their pond home, they had already started to bicker. This chill morning seemed ominous to them. The dank swamp a few houses down, breathed a malaise into the cool air. The borderland territory sometimes reeked of the refuse left by the residents of Ambrodale. Fortunately, in a manner of speaking, the borderlands were visited at regular intervals by the autonomous and elusive Horkurs. The Horkurs were a group of ragged, renegade boars led aggressively by Cap'm Thistleworts. Never considering themselves residents of the self-contained village of Ambrodale but merely outcasts, perhaps, they nevertheless helped themselves to the leavings of the tidy residents. They could also be rarely relied upon as a source of information about the goings on around the borders of Ambrodale, yet one needed solid nerve and an offering of sorts to extract all but the most trivial and useless of tidings.

Thistleworts was particularly unhelpful at times and downright challenging when it came to assisting others. His fearsome countenance made him a legend of sorts, and he counted his heritage as far back as Ol' Ivarg IronTusk, the Rooter whose origins lay back into some forgotten age.

Even knowing some of these potential dangers could not stop the Quaddling sisters or make them fearfully confined all the day long. Miriam would sometimes say, "If'n it's meant to be, so it is!" Although rather vague as a statement, Adelia, not to be bested, would reply, "And so it should be!" The chance of meeting the generally nocturnally active Horkurs never settled into her mind. It was probably considered by her that if it had not happened yet, it was simply not to happen. And it did not, that is, until the day they got hopelessly lost, and Miriam and Adelia would be forced to consider their words to the last detail.

What had started the fight between the two stubborn sisters this morning, just before their stroll, was an abundance of over-conscious gratitude when both had approached their small pond door and courteously insisted that the other walk out of the door first. Polite, respectful attitudes reverted to an obtuse and hostile rivalry between them. They both waited for the other to walk out, each being blindly persistent and impatient to deny their right for the right of the other to simply walk out the door. They both had then gotten impatiently frustrated at each other's inability to accept the simplest courtesy so humbly and self-effacingly offered by each to each. It was unbearable to consider; it was offensive, and something so given in modesty must simply be accepted. But as one can imagine today, it simply was not going to happen. The formal patience each possessed seemed to molder, and the belligerence that followed was painful to hear, let alone see, as it took place in the chilly morning sunrise. In an effort to maintain some kind of decorum, both sisters hurriedly scrambled to the door, feathers flying and with chortling voices, which ended with a series of loud, obnoxious honking. So swiftly did each finally deign to accept the other's prolonged courtesy that both scrambling birds became quickly lodged in the arched entry of their home. Before landing into the small archway, both collided, creating a certain resulting force upon which both flew forward and became stuck like a cork in a bottle. Indeed, the rush of air attendant upon their collision sounded like the cork of a great bottle of champagne unscrewed as each became stuck in the doorway. However, unlike a bottle of champagne, no toast to good fortune could be found here in their home now. Now, squeezed tight, they kept screaming as they tried to push and forcefully shove each other out of this predicament. Both were endlessly squawking, and both were saying something like, "If you would have listened to me, this wouldn't have happened!"

"Nothin woser t'en bein stuck wit' someone yer caun't stand the sight of!" "I'm nevah in favor bein' so close and alls!"

"Imagine such a dreadful thing."

"IT'S ALL YOUR FAULT!" They both squawked simultaneously, fully aware of the other responsibility for getting into such a predicament as this.

"Now, what'll we do?" Miriam asked, almost in a tearful, blabbering response.

"Oh, do hush up, Miriam, you always were the annoying one!" Replied Adelia rather nastily. "No, I wasn't!"

"Aye! Yes'm, you were! Mumsy and Popsy always never denied it 'ats why t'ey loved me more, isn't that right? No wonda why 'ose otha's had avoided you like I'm'a trying to right now! I bet even Wally has got'sen tired of you by now!"

This rude comment brought by Adelia's reaction to Miriam was such a devastated, forlorn emotional outburst.

"Fine way to say e'bout someone who makes betta muffins t'en you; at least my muffins come out of the oven all delectably plump and juicy like! Yours is anything but scrumptious, you can hardly eat it! Hard as a rock yours are, come s'out all flat and dry and unappetizingly tasteless. That, at best, your shriveled muffins are! Wallay is lucky he don't need your batch when he 'as mine, unlike yours, mine won't make him sick, it won't!" Miriam snapped in an unfriendly, undignified gabble. Both sisters had often used Wally to get at each other just by using his name for their ongoing arguments. It seemed almost ironic to squabble and serve as a tool for each sister's powerless demise.

Adelia huffed in retaliation.

Both sisters were finally quiet, with nothing more to say. They refused to speak to one another, for their displeasure at each other was evident. Though still stuck in the door, both of them continued to keep trying to wiggle out. Now, with a clear head, Adelia tightly leaned on Miriam.

"Oh, do watch yourself, Adelia!" Squawked Miriam. She was now fully compressed onto the side of the door. Adelia, turning red and with all her strength, successfully pushed herself out, making a loud popping noise. Adelia plunged forward, back first, onto the dirt path. She was now disoriented by the pushing struggle, and she was now quite unable to get up!

Wildly flailing, rolling, and rocking back and forth, almost like in a cradle, she tried and tried to get back onto her feet with no success. It was hopeless! Winded by her attempts, Adelia Quaddling was to be seen as helpless as she had never been before. She did not like to feel powerless. It all seemed rather humiliating to be caught helpless. She thought it was only fair for a lady of her stature and bearing to exit every place gracefully, especially her own home. The thought of making a blundering exit out to the world at large and ending up on the ground brought her to the brink of tears.

It was an especially poignant moment, considering that all Adelia had to do was simply accept the courtesy Miriam offered to her. It just made no sense to her at all! Watching her squawking sister rolling on the ground had made Miriam guffaw and hysterically burst into tears.

"Oh, do quit laughing, and do so help me up, Miriam, if you so kind! It isn't very ladylike to roll in the dirt, after all. Simply a revolting affair, if I do say so meself!" Cried the rocking sister.

"I don't know why I should; it's rather funny!" "It is not!" Replied Adelia truculently.

"Yes, it is! Mumsy always said yer the clumsily 'un."

"Mumsy also said allaways hulp yer elders an' im your elder by t'ree 'atches!" With this said, Miriam stopped laughing.

"Mumsy is nevah wrong; I dare say not! Fine. I shall help you! Give me your wing now!"

Adelia strained to lift her wing, vocalizing the hurt feelings of all those caught short of their own expectations of perfection. Slowly, maybe too slowly, her wing was waiting for Miriam to give her the lift. So slowly, in fact, that Miriam's unbalanced in the effort to extend and hold her wing for Adelia to grab. Miriam went down in a heap like her sister. Both now lay in the dirt path and silently regarded their fate. It was just too difficult for either to speak, especially to each other. This time, no words would suffice.

After a few minutes regarding the view of the sky above them, both still flat upon the ground, Miriam spoke at last, breaking the absurd silence:

"You don't suppose it's time to get on and move on from this place, do you, Adelia?"

"Yes, one could say so." Her voice was resigned to a kind of apathy from the struggle. "Adelia?"

"Yes, Miriam?"

"Suppose if 'e do go, then who would be left to charm Wallay? Other than us, that is?" "Well, I hadn't really thought of t'at! You are so right…"

Both sisters still stared at the sky, almost entranced by the bringing up of the Hare… then they closed their eyes and started to dream lovely thoughts…

"I do so admire Wallay… he's such a lovable-"

"Don't you forget 'bout tremendously adorable and caring!" "Oh yes, I know… so unquestionably true!"

Little did the daydreaming sisters know as they went on flattering the Hare with their verifiable conviction of infatuation for him, Wally, who had been strolling along greeting the day, had noticed the two on the ground and came to see what this situation was. Wally was already well aware of the sisters' endearment over him. He now stood over them, bidding a friendly salutation with a natural, gleaming smile. Though the sisters had thought it was all in their imagination.

"Oh, I can hear him now… what joy… what delight it is to hear!" they dreamily soughed.

Again, the Hare bid them a greeting. "Good day to you sisters! And what may I say is the trouble? You both look awfully concerned!"

With this, both sisters realized it wasn't actually a dream, but in reality, they had awakened to see Wally's face right above them. Both had awkwardly blushed in embarrassment at the near sight of the Hare. In a giggling, falsetto voice, Miriam replied.

"Trouble? Trouble? There isn't no trouble, isn't 'at right, Adelia!" "Dear me no… not the slightest…"

"You both do look like you need help up!"

"Ooh no, no, no, we are just fine down here, thank you!" Said Adelia, unable to curtsy properly and politely. She did try; unfortunately, it looked rather funny, so instead, she patted the ground. In an excuse as to why they were on the ground, they both said.

"Exercise!"

"After all, exercise is most important, you know!" "Naturally!" Miriam added boastfully.

Wally was dubious that this was actually the case and again offered his help with more persistence. Both sisters refused the offer.

"You two cannot be serious. Come now...give us a wing." Wally said gently, this time with less humor and incredulity. The tone of his voice melted their resistance instantaneously.

"Alright then, if'n you insist." Miriam carefully offered her wing to him. This time, fearing another disaster, Adelia kept quiet and waited, though her jealousy was apparent in her blushing cheeks. Wally could sense it but not wanting to call it out. He knew quite well how it might have affected her sense of personal composure, so he pretended not to notice.

Patiently, he assisted Miriam back to her feet. In a kind of stoic relief, she let out a muffled squawk as she stood back on her feet.

"Our hero! Thank you, Wally! What's a lady to do without ye?" "A lady... or two, perhaps?" Chuckled Wally.

"Oooh, do hush up, Miriam; we don't want to embarrass him now, do we?!" Adelia said.

"You too, Adelia. Come on, on yer feet, I dare say. It doesn't seem all too comfortable down there." Wally said this time in a whispering tone. Now, Adelia was noticeably flushed. She struggled at first, almost regretfully letting go of Wally's paw, and gave him a winsome smile. She did not appear to mind the inconvenience she put Wally through.

Somehow, she felt it was rather worth the trouble. Both sisters were soon once again back on their feet, brushing themselves off in an effort not to look dirty and unkempt by any means. With a graceful, coy "thank you," they clumsily shuttled away in the direction they were initially headed. The direction today was to be the Borderland. Wally had seen them off, and in a lighthearted sigh, he was off himself to meet Sampson and Booney.

"Wallay is such a kind gentleman, ain't he?"

"Don't gotta tell me! Of course, he is, kind indeedin!"

Making small talk about how the day had so far gone, they soon lost track of time, and with that loss came a general loss of their sense of direction. They walked and talked in wide circles, noting a particularly striking clump of red Sweet William flowers, and as they gazed at everything pretty. They had also started to gently collect plump and sweet berries they had seen, putting the clusters into their baskets. Amidst the carefree picking, Adelia secretly and gently placed the choicest berries in a hidden satchel concealed beneath her wing, which she had also had five buns she had baked the day before. She always felt one could be hungry at any given time, and might it be a good idea to have something tasty along the way. She often thought while wandering. It was, of course, she reminded herself, just in case the want might arise.

A trickling and winding stream they were following more or less, or some dramatic rock outcropping here and there, provided many sights to follow. Never sensible with directions even on a good day, maybe the events of the morning and the particular pleasant nature of today's sights made them unaware that they were indeed being followed. The deeper they walked into the meadows and forests of the borderland, the less they noticed the growing numbers of shadowy figures now looming closer. Some hid behind large stands of Crabapple and Pin Oak trees. Others simply stared from behind the mossy rock riverbeds that lined the stream that had now become a visible barrier. The stream had become a river's edge, and though they now knew they were hopelessly lost, they were in no way alone.

Once they stopped walking, they became silent. They could hear screaming of some sort, coupled with loud grunts and snorts. At first, it sounded as if there was a terrible struggle or fight commencing. As they listened more carefully, they began to hear laughter mixed with the chaotic screaming.

"Oh Delly, I never in me 'ole life thought such a place as this could be existin' so close to our own dear 'ome!"

"I don't think we're anywhere's near our 'ome, Miriam." "If' I says I 'as a frightened, would you believes it?"

"Well, I believes we're finding someplace 'orrible, and we can't do nothins 'bout it!" Her voice rose to a kind of shrill exclamation.

They both shuffled slowly to a clearing next to a patch of boulders—almost tippy-toe and nearly falling as they did so. Suddenly, as they approached the clearing, Miriam stopped. So sudden did she stop that Adelia could not help but tumble on top of her, sending them both to the ground in full view of the clearing. "Do watch yourself, Miriam!" Shouted Adelia accidentally. She covered her beak with her wing in surprise, hoping she wasn't heard. To interrupt whatever was happening near them certainly was not a deferential manner of introduction for two genteel, principled ladies. What they saw before them, however, horrified them both.

In the distant clearing, they could clearly see some warring or battle taking place. There were two sides, yet the figures from each side were mixed up together. There were fierce screams and grappling in the moving crowd below the frightened sisters. They could hear the tearing of clothing and the sucking and sloshing of mud as beings with large-edged horns protruding from their mouths skirmished, rising, and falling again and again.

The battling figures themselves were huge and brawny, the color of mud and ruddy red flesh. The embattled group screamed again and again, in a cacophonous unison at times. The overall image, combined with the guttural sounds issuing from the mass of bodies, made the sisters want to faint. But it could not happen, 'no, not here!' Adelia thought.

Miriam simply closed her eyes and hoped they might somehow survive it. This time, they both realized that they had gone too far.

"Did you have a good fall, 'en?" The voice shook them. The sound of the words was deep and mocking. It seemed to hover above them in a booming cloud. And the smell! It was like every sour smell on earth, and it was so close to them both. Mustering her courage, Miriam opened one eye and gasped in astonishment.

"Oin't yer prutty 'ittle oines! Evah suun a Grunball matchin' bo'fore?" Snorted the stout, mussy Boar in a foul grimace, a spiked ball cradled under one arm. Miriam's stomach churned at the sight. The Creature's face was covered in an array of piercings, these adornments clinked and jingled with every movement. His eyelids were no exception, studded with a series of rings that created an unsettling noise whenever he blinked or squinted. Miriam could barely tear her gaze away from the grotesque display, struggling to comprehend the sheer extent of the piercings.

Then, a sudden realization dawned on her. This must be the legendary Cap'm Thistleworts.

A very blubbery Boar, who also had an assortment of little piercings, lumbered forward, having been summoned by Cap'm.

"Nehvah seen the blood 'n bone flyin', eh?" The Boar wheezed with a toothy grin. "Le's 'splain how 'tis done."

Cap'm shifted the ball slightly, showing off its jagged edges crusted with dried blood. "Tha's the grun! Ain't no fancy rules—grab it, hurl it inta tha pit on their side. T'em's who carries it gets beat hard." The Cap'm emphasized his point by giving the ball a little shake with his hoof, the rings in his lips clinking loudly.

"Ya lose it? Ya fight for it back. Ain't no cryin' when yer o'pponent's shovin' yer face in the dirt!" Another Horkur added with a sharp laugh.

Before the Boar could continue, a booming voice cut across the noise. "Chumby! Come 'un see a' dis! Hyaa hyyaa!" The Cap'm bellowed, utterly oblivious to the conversation at hand.

"Aye, Cap'm. What have we 'ere?" Chumby, the blubbery Boar, slouched over with a wet snort, his rings clinking in a grotesque rhythm. His eyes landed on the grunball and the newcomers, his tongue sliding across his cracked lips.

Cap'm chuckled darkly, giving the ball a possessive squeeze. "Jus' 'bout ta 'splain Grunball to these fresh faces, ain't we?" He shot a grin toward Chumby, who let out a deep, rumbling laugh in response.

Miriam leaned close to Adelia, her voice barely above a whisper, "My goodness… look at these brutes!"

Adelia nodded slightly, too horrified to tear her eyes away from the brutish creatures in front of them. The rings pinned in their flesh swayed as they laughed, their grotesque forms towering like twisted statues.

"First team ta three goals wins—'f they ain't knocked out first, that is," Chumby grunted. "Most don' last long 'fore they're bleedin' in the pit."

"Le's not fergit the fun bit, Chumby," a third Horkur chimed in, his rings jangling as he grinned wider. "No weapons allowed—least, none ye cun see." He snorted. "Now, tha's where the real game o' Grunball begins."

Adelia shuddered, while Miriam, despite herself, couldn't help the faint flicker of disgusted fascination.

"I see it but don't belie—" Adelia started, but a rude round of laughter cut her off.

"Hyaaaaaa Hyaaaaa, MY DEARIES!" The Cap'm belched out. Miriam felt her knees buckle, ready to faint, but Adelia quickly rapped her beak with her wing, snapping her back to her senses. Miriam winced but stood firm though her stomach churned with nausea.

Thistleworts' smell was putrid, and his grizzled appearance looked ghastly and forbidding. He had not a right eye but a deep, crossed scar shaped like an "X." One of his tusks was missing, with a shorn root protruding from his slobbering maw. On the other side, a fractured, seared stub of a tusk was adorned by a stack of ornate golden bands, a mark of power and status, and accompanied by a row of sharp, crooked, and rotting teeth that jutted in all directions from his malformed and excessively dripping jaw. The hunching Boar was titanic, with long, luxuriant, tangled bristles covering his body. He was dressed in ratty clothing consisting of a soiled, shredded dark violet and indigo vest and dark pinstriped pantaloons that seemed much too tight. His large swelling thighs were beginning to tear through the tattered trousers. Shaggy, heavyset legs showed through the ripping side seams of his trousers. Dark maroon strapped suspenders seemed to strangle his shoulders, oblivious to the ludicrous appearance of his ill-fitting attire.

Fortunately, no foot apparel was evident on his chipped-hooved feet and tawny shins. A red striped stocking cap, looking more like a dirty, folded shirt with its sleeves cut out, was slouched on the top of his stubbly head. Some salvaged unique accessories were also seen, tied in different parts of his attire. Some of these items had been seen before by the sisters, but they could not recall where exactly. They had confronted Thistle regarding this "crime," citing the acquisition of the "cap" as stealing.

"It ain't stealin' if ne'er aun WANT'S it!!!" The Boar grumbled nastily. "If'n it's left in ve' trush, whoiy cant's I 'av' it anywoiys?!"

The thought of Thistleworts and his band of swine being a myth was instantly disregarded. As the Horkurs marched closer it was apparent that they too wore stacks of golden bands on their tusks, some even more elaborate than Thistleworts'. Each band glinted with the reflection of power and position within their gruff society. And though the Horkurs had never been seen or caught, the sisters had heard tales told in hushed whispers about them. They were dreadful stories, and both Miriam and Adelia feigned an interest in them when they were heard. But neither chose to take stock of the stories when uttered. Wishing to avoid any unpleasant circumstances, both sisters had a hard time attempting not to raise their assertiveness. Initially, they both greeted the ugly group with lady-like charm, poise, and sincere pleasantries as they would with anyone. With statements like 'We are the Quaddling sisters, and most delighted are we to make your acquaintances." A few other introductory sentences, though carefully phrased and elocuted, brought a kind of blank staring silence in most of the hoard. One of them was positively moved, however. He was silently watching in admiration at the sisters' politeness. He detected a kind of fearlessness borne of being considerate of others in their speech. This consideration, he knew, was poorly placed before his rough lot of swine. Thistleworts came to be immediately fondly affectionate of the two sisters, who could intuit by now his forceful, brutal passion for them both. (For did they not know his passion? Why, they themselves knew it all too well, for they had the same affection for Wally.) Accompanying his brusque, overbearing introduction, the others began to snoop and catch the scent of the berries in their baskets and some vague floral scent. The Horkurs were about to devour the contents the baskets held. In the next moment, a sudden grasping of both their sets of wings occurred, and though they did struggle for release, it was very uncomfortable for them. Try as they may, it was a fruitless effort to escape. The Boar's strong grasp was as painful to bear as the sensation of being locked in a vice. Thistleworts then began a slobbering and snuffling kind of kiss on their fair, white- feathered wings. The snorting kiss came out precisely as a long-winded sucking inhalation. And though pretending to be flattered (but honestly doing a terrible job of it) for the sake of cordial pleasantness, in reality, they were both equally disgusted by his discourteous look, appearance, and conduct. What was most offensive was Thistleworts' inconsiderate directness of such a rude, gruff, and obscene introduction! Nothing could be more important than a formal introduction to the Quaddling sisters' world. But now, it was two worlds vastly apart from where they had come. It was impossible to understand such vulgarity, considering that they had always known nothing but their own well-ordered existence.

"Oin' tells ya...why don' yar prutty, 'ittle dollies coime 'long wuth us n' we can 'ave some funs of our oin! Says, what's yer names again?" Snorted Thistle. "Is'n'it

Edilly, no oi maen Avilly en' er, uh, Mitsie?"

"It is most assuredly NOT!" Replied Miriam with almost hurt and offended feelings. "It is, however, Adelia and Miriam!" Adelia promptly corrected.

"I see, Adelby an' Mitsim, is it!?" Replied Thistleworts while pointing at the incorrect sister with the incorrect name. After repeated failures from having them repeat their names again and again, he realized that it was no good trying; the situation just could not work at all. Thistleworts had kept mixing up both sisters' names.

"Oh, do just forget it! Would you please call us by any name you fancy!" Replied Adelia, giving up in frustration (which was very rare for Adelia to give up so easily).

"And by whatever you laggard bunch of mugs mean by fun; we both would want nothing of it. We do not want anything to do wit' any of you… let alone be communiamtatin!" Now, the sisters had both become irritatingly irrational with their choice of words, both of them not in the least caring if they were to be found polite or not.

"Besides, we have our Wallay now! Who is going to take care of Wallay if'n we are gone… Hmmm?"

"So true, Miriam, so true!" Adelia inherently agreed, likewise.

"WHO IS THIS WOOLLAAAY!!!!!?" The Boar fiercely bellowed in a long, exhaling grunt. It was to be seen that by just the mention of the Hare's name alone had aroused the churlish ire of Thistleworts. It was just to be ignored, however, by the nonsensically gabling sisters as they didn't much pay any attention to the extremity of possessive anger taking place now. They obsessively and carelessly went irksomely blathering on and on (as if condescendingly neglecting whom they were in the presence of) about Wally and about how special he was, and how, in a short time, he shall be their right suitor when the right time came to be.

"Whut's Woollay got 'at oi havun't!?" Thistleworts growled stridently in his growing and lustful jealousy. The hostile tension between parties increasingly emerged into a glowering calamity.

Nor did either sister back down, for each of them had quite a lot to say, too much to say, in fact. Perhaps it was a prudent idea not to say words that would unsettle the Boar and to let kind words be exchanged instead of rash, cynical, and desultory ridicules being passed between them all.

Though presently, neither sister was much concerned about solicitude over indiscreet sentiments of their own, not in the least as of now. They couldn't help themselves to entertain their higher judgments but could only bluster out the forthright truth as they saw it, no matter how hard the result might be. The divulging truth had blurted out so quickly, like a rabbit through the fence- gate, that they couldn't help but speak ferocious condemnations in chortling remonstrations.

"Class! First off, that there in itself is a greatest of differences!" She snuffled. "I can't tell you how barbarously shabby and uncivilly behaved you all are, with this unaccountable presentation of yourselves and with what kind of rude gestures and unmannerly articulation you all forthwith babble and demonstrate your foppery with!" Pronounced Adelia in a spiteful, malicious rant.

She embodied that which was vehemently catty and aloof. "Dear, dear," she continued, "Dare I say…. haven't any of you poor creatures ever been properly edgumacated?!!" Asked Miriam with evidently profound concern. It was to be true in many cases that Miriam was the most kind of the two sisters, while Adelia was harshly pontificating and easily disgruntled by the slightest offense.

"Weez coint hulp whut weez is! Weez iz, whut weez iz!" Commented Thistleworts passionately whilst aggressively scratching and picking at his smelly, gigantic, itchy hindquarters. After his wounded defense, he gauchely snuffled the vile odor from the grubby, oily hoof that he had scratched his rear with.

"Oh goooooooooodness, and please do not do that impertinent activity you are doing in front of us; go behind a bush or tree if'n you must, but pleeeease, I cannot tell you how simply repulsive it is to witness!"

"Right, right!" added Miriam.

"' Ti's naught!" He snorted, wounded but indignant. "S'natrul behaviah in bein…" "It is most foul!" Both sisters simultaneously retorted.

Thistleworts grimaced and replied, "Soi yur buth 'un an of tose hoity-toity Rivafulk, aint ya's?"

"Perhaps we are. It doesn't really mean a lot, now does it?" She added, "Manners is manners. 'Specially before ladies!" Miriam snobbishly answered.

"Oi, yois' mam, I kner yer koind and well, oi dae. Oi, it muuns EVERYTHIN' TO OIS!"

"What does 'it' mean precisely!?" Adelia asked for clarification, somewhat prudishly with a hint of sarcasm, not having the faintest idea what 'it' meant. Thistle followed up Adelia's inquiry with a wicked, grim scowl. He bellowed. "It means that otha t'un yer two lovely lasses, no one else is allowed 'ERE... We dunt ruspec yer kind a' roonin' 'bout here in this borderland. NO 'UN boot'n oaush 'orkurs. Dis 'ere is our own TERRITORAAAHH!" He belched out emphatically.

"We dunt take 'em too kindly to strangers like yer high an' moighty Rivafooks, oo' dunt' have the slightest ruspec for us 'uns! Likewise, ta' houndies a' roonin' amook, accompanied with a bizarre lookin' fuxies and such as t'is iz!!!!" Thistle groaned.

But the Quaddling sisters had never heard of any such hounds before, certainly never near their beloved Ambrodale. As they both stood still, listening to Thistleworts' tirade, they were growing quite frightened by the dreadful thought of what the hounds were or could be. They had never encountered such a thing before as an unbridled, savage group of hounds running at will in the Borderlands with its dark forests and murky glens. Not even in a dream or a nightmare could they imagine the ragged legions of the unwanted, tearing nocturnally onto some dark destination. As regards hounds and "fooxies" in general, they could only imagine the terror of such fiends.

But of course, to make matters worse, they also had never encountered a Horkur before, either. Though they had rambled on as a pair indiscriminately through meadow and vale, protected by their own unknowing state from fear, as they traveled, this darker side of their domain was new, and all was so very confusing. If the gang of Horkurs had existed before this happenstance encounter with Adelia and Miriam, and the Horkurs were truly not a myth as many thought, then of course, to this madness, the hounds must be a criminal element also infesting this darkening wood. These thoughts, spoken each to each in whispers as they stood before Thistleworts now, began to frighten them. Their world grew vastly more complex with terrifying rapidity.

"Hounds? Gracious me, what do t'ey lookie like!?" asked Miriam, rather panicky yet maintaining her composure. As if waiting for the right moment, Thistleworts, with a twisted grin, deviously began to lure the two unsuspecting sisters into his diabolical desires as he went on in a ca.j.oling and yet cautionary tone.

"Terrble, terrble creature t'ey iz … T'um houndiez comes to tiss 'ere borderland and ravage it all for who'm kneres whut! Try 'az we might ta fend 'ems back, but t'ey's outnumba oush! Oi, battle after battle we loost, and with n' they keeps a' comin' on… disastrous casualties t'ey gives oush!" Thistle snorted in dramatic disgust while shedding some light tears. He hastily took off his cap out of respect for those fallen (though it was suspected now by Adelia that it might actually be a joking act or mock play).

"Weez'm miss ye' boyz. Brave yez were!" A snort followed the impromptu eulogy. "This iz all's we gots left!" Came a heartfelt bellowing sob. "If yez t'inkum' we are ruffian boyz, well, ye' betta not meet 'em houndiez, I say. Othawise, wha' yer gunna do wit' yorself? Ye be needin' a safe passage ye will! Better ye foun' ush out now 'fore it gets 'ins tooz late!"

In her growing confusion, Miriam let out a shrill gasp. 'What could he possibly mean by that? Has our Ambrodale grown unsafe and unsightly so close to the pond home where we live? Since when has such utter barbarity shown itself so close to our homes?' She thought silently to herself. She did not exactly know why, but she instantly thought of Wally. She could feel his memory but could not say why that might be.

Adelia shocked but less cowed, instantly felt that this whole episode must be some concoction of indiscretion. What could this absurd and disgusting old Boar have to offer? Slovenly, intrusive, unmannerly, and downright foul-smelling, he was indeed! When she attempted to think of him completing even the simplest of tasks, she simply felt embarrassed. Something seemed altogether wrong, and it made her uneasy.

"WEEEELLLL?" Cap'm Thistleworts rather belched aloud, "WEEEEEEELLLL?!" Adelia and Miriam simply gasped at the effrontery of his untimely pronouncement. It shattered their thoughts and led them away from their feelings of individual and collective bewilderment, adding to a state of general incomprehension.

"WEEEEEELL, moi sweeties, Oim 'e oines fer yer! Oi can saves yer frum yer predicat…presicat…prudish..or might'n Oi say…, Oi can hulp yers.." He now said in a sloppy whisper as he reached into the orange basket and removed their day's pickings of wild grapes, gooseberries, and pungent black currants. (Passing whatever remained that wasn't sloppily devoured by him to his eagerly awaiting companions.) With the juices of the fresh berries dripping from their loudly smacking mouths and snouts, they savagely consumed their handfuls of the sisters' pickings, grunting, and snorting with boisterous glee. As the Horkurs circled roundabout the sisters, they continued (for quite a long time now) to ravage what was contained inside of the two baskets. The sisters felt queasy at the sights, sounds, and smells of the feast.

They became indignant to witness that their handmade baskets were about to break apart from the rough handlings and nosings of each interloping Horkur. The sight of their hideous lumpy faces, besmeared with the viscous, dripping juices of the mangled and oozing berries was almost too much for the Quaddling sisters to witness. The gluttonous Horkurs went on gruffly jabbering and grumbling incomprehensibly as they sloppily gobbled, slurped, engulfed, and munched on the contents of the baskets, now shredded, stained, and ruined.

The Horkurs, being fed after the grueling sporting match, were now merrier than before. Tears of laughter fell from the corners of their disproportionately small and beady eyes. In such a state of merriment, their eyes looked unusually bizarre, considering their low or high placements on their faces, which contrasted markedly with the size and bristly texture of the bulging, bushy brows they sported. Adding to the effect of a grotesque yet somehow laughable countenance, each Horkur had huge, caved-in, and surface-irregular foreheads under which their eyes were deep-set beneath an outsized, almost comically protuberant brow.

The overall effect while observing their faces was rather eerie when one added the low, gurgling voices that issued forth from their dripping snouts as they ate. "Bes burries I 'a like ta 'ave" or sentences like "Coogy, loik'a all'ees a goots. roundalooten, suus moi!" Which was generally incomprehensible even to most of the attendant Horkurs. The correct way to picture how their eyes eerily looked with their contrasted oversized features around them might be just to imagine a man having all his facial features exaggerated and outsized and then replacing his eyes for another smaller pair, button-like: perhaps say from a mouse's tiny head. How odd he would certainly look, and even harder yet to imagine how difficult it would be to see. Their small eyes indeed influenced them, for they could see but very little. Their strong sense of smell made up for their poor eyesight, however.

Because of their acute olfactory prowess, they never starved. Rootings all the day long and into the night ensured a steady supply of food, even if putrid or rancid. For the Horkurs, even with very little utility possible from their small, defective eyes, they could mostly rely on deciphering the scents of every living creature and their leavings about here and there. It was much easier for them than that of any other to pick up a strange scent, even if it came two to three miles off. Had they not been so engaged in the battle for victory before being discovered by the sisters, the violet water both used for daily preening would have been detected long before the sisters' frantic and careless tumble in the field.

Amid their raucous jollity, an eminently hideous and visually lopsided Horkur stepped forward—Bilmey Toags, the most grotesque of the gruff swine. The only albino among them, Bilmey's pallid, blotchy skin was marred by clusters of bloody pustules, boils, and angry hives. Atop his bulbously misshapen head perched a filthy, tattered brown bicorn titfer adorned with three bedraggled black feathers. The hat, much too small for his enormous crown, slid precariously from side to side, requiring frequent adjustments to stay in place. Though an irritating effort, it served to obscure the hairless lump beneath—a grotesque protrusion, bulging and fissured with spidery, hairline cracks.

Adding to his grotesquery, a giant, beaten iron ring pierced his mucus-gushing snout, clanging absurdly against his tusks whenever he moved. As he approached Thistleworts, his stony, hoarse voice grated through the chilly air.

"Oi, I reck'm I smeels 'em houndiez shumwares!" Bilmey grunted fervidly, his broad chest swelling like a bellows as he drew a deep draught of the frigid air. His nostrils flared, wet and glistening, as he declared with conviction, "Could be a whole lot o' 'em!"

Bilmey was trying to detect the oppressive and pervading odor's location. The Horkurs perceived that the familiar reeking scent had started to intensify. Thistleworts and the others began to sniff the air with staccato bursts along with Bilmey Toags.

"Oi, we'se thinkem' yer roight!" A few Horkurs said at once. They all concurred at the moment, and with joying snorts and smelled acquiescence, they were off marching, gung-hoing, to follow the trail of scents. They marched in a kind of heavy-footed shuffle, oblivious to the underbrush, thorny scrub, and stones that lay about the field, all the time snorting, hooting, and unpleasantly croaking a martial song. They strode in pairs, bellowing proudly aloud and pitifully rasping at top volume. The effect was of a horrible-sounding march, complete with the sloshings and mucking about of their kind.

The rambling clan lurched forward and brought the poor crestfallen Quaddling sisters along as captives. The event would have seemed absurd if not for the acute pain both sisters felt at missing the comforts of their house by the pond. Before long, neither sister could utter a word of protest and was not inclined to speak whatsoever. A feeling of drowsiness and wooziness soon crept upon them both after so much walking for the day. Feeling more tired than they had ever, ever remembered feeling before (but again, they had never felt this odd feeling before. It was all new and terrifyingly unrelenting. They knew they had become helpless, indeed). The pervasive weariness was no doubt caused by this dry, bug infested heat of a forced march in the dark and gloomy bog. The Horkurs flabby bodies gave off small wispy streamlets of rising steam as they marched, no doubt due to the encroaching chilling evening. The sisters could see small strips of slivered sunlight, drably gleaming from above the dreary twisted treetops. For one, the air was so detestably stale, actually oppressively so, due to the sisters' proximity to the Horkurs' sweaty, off-gassing bodies as they shuffled onwards. The swamp air itself was also so murky they could hardly breathe at all but instead gagged and choked from its toxic impurity. However, these brooding, amoral Horkurs had long existed here; the Quaddlings had but not the slightest notion. The sisters most certainly did not like this horrible feeling at all. How they wished they were home in their pond right now, safe and cozy in their comfortable rocking chairs. Teatime had ended by now, but they could imagine baking pastries, scrumptious or not. Adelia imagined she could hear their steaming kettle singing. The memory stood in stark contrast to this dark underworld full of hideous notions with residents to match the worst of her nightmares. It was a misty-eyed feeling that nothing sinister could ever pass through or under their grassy door. (Not for the last time!)

They all continued to climb ever so steeply uphill and downhill, under and under tangled brush. Over slippery stone half-tumbled from time to time, scouring through the tortuous, unmarked, mossy pathway surrounded by small, hidden, rippling ravines, broken trees hanging limp, and ancient pillars, once standing, now crashed upon the ground in large smashed and jagged hunks. Some of the limestone chunks of stone blocked their clandestine pathway (and in that case, the group made a clumsy detour around them). The new path they tamped through was littered with desolate, crumbly caves, patches of long, prickly, odd-smelling wildflowers, and lone, stray granite boulders. The group continued on until, at last, the Horkurs' impaired little eyes finally made use of themselves and spotted a small group of Hounds in the far-off distance. The hoary Hounds were now prowling across the open field where the Horkurs were playing previously. A quiet rumble surged through the group, and all were in a mood to hunt down the grizzled Hounds just for the fun of it. A hoarse whisper could be heard by all in the ranks. It was a word of warning from Thistle to the sisters. Thistle said:

"Neow, yer two lovelies stayz put'ins, and we'll be roight back! Don'ts a' goes anaywhurs!!! By 'en I do 'ope yas caz give ain answer!" With this strongly expressed reminder, the Horkurs were off to chase their rivals, the unsuspecting Hounds. The sisters were now alone once more, awaiting and thinking what they shall ever do. Adelia, not in favor of being in such horrid company and surroundings for long, suggested they escape while they had a chance to.

"Well, if'n you askin' me, I think'n we should, by golly! Besides, o' how will t'ey eva find us? In such a big place like'n this!?

"Well, no one asked your suggestion now, did 'ey? It's all too risky if you so ask me!" Miriam disagreed with her protesting and bickering sister. "Now, I think it if we stays put like 'em 'orkurs say, it may be a safer alternative. What with'm all o' 'em hounds, foxies, and dare I say the 'orkurs millin' about!" She declared.

"Oh, how incrediabaly unintelligibly shooopid can you be, dear Miriam! We are good as dead if we stay sittin' 'ere trustin' 'em ruffins with t'ere FAKE stor'ay!"

"Stoooooopittttt? Stoooopit!? I am not stoopit!" "Oh, yes'm, you are!"

"O' no, I'm nought! On'la practical, that is! And I'm tellin' ya' I know 'e safety'est. This is 'ore safety'est t'an your crazy idea; sure is not lady-like to go as we please without at least bidding farewell, is it?"

"So true, Miriam, so true! Dear, dear, what willy Mumsy be doing in this spot!?" Thinking to herself, Adelia beamed with an answer. "I know! She would leave a note! But dear, dear, there isn't a pen or leaf anywhere, is there?!" Adelia said rather glumly after searching her surroundings. "So bein's the oldeyest and all, I am in charge an' no if's, boot's, or or's 'bout it; I say we run when we have t'e chance!" Fretted Adelia. "T'at ain't fair!" Quacked Miriam in a worrying response. So began another frustrating quacking argument about whatever they should do, not letting the other speak, and they kept interrupting each other's sentences.

On the one hand, if they did so decide to make their getaway, it wouldn't be quick, for each of them was clumsy and uncoordinatedly plodding as concerned. It would also be most unwise to have the Horkurs against them if such a plan were a partial success, and if they were to get caught, who'd know what a miserable punishment there would be? They hardly knew anything at all about this territory, and, even further on yet, what the ghastly Borderland's unknown threats were? But if they stayed put with these brutes, who knows what they would do just for pleasure?! If they ran, they would certainly be bound to find someplace to hide until everything smoothed over. Thinking it over, Miriam couldn't help but agree to escape while they had a chance to. And so, it was! She immediately begged for forgiveness for ever doubting Adelia.

With no time to spare, they started to waddle away from where they had gotten lost.

Once again, and this time with tragic consequences, neither knew where to go. When they started to waddle, they waddled in opposite directions! Adelia was walking toward the left of the path while Miriam was to the right... AND AGAIN, another argument occurred! But their argument was quickly ended. Their loud, obnoxious rambling was cut very thinly short and brought to a dead silence. They now stood trembling, and from that terrified moment, they heard the Horkurs stampeding on their way back with loud cheers and guffaws of victory! Brought on by fear of the oncoming Horkurs, both of the stammering sisters (being very close together, huddling from the fright of being rediscovered) became immediately weltered, going on scrambling, with feathers flying for anywhere they could find sanctuary. With hurried and panicky shambling, they managed to get away from the viewing spot of the field, and though not too far, they had traveled just far enough to hide.

Since they knew not the way back, they ran through the Borderland's overgrown foliage in confusion (hoping to remember something familiar, perhaps a tree or cave they had seen before becoming abductees of the Horkurs). It was wished by both sisters that the Horkurs had not been after them but rather still pursuing the Hounds, how they wished it!

They tried to conjure up happy thoughts of home in the growing darkness of the Borderlands. (They were both trying to drown this present woe with the pleasures of dreaming.) Yet, almost rudely awakened, they fled harder and further when they heard the horrible screeching of Thistle that followed when he returned, expecting to find his 'dearies waiting for their hero's return from danger,' he thought rather stupidly. In cold reality and to his blighted obtuseness, he found them gone.

"WHEEEEEEEEEEEEERE ARE THEEEEEEY!!!!!!!???" Screaming and cursing in vulgar absurdity, with howling rage, the lugubrious Cap'm shrilly screamed out, "FIND T'EM AND BRIIIIING T'EM TO MEEEEEE!" To hear the menacing, yammering Horkurs stamping, snuffling like bellows, and trampling in the underbrush as they began searching after the sisters like raving predate beasts (as they well were) made Adelia freeze momentarily. The game was real. This was not AMBRODALE. There were no rules for etiquette. No considerate words, no comfort from the cold, and no need to win anything. The realization of how alone she had truly become made her look at Miriam. Miriam was shuddering and ruffling her feathers ever so slightly to keep off the chill.

Miriam was doing her ever best to appear composed. In Miriam's eyes, she could see how much she had misjudged her sister. Her sister had always been a reliable friend. She was not particularly quick-witted, perhaps, but Adelia could see in Miriam's darkening eyes, yes darkening, almost tearfully afraid, that Miriam could and would never leave her. Not even if fearing the worst. They were both alone now. In the darkening woods, twigs snapped from behind. It seemed as if the Horkurs were catching up to them. Snorts and shrieks echoed off of the greenish-grey slime-covered boulders throughout the Borderland where both sisters stood.

The scenario was all too terrifying for such simple folk of the Bromby River. Adelia knew now why folks of Ambrodale had never bothered to acquaint themselves with this place. The Borderlands and territories beyond the village remained a vast and terrifying unknown.

They could see the advancing, ever-growing, tall, and lank shadows approaching from all sides. Looming and sulking, closer and so ever closer to them, these growling shadows seemed all too recognizable to the sisters, like the ones they had seen when they first arrived there. As they fled, Miriam, with all the fear in the whole world, welled her consciousness into one driving thought. Her former attempt at happy musings was abandoned. Miriam screamed: "Come ooon, DDDEEEEEEEEEELLLLLLLYYYYYYYY!!!" She could not help but run ahead of poor Adelia, who had such a terrible, terrible time trying not to be slow (but in vain). With long, wheezing breaths, Adelia quickly fell behind her fleeing sibling. They ran and ran rather naively through the shrubs and prickly weeds until, miraculously, they spotted a winding path downhill that became familiar to them once again. Now on the verge of well-being, they still heard the screams and curses of wrathful Thistle and his horde. Distant he was, yet so frightening them even more. Miriam was so flustered by the Horkurs' pursuit that she did not even turn her head to see her sister trailing behind her.

She rapidly deduced that her sister was right behind her like she always had been. But when she finally reached Ambrodale's entry hedgeway, she turned once more, wanting to see Adelia. To her timorous and breathless dismay, Miriam saw nothing... and she heard nothing. Miriam desperately called out her sister's name, awaiting the high-hoped minutes that turned into distraught, miserable hours. The sky, once streaked with buoyant colors, transformed bleakly and morbidly into an odious grey. With the coming of a booming storm, its pale clouds, and the light drizzling of cold rain, the atmosphere soon devolved into a heavy and oppressive downpour with raindrops slick and gelid. The rain beat on in a hammering shower as lighting flashed blue streaks in the dark, withering sky. Now and again, the sky was stained with purple bursts of electricity as the erupting thunder roared. The gusts of strong, moaning winds swept the little valley seemingly upside-down, knocking the feeblest of the scurrying figures from the village off of their feet. They scrambled about as they hurried indoors to shelter as the surrounding cataclysmic tempest (the kind of weather to get you bedridden if standing out too long) went on and on.

Completely soaked by the heavy rain that ruffled her feathers with its icy cold shards, poor Miriam shivered from the effects of the tempest. She did not worry about it or her own safety, but worried for her sister's safety, wherever she could have been. Patiently and with remorse at her blind hastiness, Miriam waited long for a sign, for at least a response, of Adelia's safe return. She hoped for it, but no comforting response echoed back. Nothing could be heard at all but the cold wind nipping at her tender webbed feet. It felt as painful as severe frostbite, and countless times during her watch, she was to be forcefully dragged away by the great, blustery gale. It moved her from where she stood to whatever the closest object might be able to stop her. The blowing wind carried her, but countless times after, unsteadily, she fought the violent gush as strong as a devoted sister might. Adelia would have done the same for Miriam; she knew well.

Still, she waited… alas, even so, no response came to her own tearful, pleading calls. There was no sight of her sister anywhere, but in her mind's visioning, she saw images from her own frightful imagination. Her thoughts were infused by the memory of the reeking and frigidly cold Borderlands. She stood transfixed, staring across the fields into the smoldering pitch-black night. The dreaming had almost reverted into a forlorn nightmare. She could not even speak to anyone else about the horrendously twisted and now hazy sights she conjured as the savage storm raged on even more viciously. Adelia was gone… Adelia was missing! Such a thing had never happened to her or anyone else she had ever known. It was painful in the extreme for her to realize that it should not happened and altogether could not be in a place like this. It felt especially true for two close-paired sisters who never had ever been separated since hatching.

Now, for the first time, Miriam stood alone and realized that both were lost. Both sisters were on their own for the very first and only time!

A Stormy Story

The ferocity of the storm relentlessly shook the dark valley, in its uproar tantrum as it shrieked and appallingly wailed through its speeded untamable gale that whiiiiiiiiiiiiiiiiiiiiiipped across the fields. Thunder CRACKLED and RUM-RUM-RUMBLED in hellishly tenacious reverberation. Jagged bolts of lightning FLAAAASHED in unbroken chains of bright and blinding flares, ripping the dropping black sky apart and dividing the innocent airy children of the BOOOOOOOOOOOOMING angry hovering clouds. Persecuted by this disaster, Ambrodale, deluged within a ferocious display of destruction, had cried out in its plea fearing a none-to-happy outlook ahead. The cruel storm with its feral superiority disdained the valley's miserable exhortation for a stoic mercy to be granted them. Their plea was abortive, for the raging tormentor savaging the land had no intent of stopping nor showing pity.

Inhabitants huddled in their tiny homes prayed for their safe being. Of others, hearing the cannonade of furious rain hammering against all corners of their leaky homes demanding to enter in its detrimental dictating pish push poooooosh, it thrummed. Random debris flurried about from outside. It scraped and whirled objects in the barbarous gusts, creating a deadly vortex of destruction. Objects including stripped roof shingles and cracking shutters suddenly ripped from their bolted windowed places and joined the deadly whirlwind of flying objects. The winds and driving rain even ruined garden beds and uprooted plants in pottery left outside, crashing into many a home. All was a catastrophe. Storms like these were the only terrible downfall of Ambrodale. They happened so frequently that it became almost an inevitable drill for all to instantly rush into their homes when there was a bitter chill or a bizarre stirring feeling in the general atmosphere. The residents would invariably await the storm's arrival and then fearfully wait for it to subside. Still, alas, storms last very long in Ambrodale, not a day or even two like some in other valleys but stretching on to a week or surprisingly more. After the exhausting and anticipated departure, everything would appear ravaged, and the Riverfolk would rebuild what was lost during its path of ruination. In the middle of this particular malevolent rainstorm, where no living being should be out, there was but one... sad, miserable, and completely distraught was she... poor Miriam Quaddling. After a long mood of dolor and with freezing hours, exposed to the night's dreadful weather (She was at a marked risk of catching something more sinister than a common cold or flu could be), Miriam was still waiting and looking for her sister. Adelia was nowhere to be found. She had not a hope left as of now. Miriam had succumbed to considering anything that could have indeed happened to Adelia, her beloved sister, lost in that horrible borderland or worse yet kidnapped by those wicked clan of Horkurs. Who knew what crimes she imagined were being committed against Adelia?! And with this terrible thought, they were both lost, not only Adelia but Miriam as well! For she was always with her sister. They had depended on each other to do anything, and poor Miriam had looked up to Adelia for guidance, but guidance had not come.

Nothing came but the grief of being alone, and she was exceptionally afraid of being alone. Thus, by the storm's imperiously cruel amusement, Miriam was fraught by an obsessive illness that came on suddenly and acutely. The storm was a viscously baleful, remorseless supernatural malefactor.

"O' Dear Delly, O' where are you?" She mourned with an abundance of swelling tears that ran down from her glassy, stinging, tender eyes. At the same time, her heavy and crackling lungs, clogged and congested, let out infectious-sounding gags and sharp, trilling wheezes with a painfully dry barking croup. Her scratchy, virulent sore throat had severe burning inflammation as if it were clawed from within by monstrously stinging little creatures. The grinding and rattling of her frail bones gave Miriam a miserable time. How hard it must have been to stand the racking pain in her tiny frame for such interminable hours. Her weary patience gave out in this wretched, chilling thunderstorm.

Her spinning head was devilishly racked with panging and dizzying discomfort. Her head had tremendous and inevitable hazy fatigue and an overwhelming affliction of blurred and bleary vision. She was likewise suffering the most vilely overwhelming tossing and turning of her stomach. This malady dealt in nausea and debilitating cramps. She could no longer withstand the grueling hardship in weather like this, especially in her frail condition. Deciding to continue the search for her sister once the storm cleared, Miriam lightheadedly staggered and reeled, unable to see anything. She blindly followed wherever her feet led her through the empty paths of Ambrodale. Surrounded by mortal dangers from the whirling debris of the storm, objects hurtled by, threatening to strike her down. Yet, she avoided these hazards by some miracle, still bravely venturing through the blustery paths, fighting against the forceful winds.

Her destination? Home. But poor, sickly Miriam, without her sister Adelia's guidance, didn't know exactly where home was. Adelia had another pair of eyes, so they both relied on each other's wandering gaze to find their way back to their pond. Miriam would look one way while Adelia observed the other, their constant arguments over directions often proving just enough to get them home. Now, coughing and violently sneezing without so much as a handkerchief to use— Adelia had always carried it—Miriam unwisely meandered in circles through the outskirts of Ambrodale, making no progress. After three aimless loops, she ended up right where she had started—lost and utterly confused in the unforgiving storm.

Desperate, she tried to think of what Adelia would do, but sadly, she could only recall their last moments together. Little did she know that each time she made a roundabout, she had passed her home three times without recognizing it, mistakenly believing it had vanished. On her fourth attempt, as she approached the end of the pond where their grassy home should have been, something caught her eye. It was the reason she hadn't found her home earlier. The doleful, indiscreet sight that greeted her was one of absolute horror. Already overwhelmed by her sister's disappearance, she was now struck with devastating grief at the sight of her home in ruins.

She had no idea where to go. Sick and exhausted, Miriam wearily trudged through the wicked storm once again, heading to the only place she could think of that might offer her refuge.

Through the deep-set circular windows of Wally's quaint tiny home, faintly lighted by a roaring and crackling fire in which the Hare had started to keep all in his little home nicely cozy and warm on the inside. Everything went ragingly crazy from the outside! Thankfully, all was safe and secure in his well, reliable, comfortably toasty bungalow, with (of course) such periodic occasions of rattling and crashing impacts that struck the dwelling from without. Battering, scratching, and thumping could be heard and tremblingly felt as Wally braced for the sudden ramming at any spot of his home, demanding a notable breaching entry into his warm domicile. Wally was not alone either; his friends, a good and pleasing company to spend enjoyable time with, had been lodging with the Hare since the storm's arrival.

Booney, the speckled Frog, was enjoying the jar of delectably juicy and crunchy flies he had brought to share with everyone. Still, in total honesty, even he knew; except for himself, no one had an appetite for a jar of flies immoderately and grossly smothered in a mucky green pickle juice. The 'treat' had a peculiarly putrid, sour, overwhelming odor and a vaguely distinguishable smell of a moldy travel stocking. When passed around, Booney excitedly exclaimed, "Go on 'en, take some, t'ere a plunty to go round and back again for more, sure makes the blood run thicker on a cold, windy night, oh my, so scrumptiously tasty!!!" Booney was the first visitor to drop by Wally's home this night. Once there, the bombastic speckled Frog was still sitting in front of a mirror, mindlessly spellbound by his own reflection. "Beautiful reflection," he called it, overbearingly affectionate towards his doppelganger that gaped back all googly-eyed. As usual, he carelessly swilled the pickle juice straight from the mouth of a slimy jar. His natural quaffing skills were lacking, and instead of getting most of the drink into his pot belly, it splashed and dribbled from his wide-open chops. The juice overflowed, splattering and staining the carpet with its smelly odor.

When Sampson, the second visitor, arrived, he sternly lectured Booney on the mess he was making. He advised the Frog to be more careful with food and drink to avoid the trouble of cleaning up afterward. But as always, Booney was too absorbed in his dreamscape fantasy to hear Sampson's momentary mentoring. For the Frog's inner-world sanctuary was a place where no one could enter without his express permission.

As one might expect, Sampson was never going to be permitted by the Frog. When Booney finally began to hear Sampson's obnoxious, unrelenting instructions, he did what he always did to escape the real world—and Sampson's lectures. He began to sing his own song, adopting a dreamy, lazy tone to drown out the tedious lectures he received. This was a long-standing habit of his, developed specifically to evade the Moose's persistent nagging.

The song worked like a charm. Sampson, whom Booney considered dimwitted, didn't notice the Frog's absentmindedness and continued his lecture, directly addressing a carefree and abstracted student. As Booney sang louder and louder, his voice competed with the booming thunder and Sampson's lecture. To the Frog, Sampson's words seemed like a meaningless waste of time rather than a serious lesson.

When Sampson finally realized that Booney was ignoring him, it was too late. The Frog was too engrossed in his own image and imaginary world to pay any attention. Sampson's attempt to refocus Booney's attention on his preaching failed. Frustrated, Sampson grumbled and growled in irritation. Booney's song, intended to provoke, had succeeded in making the grumpy Moose even more cantankerous.

"I haven't a care, Feeling happy and fair,

This whole world revolves 'round me Just me..

No, I haven't a care at all, Not at all.

And o', what a thrill! My worries are nill! I've time yet to kill!

For comfort and pleasure Without burden to bear,

No, I have not a care, Not at all

The sunshine is bright. I'm filled with delight.

With no such fright to be fearin'! I haven't a care,

Just merry cheer, Plenty a smiles! Plenty a laughs! To go 'round…

Let naff reign and not be ashame, In my cool chaff-chuffy style.

I am one to be…in mirthfully glee, My adventurous spirit a'roiled!

I have not the simplest care at all! No, not at all…

Comfort is easy.. Enjoyment is pleasey…

O' what be the most marvelous… bein alive. Alive, alive, ALIVE I DO CALL!

In a celebration.. Without cancellation..

This golden day spent napping Goodly knowing, I'm clappin'

I haven't a care… no nary a care here at'll!

Sampson, grouchy and utterly disgruntled by the speckled Frog's lack of responsibility, finally snapped. He confronted Booney, harshly bombarding the rascally Frog's resistance to his admonitions, abruptly pulling him out of his fantasy world and into the cold reality of the storm still raging outside. Booney, displeased by this intrusion, fought back with mocking and scornful witticisms, sparking a dispute. As Sampson preached, Booney derided him, the two of them bickering incessantly in one corner of the room.

Meanwhile, in the other corner nearest the doorway of the cottage, Wally and Whyles observed the tedious wrangling between the Moose and Frog. The discord between Whyles and Booney was also marked and relentless. What had once been a mere trifle had now burgeoned into a tempest of sharp exchanges and fierce confrontations. Whyles, plagued by paranoia and with a rough history of his own, was deeply unsettled by Booney's mocking remarks and irreverent behavior. The Frog's calculated jabs and sardonic quips constantly undermined his attempts to maintain a semblance of control and decorum.

The air frequently crackled with the tension of their encounters, each skirmish more biting than the last. Whyles would react with flares of irritation and mistrust, while Booney, clad in his conspicuous red velvet jacket, responded with a smug grin and cutting comments. It seemed that no effort could bridge their divide. Despite Wally's boundless patience and earnest goodwill, his attempts to mediate between the two and soothe their animosity met with little success. The enmity between Whyles and Booney was simply too entrenched to be quickly dissolved.

Yet, Whyles was not the same as when he first arrived in Ambrodale. He was no longer a stranger; he was quiet and rarely spoke but had found peace within himself. For the first time in a long while, his thoughts were secure, not scrambled. He had experienced something new in these past weeks—compassion. He had both received given such and now, no bitter thoughts were seeping into his sleep. Once filled with ghoulish nightmares, his nights were now as calm as a boat floating in the river. The dreadful memories of Kaliber, his underworld gang, and the terrifying Clovis Kaine seemed like nothing more than an appalling nightmare from which he had blessedly awoken.

His days in Ambrodale had been marked by hot, steaming vegetable soups and with an abundance of nourishing side dishes—meals far removed from the bloody, raw carnage laid out amongst ravenous savages. Whyles was no carnivore by any means, and the sight of such fare had always repulsed him. He had not visited the underground mound for ages and felt no concern about it. He was now considered part of the river country, something he would have never imagined happening. A distinct change had occurred for the better; a new and better life had begun, and Whyles had finally come to understand what had been lost to him before belonging.

There were no second thoughts for Kaliber and his crude company until the Fox's gaze was drawn to a sight outside that shattered his composure. Peering through the rain-streaked window, Whyles beheld a scene that struck him like a sudden and brutal blow. Miriam Quaddling, struggling through the tempest with great effort and visible pain, was fighting her way toward Wally's home. Her appearance was almost spectral, her form only discernible when the lightning rent the heavens, vanishing again into the misty downpour. Her frantic movements, coupled with her solitary state, were a shocking anomaly, for she was never seen apart from her sister.

The storm lashed around her as she waded through puddles, her resolve faltering. Whyles, seized by a paralyzing wave of guilt, watched with growing dismay. His heart pounded furiously, and his brow dampened with anxious sweat. The storm outside seemed to mirror the chaos within him; each clap of thunder echoed his mounting remorse, and the shadows cast by the storm grew menacing and distorted. This only served to amplify both his guilt and his despair.

His hard-won composure began to unravel. The storm, a timely reflection of his inner turmoil, intensified his dread and sense of failure. His breaths grew shallow, his mind a whirlpool of regret and helplessness, as though the storm itself were passing judgment on his soul.

At that crucial moment, Booney, finally breaking off his argument with Sampson, caught sight of the beleaguered Miriam. "O'ley Whompers!" he exclaimed in alarm. "Wally, is that not your fair Miriam battling the storm outside? Indeed, it must be! I dare say she looks absolutibbley wretched!"

Wally and the others were jolted into action by Booney's outcry. As they peered outside, Wally's initial shock gave way to a chilling realization. Miriam's solitary presence in the raging storm, when earlier she had been inseparable from her sister, was disturbing. A dreadful certainty weighed heavily upon him—something was terribly wrong.

Amid the rising turmoil, Whyles, overcome by a crushing wave of guilt and anxiety, retreated into the shadows. His mind churned in a turbulent whirlpool of remorse and despair, the weight of his guilt smothering any hope of solace or peace.

In a hurried scramble, Wally directed Sampson and Booney to help Miriam inside while he hastened to prepare a bed. His thoughts raced with mounting concern, the terrible awareness that something grievous had occurred, began gnawing at him.

Booney and Sampson rushed to the door. When they opened it, a strong gust of wind blew through, so powerfully that it knocked down the rattling pots and pans from Wally's shelves. The violent gale pushed the heavy rain into the cottage, extinguishing the glowing fire, leaving only traces of its warmth in the form of tiny sparks and glimmers of burning embers that quickly fizzled out. The rush of extreme air nearly lifted Booney off his webbed feet, but Sampson, with the quick reflexes of a seasoned catcher, grabbed the Frog just in time.

"You must be cautious, my little friend; this isn't a time to be a hero alone," the Moose sternly warned.

Booney huffed, maintaining his recalcitrant demeanor. "I didn't need any help, especially from an old codger like yourself! I would've been just fine without you, thunk you!"

"A fine way to show gratitude!" Sampson retorted.

"I ain't gratinfie! Who says I'm gratinfie?" Booney snapped nastily, demanding to go out first. He deliberately stomped on Sampson's hoof as he passed, but the Moose felt nothing. The stomp bounced back at Booney, causing him more pain than it did Sampson. Gripping his boater hat, Booney stamped in defiance as the Moose chuckled. Booney then rushed outdoors into the heart of the furious storm, waving at Miriam, who didn't respond. She had no strength left and suddenly collapsed into the muddy puddle she had been standing in.

If not for Booney, she would have made a splash like her basket. The Frog struggled to support her leaning weight, his webbed feet digging into the mud as he pitched himself at a 45-degree angle to keep her from toppling over. His skinny arms trembled under the burden, and he groaned loudly as he began to slip forward into the mud below.

Seeing Booney's predicament and admiring his bravery, Sampson lumbered forward, chuckling to himself as he sloshed through the wet, gloopy mud. He arrived just in time to relieve Booney of his burden. "I'll catch our Dearie now! Give it a rest, Booney," he said, and as the Frog let go, he slipped and fell into the puddle himself, cursing and blathering in the rattling rain, now covered in the icky mud.

Sampson positioned himself between Miriam and the muck. With one gentle sweep of his giant antlers, he lifted her onto his back, where she shivered in her sleep, bitterly cold. Sampson knocked on the door in three quick wraps, relieved when Wally opened it with a worried face. Wally quickly led them both inside and instructed Sampson to set Miriam down in the cozy bed he had prepared. Poor Miriam, still unconscious, faintly muttered about the Horkurs and the storm and called out for her sister, Adelia.

"Poor 'ittle love, she's had quite enough, I'm sure!" Sampson murmured as he gently placed Miriam's quivering body on the bed. Wally tenderly tucked her in afterward, but even as she lay comatose, Miriam looked insipid and continued to groan, tearfully mumbling broken, shaky sentences. "Poor ittle home, deeestroyed by—by s-s- 'orm! O' where are you, dear sister? 'Ose wicked Horkurs…"

Wally and Sampson exchanged a glance, connecting the pieces of Miriam's disjointed words. The poor Quaddling, infirm and oppressed, drew their whole-hearted pity. Yet, she wasn't the only one feeling the weight of oppression. Whyles, standing apart, twitched suddenly, harshly leering at the ailing Quaddling from a distance. Surrounded by trustworthy, compassionate friends, Miriam's forlorn state triggered something dark within him. He knew all too well what had happened, but with his prior orders, he remained silent, keeping the truth locked away. His mismatched eyes glinted with a menace as if preparing for a battle within his mind—a war he had fought many times before and had lost.

Whyles' consciousness wavered, retreating into a mire of depravity. The dreadful feeling consumed him as the maddening disorder clawed its way into his thoughts.

Clovis Kaine, that insidious fiend, bombarded Whyles' mind, penetrating his deepest fears. The Fox could feel Kaine's brute presence lingering within him, his mind going blank as it was shrouded by a nefarious force. Perhaps it was just a hallucination born from the terror of seeing Miriam alone, without Adelia.

But nevertheless, the terror was real. Kaine, with his possessive power, disarrayed Whyles' thoughts, replacing them with devilish schemes for the demise of all who stood in Lord Kaliber's way. Kaine's influence left a calling card, a reminder of his presence, as he snatched away Whyles' sanity and ran off with it. What could the Fox have done to resist this inevitable breakdown?

Clovis Kaine had captured Whyles' sanity, which was now the Fox's most treasured belonging. Clovis held it for ransom. Clovis also knew that without the strength of lucidity, Whyles would be entirely vulnerable. Without sanity, self-victimization and blind loyalty to those promising a solution would follow. Owning the Fox's sanity was a tremendous advantage for both Clovis and Kaliber. All Whyles could feel for the poor, half-dead Quaddling was begrudged acrimony, and who knew what had become of her sister, Adelia? Whyles himself was the key to her disappearance, but the key was rusty and told nothing of its master's secrets.

"Come, let's not disturb her rest. She's been through a lot today." Wally said softly. With that, both Sampson and Wally left the bedroom, leaving Miriam still muttering to herself, her deep, dry coughs and retches were agonizing to hear, as if she were choking. They all gathered around the fireplace, where Wally began to stoke the embers, gradually bringing light and warmth back into the room.

Whyles, however, did not flinch. He continued to gaze intensely at the ailing sister, the missing Adelia weighing heavily on his mind. A morbid expression began to alter his face, giving him an uncanny resemblance to a felon on the run, a criminal yet to be convicted. But as the flames from the burning logs climbed higher, the crackles seemed to call to him, and the dancing sparks mesmerized him. Drawn closer to the fire, his face lowered into an expression of mortification, fully forged by the horrors he could not escape.

The front door, left a.j.ar, slammed shut in fury as Booney marched in, disgruntled and carrying Miriam's wicker basket. With a burst of anger, he hurled it aside, his muddy face etched with frustration. The Frog, from his small head to his wiggling toes, was drenched in slimy mud, his red velvet jacket smeared with stains, his boater hat splattered with grime, and his face so heavily layered in wet, gloopy filth that it was barely visible. As expected, the Frog's arrival was met with loud, galling complaints. Booney, waving his arms irrationally, yelled and cursed despite Wally's pleas for quiet while Miriam rested. The Frog only laughed and complained even louder.

"Always seeking some kind of attention, aren't ye, Booney?" Grunted the Moose.

"O' do hush up, ye baggy CODGA! Can't you SEE this filth on me!? Absolutibbley revolting! Iiiiick! I feel all slimy and gross!" Contested the Frog nastily, a foul frown on his face.

"How awfully childish! I don't know why you're complaining about grubbiness. You eat like a slob, and what you eat is slimy at that!" The Moose commented cynically.

"MEEEE, CHILDISH? HAH! That's a laugh; if anyone is childish, it's YOU, leaving me in that mucky mudhole!"

"YOU WERE BOOOOOOORN IN A 'MUCKY MUDHOLE!!!" Chortled Sampson. With that, the zounderkite speckled Frog charged at the Moose with extreme choler. Springing around the Moose in circles, Booney put on his best-swinging boxer stance, fury radiating from him as he screamed insult after insult, even making up a few on the spot! "Take that back, ye ol' dastardly buffer! Ye, ye, ye CUMBERWORLD!!! Ye DORBEL!!! YE DRATE-POKE!!! Ye

YELLAFINKA! Ye cowardly STAAAAAAAMPCRRRRRAAAAAAB!!!" Running out of insults, the tongue-twister spouting-speckled Frog stopped to catch his breath, having tired himself out more quickly than he could spit out the words.

Now, it was Sampson's turn. The Moose began rolling out his own insults: "Unteachable FOPDOODLE! YOU rapscallion GOBERMOUCH!!! NOTHING MORE THAN A LOITER- SACK, LUBBERWORT, MUCK-SPOUT, RAGGABRASH, SCOBBERLOTCHER, SORNER, BOBOLYNE, QUISBY, LEASING-MONGER, KLAZOMANIAC WHIFFLE-

WHAFFLER!!!!" Alleged the Moose.

Booney, not to be outdone, impulsively proclaimed in a top stentorian volume, "Well, at least I'm no DEWBEATING, HONEYSUCKING, SADDLE-GEESING, BESPRAWLING SNOUTBANDING BIPPY!!!"

Before anything else acrimonious could be further vocalized, Wally intervened, imploring both of his friends to cease this useless slandering feud, calling it "a clash of words." After a somewhat awkward pause, he fervently suggested an idea neither could refuse: to tell stories to pass the time as the turbulent storm howled outside. Whyles, skittish as ever, jumped at the eerie howls, his thoughts solely on Kaliber.

They all settled down, awaiting Wally to begin. The Hare packed his pipe to the very top, dusting off the excess from the bowl. He sat in his reddish-brown velvet chair nearest the brightly glimmering fire. With one swipe, he lit his pipe, taking small, slow puffs. He enjoyed each drag of the thick, sharp, chocolatey smoke with its pacifying fragrance—a refreshing yet dense blend of woodsy fern and spicy citrus. Gazing deeply into the fire, he beamed a broad smile, ready to tell a story of his own.

And so, Wally began a fable about an orange cat named Strifer, who, to Sampson's private belief, bore an uncanny resemblance to Booney—perhaps too much similarity, he thought. Strifer was a rascally swindler who took great pleasure in stirring trouble for his friends, playing foolish tricks on them. But each day, as Strifer's pranks continued, he lost a friend. Strifer didn't much mind losing one friend; after all, he had many more to prank. But eventually, all his friends grew tired of Strifer's incessant ridiculing, and at the very end, Strifer found himself alone. The fable goes without saying: if you prod for attention with critical jests and take it too far, you may end up alone, with no one left to tell your tales to but yourself. Along with the story, Wally had composed a ballad—a ballad of Strifer, who, by misusing his amusement, gained nothing in the end but loneliness.

Ballad Of Strifer

There once was a cat named Strifer. In his sack was a rusty ol' knifer.

He cut, and he cut,

Whittling down the friends he had,

'Til his very last day, O' what a naughty cat,

O', what a naughty cat (was he)! There once was a cat named Strifer Causing so much trouble,

He fooled around, Upside down,

Fell anything in his way, On and on,

Oh, every day, Oh, every day,

He laughed, and he laughed, Rolling on the floor,

To see such pain and fear, O' he played his little games,

He played such little games! O' what a nasty cat,

O', what a nasty cat!

There once was a cat named Strifer By golly, was he a lifer!

From all his gags and tickle butts too, All his friends grew tired and blue,

All his friends, so blue,

One by one, and two by two, They shooed away early one day,

Such a sad, mewling cat left alone Hanging his head in shame,

Who hung his head in shame, Alone 'neath the shining moon.

Yet the moon, with its bright face,

Turned away, ignoring the lonely cat, It hid its face from him who had

Cut his life away, away, Cut his life away,

He cut his life away!

O' what a friendless cat was he, O' what a friendless cat…

By the story's end, the room fell into a heavy silence, with all exchanging glances, sensing the tension thickening among the listeners. Suddenly, a frantic squawking broke the quiet—it was Miriam, abruptly jolting back to life, screaming hoarsely as if her throat had been strained to its limit. Her head throbbed intensely, spinning more violently than before. Through her bleary, stinging eyes, she thought she saw Wally rushing to her aid, with Sampson lumbering in behind him. Panic surged within her; she feared it was all a hallucination, for everything around her appeared vaguely golden through her bloodshot, tear-filled eyes. Dizzy and disoriented, Miriam believed she had crossed into the afterlife and perished in the storm's fury.

She grew hysterical at this terrifying thought, crying out in delirium so hard that she began to gag from the uncontrollable sobbing. Wally tried desperately to calm her, but she only wailed pitifully, her voice trembling.

"Am I dead… are we all dead!?" She cried out, her face ghastly pale, as if it were a miracle she had survived nature's wrath.

"No, no, my dear, you're safe now," Wally reassured her, tenderly stroking her damp forehead, which was burning hot to the touch. "Everything is fine… you're in my home."

"Delly… Adelia… is she here?" Miriam's voice trembled as she asked.

Wally handed her a warm, steaming teacup. "Here, take some black currant feverfew tea. It's what you need right now."

"DELLY… D-D-D-E-E-LLY…" Miriam's voice cracked as Wally supported her back, bringing the cup to her chattering beak. She drank half of it in one gulp, then reclined back onto the bed, her fever beginning to subside. Wally murmured gently, "We don't know where Delly is. We thought she might have been with you. Do you remember what happened?"

Miriam's pale face grew even more ashen. She moaned weakly. "T-they took her…"

"Who took her?" Wally asked urgently, but Miriam's mind was a fog of confusion. She couldn't recall what had happened before the storm; it all felt like a bitter nightmare. The more she tried to remember, the more distressed she became. Suddenly, in a moment of clarity, she wailed, "Oh, how utterly awful it was! I can still see their horrible faces! They must've taken her! My poor sister, my sweet Delly, is gone!"

"Whose faces, Miriam? Please, try to remember!" Wally urged, but Miriam only cried louder, pulling the blankets over her head. After a moment, she bravely continued.

"Who else but the Horkurs! They came outt'a nowhere while we were mindin' our own business, pickin' the freshest berries. And let me tell ya, they're savages, they are!"

Sampson dismissed her claim quickly. "Outlandish," he called it. "No one's ever seen a Horkur, let alone spoken to one. It's all a myth." He suggested that perhaps her memory was playing tricks on her, but Miriam was deeply offended by his disbelief.

"It wasn't a delusion! Right, Adelia?" She said automatically, turning as if her sister was right there beside her. Realizing her mistake, her voice grew more insistent, "It's true! Undoubtedly true!" She spoke as if Adelia herself were confirming the story.

Wally begged Sampson to let Miriam continue, regardless of whether or not Adelia was missing. Whyles, upon hearing the mention of the Horkurs, stiffened. Miriam described them as massively fat, with black sticky ooze dripping from their greasy folds of flesh—vile creatures who were uncivilized and guilty of kidnapping, or as she called it, "ducknapping," her sister.

"The Horkurs, they are! Never in my life have I seen such fiends. Cruel they were, too. They wanted us to go with 'em, to have fun. Whatever that meant, we wanted no part of it. But then, I remember, they ran off after something... a 'houndie,' that's what they called it."

Whyles froze, every fiber in his lanky frame tightening. His stomach twisted in knots, and cold shivers raked down his spine. His legs, weak as boiled noodles, threatened to give way beneath him. Sweat trickled down his face, thoughts racing. 'Is it time to run? Should I vanish, leave no trace—alive or dead?' If Miriam remembered the Horkurs mentioning a fox and hounds... What then? Would he be accused? Punished?

"Whoever those Hounds were, they sounded horribly dastardly!" Miriam said, oblivious to Whyles' distress. As she continued, she described shadows following them and how, in her panic, she had run ahead of Adelia. When she reached Ambrodale, her sister was gone.

"It's all my fault... I should've slowed down for her," she cried. "They Horkurs must've taken her, Wallay. I know it. Why it's a sister's intuition!"

Sampson's brow furrowed as he remembered the instances of Riverfolk vanishing in the night, never to be seen again. "I'm not sure of that," he muttered giving a wary glance at Whyles.

Wally voiced his concern. "Things haven't been right lately... it's most certainly troubling."

Meanwhile, Whyles recoiled in the corner, twitching uncontrollably. His mismatched eyes flicked wildly, seeing faces from the past—specters he thought he'd buried long ago—now staring back at him with cold, unrelenting judgment.

His heart raced, pounding like war drums in his chest, and his fingers clawed at the floorboards, desperate to hold onto something real as his mind frayed. The room twisted and warped around him, the air thickening like a noose tightening around his neck. He gasped for breath, but his throat seized, strangling any sound, leaving him voiceless in his panic.

He wanted to scream, to break free, but nothing came. His voice, his strength— gone, locked inside a prison of his own making. His limbs curled in on themselves, folding into a pitiful ball as the shadows crept closer, stretching their long, spindly fingers toward him. They whispered the same damning refrain over and over, gnawing at what little was left of his sanity:

"It's all your fault… it's all your fault…"

"Oh dear, dear, oh, I do hope Delly is all right wherever she may be. I must find her, no matter what!" Miriam cried, her voice full of desperation.

"You mustn't find her right now!" Wally pleaded, trying to keep her calm. "I don't see why I can't go! She'd do the same for me! We haven't been parted since we left our Mumsie, and she said we'd take care of ourselves and entrusted Delly to keep watch over me. I hardly know why, considering I'm not the one lost! But a sister as close as we can't be left alone. It's not the CORRECT way! Lemme go; I must find her before something happens to her. And if anything at all happens to Delly, dear, I'd be to blame, and surely, more than ever, I'd be dead too. Without me, sister and all, there'd be nothing left. No fights, no baking treats, tasty or not! I must find her, I tell you, Wally!"

Miriam's fervent devotion to her sister was clear and earned her the respect of her friends. Whyles, watching her intense quest, wished he could reveal the truth. He knew Delly wasn't truly missing, but he felt unworthy to face the consequences alone. Despite his own fears, Wally continued to dissuade Miriam from undertaking a dangerous search in the worsening storm, promising to investigate her sister's disappearance once the storm passed.

"But please do tell me, Miriam, one last thing if you can?" "What is it?" Miriam asked.

"When I reach the Borderlands, how will I find the Horkurs?"

Miriam's face shifted from sickly pale to a dramatic shock of fear. The image of the hideous Horkurs, all beastly smiles, filled her with dread. "Oh, dear

Wally… they will find you in a matter of minutes. You don't have to look far, but if they capture you too, I couldn't help but just perish in my own wrongful guilt! You mustn't go; I must! It's my duty. We are flesh and blood! Delly means the world to me. She is my best friend and the only friend I have, but somehow, Wally, somehow, you mean much more than that. In another strange, funny way, I can hardly describe it without going red in the face!" She squawked, her voice quivering with emotion. Miriam's heartfelt confession was a revelation she could no longer keep hidden. If Adelia were here, she would have scolded her sister for such an admission, but Miriam had nothing left to lose. Her home was destroyed, her sister taken, and she couldn't hold back her feelings any longer.

With a soft whimper, Miriam took Wally's arm, and he gently wiped her tears away. Without hesitation, he placed a tender kiss on her forehead. Miriam's face flushed a deep red at the unexpected gesture. What seemed like a simple kiss to others was much more to Miriam.

Wally's kindness was a precious comfort she could no longer deny.

"Rest easy, Miriam. Things will be just fine. You can count on that!" Wally assured her with a warm smile.

Booney, witnessing the tender moment, made a playful gag and stuck out his tongue. "Oh, now I've seen everything—gross! Cooties and all. Let's get back to storytelling. I've got mine to share, and I'm sick of all this mushy stuff! I'm so glad to be free of this sappy drivel!" Booney quickly retreated to the fireplace, eager to share jovial stories.

Soon, the Fox, Sampson, and finally Wally joined Booney. The Frog greeted them with a mischievous grin. "Here comes the groom, unaware of his doom!" Booney teased.

Sampson added. "Let me tell you, you've caught my dastardly cooties. They'll make your life all topsy-turvy!"

"Watch it, old coot!" Wally retorted.

"And for what? Just to keep your wifey happy without a reward? Being tied down is the worst!" Booney boasted.

"That's because you're only interested in yourself. No one else is even bothered by you!" The Moose commented with a hearty laugh.

Booney cast a sideways glance at the Moose, who answered with a playful raspberry. The Frog, with his speckled green skin glistening in the firelight, stretched out his arms in a lazy, boastful sprawl. "I'm me own, aye! Not one to be shackled nor strung like a puppet. I roam free, do as I please, and if life be a song, then mine's a merry tune."

Whyles, seated by the fire, eyes fixed on the flames, said nothing at first. He let Booney's words hang in the air, like the smoke that curled upward, twisting and distorting in the night sky. The firelight flickered across his face, casting long shadows beneath his eyes.

"T'at must be a fine thing," he muttered at last, the words heavy, like stones dropped into a well. His mind wandered—no, fled—from the moment, to a place where peace might still exist, a quiet hill overlooking a wide valley, where he could stretch his legs and breathe without the weight of his sins clinging to him. But the vision dissolved, as it always did, under the looming specter of Clovis Kaine and the grin of Lord Kaliber, whose hands were stained with the freedom Whyles so craved. Freedom, but at what cost? A traitor's life, a turncoat's heart, a soul hollowed by the weight of betrayals too numerous to count.

"Freedom," Whyles said softly, "may be the cruelest joke of all."

Booney, lounging beside him, turned his head sharply, eyes glinting. "A joke, you say? Well, if it's a jest, I'm the only one laughin', it seems."

Whyles' gaze shifted from the fire, darkening. "Aye, laughin' like a fool who knows not what he's lost."

Booney sat up, his grin now more pointed, sharp with challenge. "And what've I lost, Fox? You speak as if you're some grand philosopher, when all you do is scowl and plot. Maybe you'd enjoy life more if you didn't bury yourself in miseries that ain't even yours to carry."

Whyles' eyes blazed, and he rose to his feet, his paws trembling with anger. "Ye think it so simple, don't ye? A wanderin' vagabond like ye, free to drink and dance while others rot in chains of their own makin'. Ye know nothin' of burden, Booney. Ye know nothin' of fate."

Booney, now standing too, met Whyles' fury with a shrug and a careless smile. "Ah, Whyles, all yer heavy thoughts have turned you bitter. Freedom's a thing to be taken, not lamented over like some lost love. If ye spent half the time actin' as ye do broodin', maybe ye'd have some joy left in that wretched heart of yours."

Whyles' voice dropped, low and dangerous. "And maybe ye've spent too long livin' in a dream, Frog. Freedom won't save ye when the wolves come knockin', nor will it mean a thing when the truth catches ye at last."

Booney's laughter rang out, sharp and mocking. "Truth? What truth's that, then? That you're nothin' but a pawn like the rest of us? I'd rather be a wanderer than chained to the likes of you, spinnin' yer webs and thinkin' ye're clever."

The fire crackled, and the two stood face to face, eyes locked, their words like knives, cutting deeper into the rivalry that bound them. The night grew increasingly tumultuous around them, the storm's fury intensifying as lightning slashed through the darkened sky. The stars, obscured by the roiling clouds, seemed indifferent to the conflict below, as if they watched from a distant, indifferent realm, their cold light swallowed by the tempest.

Miriam sat in the other room, snugly wrapped in a blanket, her cheeks still flushed with a hint of fever. What might have been perceived as a mere inconvenience—being confined to bed and attended to due to illness—had, in fact, transformed into a source of unexpected joy for her.

Despite the discomfort, she found herself delighting in the attentive care and concern lavished upon her. The fussing and nurturing she received, though once seen as a bother, now felt like a cherished indulgence. Miriam couldn't help but revel in the warmth and attention, feeling profoundly satisfied by the care that made her feel so valued and cherished.

"I certainilly 'ope I gets sick mo' ofen to get splendid trutments," she thought to herself, giggling. "I can get used to this; I can!" Despite her amusement, a sudden shift in her mood revealed a deeper concern. The reality of being alone, without her sister Adelia by her side, became painfully clear. She imagined how Adelia would have reacted to witnessing the kiss they had both dreamed of for years; Adelia would surely be furious and resentful, given her longing for such a gesture. Miriam's heart ached with the thought of her sister's absence, and though she felt somewhat comforted by the care she received, the loneliness began to overshadow her delight.

The harsh truth of Adelia's absence made the much-anticipated kiss seem like a distant memory. Miriam felt the weight of her sister's absence more keenly than ever. "If'n, only Delly, was here to see me now, if only," she mused wistfully.

"However, I do suppose she would be indeed frosted by it, so probably it's for the better she's not. How of'en can I get special single attention? It's usually Delly who gets mo' than me!" Despite her whimsical thoughts, Miriam was deeply unsettled by the solitude, a sensation she was entirely unaccustomed to. The storm raging outside mirrored the tumult within her, each crack of thunder amplifying her sense of abandonment.

As the storm reached its peak, the thunder boomed causing trepidation, Miriam screamed in fright. Wally, concerned, periodically checked on her, trying to offer reassurance. The storm seemed to embody the inner turmoil both Whyles and Miriam were experiencing, their shared demoralization reflected in its ferocity. Meanwhile, Booney, exhilarated by the storm's intensity, leaped up and exclaimed with enthusiasm.

"Terrifically fine bogey tale perfect for this here, sturm!"

"Well 'en, let us hear it t'en!" Encouraged the Hare. Whyles slinked by the corner, not too keen to hear a bogey story but unwilling to protest.

"Wit' me pleasure!" The speckled Frog enticed them all to gather nearer to the fireplace as he began his tale.

"This'n is e storay passed trough genermerations of me Wiggans kith an' kin, true it is too! Te gooey Bog Gubbler! Firstie spotted by me own greap grumpappy Wiggans. Yah, sees, the Gubbler is a fiendish devil, all slimy and gunky it is! Puffed up like a bag o' gas, with black dotties a'face an' ol'a' oily spidery legs 'n' all. Me grumpappy suun it a boggin as it be. It rose from the mire all mucky, lookin' like a lot of faerie lights in the mist... but as it floated closer to me grumpapps, it let out a hissing steam n'n' all... an' it don't have any lights at all... twas its eyes, lots and lots of loomy oiyes a glowin' like embers..."

As if on cue, a shrill gasp came from somewhere outside the room. The three in the room gasped as Booney himself shuddered. "'An' it gets a closer... an' closa... but papster couldn' nae see no mout an' all... just eyes, just black pinhole 'ittle bitty eyes all 'bout it, a-glowin' like coals in each globbly oiye! ...' he realized he was stuck, 'cause he knows no un ever saw this much before t'ey wus gonz. Me couragabus grumpappy gave it what for! So, he steels himself all hard and sucks deep on his ittle clay pipe, and what did he do but stick its burning bowl into the oiye nearest him. WEEELLL, the mucky Bog Gubbler lets out a hissin', and it shrinks to a flap like some misty ol' balloon. So, it shrinks, maybe even shrieks, but me papster is not moovin'. He figured the Bog Gubbler is a coward a hidin' self—alones in a swamp like t'at. He neva knew if it had A MOUT AFTER ALL, BUT HE KNEW IT WAS A HOMELY LITTLE GOBLIN

WITH NO BRAGGIN RIGHTS WHATEVER!!!" Booney let out a loud belch of his own, sounding like he had a lot of wind passing through his croaker. "An' it's shaped like… like a boggy glob, it is, wit' a glowin' yullaw antenniya stickin' on top of its hed! …And tun greenie oiyes or evun hirteen as I rucall—"

"I t'ot you said tis gubbler has all eyes, but now you says it just has thirteen? How's ye pap 'uppose to count them eyes in te dark if he was undee attack? It's a bunch of gubblery nonsense to me!" Sampson grumbled, seemingly unaware of how his antagonistic tone contrasted with the Frog's own boisterous demeanor.

Both of them were projecting their habitual provocations. That much was easy for Wally to elicit. The Frog then further blurted out, "you ol' nitpicky bruin, 'tis me kin's storay telled to me- by-me Wiggan Papster, and if'n ter's errors in te tullin' it don't mean it t'aint troot!"

"Hmph, I still t'inks it's a lud of blarney!" Said the unconvinced Moose.

"T'ink whut ye wunt! Yeh's simply naff. Yer a boggler in yer own right!" the Frog shot back at Sampson.

"Keep yer pointless tales to yerself, ye barmy plonker!" Sampson bellowed back in obloquy.

Wally, wanting to restore order, intervened as he always did, bringing along a well-composed negotiation. "Come now, fellers, where is your manners? Poor Miriam is sick and is resting in the other room. She does not need to hear us bicker! Surely, we can continue on with an argument later if we must. But now is not the time! Can't we all agree?" Wally voiced in reasonable terms.

"Very wull," Sampson grumbled, agreeing not to bicker—for the time being. In contrast to Sampson's acceptance, the Frog merely smirked.

"Bickering? Who's bickerin'? T'is moraloizin' galoot is more frightening wit' 'ull his grumbling t'en me wit' me own bogey storay! And I certaintitty ain't gunna fintish it neither…not witout an apology t'at is!" Booney snickered, desiring some sort of self-gratification.

"Apologize? Apologize? For what, may I ask?" protested the obdurate Moose in his mulish pout.

"If you would, Sampson, it would be most, most appreciated!" suggested Wally, always the peacemaker. Booney thanked him, yet Sampson still continued to grumble. "Apologize... hmph apologize, how utterly humiliating! How intolerable, how ignorant, how bullheaded!" Sampson proclaimed, and he was most certainly right! Booney waited tensely to hear the Moose's apology. "And it must be sincere!" Added the hotheaded Frog, his hand cupped to his ears.

"I don't heeeeeeeeeear 'unytin!" Booney retorted curtly. Booney was ceaselessly pressing "sincerity" as being of great importance, toying with Sampson's sagaciously strong-willed and cantankerously unyielding and wounded belligerence.

"A'right, a'right, Booney Wiggans! I sincerely apologize for listening to ye foolhardy tale and actually payin' attention... tryin' to savvy such an uninspired tale... and futermore I am wholly sorry for ever knowing such a chuffer bumpkin!" Snapped the Moose without the slightest remorse or hesitation. Booney was not in the least clever enough to fully understand the judicious and torpid Moose's witty remark, which seemed to go right over and beyond Booney's smug lack of discernment.

The excitable speckled Frog went about continuing to describe the Gubbler with silly gestures and lusty calls; the howling eerie wind made sure the story Booney was telling came to a sort of reality as torrential precipitation abraded and whipped across the little home. The dwelling was abruptly shaken by the hammering rain, which sounded like unending rattling gunfire, scaring not only the three listeners but also the storyteller each time they heard these strange sounds.

Booney would yelp in unrestrainable fright with his stammering and excitable panic. Booney hopped straight up, startled by each effect the storm had brought, banging his head on a copper bed warmer and falling fat on his bottom, tipping over an urn of gathered sticks rolling across the hearth; what was even worse, the candle sticks suddenly extinguished. Booney exclaimed that they went out on their own! Luckily, the fireplace was still burning, and the room had enough light to see. With a rush of adrenaline, he continued to tell his tale through his excellent talent for shadow puppetry. "Now the legend has it t'at this Gubbler lures unexpected travelers into its own swampy domain by its long and terribibble babyish-like screech. "ka.j.oooooooooohooo." The wind then suddenly echoed the Frog's screech, propelling the already neurotic Frog into a frenzied tizzy, "Whun it spots t'ey victum, it emerges from its moocky hiding 'ole, a master of disguise it is! While the poor victum is a' searchin' for a way out since t'is crature got 'em los' in t'ey firs' place! It AMBUSHES 'em frum behind, snaggin' the sucka' wid' it's spidery legs as far as it can stretch 'em and drags 'em down deep into the moosh where t'ey is nevah seeney again-"

Sampson, now hearing enough of this "preposterous tale," was highly doubtful of the sworn veracity of the tale spoken by the narrator. Rather, he interjected scientific logic into the preposterously unverifiable subject matter. "How utterly absurd! This outlandishly fopperous bogey tale is nuttin' more than a farcical whopper solely founded on droll debauchery! Tut-tut, don't goad my good intelligence for such an indecent, unethical display of ignorance of low and insubstantial morality!" Sampson pronounced. All the while, he asked the Frog if there was any proof of this here creature called "The Gubbler." Booney, quite annoyed by this common query, nastily replied, "HUSH UP! No 'un 'as ye' scientiffy piffly belieffy! listun, an' listun wull, ye Ol' piffer! Ye insult me! Me proof is in me words, you ol' GAFFER! Me Wiggan papster wud nuvah loi. He has always been a most uprightibibble, respecabibble an' 'ut mure unimpeachibibble fellar evah t'ere was!!!" Yelled the frazzled Frog. "God rest his ol' bones an' pure soul! Besides, he had evah te mark of te Gubbler on his right leg. T'was a large red splotchy, not doubtabee frum his bruve rumpypus wit' none otha t'an ey Gubbler!"

Sampson just chuckled, "I'll tell yer an actual fable wit' virtue embedded isn't and not sum flippant and improper fib to while away the hours to make a cheap senseless thrill. Mine will be equally enjoyable and, in addition, add a bit of knowledgeable enlightenment. Sumtin' you can't provide, me fruggy frund, puffed up wit' your stories of ribald nonnysense! If yer granpappy told ya such te dribbling stories ye jus' told while you were a mere taddy, 'tis no wonder why ye turned out the way ye did! Sampson declared. Just before retreating to the enveloping darkness, the Frog sulked in the corner like a shadowed specter. In a fit of scornful retaliation, he whirled towards the Moose, who regarded the scene with an air of amused detachment. The Frog's wild, spinning strikes missed their mark with every desperate swing, his movements becoming increasingly frantic and erratic. Finally, with a wearied and dizzy collapse, he fell to the ground, the wet thud echoing his defeated and disoriented state. Ol' Sampson cleared his gruff and itchy throat and began to recite his allegory.

"Once t'er wus a 'rabblerousing slicker Wusel who wus always 'ungry an-"

Booney then interrupted, asking a trivial question about this certain "Slicker Weasel," why he was always hungry, and where he came from. "I wus' jus' 'bout 'ady to get to t'at ye pestery bungler! Neow sit tight 'efore I muss crown ye for ye squirrelly shenanigans!" Moaned the Moose in agitation from Booney's lack of forbearance. Booney only laughed and kept asking even more questions. A friendly, sporting match of insult-endurance between the two commenced as they had been so accustomed when they habitually attempted to outdo each other.

"Don't mind him, Sampson, go on with ye storay! O' how I do so want to hear it!" Wally kindly intervened. Sampson thanked the Hare while Booney crossed his arms and legs.

"Now tis 'ere Slicker- Wusel wus always 'ungry because he wus always grookin' for a free mealsey fare. 'E' never worked for it, mind you! A common, crass swindler!"

"Well, I find t'at very admiribibble!" The Frog wholeheartedly announced. Booney went on applauding, though, with almost aggrieved feelings towards the Moose's scrutiny of this certain Weasel. The Frog fwas not crass in the least this time but rather deftly quick-witted and clever. "Well'n if he's a such a crassy 'un like'n you say'n, how can he fools all 'a' rest!?"

With this question brought up by the questioning Frog, Ol' Sampson appeared stumped in a moment of awkward silence. Sampson stammered, much to his own chagrin. He replied, "There is no clear answer! In fact, what difference does it make? It just is what is!" The Moose hastily declared. "Oooh hooo hoo' It doesn't sound too promising, you ol' codga'! Now, does it? I mean to be outsmarted by a mere crass Weasel! Actuality-wise, 'e sounds most cleva' and all 'eh rest sounds crass." Replied the smirking Frog.

"You misunderstand me, ye' slime ball! What I means to say was, he was always hungry because he nevah could nay outsmart any, so he was always 'hungry because he was nevah lucky with his swindles. In fact, it caused him a lot of trouble; it did! Like that time, he tried to catch a 'little, bitterly Crayfish! T'at poor Wusel had it comin', he did!" Sampson bellowed.

Intrigued by what indeed happened to the crafty Weasel and Crayfish, Wally urged the Moose to keep on telling his story. Ignoring the speckled Frog's moaning, groaning, pouting, and complaining of how 'dull and tasteless' the story was, Wally continued to pester the Moose, pleading with him to continue. Clearing his throat with a sonorous grumble, Sampson began to tell of the tale of the Weasel and the Crayfish. "Well 'en this Slicker- Wusel was on the hunt for sum quick grub an' he sputted a small Crayfish stuck in-between some little rocks an-"

Booney, who was wheezily napping in a hoaxing, slumberly – ruse in his cheeky grin, commenced to snore loudly, interrupting the progress of the story. Booney was snoring so loud, in fact, a sickly green booger bubble began to form on his tiny puffing nostrils.

Sampson falling for Booney's deliberately galling provocation worked its iniquitous magic; fooled by the Frog's sneaky trick, the saggy Moose, quick in anger, hollered in strict discipline, awakening the already awoken Frog, who sprang in surprise. In his failing effort to maintain deferential conduct towards the frivolous Frog and the rest, Sampson's yelling grew louder in his chiding manner. The Frog countered with railleries as loud as the blustery storm itself. The little home shook, though it was unclear whether the tremors were caused by the tetchy Moose's fierce vociferations or the fierce blustering gale demanding an unwelcoming ingress, as the bedeviling tempest battered in ultimatum with a pernicious warning.

In any case, amidst all the pandemonium, poor Miriam was absolutely terrified by the sounds, which to her in her hysteria, awfully resembled the terrible bellows of the Horkurs. With the shadows cast upon the walls, she tearfully absorbed the chaos and began to cry, shrilling for mercy: "T'er comin fo' me, t'er comin! Poor Delly been taken, away, away, gone for good an' I'ma next! Get out, ye brutes! Don't take me—I've done nothing wrong, NOTHIN! Get ooooooouuuuut, pleeeeeeeeeease, please, poor Delly…"

All four overheard the mournful wail of the Quaddling sister, and Wally, now stern in his care for Miriam's wellness, recognized her distress was already critical and in dire need of self- restoration.

"I have heard enough of this; Ye both shud be very ashamed of ye selves!!!! Having no consideration for poor Miriam, who must I remind already in grief, she doesn't need to hear us fight! Sampson, you, a teacher in your trade, should know betta not to be so easily upset by simple immature silliness, and by golly,

Booney, why would you keep on bugging Sampson? You know all too wull it upsets him so? Now, friends, I do not mind all that much breaking up arguments, but time and time and time again, I must keep bringing order when things get outta hand, and now we have sick company who is in desperate need of rest! In no way is this the right time to have yet another time-wasting bicker... save your needy bickering for later! But right now, is not the time! Now, if we can presume to tell stories without any more trouble, it would be much appreciated for the sake of Miriam's well-being! Said Wally, scolding the Moose and Frog, bringing sensible order to the mayhem. Sampson, shamefaced, felt wholly responsible.

Hearing the distress of Miriam's withering call, Whyles slipped away from the three friends who finally coming to an agreement. The Fox gingerly snuck to where Miriam was resting, treading with extreme prudence. The door creaked open, and Whyles cautiously skulked into the room that was alternately cold and dry then humid, and altogether steamy. The room was faintly illuminated by a low, dimming candlelight next to the bed that was fading very quickly. Miriam, wrapped tightly in her blankets, stared tearfully at the wall above her head, her eyes swollen and red from relentless crying. Small leaks in the wall allowed raindrops to sprinkle onto her beak. Each drop, a cold reminder of her discomfort. The bleakness of the storm outside seemed to deepen her sorrow.

Whyles, in stark contrast, wore an expression of deep, unsettling guilt. His face, usually sharp and keen, was now drawn and pale, marked by a look of profound torment. Seeing Miriam in her state of distress—shivering under the weight of her misery—was a heavy blow to him. The realization that he was the cause of her suffering compounded his feelings of remorse. He felt a deep sense of responsibility for her plight.

Attempting to avoid further confrontation with the ailing sister, Whyles tried to slip away into the shadows of the room. But he was caught off guard by a heart-wrenching question from Miriam. The question, full of raw, desperate emotion, sent a chill down his spine and broke through any remaining resistance he had. It was a moment of intense vulnerability for Whyles, exposing the full impact of his guilt and the weight of his actions.

"Is at you dear, dear, Delly? Where you b-b-b been?" She half croaking whispered in a sanguine tone. Now alert from her sudden awareness of the Fox's presence, Whyles stopped dead in his tracks, turned, and approached Miriam, who drowsily lounged severely, wheezing and hacking a congested lung with labored breathing as she agonizingly lay, awaiting an answer. Whyles, kneeling beside her, instinctively laid his roughly pitted callused paw gently on her moist wing, drooping off the bed that flinched at first touch.

"Im sooray, but it is not." Whyles regrettably denied her simple, innocent request, and his heart sank when he heard Miriam dolefully whimper; Whyles could no longer hide his tears and had started to sob and how those tears had stung. "I'm sooray, im soo very sooray for every t'in…"

"Sorry? Sorry for what?" Asked Miriam, "I'm t'a un who's sick!" Whyles didn't say anything, avoiding asking that certain question. "I'll fix it; I swear, somehow, I'll fix everything! I'll make everything right," the soft-spoken Fox vowed. "Tell me what 'wud ye say ta your sister if I were to relay a message to her?" Miriam wondered briefly, then exclaimed, "I would most certainly ask if'n she is comfortable and safe wherever she may be! You wouldn't 'appen te know wherever she certainly is?" The ears of Whyles sprung up. "I may... but I can't say nuttin' more!"

Drifting off to sleep once again, Miriam thanked him and soon departed to the land of dreams. Whyles cautiously pussyfooted away from the steaming dark room, trying to avoid waking or rather starling the sleeping sister to consciousness. Returning to hear more stories but not without grabbing a sweet bun from Wally's pantry first to make it seem less conspicuous, to Whyles's surprise, his transient disappearance was gone unnoticed by the three friends; thinking of Miriam and his promise, he took a large vigorous bite from the bun. His decision to seek out for Adelia on his own was final, wistfully he knew exactly where she would be locked up.

"Now, if'n eveyt'in' is settled, Sampson, please go on." Wally granted permission to the Moose, and the Frog, about to interrupt, was for once shot down by the Hare; Booney turned around, facing his back towards them all, hearing the Moose start to tell his unfinished tale, the Frog, like a mime, started to mock the Moose with his shadowing puppet handwork. "Now, where was I? Ah yes, I rumember!"

"Wish ye didn't ye oaf…" Booney, rolling his eyes, spitefully scoffed once again, being hushed by Wally. Booney agitatedly snorted and stuck his tongue out, then went back to play with his shadow puppets with wounded sniffling, defining his dispirited feeling.

"So dis 'abbleousing slicker Weasel was out for ey hunt searchin for a meel, an' when he spotted te ittle Crayfish trapped in between two rocks by t'e side of a riva, the Wusel jumped for joy in such a sight for he huden't eaten anytun' in days, Appruchin' the cray, who started to panic more when he saw the slicker lungin' toward him wit' eager eyes an' a wide smile and a grumbling tum tum. 'You lookie mighty scrumdidyumptious for I haven't eaten in such an 'ery looong time, anytun' looks appytizin'! An' so the Crayfish wit' nuttin to do to stop the Wusel from eating him pleaded with the Weasel to let him go free if there was a little gamble first and if the Crayfish one the Wusel would let him go. The Wusel was fonding of gambles and surly tought he wud certainly win and so he agreed to Crayfish's gamble."

"What did t'ey bet on?" Asked Wally.

"Ah, a very good question indeed!" Sampson said, clearing his throat once more.

"The 'ittle Crayfish had bet if'n the Slicker Wusel could lift the rock why'd he'd be his to munch 'on, an' so to ay Wusel it seemed quite easy 'nuff. So, The Wusel grabbed the rocks by his two paws, and whun he was 'bout to drop eir te 'ittle Crayfish jumped out of 'ey water and pinched the slicker on his nose, not letting go, squeezing it toight he did, till the Wusel's nose was al red an' whun t' Wusel tried to snatch the Crayfish off his nose,' he dropped the heavy stone on his foot! While t' Wusel was yelping in his pain, holding his footy, hopping on one foot why the Crayfish released himself and leapt back into the water. He was givin' a good splash of water on the Slicker Wusel before swuimin' away!" Sampson now finished his tale asked his audience "now what ave we lurned 'bout t' Slicker and the 'Ittle Crayfishie?"

Booney, just started to shout crudely when Sampson interrupted the bouncing speckled Frog, quoting:

"Ye cannot be heard without raisin' ye hand. First, it is simple and only fair; everyone must have a turn!" The Moose clarified; Booney, agitated by the interruption, thrust his spindly arm high in the air and stood on his tippy toes. Sampson, ignoring the speckled Frog, briefly asked anyone else for their answer. "C'mon c'mon you, ol windbag, ye are purposefully snubbing me, and that un't very nice, no it ain't!"

"Hush ye dingbat Fruggy, I sees ya', I ain't snubbing! But ye must learn patience if ye eva' want to be well-liked, why it's only for common respect and not to be rude!" Booney disregarded the Moose's practical counseling, the Frog huffed:

"Well'in, I tell ya' un' most needs patience for his blarney yarning! But I tell yaw wut I've lurned!"

"May so then, what have you learned!?" Replied the Moose. There came a loud hysterical laugh from the Frog, upsetting Sampson.

"I've learned absolutibbly nuttin', nuttin' at all, w'ut a tale, tale of jejunity, of bigotry, says the Weasel had it comting, the Ittle Bitty Fishie had it comting whun he got stuck in 'ey rocks! The Wusel was ungry like any other and so a quick bite indeed! Ye story can onla entertain the deaf! Why's, in fact, ye wuden't evun know if or whun a good storay came and bit ye, or even how to tell it propibibbly!" Rejoinder the laughing Frog; Sampson made the wisest choice and did not bother to enter Booney's spoken lure into another fight, yet Sampson most correctly phrased with proud credence:

"At least you tried me, Fruggy friend! That I give credit for!"

Whyles carefully analyzed the tale as told, thinking hard and clearly. Whyles was very sure he had come up with a possible answer; he raised his frail paw. Whyles said, "I think I got a fine answer, if'n ye don't mind me saying it t'at is!" The Fox shyly mentioned while hunching in the corner. At first, he was hesitant and kept raising and lowering his twitchy arm, being very unsure of himself. He kept stuttering as he went on mumbling in a jittery fashion to himself. Ever a friend to all, Wally charmingly voiced in and motivated him to speak, saying to Whyles that there was no wrong answer for its all up to the listener to decide what it meant. Sampson, along with the Hare, invited the Fox to speak plainly what he thought, both were intrigued by what Whyles might have to say. The topic that would proceed was as follows.

"Well'in, I t'inks 'ey Weasel wus so full of heself he cud do anytin' he so pleased, witout bein' questioned t'at is because- bec-" Whyles faltered, his voice trailing off into extreme reticence. He lost his confidence and his train of thought, departed, his mind went blank. He struggled to find the right words, perhaps overwhelmed by the crashing storm outside. His speech began to slur, becoming incomprehensible.

Offered assistance from Sampson, Whyles kindly refused, desperate to express what he needed to say. The experience was new to him, complicated and challenging. His mind was foggy, and though he wanted to articulate his thoughts, the words stubbornly twisted on his tongue, refusing to come out clearly.

"Wull wut I maen te say is, t'e Weasel wus... wus." Then it clicked, and the words magically untied and rolled themselves out: "T'is Weasel wus blinded by his uwn past accomplishiemunts he got ahud of heself and made action before tuat!" Whyles proclaimed, visibly proud of himself. He gleamed with an uncharacteristically whimsical, almost cheeky smile so broad and vaguely formed that with his squinting eyes, his wide face appeared flatter somehow. The effect produced a kind of strained look on Whyles' face. It appeared as if his facial muscles, which had atrophied from long disuse, created a strained look. It was the first smile any of them had seen from the embattled chap. Why, they HAD all thought the Fox didn't even know how to smile; oddly enough, it was quite an awkward one, a gummy smile showing his infected canines that were sickly coated with yellow slime, not having ever been well-cleansed. The ol' Moose laughed jovially and then congratulated the Fox on his theory. Sampson then further explained that the morale of the tale was "If'n ye t'ink n' act such like ye are smarter than anyone else, you'll be dead wrong because t'er always be smarter fellows that yeself. Most importantly, if'n ye dare challenge t'em wit'out knowin' it, you just might get ye nose tweaked by ye cockiness by meddling in sum'un's affairs t'at don't t'at all concern ye!"

Booney, now tired of hearing Sampson and his morale tale, which to the speckled Frog was a fruitless attempt at storytelling, brashly intervened:

"Where'd you dig up that drab and drull tale, ye ol' dullard, ye tell tales of stodgy principibbles? A crub tuller a' loosey words manin naoght! Boshh it all!"

"At least mine tell it all in a cordial and appropriate setting; it ain't unethical and amoral!" Both Frog and Moose expressed their views about how stories should be told. Sampson thought it best that a story of purpose aught to have a lesson in it. Booney didn't second the notion as his own credo was that stories are solely meant to entertain the audience and not put them asleep. Rather it aught to awaken them with marvels and dangers! Both were exclusively committed to their own belief; they didn't even think logically that stories could work both ways if told properly!

"Wull, anyway, since ye story was very good at putting me to sleep, I may as well awaken every one of ye up with another fine bogey tale, again passed tru me Wiggan kin!"

"And what may t'is marvelous Wiggan tale be entitled?"

"Ta Mush Mooga!" Booney proudly announced. Sampson, already expecting another flop of an immoral fool of a tale, snorted loudly as he loathed such a telling again. He deemed it unnecessary for the story to be told.

"And why can't it be told!? I'd like to knows."

"Because it has no purpose involved, without logic, such a story would be false and flawed, besides t'er's enough mugging out and about, there is no need to be flapping about wit one of ye drawling purposeless yarns! T'er has been too many mugginses happening lately!" Sampson claimed on behalf of poor Miriam and her dilemma of her missing sister and the other folk; Booney protested against Sampson's statement and claimed the Moose had put his story on trial with no jury.

"To vote for my story or not!? That is what I ask!" the outcome of the vote among the friends was against it; all agreed but Booney, who was shocked that they declined the telling,

"Not the right time, Boone." Said the Hare. The speckled Frog huffed and nastily declared: "Wells, I'm tellin' it anyway!"

"Oooooooh, no ye wunt!"

"Ay yes, I ca-" But just before Boone could say another word, Whyles voiced sheepishly, "If I may, can I tell a story? I haven't told any yet, and I do so love stories, hearing all the thrilling tales, I would so love to share mine!" Wally and Sampson supported the Fox and waited to hear it, unlike Booney, who groused in resentful antipathy. "Well, let me see here, I ain't too good at tellin' un, but I will try me best!" Whyles said, bashfully expressive.

"I'm sure it'll be just splendid; please just go on!" Wally cheerily chuckled; with a warmhearted reception, the Fox, in jitters, began to tell his tale timidly.

"Well, it goes like—" Whyles began to slur again. With all the attentive eyes on him, he grew increasingly uncomfortable and fidgety.

"A wee bit nervous, are we!?" Booney snickered arrogantly.

"Just a wee bit!" replied the Fox, his head downcast and eyes fixed on the carpet as he kicked at it in frustration.

"Serves ye right, interrupting such a fine storyteller as me. An amateur mistake!" The Frog declared coolly.

At this, Booney was sharply slapped on the back of the head by Sampson's hoof, accompanied by an irritated glare from Wally.

The Fox, flustered in thought, replied, "I'm very sooray; I don't know whut got into me; I just guess I got carried away for a moment! Wun't huppen again." Whyles, once again withdrawn himself and chokingly excused himself from his story, closed his narrowed eyes and rose, briefly staring at the hearth. Now hunched over, he gawkily strutted toward the pantry. He took a mouthful of another sweet bun. At the same time, both Sampson and Wally scolded the Frog's insensitivity; Whyles peered through Miriam's doorway, where she still lay wheezing. Whyles then joined the three friends who were in the process of scolding Booney.

Booney puffed out his chest defensively. "Hey now, I was just speaking my mind. No need to get all worked up."

Whyles glared at him. "Speaking your mind? Ye been nothing but a troublemaker. Ye done nothing but disrupt our storytelling and turned it into a farce."

The Hare added, "We're trying to focus on the tale, and your antics are making it impossible." Booney's bravado faltered under their combined rebuke. "Alright, alright. I get it."

As the storm outside raged with relentless fury, the room fell into a tense silence, broken only by the harsh sounds of the tempest and the crackling of the fireplace. Whyles, taking a deep breath, cleared his raspy throat. He loosened the red tie from his rough, raw-boned neck and prepared to continue his tale, determined to keep the story on track despite the chaotic atmosphere.

"Wull, it seems like it all started some time ago! And so it starts like this..." Whyles began, his voice quivering with a blend of anxiety and determination. "T'er was a tiny hamlet 'neath the blue skies and on the corner to the mysterious woods. There were peoples that lived there, good folk, for they cared for one another."

As he spoke, Whyles' face took on a troubled expression. "But over the fen, over the happy grounds t'er in t'e scary borders, where the bad people dwell... t-t-t-t'er's sum that doesn't anything good happening. They hunger fo' power an' riches no matter the cost. T'ey... t'ey..." Whyles shuddered, his voice faltering. "T'ey harm... t'ey, t'ey punish for wealth and respect, abuse their loyal followers, t'ey do! T'ey think they deserve a slice of the good life as this place does, I mean the h-h-h-hamlet, so t'ey take it for their own, t'ey ruin it!"

The group sat in rapt attention, eyes fixed on the Fox whose eyes glowed eerily in the firelight. Booney, however, was visibly uninterested, his Frog head resting on his slimy palm. He yawned exaggeratedly, kicked his legs with childish impatience, and bounced his feet as if he were a toddler. Whyles was clearly longing for distraction from the storm raging outside. If not for the tempest, he would have happily hopped off to his log home or Phenny's pub for a drink and some more mischief.

Suddenly, a blinding flash of lightning jolted Booney from his daydream. At the same moment, Whyles, in a fit of tearful frustration, shouted out to the Frog, his voice trembling with emotion. The deafening crash of thunder accompanied his outburst.

"I KNOW I'M NOT A GOOD STORAYTELLA, BUT DON'T LOOK AT ME LIKE THAT!"

Whyles cried out, his voice cracking. "I DON'T KNOW HOW TO SPEAK BEFORE OTHERS LIKE YESELVES, good folk an' all. I'm doin' t'e best I can! The very best!"

He scanned the room, his gaze particularly harsh on Booney, who recoiled at the Fox's unanticipated fury. Booney, stunned, quickly pulled his head into his patched jacket and placed his boater hat atop, hiding his face but peeking through the small opening where the buttons went.

Whyles, now visibly agitated, lashed out defensively as Wally tried to calm him. His mind, a storm of its own, was plagued by hissing voices, jumbling and incoherent, further fueling his disoriented rage.

"Sees whatcha' did 'ere ye bumpkin… muddle things up as ye always do! Can't ye ever keep ye trap shut even if ye knows what good for ye!? How very shameful ye gormless gobermouch!" Sampson chided the shrinking Frog.

"Why don't nobody eva' listen to what I'm gets to say? I'm just a looney I am! N-n-ne-nev-nev- never has any'un 'eard my soray… I sits in 'eys cornah watching, learndin', but never bein' able to join in as I sees the fun." Whyles wistfully bleated, his voice wavering, though something in his eyes hinted at a longing he dared not voice.

"Come now, Whyles," Wally said with gentle insistence. "You're among friends here."

The word "friends" seemed to unsettle Whyles, but not in the way it usually did. His fingers twitched as if wanting to reach out but instead tightened on his tie. He glanced up with confusion and discomfort, masking something softer beneath his defensiveness. "Friends? I never needed any, and I still don't want any."

The room fell into a moment of tense silence, the storm outside howling as though it echoed the storm within Whyles. His eyes darted nervously from one face to another, as if half-expecting them to turn away in disappointment—but a part of him wished they wouldn't.

Wally smiled gently. "We're all in this together, Whyles. You don't have to be alone anymore."

Whyles shook his head sharply, his throat tight. "No, no, ye don't understand. I've managed just fine on me own. Friends—why would I need 'em? I'm used to bein' alone." But even as he spoke, there was a flicker of hesitation, like he didn't believe the words as much as he used to.

Booney snorted, breaking the tension. "See? Even he's not falling for this whole friendship charade. It's all a load of nonsense." But behind his mockery, Booney gave Whyles a quick, almost imperceptible glance, as if testing the waters.

Sampson cut in with a sharp look at Booney before turning back to Whyles. "Booney's just being his usual self. We're not forcing anything on you, mate. We just want you to feel welcome."

Whyles's eyes softened for a brief moment, but the shift was fleeting. "Welcome? It's all strange, this talk—" He hesitated, almost wanting to say more, to reach out, but fear got the better of him. He gripped his tie, holding himself back.

Wally nodded, his voice calm and reassuring. "You don't have to give more than you're ready to. But we're here."

Booney rolled his eyes, clearly unimpressed. "Yus, yus. Let's move on, shall we? This whole emotional scene is getting tiresome."

Whyles let out a breath he didn't realize he was holding, his heart aching at the offer of connection he wasn't quite ready to accept. But, for the first time, maybe—just maybe—he didn't hate the idea of friends as much as he pretended.

As the storm outside continued its relentless assault, the crackling fire inside seemed almost to reflect the inner turmoil of Whyles. The Fox stared into the flames, lost in thought, his mind wrestling with the uncomfortable notion of companionship that he had long resisted. The room's warm light and the storm's cold fury created a discordant backdrop to his inner conflict, highlighting the stark contrast between the comfort of the hearth and the isolation he so fiercely clung to.

"Well...if'n there good uns, yes there's bad uns too. They're bad, so they're all sittin' and plottin' and thinkin' and torturing and thinking and thinkin' 'bout what they can 'ave that ain't there's by any rights—no claim for them to take WHAT THEY NEVAH EARNED AT ALL. Just sittin' there greedy... eatin' …hittin'… swearing doom on the innocents, never harmed no un. Nevah could…"

By now, Whyles had entered a kind of personal delirium. Everyone noticed Whyle's eyes had grown fixated on the hearth. His eyes glowed, one eye red, one eye green as they did in the sunshine. He went on.

"If'n a body knows the good 'uns don't have a chance to win, he could go mad ...if he .. if he… if heeeee-"

"If he what, Whyles?" Sampson asked in a deep, resonant voice that filled the room.

"If heeee…heeee…. L-l-l-l-lo…" Whyles could not continue. He broke into a muffled sob and cradled his maw in his arms. "I HEEEE…. L-L-L-L-LIIIKED 'EMS….. ALL!!!" "Aaaaalll!" He repeated softly through his dazed tears. "If he liked them's all…."

"It's alright, Whyles. It's only a story. We understand that there is something that cannot always be told easily," Wally said, somewhat frightened by Whyles' current state of mind. He put his paws on Whyles' shoulder, and Whyles instinctively jumped. Whyles continued to stare at the hearth. His look was intense, yet it had softened a bit. He whispered to himself in the firelight, "That's what you think… that's what all you think."

Wally, though his cheerfulness was somewhat forced, asked with a bright yet strained smile, "Come someone, it's time for a good cup of tea. Maybe a snack? Can anyone lend assistance?" His words were almost perfunctory, revealing his genuine desire for solitude.

"I'll come." Sampson rather glumly offered. As Wally shuffled through the many breadboxes and jars of goodies, he and Sampson both grew increasingly suspicious of Whyles and his erratic behavior.

Whispering cautiously to Sampson, Wally voiced his concerns in fear of being overheard by the Fox, who was eavesdropping with his ears pressed against the wall.

"Well, my old friend, it does seem strange about Mr. Whyles' unusual dilemma. I've never seen such a case!"

"Neither have I!" Groaned Sampson, reaching for a vine of plump juicy grapes. Wally poured the tea, suddenly struck by the unsettling realization that their new acquaintance might not be as friendly as he seemed. The Fox's secrecy and the strange events surrounding his arrival had made Wally uneasy.

"Dare I admit I was a bit too hasty and open-minded, letting in a stranger without much introduction. He seems ill somehow and on the verge of near mania. I fear something, something I've never felt before, something much bigger than we can solve on our own. Whyles, a curious and sometimes friendly fellow, is much more of a danger and rather sly. As good as he is, there seems to be something loathsome about it. I fear it... I fear not only the Fox but also the secrets he hides and his scheme. My geniality may have got the better of me and my judgment. I pray not, but I do not trust this Fox now. Something seems upsetting ..the way the Fox carries on... he doesn't seem to be all there!" Wally voiced in concern.

Sampson added, "I'm afraid not! And as I recall, Booney, as much of a fibber he is, must have told the truth, as hard as it is for me to admit. But when he saw this stranger approach the Gorse and met those Hounds..."

Wally then remembered what Miriam had said about the Hounds, told by Cap'm himself, and how they were no good and were spreading terror. This made Wally deduce that Whyles, as secretive and dangerous as he was, most assuredly might indeed be associated with that bunch. Wally felt awful, his stomach turning with the assumption.

Unaware that Whyles was eavesdropping, the Fox was piecing together fragments of their conversation. The ghostly faces in his mind seemed to loom, their presence unsettling.

Overwhelmed by the sensation, Whyles felt a surge of unease as the unseen eyes watched him with relentless scrutiny. Interrupted by Booney, who was eager to grab some treats, Sampson and Wally broke off their conversation.

"Keep a watchful eye on him, Sampson," Wally instructed. Whyles, feigning ignorance, dashed back to his previous spot.

"Well, it's about time; my tum is rum rum rum rumbling!" Declared the Frog, patting his stomach.

"Sorry 'bout that, Booney, but it's here now!" Wally replied, serving the Frog with a silver platter.

Booney grabbed a couple of pieces of candy, gobbling them up quickly and taking more. "Well, it's due time for it!"

Sampson and Wally kept a close eye on the Fox, who pretended not to notice and kept his head down. "What seems to be the dilemma 'ere?" Booney asked, wondering about the awkward moment. Caught off guard by the Frog's question, the Hare answered, "nothing, nothing at all…" as he focused on the quiet Fox.

"Nothin' we DON'T KNOW of at least…" Sampson harshly asserted, still focused on Whyles. The sheepish Fox felt as though he was on trial, his heart engulfed by angst. He was exposed and uncomfortable, his sentiments concealed as he slumped into the corner, staring into the fire.

The room fell silent, save for the howling wind and the pitter-patter of rain outside. Suddenly, a peculiar pinging sound erupted, followed by a small flickering ember darting out from the fireplace. The ping reverberated within the hollow of an old bed warmer pan.

Startled, Wally exclaimed, "My oh my, what an unusual and marvelous sound! It could be music if well executed! A perfect idea for a perfect moment. Never a dull moment to waste; something's gotta be done about this!"

With a quick burst of inspiration, Wally handed three pans to Sampson. "Ere, Sampson, I reckon ye can play some percussion on this!"

Sampson, examining the pans, agreed, "Seems feasible!"

"Fabulous, absolutely fabulous!" Wally cheered. Sampson's first attempts were abrupt and loud, resembling a heavy suit of armor tumbling down a narrow staircase. Laughing heartily, he didn't seem to mind the clamor.

"Hard even with ol' rackety pans, eh? 'Ere 'ere, 'ave a real pro show ye how to play good and loud music 'round a hearth, will ye?" The speckled Frog caustically yammered. In his usual style, Booney challenged the Moose to a friendly competition. Sampson graciously accepted, bringing a loud, merry laugh from Wally.

"O', let's see 'em, let us see! This should be very interesting!"

Booney, eager to prove his point, pulled out his jaw harp and began to play. As he added his rhythm, Booney spun and twirled, creating a lively atmosphere. Wally, unable to resist, retrieved his harmonica and joined in, producing a train-like melody that complemented Booney's harp.

The music grew louder and more exuberant, blending with the storm's fury. Whyles, though initially reluctant, was drawn to the lively scene. Despite his reservations, he felt a compelling urge to join. With the group's encouragement, he could no longer resist.

"Music heals all souls, even the broken ones!" Wally declared, turning to Whyles with a gleeful smile and a wink.

Booney cheered along, "Keep it up, keep it up!"

"Dun't think I can't see ye, Mr. Whyles. Come join us, too! There's more 'n enough, come on, don't be blue! Be happy! Be true!" Wally called out.

"Ey, I ain't one to dance. I've got wobbly legs, I do…" replied the Fox, his voice gravelly and hesitant.

Despite Wally's insistence, Whyles was reluctant, finding the festivity foolish. Yet, a part of him yearned to join. As the music grew more intense, Whyles finally gave in. He scrambled toward the circle, fumbling for his fife. With the flutter of notes and a soft whisper, Whyles played with a newfound vitality.

The friends rejoiced, dancing and singing to the storm's rhythm. Whyles, once isolated and anxious, was now part of the merrymaking. As Wally stepped aside to let Whyles join the circle, the Fox played his fife with graceful agility, releasing his bottled pain through the melody.

The sweet, expressive notes filled the room, and even Miriam, despite her illness, joined in from the edge of the room, swaying to the rhythm.

"Celebrating at this late hour?" Miriam asked. "Why shouldn't we celebrate?"

Wally laughed.

Miriam, smiling despite her troubles, asked, "What may I ask are we celebrating?" "Nothing particular. Do we need a reason?"

"Aren't there reasons for everything?"

"Come, don't be bashful! Join the fun!" Wally coaxed, and Miriam, despite her initial hesitation, danced with the group. The music brought respite and healing, even to Whyles, who found himself swept up in the celebration.

As the night wore on, the friends danced and sang, their joy amplifying with the storm outside. Whyles, finally immersed in the festive spirit, let go of his anxieties and joined his companions in a joyful celebration that seemed to make everything right.

All the frolicking friends started to taunt and mock the storm and merrily danced to its furious tantrum with a song they all started to sing in the endless night soiree.

Blow as ye might, ye Chilly Northwind,

We are not in fright; we're in the warm light.

Where lanterns glow bright, look! Our spirits in flight! O' bitter Northwind, hear our delight!

Come, come, with your frosty, nimble fingers. Knocking on the door, your cold breath lingers. Stalking through the trees with howls that seize. This glossy night full of dancing glee.

For ye cannot enter nor chill our cheer.

O' prowling Northwind, ye must stay clear. Hush, hush, stay out of sight.

Rush, rush, flee from our revelry's light. O' fearsome Northwind, can you not hear? We're singing loud, with voices clear.

Ye that glides with rime on the glade. Our joyous cheers will not be swayed.

O' crotchety Northwind, with your whirling blindside, you cannot touch our frolic or our pride.

In this endless night where we dance and play, your icy wrath is kept at bay.

The Toller

Shrouded in a distressing mystery, bottled in a darkened void, Whyles was alone and blinded. He did not know where he had been transported to. There seemed to be an invisible but discernable noise of a crowd hovering above him. In a vicious pillory, they were laughing, taunting, and shaming the Fox. He wanted to wake up and desperately tried to escape the black room. He kept running, but some barrier kept bouncing him into the center, a barely distinguishable space. Alas, he could not open his eyes. It was as if they were glued shut by the thick darkness itself. He was trapped in such an unrelenting torment with the feeling of wanting to run but not knowing how or where to go. Shadowy forms of some vague familiarity appeared. They all circled him without a word. Then began their speaking with familiar voices to him. They were the voices of Wally and the Quaddling sisters. The experience was draining his willpower. They spoke to him. "Why have you forsaken us, left us to die, to suffer?"

"You are a MONSTER!" "No, I am not!"

"You have let bad things happen to our home!" "I Didn't mea...'"

"Left us to perish in flames!? Why?" The shadow figures gathered around, circling the helpless Fox. "Left us to die. You are to blame! WORTHLESS, WORTHLESS!"

"N-no, I'm not! IM NOT!!! ITS NOT TRUE!!!! Stop... stop, p'ease stop I'm begging you!!!'"

The Fox pleaded as he shut his ears and crumpled up, weeping now. "I promise to you all... I'll change, but please stop this madness! Let me be. Let me be!!!'" He screamed. The shadows had vanished, but his crying began to echo as the sound got louder and louder... "W-w -w -w-Wha wha whats happening!??" Smoke had arisen from beneath his shaking feet. He was swallowed whole in a pit, in a situation of dire judgment being placed upon him. Winds as if from a tornado swirled about him now. The toxic and acrid smoke slashed at him as it hissed madly. "You can't escape from yourself. Nor your fate... but you can definitely change it."

'How? How to change it? P'eaaassse...'" Whyles implored.

The whirling smoke split open. As wings unfurled, in the center of the smoke circling around, like a wall of a tsunami wave, was a meager hooded figure with a carnival mask. It was like the masks of some forgotten time in Ambrodale he had seen one afternoon. When he had asked Wally what it was, Wally had no answer. The mask before him was pale like chalk with colorful splashes on its cheek. They shone as crimson in the dim light. 'Loos like blood,' thought Whyles fearfully to himself. The figure's hooded robes were tattered and ragged. They were not dirty but rather clean; it seemed like the robes had existed forever in this state, like time that seemed old but never died. There then came a blinding bright white flash spotlighting the mystery figure.

Lurching forward, he pointed at the dazed Fox. "You and I are the same; we are weak in a way; we have no morality... have we no honor? No shame?"

"Wh-wh-who are... are... are… yooou? Sh-sh-sh-o-o-o show yourself!?" "Must I? Why may that be?" Asked the masked figure.

"Be-be-because I wish not to speak to those, I don't trust… and to see what is underneath… I am curious..."

"If you wish…" the figure slowly unraveled his disguise, and Whylcs was completely shocked at the presence.

"Ye... Ye look like maybe me fauther. Like. No... Like me???"

Indeed, the hooded figure had an identical form of Whyles. It was like staring into a mirror. However, the copy was eyeless... Whyles was in disbelief.

"But of course, I am he whom you have created…. Behold! I am your fear, your pain, and pleasure, Fate Toller, the bringer of your destiny." He continued, "Come tell me, how does it feel to live life so fearfully? So blindingly? Give yourself away voluntarily!"

Whyles swallowed hard and, in a shaky voice, stammered. "It feels miserable; I am a miserable coward... I hate meself!" As the last words escaped his lips, a profound and ruthless anguish seized his stomach. The Fox's shriek of despair cut through the silence as he doubled over, clutching at the source of his torment. The pain, relentless and searing, spread through his head, making it feel as though it were on the brink of shattering like an egg upon a red-hot griddle. His thoughts were stretched and distorted, leaving him adrift in a sea of confusion. The relentless, stabbing sensation in his ears was akin to needles driven in with cruel precision, and his vision danced with flashes of torment, leaving him reeling and disoriented with shining colorful dots that surrounded him. He squeezed his eyes shut to be rid of the visions, but it was no help. He realized that the spots existed within himself. "What are you doing to me!?"

"Nothing more than what you say..."

"BUT IT'S TRUE! Wherever I go, I only bring disaster..."

"I can sense your burden. It is unyielding, and I pass my sympathies on to you. However, my pity cannot grant you the sanctuary you seek. It is now up to you to save yourself."

"I could never, eveeer!" Cried the Fox.

That is past," intoned the Fate Toller, "yet life persists within you. Do you wish to forsake it all now? Leave both foes and allies in the dust?"

"Enemies, indeed, I have many," Whyles replied, his voice laden with a deep-seated bitterness. "And what of friends?"

Whyles's face contorted in despair. "I HAVE THOSE THA' PITY MEEE!!!!" He howled, his voice cracking with a tortured, desperate fervor. "Yet their pity is but a fleeting balm—nothing eases this relentless torment!" He gripped his midsection, the pain surging through him, a seething agony through his being that seemed to engulf his very soul.

"Do you still crave their pity, even now?" The Fate Toller's inquiry was both tender and probing, a mirror to Whyles's deepest afflictions.

Whyles fell into a stunned silence. The violent tremors that had seized him slowly abated. The torment in his stomach receded, and his throbbing headache diminished. Only the flickering, ghostly lights remained, drifting serenely around him, casting ephemeral glows that seemed to dance in silent sympathy with his enduring anguish.

"I never wanted or needed pity," Whyles muttered with a slight air of resignation. "An' friend, yes, I suppose I have em."

"Is that enough to continue on? For their sake?"

"I'm not sure!" As soon as he said it, the pain within him began to rise.

"I'm also sure." He felt better. 'I'M SURE. I'M SURE! In fact, in fact! "Yes? In fact, what?'

"I love them, even that darn fruggy; I ADMIT it!" The Fox declared. The Fox's declaration rang out with a mix of defiance and relief.

"If you leave me, you must return to finish what you have started. Can you do that?" "I can't do that…"

"Why not?"

"I don't know why… that's me problem. I'm betta off disappearing!"

"Try to run, run, and run, but you can't escape yourself, but in fact, it will surely worsen your hardship. Do you think you can get anywhere by running maybe to other locations? But nay, you are stuck in the same dilemma! Change is never easy… yet there is always chance of resolution; each day comes with as many chances as there are ideas and desires. Determination is the key. "

Whyles stood silently; He had no answer. The Toller beckoned him forward. "Come forward; I have need to show you something."

With a confidence unusual for Whyles, he strode forward. Behind the Toller was a large glimmering silver table.

The Toller held out a bag in which he pulled three packages and placed them on the table. The Toller waved them to him. "Choose just one " he directed.

"Wh-wh-what are they?"

"Haven't you the curiosity to find out?"

"But what if I pick the wrong one?" "Then you do… Choose wisely…" "Im afraid…. im very af-af-afraid…" "What's there to be afraid of?"

The Fox carefully examined each box; they all looked similar. However, one felt light, the other felt somewhat heavy, and the last one felt extremely heavy. Upon lifting it, Whyles thought, "There mus' be golds in here".

He shook the boxes, and the first box made a light tinkling like the noise of wind chimes hanging on the eves on a house in Ambrodale on a summer day; this reminded him of how many times the Quaddlings had prepared something special for the guests they so often entertained. He smiled when he thought of how much they had given to others; even though they had sometimes complained, their heart was always in the right places, he thought silently to himself.

Shaking the middle box, something slid across the bottom of it, making a shrill whine. For some reason, Whyles found himself disgusted and not been inclined to pick up the box again or to choose it.

The third box made not a sound, but when he placed it down, it hit a table with a large cracking noise and thud. The noise gave Whyles a startle. This was clearly not his choice.

He then smelled each box. The first box smelled of fragrant meadows and sweet treats as the odors that escaped the Quaddlings' kitchen did.

The second box had no smell.

The third smelled foul and poisonous as if something was burning. Whyles knew he was right to avoid it entirely. Then he pressed his ear and listened to the sounds each box contained.

The first box held the sounds of laughter and cheers, a call of celebration.

The second carried the noises of a blowing wind as it wrapped around some jagged rocks. Finally, the third contained the sounds of chaos and destruction. He could hear cries not of joy but of misery. He felt no need to listen more. He retreated from its presence as it seemed to glower at him in the darkness.

"I have made up me mind…" "What do you choose?"

Whyles gestured to the box that spoke most to his heart as a mystical force unwrapped it, "Did I pick right?"

"It is not for me to say…"

"I have but one final word before you awaken!" "And what's that?"

"Peace may be thine by actions you shall take from hereon… I bid you farewell."

The little spots of light that were around him when he met the Fate Toller began to glow brighter. Then, they began to grow larger, merging. The image of the Fate Toller became indistinct and faded into a spreading light. Glowing spots of light drifted closer, revealing familiar faces. First, he saw Miriam and Adelia, then Wally, old Sampson, and last to show was Booney. As the lights merged, he found himself enveloped by their glow. He began to glide effortlessly, closing his eyes and letting the inner light guide him. The sensation of weight disappeared, replaced by the comforting presence of his loved ones, guiding him through a sea of radiant light, one resembling the unmatched brilliance of many suns shining together at once.

Shining Hearts

Whence the horrible storm had ended its savage tirade that had aggressively oppressed Ambrodale for much of two disastrous weeks; no one wanted to remember. The humble populace stepped out of hiding in their crumbly homes and stared into the inevitable wreckage. They set about tidying their small community with commendable zeal, each one taking up a task and working in harmonious unity. The devastation was far more extensive than they had anticipated, with ruin strewn in every direction. Yet, no grumbling arose among them; this was not the first time they had faced such destruction.

With the departure of each storm, homes and gardens lay in tatters, but the children, guided by none other than Booney, rose to the occasion. The sprightly Frog, ever the enthusiastic leader, had convinced them of his innate talent for such 'heroic moments'. They eagerly took to collecting the scattered debris, bringing it to the adults for further instruction.

The hoppity Frog regaled them with the bellows of his croaker, gleefully hooting as the crew of children busily tidied up. Little hands worked diligently to replant the surviving garden beds and sow seeds in the empty spaces. Homes that had once provided shelter from the storm now bore gaping holes, shattered doors, and stripped walls, their contents strewn about like festive banners. Debris lay scattered across pathways and hidden corners, evidence of the gale's fierce assault.

Despite the chaos, they labored tirelessly, salvaging what they could and rebuilding what they could. Amidst the disarray, Father Tree stood resolute, a steadfast symbol of endurance and hope in the face of such adversity.

Wally kept his word to Miriam and was already well off to the borderlands in search of

Adelia. By the time Miriam, still plagued by illness, came to her senses, she found herself awake but scarcely recovered. She discovered Whyles standing vigil beside her, his presence suggesting he had observed her throughout the night. Miriam offered a faint smile, her vision obscured by the crust of sleep, yet she could discern Whyles' hunched and ragged form through the haze.

Inquiring about Wally's whereabouts, Miriam was informed by the Fox that Wally had departed, leaving Whyles with explicit instructions to watch over her. Grateful, Miriam thanked him and admitted to a rapid improvement in her condition. Eager to return to her routine, she attempted to rise, her forgetfulness momentarily making her overlook the fact that she had no home to return to.

Whyles, uncertain of her full recovery, halted her progress with a firm insistence that she return to bed. Like a protective sibling, he decreed that she should rest, prompting Miriam to comply, albeit begrudgingly. As she settled back into bed, the two exchanged glances without speaking. Whyles, visibly agitated and twitchy, averted his gaze, his eyes darting downward in an effort to avoid further contact.

He was surprised himself at his tone owing to his concern for her.

"You 'ookie 'ike te 'lonla type." The Quaddling announced sympathetically. Whyles backed off. "Why yez care?" He retorted.

He went on. "Well! Yez are vury much wrong! I'm sure NOT!" He vehemently denied such an accusation by his usual attitude of feverish alarm. Though even in his mind, somewhere, it rang of truth

"You don't have to be afraid of me, uny friend of Wally is a dear friend of mine. Besides, after all me and Delly have taught, ye mean much more than a friend to us, why you are our dearest family! We will die for ye we would!" Miriam uttered as she hacked away. Whyles, hearing Miriam's honest statement, felt their devotion and the love that she shared for him. Whyles started choking up. He tried to hide his emotions with one big swallow. He didn't much like emotions, much less understand them. In his rather misguided logic, those who become bonded only suffer from heartaches when something bad eventually happens. For the Fox, it seemed a far better solution to try to avoid such goodwill.

"Friends? Family? I don't need any. T'er is no point in it. 'It's all truly useless," he declared, his voice echoing his internal struggle. After saying so, he felt a flush in his face, betraying the lie he was telling himself.

"T'at's not true, not one bit! Why everyone needs a somebody!" She said wholeheartedly, "Without friends, why t'ere be no 'un to be wit, and it's awfully hard to be a 'onesome fullow…I can't help but pity ye, Mr. Whyles; I don't know why. Ye always seem to have a sompin sad 'bout ye. Come dear, don't be afraid. Please tell me ye trubbles. Ye do look so burthened by it all!"

"I really don't mind it. I'd much rather be alone with nuttin' but meself to 'orry 'bout, it's easier that way!" Whyles then became irrationally temperamental: "A-a- an anotta' t'ing is, I don't need uny un's pity, im much fine the way I is! It doesn't matter nuttin' to me."

"Dear, oh dear, but are ye really? I don't mean to meddle where it's not me place, but I mean with all fair goodness that I must say that it really does matter! Ye only hurt yesuf if ye pretend not to care. Life is much too short to go about it all alone, and it's much too short to dwell in misery!"

"If ye only knew, if ye 'ony know what I do!" The Fox mumbled to himself.

"Why does it matter anyhowy? Falling for hearts is a fool's gamble! I want nuttin' to do with it." The Fox harshly cried out.

"And what a gamble it indeedin' is! Some for the better, some for the worse! It is all about how ye lookie at it! It is a gamble, but at the very end, it's all for a purpose. T'er is no reason to hide anything ye feel. In a way, we are all the same. We share fear and joy; ye mustn't be ashamed of emotions nor change. It's all natural! If'n, ye hide it, it aint'm healthy. Beware of the many tricks' isolation brings. It's not all ye t'ink it is."

"Isolation is wonderful!" The Fox snapped back.

"Isolation turns one bitter, dearie! Ye mustn't let misery control ye; always remember ye are the 'ony one to free yersuf. Ye must be brave!"

Unwilling to change his disdainful view even in view of what Miriam spoke, Whyles needed to hear those words! He didn't want to change, but he could not resist the ideals she professed, either. All he ever knew was how to pretend; it kept him safe. He admitted to himself with change always comes the imposing pain of coexisting with truth, and he was not yet prepared for that day. It was too sudden to realize the import of her words. Something in him knew, however, that what was taking place in him and around him during his time with Kaliber was absolutely wrong.

To pretend and to lie it all away would never fix the dilemma he felt but only hide him from the reality that was unfolding within him. He blindly took part in his life with Kaliber and the Hounds as well as that wretched Clovis, from fear and from fear alone. He felt guilty after seeing their hateful deeds against the Riverfolk. By Miriam's kind words and guileless manner, he could begin to predict what was about to unfold. It was truly devastating to him to realize that he was the key to success or failure for either side this time.

It began to tear him up inside. All these years, he had grown used to acting through pressure from others and his own confusion regarding what he should or might do. Always he failed to stop something awful from coming forward. And that awful, awful Clovis! Where did he come from? He was unlike the rest and seemed to feed off Kaliber now. Kaliber used Clovis to make his plans go through. But could Kaliber not see in Clovis' eyes that Clovis could care less about anyone? Why did Kaliber dive so deeply into destruction with him? By what import had Clovis' gloomy countenance even turned up? It was like a bucket of filth had been dumped on himself, Whyles thought. Clovis' acts were unpredictable and always set to the maximum destructive effect any being could deliver. Whyles hated him and his crony Hounds... When he considered Kaliber and his 'kindnesses' to Whyles, Whyles involuntarily shuddered. Miriam and Adelia, Sampson, and especially Wally.

How they had been kind to him in such a short period of time without Whyles feeling guilty or small about anything that transpired between them. Now, he saw his own acts weighing in before him. His indecision no longer wavered before him. What he had received from perfect strangers for these past many moons made him feel appalled by his own past. The prospect of opening his heart was almost a distant desire, but yet its' VOICE COULD NOT BE QUELLED. It would not leave him alone. Still, now he felt there was hope for him as he remembered what the Toller had shown him. He knew what must be done. His heart quavered. The same feeling of nausea beckoned, but he would not move this time. If the feeling came, so it came. There was now a place in him that seemed like a long-sought sanctuary for a soul on the run. He knew he somehow had to stop what was about to happen at any cost. He plainly admitted to himself that he didn't want to see these folk who had done nothing wrong, who, in fact, took care of those they loved, fall into a dreaded subjugation.

He knew the feeling all of his life. The Riverfolk he loved was at the wrong place at the wrong time, through no fault of their own. This was their home; why should they give it up? They were not for Kaliber to control OR HIS WRETCHED HOUNDS TO DEVOUR. To speak nothing of the evil Clovis. He knew that now. It was time to act and resist, not to pretend, not to hide, and not to let his mind rot in misery and corruption. His mind was clicking and turning. He had already started to adapt to the bold idea, though it had not yet settled in. He steeled his mind in the understanding that this must not continue. However, with each thought of resisting them, his body, through habit, would still react in an unwilling resentment towards his new motives. The dawning realization of doing what's right for once had almost made his physical appearance temporarily unstable. He could not, however, say no this time. It was time to change for the better; he wanted nothing to do with Kaliber any longer. He, out of sheer good fortune, timely advice, or perhaps fate, had found his true family. Nothing would or could ever take them away from him. 'NOT AGAIN!' his mind screamed at him. All these thoughts of sacrifice and valor came flooding in again. All these inner emotions clashed, rending their booming voices within him. It was a strange effect, and it was almost like he was being directed and not purely manipulated this time. A decrease in the nervous tension that had always plagued him settled within him now. A boost of adrenaline streamed through his body and soul. He had to act fast before the impetus to act would be replaced by his previous wounded spirit. 'THEY ARE NOT HIS, THEY SHALL NOT BE HIS, THEY ARE FREE, THEY MUST BE FREE, FREE THEM

ALL!!! It's NOT TOO LATE,' the voices of his consciousness railed.

He then told Miriam, who was before him on the bed, that he had to do something and wouldn't possibly be returning soon. But he had sincerely thanked and praised her for those blessed teachings. Just before he left, Miriam beckoned him over to him.

"Now, Dearie, I don't know what ye are getting into, and I doont a' like it. I must be honest, I doonty like it, no, not one bit. But if'n ye must go, t'en it must be for a good reason."

"A vury good 'un!" Whyles fixed his eyes on her in a long and gentle stare regarding her. In a gentle and unwavering voice, he said softly. "But p'ease ask me no more; it must be done."

"And who I am to force ye to stay put, but wherever ye are goin', please brins' this along for faith. I think you'll need it!" Miriam said, uncomforted by the thought of his passing. She asked to extend his paw to her. As she gently grabbed it, he was trembling slightly. She had then instructed the Fox to close his eyes. He did so, yet squinting with one eye open. She had then pulled something small from her wing and plopped it into his palm. It felt cold and smooth.

"May I open my eyes?"

"Ye may!" Miriam chuckled. Whyles popped open his eyes and examined the gift he had received. He was most befuddled by it.

"It's just a little rock?!" Whyles declared, not seeing why it would grant any protection. He looked harder at the polished, speckled pebble. It was no bigger than a raindrop.

"Why dear, it's not just any old pabble, ye see, it's a very special pabble. This 'uns me favrit ...ye see it dunt lookie like much but whin ye looks closer there are lots of white and dark specks in it. Looks like a dirty ol ting from a distance, but behind ye look closer ye sees the bits is all shinin' like lookin' at a gem. There's no tellin' 'ow old it is or if anyone else ever owned it. To some, I'll bet it looks like a right bit of rubbish, but the rivers run it smoothly and the very sands of the banks what's in it. Seems special to me and diffrunt like about the folks that are here at Riverbank. No telling they could be worth something t'other. The precious ones there too, in this here old river. This 'un hasn't done much good for me, but it seems there's memories in it.

Perhaps it may shine on you where you are a'goin..." "I'll take care of it..."

"Promise?"

"Promise," Said Whyles in response.

Whyles pressed the pebble to his chest and set off with a slight smile. The little pebble was light. It fit snugly in his pocket, right next to his heart.

Wally had made a daring effort venturing off alone to the borderlands in search of whatever he could find. A clue? Hopefully! An answer? Wishfully! With just a map, he was sketching out for future generations to come and with some brave yet cocky sense of morality. He was charting out what was never fully documented! These lands were demented and thought to be destructive to those innocents who were fraught with fear. They could be afflicted with the fear of the unknown, the blackest fears that grip the shaking bodies of those enfeebled by a gripping torture that simply would not relent or release its nocturnal hold on them. Wally was not one of those types; he always did what he said he would do, and so he found himself doing them. Maybe his fearlessness on this matter was tied to this obedience to the decisions he made. He was so concentrated on the hope of finding answers to this mystery that he was completely oblivious to the fear that Sullen Fields brought. Every path, every dark cave, and every knotted tree he saw, he marked and double-checked on his giant dotted map made of mulberry bark paper. Crudely fashioned by some ladies in the village, it held up under considerable stress. Though no one knew how they made it, Wally had come to depend on its durability. As he was investigating the Borderlands, which seemed to screech and holler noises from every way he turned, something had caught sight of him. He traveled more swiftly now AS he discovered a devastating clue.

"Oh no, no, no, whut coulda happund here?" The Hare had come across a tattered and destroyed little handcrafted basket. It was cleverly named- tagged 'Adelia D. Quaddling' in a tight cursive script. The crushed crimson berries oozed from below the crushed, unweaving basket. He then quickly surmised that it was her own blood as he inspected the wrecked contents settling into the muddy ground.

"Poor, poor Adelia whut on eart' di' ye get yersuf into, I hope wurever you are, you are safe…"

Suddenly, he felt a huge rumbling where he stood as if the ground was cracking and submerging below him. 'No time to stop! Must find her!!' His mind screamed at him.

Wally dashed as fast as his springing legs could lift him. Trekking deeper into the Borderland in dire hopes of finding the lost Quaddling wherever she may have been. He continued to map out his journey upon finding safer ground. While he was continuing to explore, he was unaware of the many traps hidden in obscure spots. The traps were crude attempts to capture any unwelcomed, unfortunate interloper who so dared to come for a visit. By some strange luck, he had not noticed these planted booby traps, so he proceeded and evaded them completely. He went freely about, hopping through the thickest, most dangerous foliage. This continued, however, until he had placed one foot on a pile of sunken leaves, whereupon he tumbled over headfirst into a deep pit. The fall forced him to drop his map to the ground. Almost as a vicious mockery to his unsuspecting fate, the drifting wind seemed to almost grab the parchment map right from him, flinging it long away from him as he fell!

Down, down, down he helplessly plummeted (It felt like an eternity precisely because it hardly felt like time existed at all during those moments of extreme trial) into complete darkness until, with a large CRACK and THUD, he finally hit rock bottom and went unconscious.

He had then awoken a short while, with a giant lump in between his floppy ears, to the sounds of vulgar curses and maniacal bellows. He now saw, by looking up, the sharp edges of what appeared to be at least three ruddy spears. He quickly attempted to climb back up but with no luck whatsoever. He just slipped down with one step as he couldn't find a good mooring; he now felt he was hopelessly trapped. He called out to whatever he had thought he heard, but there was no answer. Brutish bloated heads with squinting eyes peered down and stared at him, proclaiming aloud with a peculiar joy what they captured.

With their puny, lazy, non-orbital eyes, they just stared dumbly until one yelped, "Oaz Bilmey!!!! lookie lookie whad weez cugty! Dib we dae gud?" Said the sloppy voice.

"Yud'm did! Bris' him up! Oaz! Fenger Rew, Oual Corkus, Thraw Duun!!! Bilmey commanded. The rope dangled down as Wally tugged on it, making sure it was safe.

"Whutcha tugging on it fer? Weez gotz it, now boaz on me mark weez 'pou!" The group of Horkurs made ready as Bilmey gave the word. With one gruff order, they pulled Wally up so fast and strong that he felt like he was briefly flying skywards as if already passing on to the next world. With a scraping 'POP!' He landed right back on his feet again... Now standing, he gathered his scattered senses after being so rudely flung up from the pit he had been trapped in. He realized that he was now surrounded by five mammoth and shaggy Boars clad shoddily in ratty outfits and gripping knotty clubs and twisted poles. Led by the most slovenly and aggressive Bilmey Toags. Bilmey was in charge of all the scouting expeditions along with his own group of loyal comrades.

These daily expeditions were organized expressly to capture any and all trespassers; no questions asked, no pleas honored. The ragged team was charged with bringing them back to Cap'm Thistleworts for a sentence to be pronounced always in the Horkurs own favor. The Judge and Jury were seated in the ancient ruins, deep within the Borderlands, which they heavily colonized for their own uses. They were all disgusting, all disheveled, and all uncaringly crude. Their saggy, malformed, grimacing faces gave off an unappealing nausea-inducing odor to the Hare.

He did not know what to make of it. Seeing an actual myth told to frighten the young children never to stray too far now made him shudder.

Never did he think those scary myths were true until now. He spotted his now dirty map and claimed it before the towering horde. Being of a polite nature, he had just begun to thank these repugnant and slobbery rescuers who had a malicious smirk rippling amongst all of them, further distorting the mess that their hideous faces presented to him. They forcefully seized him, and with one of their large poles, he was bound with the same rope that saved him. He was even blindfolded during the process, adding to his frustrated sense of indignity! Yanking the map out of his paws, they all stared at it rather dull-wittedly.

"Oaz whuts all t'ese squigglilies and dotties?!" They clamored among themselves. They huddled around the map, examining it with intrigue as each one of the Horkurs tried to decipher it. They angrily ripped it out from each other's hooves, and they began to fight for it! Their tusks were jabbing, and their clubs smacking their fatty flesh with a loud squwooshing noise. They grappled and bit and flipped and snapped

"Please do be careful with that! I work awfully hard on it! it means ever so much to me!" Wally whimpered, genuinely concerned for the map's physical integrity. The Horkurs had stopped their fighting for the moment.

"Wellin in t'at case!" Wally had heard the terrible sound of his most cherished handiwork as the shredding of paper. The map he had so carefully rendered and with which he had been wholly engaged in making these many years was torn into little pieces. The pig-footed tribe had done their corpulent shuffle about it while laughing at Wally's wounded outcry.

"Take this nosey tussypusser back to Cap'm and sei whit ta dae wea him!!!"

"Onwards, HO!" They all cheered as Wally pleaded with them to set him free.

"I meant no intrusion. I assure you, please, I am looking for someone; it's very urgent that I find her quickly!" he blustered.

These pleas were unheard or flatly ignored by the rowdy rabble. As the poor, disoriented Hare hung upside-down, he was being shouldered by two hefty Horkurs, Kusnus Utag, and Gredd Chusser. These two stoutest plumpers were the bearers of the pole.

"Where am I going? You must tell me...Where am I going?!" Wally protested ineffectually. Frightfully pestered, the forlorn and forgotten Hare demanded answers.

"Quit ye blubbering! Ye bampot! We shull smather ye if ye dun't kup ye mout shuut! Ye wei find oot suin enutt!!" Was the threatening answer angrily delivered as they began to shake the pole violently.

Wally was strapped tightly, and each motion threatened to force the breath from his wheezing lungs. The grizzled company trekked deeper and deeper into Sullen Fields and over its twisted and confusing pathways. Over hill and across hazardous ravines, they trekked intently with hardly a thought to their own comfort and most certainly not Wally the Hare's.

Unbeknownst to Wally, who was buried in his woes, strapped like a carcass and quietly mumbling a few prayers, they were nearing their destination. In a massive silhouette appeared the outlines of the ancient ruins. As they kept to the rocky trail, crumbling stone columns were scattered as if rolled down the hillside. Wally, parched by the extreme heat, asked for a bit of water. One of the escorts, Snarolf Kovy, lifted his scarred and pockmarked arm to his shoulder and grasping a weather-beaten skin bag of who could tell what had fallen unfortunate to its creation and indecorously shoved it into Wally's gasping mouth.

Wally was beyond understanding what the taste of the ichor was. He could only swallow a' liquid as thick as the uncured stucco he used on his house after a long winter. He hopelessly thought at the drought, 'If this doesn't kill me theeen…'

His thoughts ruptured as he was thrown to the ground, pole and all, onto his aching back. The troupe took a brief pause and, lifting with haste, stuck the poll into the mushy ground.

SLOOOSHH baaaamuuuuck! The pole slid into place, staining any clean and dry patch on Wally's attire. Oual took out his well-used canteen and crammed it in the Hare's mouth.

"This'll suit yas better. Least its waaattaahhh!" Wally chugged it down till his thirst was at least slaked; however,' Wally had to spit it up afterward upon realizing the water Snarolf gave him at first was foul slime; the raucous Horkurs laughed, taking turns roughly walloping him around 'Jus for rawkin' of it ael.' With their clubs, as they did with all captives, they hit him again and again. For he was stationary and could not resist. He hovered above them on the pole.

Motionlessly. He accepted each brutal hit. That was until Bilmey stopped the ordeal and gave the final blow… "Wut is it not tasty enout fer yer?! Ye dunt look so weel!"

"Well, you see it-"

"No more catter! Coom on! Luts goot muving aguin! Boofur' it goots dawrk!"

Bilmey ordered as the five continued to trudge along. "Wez are naurly 'der now I can smeel oit!" added Chusser in excitement. The path shot straight, and the group climbed ever so slightly over broken stones, undergrowth and other inconveniences that were crumbling before them. It seemed this hike was taking for hours until they had reached the final mile. They came upon two gigantic and gnarled willow trees on opposite sides. Their enormous branches were contorted and hung over the path.

Their large, entangled branches were shaped like a twisted, prickly shield. The branches safeguarded what was hidden on the other side.

They crossed over in a slumping battalion, and finally, at last, they had arrived. The Horkurs yanked the blindfold off of the dazed Hare and untied him from the pole only to then drag him by his floppy ears (His tattered and scraped body was now a pincushion for shards of broken glass and briar-like weeds). The sloughing and panting crew went on tramping through the sullen stone entrance archway, which was pinned by shredded flags. The impaling flags led up to a massive landmark that resembled images Wally had seen in his old books.

'It looks like a crypt of the ancients.' He thought to himself, not exactly knowing what had triggered the thought or what it might actually mean. Wally was extremely astonished by what he saw in the mysterious and enchanting wonder right before his weary, searching eyes. Like a spark in the night, he had a flashing desire to learn all about this new place. It was an extraordinary yet extremely daunting edifice. He was surely amazed at the prospect of seeing this place for the first time. His imagination ran back to the time of his childhood when his father had described mysteries but would not explain them to Wally. In place of direct answers, he left or rather bequeathed a large library which, it seemed to Wally by now, must indeed contain answers for what he was seeing. Moving slowly to examine and let his eyes adjust to the space before him, Wally felt a hint of dread. Maybe his father would not tell him because he was not ready to understand at the tender age when his imagination began to grow. As Wally moved forward with the trepidation borne of a natural awe at things unknown to him, a colonnade with five colossal decaying, wobbly spires stood above him. The columns were like the necks of five stone giants, hair-dressed by twisted vines that bore a glossy dark fruit that smelled of pitch. The site greeted them with thinly-splintered support beams and columns below a gigantic and encircling ancient temple complex. The place where he stood seemed to afford a view of the entire complex as if to awe the newly arrived visitor of ages past. Many crumbling buildings, now laid to waste, encircled the entire plateau where they stood. Most of the structures might have been residences built in clusters with what looked like central great rooms like those he had read about in the Records of Battles Ancient. That volume remained among Wally's favorite tomes as a young Hare. He would thrill to think of entire cities with so many thousands or millions of people in them. Yet what he could interpret now revealed but little. The destroyed buildings, scattered debris, scribed monoliths, smashed archaic limbless statues, and sculptures forged from marble, he guessed, were not a rare sight to see here.

Underneath these primitive ruins grew clusters of stunted and wilted flowers that, despite the names given, could only be received as rank, stinking weeds. Among these sour plants were many begrimed and rotting bone remnants of ages past, now only valued by the swarms of flitting insects in their frenetic buzzing and flying. When viewed from the distance where they stood, Wally could easily see the remnants of the city, if such it had been, formed a ring-like maze. In the center of the maze was one massive and deeply deteriorating temple fifty stories high and wide as a volcano, Wally guessed. Its ornamental and obviously breached walls had been defaced by the Horkurs' own interpretation of art. Wide swathes of broken and mud- smeared walls were an awful stain on this campus' former beauty. Mixed in with the crude mud stain decorative washes were sections of walls bedecked by moss and grubs. Many strange humanoid deities had been sculpted on the saw-toothed pediment of this temple. On the grounds of this temple, the rest of the eighteen Horkurs were to be seen in separate and private groups, having their own party. Some had stomped on the long snakes that infested the ruin. Small rows of monstrous tribal drums, uniquely crafted, were being smashed by huge pounding mallets by others. Yet others amongst the arriving horde had dug giant pit holes and filled them with mud. They began relaxing in their own filth. The rest of them brawled and destroyed pillars, testing their brute strength. The entire group ate rancid scraps of dry meat still on bones, stripping them clean. Mixed in with these scraps were to be found shriveled fruits that lost their colors and turned sickly.

All stopped what they were doing when Bilmey and his comrades came lumbering back. All were attracted to the sight of yet another captive. The group eagerly followed them from behind, wanting to hear the Hare's imminent conviction from the Cap'm. The rooting horde marched their way up the seemingly unending flight of fragmented steps that led to the temple proper. The steps kept escalating higher and higher still as it felt quite a bit higher indeed than the clouds themselves.

A series of deep, loud, and blaring horn blasts had stopped them all momentarily. This bombastic and resonant melody of a giant horn mightily vibrated the temple itself from where it rang from above. The ongoing, jarring blasts made the grounds tremble. Many of the wobbling structures down below, which had begun to collapse in ages past, shook yet still with the reporting horns, shaking the temple, which had started to crack off in large chunks.

Finally, when they had reached the highest peak, Wally looked down, though not really wanting to. He was surprised when he found himself looking down below. He knew he shouldn't have, but it was only natural to be curious, maybe dangerously so. From where they began the hike, he could not see anything, and at this high altitude, he also felt out of breath and extremely sick.

They were at the foot of the skillfully embellished entrance of a carved and monolithic entry. It appeared to be the oversized cavernous portal of a freestanding ziggurat-styled stepped mound of limestone blocks. The blocks were covered in moss and dirt, but a worn path to the center was clearly evident. That the place was a temple was Wally's inevitable conclusion. To whom or what the edifice honored or was meant to serve remained a mystery, especially in his present abducting company of brutish Boars.

There was a pair of stone fire pits in front of the temple. The charred and moldering remnants of some indescribable offering, thought Wally morosely. A Horkur had grabbed some of its filthy ash, left over by the last supplicant present at some point in the past. With his huge, greasy hooves, he whipped a clump of it at the poor, bruised Hare. More than bruised at heart, he was now coated from head to toe with musty soot as he gagged from the overpowering taste of ash in his mouth. All the while, Wally was blinded by the force of the dust in his stinging eyes even as he tried to wipe them. They all marched into the dank hall which now stood before them. By Wally's estimation, the smell of mold and mildew meant lots of moisture and not a lot of use within. 'It must be a temple, surely,' he thought to himself. "I don't really want to know what for," he said in a mumble.

"Soilleeence!" His captor attendants said with a shove. Quickly, they came to a dingy altar room that smelled to Wally like camphor and burning paraffin. In this room, which was wreathed with the sheds of dead snakes, was a tribute mound of sheared tusks. Within the mound were placed shining shards and pieces of dulled metal. Above this bed of fragments, there seemed to be resting an ancient war club. The giant war club's handle was wrapped in shredded leather. This anomaly of war was the sacred weapon used by the legendary Ivarg Irontusk. He had succumbed in battle at 105 A.O.I. His death was the end of the First Age of the Horkurs (that started the Age after Ivarg), when Ivarg was not known as Ivarg Irontusk but rather as Ivarg the Invincible. His moniker was well-earned, for no blade could cut through his resilient hide. Through many battles, he had led his Horkur brothers to victory against their overlords, who had chained and slaughtered them for sport. The Bloody Age continued prior to the Horkurs' revolution against the oppressors. In a show of enduring resistance, made possible by the strength and courage of Ivarg, just before his own defeat, these overlords, the Trisengias, had cursed the Horkurs Clan. In their own brutal downfall, the eldest of the oppressors, Sardes Alatrem, uttered in his own dying breath that one day, the Clan of the Mighty Ivarg would fall. He cursed that a betrayal within the Horkurs Clan would leave the Horkurs crashing down powerlessly for lack of their own obedience to the Trisengias, their oppressors.

This giant club before them was now like no other. An iron crown was spiked and hammered deep into the crest of the club. Its beaded roundtop was, at one time, jaw-crushing by the sheer weight of its descent upon its victim. This club was extremely heavy as well. It was a perfect representation of its mammoth wielder's skill-at-arms. Only Ivarg had the strength to lift and crush his foes with it. It was distinctive, as the crown of the wooden club had two ogre-sized tusks rammed in deep on both sides of it. These twisted claw-like tusks were once used to gouge his enemies' eyes out just before he came to his death. Otherwise, the enemies of Ivarg were often crushed by the blow of the weighty shaft. How and why these tusks were crudely wedged into this massive club was recorded upon the Horkurs' temple walls, which enclosed them all.

Just after the curse was put upon them, the conflict was finally ignited, bringing death to Ivarg. Surrounded by archers of the Trisengias, Ivarg, fallen in battle and bound by a pledge to blind Sardes, excruciatingly removed the tusks from his own battered jaw. The Trisengias thought his motions were an honorable suicide. The ripping shout of pain as he grabbed each bloody tusk and tore it from his jaw rent the battlefield. Ivarg, hastily embedding each one in his battle club, had the archers perplexed. The archers could down him in a minute's time and would shortly do so. Why, they thought, would he torture himself in this way when his end by them was assured? More mysterious yet was the drilling of his own tusks into the battered wood as he bled in mortal pain.

As Ivarg rose once more, the archers fixed all arrows upon him, as their dead lay beneath and around him, crushed by his mass as he stood. His eyes fixed upon Sardes. Ivarg silently lofted the club, which made a shrieking sound. With deadly accuracy, the war club flew onward to its intended target, the mocking eyes of Sardes. Before he could draw another breath and scream the cry of the defeated, a deadly rain of arrows felled Ivarg instantly, though no historian ever knew if he had given up the spirit before even a single arrow reached his flesh. He did not live to see his tusked projectile find its home in the head of Sardes. In a twist of irony and in deadly earnest, each embedded tusk ruptured each reddened eye of Sardes instantaneously as the head of the club savagely burrowed into the massive skull of the oppressor. Nor did Ivarg hear the curse that preceded his leagues-long throw at the enemy. Neither did the Horkurs know that their fate had been delivered to them on this searing battlefield despite the dying bravery of their leader, Ivarg the Invincible. The club itself was properly and posthumously named Irontusk in the annals of Horkur Histories to follow that age. And so Ivarg, its wielder, was granted his new title after his own death.

More shocked yet were they, when Ol' Ivarg had died by his bloody wounds and left the clan leaderless, it was Demtis Yarg who stepped up for the position first; this act galled a number of Horkurs who all greatly craved to be the chieftain or how they say "Krodyr," particularly a jealous and spiteful Horkur named Borkul Dorgum who had spent a great deal of time corrupting and pillaging as he had tried to frame Demtis for the many murders he had sinfully committed. Starting from 305A.A. They all became mistrustful as they turned on each other, and soon, there was a great divide amongst them. They all formed many little tribes, and eventually, with each division clashing for the same power, there came bloodshed spanning many lifetimes, titled the Great Tuskal War. It had seemed to never end; it was a perilous war. It seemed to have no winners, and very few tribes had remained until one massive battle had decided the clan's fate. Yet here they still were, carelessly surviving, not as honorable nor glorified as they once were.

Then, there came these echoes of grumbles and laughter from the distance that made Wally shiver. Nearing the next chamber, they saw a huge outline of what looked to be a giant; as the deep, gurgling voice called them over, the room was dimly lit like a dying hearth. Its wall was colorfully painted with murals all depicting the glorious golden age of the Horkurs clan as these elaborate murals expressed their stories of battles and valor, of sacrifice and betrayal. Etched in white ash next to these murals were requiems and odes to their immortal ancestors... especially Ol' Ivarg Irontusk, the founder, was highly lauded as a god in the many inscriptions, as one particular poem read.

Ode to Ivarg Irontusk, the great Rooter

In chains, we were slaves,

Till thou, Irontusk, with might, broke free. O' Ivarg, our savior, we give thanks.

O' Ivarg, the brave, we honor thee. May he long live and reign,

Lead us to victory. Gift us thy guidance, Gift us thy wisdom,

SHOW US THE WAY.

Smite with thy club,

Boom Boom!

He who slays tyrants,

He who sends the fiends to their doom. We obey,

We humbly obey.

Thy sons and brothers are at thy call and roar, We are ready to make war.

Hear our thunder, We take our plunder,

The cowards are put asunder.

Till the sad day shall finally come, When ye forever lay.

But nay, worry not of a blunder, Thou shalt never be forgotten...

Beyond the cloudy sight,

Past the burning stars so bright, Come day,

Come gloom night.

Thy tombed in a fortress of glass,

The name Yollgikkos bowered within a jeweled barrow, High o'er a shimmering sea of gold.

A mystic kingdom of yore, Showered by riches foretold.

Ye shalt rule the fallen where they dwell, In deep crystal halls of old.

May the rolling drums beat on, Shattering the cold mirrored walls. Hark! Hark!

The cheer of glories!

Come, let us regale upon our gory stories, Of battles fought,

Of blood spilled, Of tears unshed. Drink, drink,

Be merry, for all our foes are dead.

The overflowing fountain of ale never dries,

The blazing hearth is eternally ignited.

The shrill forges are steaming, The bells, the quivering bells, Faithfully knell.

Blow the gleaming horns, let them be heard, The rising day of reckoning nears.

At arms! At arms!

At last, thy luminated army shall return, Storming forth, raining their spears once more! In great ire, Ivarg shall cast these lands afire.

The rest of the room was piled high with broken artifacts dating back to the very beginning of the Horkurs clan. In the center of the treasury was none other than the imposing and welly Cap'm Thistleworts. He sat on a throne bathed with filth. Mounted on this throne were several tusks from the past clan leaders, for once the leader has been laid to rest, their tusk must be broken off and be mounted on the throne in memorial.

In his lap, he cradled what seemed to be a tarnished brass horn turn green; this gigantic horn resembled a double bell tuba. This horn, which was titled the Vuggahorn, was greatly revered by the Horkurs and passed down through the ages. The Vuggahorn was one of a kind, only forged for ownership by the chieftains of the Horkurs; Ol' Ivarg Irontusk gave it to Demtis Yarg, who, after his untimely doom at the hands of Borkul, Aggar Verag claimed it and chieftain after chieftain handing it down each generation as a gift of leadership as it presently resides with Thistleworts, the scummy horn was rich with history. Cap'm had set the impaired Vuggahorn aside, boorishly slurping from his giant drinking horn from one beefy hoof. In the other hoof, he grasped a long, thick, but stale cigar between his blistered knuckle, whiffing its harsh and pungent odor; its acrid dregs seemed to be clinging to his flabby mass. Deeply drawing in powerful puffs rather excessively, quickly savoring the spicy and nutty flavor in short heaving bursts, and in due time, exhaling quite frenetically, as billows of musty smoke waltzed out through his ruddy snout, the flakes of tobacco and ash sprinkled like patches of sand on his jouncing paunch.

Strangely he dunked the smoldering cigar into his drink and started to rapidly whisk it around, as whatever brew he was mixing spilled and sploshed on him, but it did not seem to matter; he then lifted the soggy cigar giving it a few good whacks on the edge of his horn, and like a straw, Thistleworts mightily sucked it dry instantly destroying the stogie as it crumpled into big chunks, and in a routine, he resumed guzzling his dark beverage, licking the last few drops in a great effort of squeezing his bulbous head as much as it would fit into the horn. He turned his attention to his horde that begged his presence.

Now clouded in a grimy soupy haze, opaque by everyone but himself, the blotto Cap'm asked Bilmey where they had found this unfortunate soul. "I cugt him snupin bout owr territorah!" To which the Hare kindly replied, "I did not mean to snoop only looking for someone, please let me free. I did nothing wrong!" pleaded Wally.

"Silence, I'll be ta judge of t'at!" Cap'm shouted, barreling out of malodorous the cloud toward the mob; as he went about studying the groveling Hare, Wally could say no more. He was subdued as the horde grounded him on his stomach with their dirty feet kept on top of him; leering over him, Cap'm Thistleworts overpowered the Hare with his reeking breath. The Hare was doused by the involuntary dribble of the Cap'm slobbery jaw.

"Who are you looking fer, moight I ask?! Ye come a long way frum yer nice river home to search!"

The Horkurs crushed the Hare tighter with their chipped feet as he squeezed out the answer. "A very dear friend, I am awfully afraid she is lost and is in danger! I must find her; please have a heart!"

"Well, Woollay!!!!!!!!! Your Frens, Adel and Mistum is it? Isn't here!!!!" Cap'm grunted in anger as he commanded the Horkurs to crush him harder. Wally, enduring the severe pressure, was about to break into two parts! He felt his bones start to snap. Cap'm knew darn well who this intruder was from the first moment his tiny eyes saw Wally. When Cap'm saw Wally being dragged in, he realized instantly that it was certainly the one the Quaddlings had praised. At this recognition, his blood boiled, smitten with jealousy at the sight! Oh, how he wanted the Hare's guts to be spilled. He had not believed a single word from Wally. To Cap'm Thistleworts, it was a trick for snooping. In his reluctance to pass an initial sentence on him, the old grubby Boar was quite curious, in fact. He deeply desired to know more from this foolish Hare. Wally was most shocked when he knew his name and asked the malformed Cap'm how he had known.

"Aye, I nevar fergut a name or story, Woollay!!! Tey is VERY fond of you, and I HATES it!!!! Tell me why dae ya t'ink t'ey is hure!? We ain't un tae be kidnuppin ony prutecting this territoree of owrs! You've bun sadly misinformed! Ye koind has always disliked 'ush evun dogh we kupt to ourshulves un ye keep comin to tus here TERRITORY AND BOTTERIN US!!!!!!!!!!!!" Cap'm bellowed, enraged by such a discernment.

"I did not mean to offend not the slightest. I'm just trying to fin-" Wally was cut off by the interjection. -

"Wez dunt l'oik ye snooping koind roonin amook in our terriortoree ye hear!!!?"

"Well, that is fine, of course, ye are entitled to it, but let's keep our differences aside on behalf of the Riverfolk. We don't mean to intrude or be rude. My presence here is just a mistake-"

"A MISTAKE!!!!!? BY IVARG, I am not Glaikit! I understand yer point... yer tricks won't work with me WOOOOLLAAAY!!! What oi cun tell yer is... yer aint nottin to us Horkurs... owr rules are owr oun... weez takes what weez want when weez want it! Us Horkurs are owr oun ere in this borderlands thut imtae true wun ruler. Weez don't takes too kindly to yer fulk! Dae make mesulf clur?" T'ose sisters havered on aboot yer like an idol and to be perfectly honest I hate it...it makes me angry and yer wudnt wunna sae me angry... wut to dae wit ye, wut tae dae?

Wull, I can't have ye dauner away!"

"But I swear to you this is no trick! Why would I travel so far? She and, in fact, a great deal of others have gone missing, and im here to find them, nothing else!"

"LIE!!!!" Bilmey Toags refuted.

Cap'm thought then his malformed face grimly twisted with an awful idea "I knar wez wull toss him auf and SPLAT!!!!!" The Horkurs all busted with roars of zealous cheer as they picked up the poor Hare overhead, and the gruff tribe marched outside chanting "Ye 'ave come tae ye death zaa o o o raaaaa, ye 'ave come tae death, waa nan, a nan allay nan allay!!!" They lighted the fire pits.

Wally, knowing this might be his last moment, had brilliantly thought of an idea that required a skillful form of charismatic flattery. 'It may just work,' he quickly thought to save himself from this impending doom. "But please, before I am to be thrown off, may I have but a few last words?'

"Fine! But make it fast!" The Horkurs all groused upon Cap'm unanticipated acceptance.

"Listen, when I say something strange is stirring, and im trying to solve it! But I do need help! In all truth, I was fully hoping you were indeed here; you mighty Horkurs are quite the glorious bunch as such myths say I am wholly in awe."

"As ye shud!" came the gruff bellow, Cap'm said as he was easily charmed. Wally, now with a smile, continued to praise them.

"I'm not one to be noisy, but is it a crime to seek mighty warriors such as yourselves in time of need heroes such as yourselves?"

"Ah, how vury true!" Cap'm happily gloated. "And great warriors must have a righteous code. Am I wrong? For Adelia's sake and safety, since we both care for her, will you not let your grudge against us be set aside for now? You know, as much as I do, the only hope we can find her and the others is if we band together to fend off whatever is happening here… I cannot force you, but please do consider it wisely, do what you must of me… I am not… afraid…

"AYE, YE SHULD BE! YE FLATTERING SCRIMP OF A HAAAAREEE!!! Yer LYIN

PILLICK!" Thistleworts felt a surge of rage looking at the helpless Hare entirely under the Horkurs' command and control.

Wally lowered his voice but did not stop this time. "As I said … I am not afraid… But afterward, please, you must find Adelia along with the rest!" Wally pleaded with the brutes.

Annoyed beyond his patience, Thistleworts reached for the brutish club bat at his side. He muttered. "I don't truuust yeeerss…., you need to be…" Cap'm Thistleworts stopped mid- sentence. "You aul NEED TO BE…" He stopped for good. Beyond Wally's head, at an odd angle, the smoke from the temple offerings began to rise. Cap'm was deadly still. "By the long Tuskers of Yollgikkos, me

Krodyr, what is happnoin?" The smoke behind Wally was thickening. It became a kind of vapory wall. As Cap'm stared, the wall became a scene of the fallen. Things he had not seen formed in the eddies of the smoke. "I must be... I muuust be..." But the scene continued to unfurl in smoke. The rest were silent, watching Cap'm. The smoke came out in many colors, but the darkest blue plumes were the ones Cap'm dutifully regarded. In the billows that formed, Cap'm saw lots of figures he did not recognize, twisting, writhing, and leering.

Rather than questioning what he saw, and without bothering to wipe his streaming eyes, he beheld a figure adorned in ceremonial garments woven with scarlet and gold threads. The attire was complemented by ancient jewelry crafted by the great jewelers of the past hinterlands, who had remained outcasts for centuries, even unto this fateful day.

Among the swirling images, one began to take shape—a dark purple wash of smoke. It formed slowly at first, then began to solidify. It was him. It was Ivarg the Great Rooter. Ivarg Irontusk. Ivarg the Invincible.

Cap'm was accustomed to things that might perplex him, and he hoped the others would not notice as he stood in contemplation. The spectral image did not dissipate; instead, it began to consume all the other images in its encroaching blackness. Only the form of Ivarg remained, hovering before him and visible to no one else. "I musss be maaaad," he mumbled.

As he stood there, deep in thought, he heard a voice very clearly, saying, "NAR, noot, mad. Nevee. Tiss aon before is raal. Listen. Da noot daar tae strike him. Listen tae him. Listen…"

Unable to raise his eyes, Cap'm looked down. The silence was gently broken by Wally's voice. "Cap'm… Cap'm Thistleworts… you were saying… are you alright?" he asked softly.

"Yus'm alright... say no more. I've hurd enough." Suddenly, Cap'm' had slowly realized regarding the now vanished image of Ivarg, which had become so diffused as to be just ordinary smoke from a firepit. What if what this Hare said could be true, and if indeed these threats were luring them all in? Part of this chaos was not only for them, the Riverfolk, but also for the Horkurs. It dawned on Cap'm suddenly that there would be no choice but to do the right thing and collaborate, even having his grudge against the Riverfolk. Though they had cast him and his clan out ages ago, he couldn't let terms of peace be unsettled. He commanded the Horkurs to let Wally go, and they reluctantly did.

"Weez are honor bound. Woooollay! We have lost owr ways an' forguteen owr pride, WE HAVE BEEN WRONG… but no longer, I have seen what we must do, I think its aboot guud time ta reclaim owr loost ruspet once again!!! This is owr chance! If ye have spoken thar troot thun by great Ivarg himself who is ta Horkurs tae let things go wrong, we stand by ye brave Woollay, wit' owr miht and tusks this land will neva be plundered!!! Horkurs let oush find Adelum and the rest, let oush unite with tase riverfolk, FORSH TA GREATA GOOUUUD!!!!!! Turn this whole borderland upside down if need bey! Bilmey! Chumby Whurn, escort owr neefond frun' back where he belongs! This is no job forsh sufthearts! And don't ye worry Woollay whurever tey is we will find t'em an' bring tem back! Ye have haur word…" Cap'm Thistleworts bellowed.

"I sincerely thank you…you are mighty heroes, as I would have expected." Wally praised them as the Horkurs all hollered, and by Thistleworts command, they all divided into small hordes and started to march their way into Sullen Fields, scouring for the missing residents, and escorted Wally back home.

While many Riverfolk were tidying and counting what was lost to the storm back in Ambrodale, to their dismay, they left Booney in charge of their children, his newly found band. They scoured any remains from across the bridge and into the borderlands; the cheerless children were most afraid. Their little paws collected as much as they could to rebuild their homes. In a V formation, they marched whistling a little tune. Booney, upfront, continued his hopping and, at times, continued throat-bellowing, excitedly leading them as he twirled his walking cane like a baton. They trekked deeper towards and eventually within the borderland as on a scavenging hunt they went. All went well, too well, until Booney called out attendance to find three of the ten children missing!

Booney was most fretful, "Wull we can't 'ave this, Oh! BOLLOCKS!!!!! WHY MEEEEEE!!!!? OH BOLLOCKS! T'ey mums will ring me poor neck, t'ey will, if'n anything huppuns!!!" The children started to cry. Composing himself, Booney reassured them all. "T'ere is no need ta blubber; we'll find t'em! It's a game, afer all 'ight?" Booney coolly tried to boost morale among them.

Booney, along with the rest, had then called out the missing children's names, hoping to find them, but to no avail. He tried to do a horn-like alarm from his croaker, but little one named Nissie began to cry upon hearing the sound Booney had hurriedly produced. She had said it might scare the lost ones yet more to hear such an unwarranted blast. "No hidin' and seekin', no tricks!" Booney hollered. He collapsed a bit from the effort, having exhausted his supply of wind. As he lay down for a spell to recover, he suddenly felt quite alone. The many children who followed the Frog one by one were quietly being snatched and stashed into brown burlap sacks. As this occurred, they squealed in muffled tones to be set free.

Unfortunately, the scenario went unnoticed by the winded Frog until he was finally alone. "It's awfully quiet!" he said at last as he turned around to find every last child gone! Booney finally threw a stuttering tantrum, yelling at the top of his little lungs, "N-N-N-N-N N-O-O-O-O- NO… NO, G-G-G-G-G- A-A-A-MES N-N-N-NOW, COME ON OUT WHEREVER YER ARE! W-

W-W-W-E-E-E HAD OUR F-F-F-FUN NOW!!" As he let out one last croak, which tapered off like a leaking balloon. Just before he could inhale to say anything else, a group of hidden figures came from behind and snatched him up in haste as well.

Chapter Nine
An Ugly Truth

By the time Wally had been captured by the Horkurs and was presently negotiating, Whyles was well far off on his own intrepid and lonely expedition. Clenching the speckled pebble gifted by Miriam, his ambitious goal was to find a hidden grove in Gorse-End, which lay just beyond the Hounds' encampment. He had overheard the Hounds speak of their guard duties there. He had been sorely forbidden to ever visit for menacing consequences in that breach of trust, warranted expressly by Kaliber.

"I'll get her back; I'll get them all back. I don't care what happens to me..." The Fox declared with a chivalrous spirit, but yet there came another voice that beckoned his attention.

'Turn back...turn back. YOU owe nothing... Save yourself...now's your chance... Kaliber has what he needs…… Run...Run…. He won't find you. No one needs to know anything….be free of them all …be free!' These inner conflicts would not stop him this time, he assured himself as he strode forward.

"Owes them much more than I can give. I am done with runnin'!" He said briskly and with more than a hint of anger. He was, in fact, absolutely incensed this time around.

He soon sadly discovered, however, and to his tired vexation, that the grove he was trying to reach was obstructed! It was barricaded by a sizeable forticated palisade with walkways, where the guards kept a garrulous watch. The palisade was crudely assembled with jagged and serrated metal sheets ringed with rust spots and ribboned with barbed wires. There was no visible ground-level entry. It all looked like a large and jagged unwound spring coiled inside one of Wally's many antique clocks that he had broken on several occasions as he tried to understand the workings of such things that chimed with no visible instruments. The encampment stood before him as an evil stockade full of the unmentionable things he knew well. The things deep within the earth swelled in nightmarish writhing, awaiting their own turn to work evil. Perplexed by the magnitude of the puzzle before him, he briefly paused.

"How am I gonna get through?" He asked himself for a few long moments as he envisaged a plan. The walls were much too high to climb without leverage. Even if he managed to scale it, how could he go undetected with the number of guards at the ready, watching and leering on the main road? Maybe there was a way to trick them to let him up… but how?

"Hullo up t'ere!" he called to the guards. The guards inspected their surroundings and gaped at the Fox.

"Oh. It's you. We were wondering when you might show up agin'. ISN'T IT THAT YOU'RE NOT SUPPOSED TO BE HERE, YOU LITTLE TWIIT!

Betraying none of the habitual fears, the Fox said confidently with a burst of enthusiasm. "'Ave you not heard? What do ye sit all ta day for nothing?'

"Bollocks, ye crumb of spittle!" Laughed Grendower, the stupidest of the Hounds and somehow given the most critical job. Fit for still sitting as a sodden drunk his entire life was his stock in trade.

"YOU DON'T KNOW DO YOU? I would not talk to me in that tone. Kaliber said this fortress, if'n you call this pile of waste anything special, he said it's got weak points, and he wants em fixed NOOOOW!" Grendower blanched.

'YOUA SLIMY LITTLE NO-GOO RUBBISH EATIN, ' PELT A' PESTILENCE, YOU SON OF A FLYIN' PIECE OF TU!"

"Shut yer dribblin' trap, you sluggard! Whyles interrupted the rant. He was cooler and calmer than he had ever been. He shook not and glared at the stupid Grendower. He could only stand mute in response, Alarmed at the Fox and his boldness.

'Well, when did he say it, and why do you, you little!"

"AS YOU SIT HERE ALL-DAY DRINKING, DO YOU KNOW WHAT GOES ON OUT

THERE? Have you ever even talked to Lord (Whyles tried not to snicker when he added Lord to Kaliber's name) Kaliber one-on-one?"

Grendower was struck by this. Everyone knew Whyles saw more of Kaliber than anyone else.

Whyles continued. "Have you been told about the workings of the Riverfolk? T'ey's not stupid; they are figuring things out; they are NOT ALONE, YOU SIMPLETOON!"

Grendower swallowed hard. Whyles suddenly saw an opportunity: every device has a weak spot, and instead of taking the obvious approach, the key to damaging it might be to exploit that central mechanism's vulnerability. Whyles knew he could manipulate Grendower's lack of insight to his advantage. "WHAT ARE YAR LOOKING AT? Idiot! What is Kaliber telling you to do? SHOW ME WHERE THERE IS A BREACH YOU SLOB!".

Grunting, Grendower came down the side of the twisted ramparts. He spoke quietly. "Look here, Foxy. I bleve's yar. But if anything happens here, It's yer skin I'll flay. Unnystand?"

Whyles did not so much as blink. "It's ok for me to save your skin from Lord Kaliber's wrath by telling you this, but you want to do me in for it. YOU shameful bucket of bile!" Whyles hissed.

"Get on with it!" He snapped in Grendower's ear.

Grendower walked almost sheepishly. 'Well, only I know the details here. They approached a low wall barricade. "T'e Hounds, us, I means. Well, we gort tired, and we didn't do this right. It's breachable alrigth." Whyles looked on. There was a gaping hole hidden by a partial full- height wall. From a distance, it looked completely sealed, but if one got closer, the hole was rather large.

"How long will it take to repair?" Snapped Whyles, pointing at the many piles of tools scattered across the barricade.

"'Boud a week or two with this lot! They're mostly drunk nights, but don't tell His Lordship. I'm trying to work to keep them on their feet. Least the watchmen on the wall." Whyles saw there were no watchmen at all in the area as it was concealed from view even from the highest platform. It did appear imposing and impregnable. In reality, Whyles now ascertained that there were huge gaps in defense.

"Please don't be too hard on us when ye tells Kallyburr nuun of us want our paw or sompin worse chopped off ...I'M BEGGIN YA..." He hated begging; Whyles was very impressed with this certain achievement: "Well then, fix it and make it snappy before the Lord hears of it!

Besides, no one can see it... 'cept me, and what can I, a mere weakling, do?" Whyles skillfully interrupted... Sounding official, he asked, "How long and how many workers?"

"Why maybe hulf the guard and maybe two... no 'ree weeks. But we'll do it, we will!"

"For morale, be quiet about this. Get only a few Hounds at most, and don't work nights. It will be very suspicious if Silas catches wurd. YOU will all be dead. Too suspicious. IF Kaliber knows the extent of this, I am sure you all will be replaced and certainly executed."

'YOU have me word!" Said Grendower with a kind of fearful sincerity.

"Good. Get to work. Be smart! Don't betray your guard by acting stupid and showing off. I am sure you will all pay dearly if you act like a fool. Good day!"

Whyles did not turn around to look at the sniveling and grumbling Grendower. 'Two weeks at best.' He thought to himself. 'Too easy. These fools.' He heard himself laugh out loud, but by now, he was well out of earshot. 'Now is the time!' He thought, racing towards a secret little nook he found not so far from the barricade, and this was where he kept a watch over things until he was ready.

Nightfall came. It was a clear but cold night—the kind of night when he knew the guards drank. Whyles crept toward the barricade, but he was in for a rude surprise upon seeing the Hounds positioned along the exposed wall, their low murmurs drifting in the crisp evening air.

Whyles withdrew into the shroud of darkness and then dropped to his belly, the cold earth pressing against his fur as he began to dig. His forepaws clawed at the damp soil, sending clumps of dirt flying in all directions. The rhythmic thud of his digging echoed in the silence; each stroke driven by a desperate urgency. The barricade loomed above him, a heavy reminder of the obstacles standing in the way of freedom, THEIR freedom

As he burrowed deeper, the dampness of the earth clung to his paws, and the sweet scent of moisture mixed with decay filled his nostrils. He felt the soil give way beneath his determined claws, his muscles straining as he fought against the weight of despair pressing down on him. Sweat mixed with the dirt on his brow, but he pressed on, his heart pounding in time with his efforts.

With every handful of earth he tossed aside, Whyles envisioned the prisoners just beyond the barricade, their weary faces urging him forward. He focused on the task, the tunnel slowly forming beneath him, a small passageway that could lead to hope. The noise of the world above faded, replaced by the sound of his own breathing and the scrape of his claws against the earth.

The minutes stretched into what felt like hours, but Whyles' determination never wavered. He was a blur of movement, a creature of instinct, digging and pushing through the damp soil. Each clump of dirt was a step closer to freedom.

With a final flurry of movement, Whyles pushed aside the last clumps of dirt, his heart pounding in anticipation. He paused, feeling the rush of cool air against his fur, a tantalizing hint of freedom. Taking a deep breath, he braced himself, then poked his head out from the freshly dug hole and saw the many cages.

As he approached the cages, he avoided any interactions, only to be confronted by the horrifying truth: there were far more prisoners than he had ever imagined. The sight was a painful shock.

How had so many been captured? How had he forgotten about this? The guilt was overwhelming. He recalled the complaints he had overheard in Ambrodale, concerns he had dismissed out of hand. Now, seeing the suffering he had a hand in causing, Whyles was filled with profound regret. He felt sickened by his own callousness and fear, realizing too late the full extent of his actions and their impact on those he had betrayed.

He knew well he had been played like a pawn enabling this travesty. But here and now, they were there. No excuses could justify the shackled, starving, and haunting faces, once golden and showing jolly merriment, now sickly and sunken, wearing their approaching doom in great misery. Worse yet, the poor prisoners were choked by tight metal collars locked around their necks, but it was just more than any degrading collar; these were specialty torture collars. There were embedded iron spikes that pierced into the gashed necks of these unfortunate souls. Sadder yet, some of the more talky prisoners were muzzled to keep them quiet and hungry. Whyles could not bear to see them suffer any longer in these cages made of wire. He could not help but blame himself, cursing his very existence. But now was not the time to contemplate or condemn himself. He knew that freeing all of them at once would be no easy task. Where would he bring them to? Where would they all be safe from the wrath of Kaliber? It would require time, and time wasn't on his side.

He silently crept to the cages, avoiding any open areas, and tried to jiggle the doors. They were, of course, locked. The many prisoners had pleaded with the Fox to set them free. "I'm trying, I'm trying, just please don't make a fuss I'll get you all out, I promise!"

"There are so many of them," he muttered to himself, thinking of a way to free them. Scanning the area, he then heard an oncoming assembly of Hounds fully equipped with an arsenal. In fear of being spotted, he crawled behind the cages and hid beneath the bushes nearby. He counted the many Hounds assigned to guard the prisoners by order of Lord Coveton. But what could Kaliber have wanted with all of them? Whyles questioned. How wicked and cruel young Kaliber Coveton indeed was! Had he not a soul!? He had then heard a familiar voice coming in front of the bush he was hiding in. It was a dispirited whimpering that sank his heart, and when he peeked over to see who it was. In his correct assumption, it was Adelia D. Quaddling slumped in the corner. She was unrecognizable. She was unduly gaunt. Her once pristine feathers, which she had spent incredible time and generous self-admiration preening, had been ruffled and shorn of their once natural luster. Like the rest of the razor-shorn prisoners, the dress that she had worn previously was now replaced in the same fashion as the rest. They were all dirty and tattered burlap uniforms with flax woven caps printed with labels and numbers. Motionless, she contemplated, fearing she would never see Wally or her home, her dear sister, or never bake, never again. Morosely, she quietly nibbled on a stale pastry she had baked in her home and had hidden in her satchel beneath her wing before all of this mess. However, fearing others who have been going hungry might find out and expose the treats, she quickly tucked it back in after a few nibbles.

Whyles called her attention in a whisper. She startled. "W-w-w-w-hoooooo's there?" She trembled.

"It's me!"

"Who's me?"

"Who do you think!?"

Adelia started to guess, only to be cut off by the inpatient jittery Fox. "No time for guessing games! I'm here to rescue you!" Whyles declared.

"Oh, that's nice…" Adelia moaned despondently.

"Didn't you hear me?" Whyles asked, surprised by her answer. "Of course I did, but " the sister stopped.

"But what?" hissed Whyles.

"But YOURE the reason I'm here, the reason we are all here!"

Whyles stiffened, turning white and clammy, and his face became twitchy. His heart stopped beating as if dead. He wished he had been dead. This she knew, she knew everything. Her eyes showed the great fear and the mistrust she had for him.

"How do you know?" "The Wolf…"

"Yes… yes, go on!" Whyles rushed her for an explanation.

"I overheard him talk to those houndies on what to do with us just before they shaved our beautiful coats…and choked us with these collars… we can hardly breathe," she gasped. "They spoke of you… they are not who you think they are!"

"I-I-I kno-kno-know that now…" Whyles gulped involuntarily.

"I t'ink you should leave; visitors are not allowed … RULES ARE RULES," Adelia shot back at him.

"A' Hell with those rules, I am not leaving without you, or any of you…" "Just please, leave us in peace; I can't bear to talk to you!" Adelia sobbed.

"Wull, you'll just have to bear with me a little bit more, I'm afraid..." Whyles smiled a broken tooth smile.

"It's too late for that."

"It's never too late to try, as someone special said..." Whyles said, trying to win her over

"We believed in you, Mr. Fox, such high hopes; guess we were wrong; it was all just a cruel hoax..."

"I can't defend for what I did; I meself lived in fear of such punishments, and for that, you have now... my full apology. But I'm different now; you can trust me; you MUST trust me; I am here now; I can't let you all rot. I am here to free you, P'-P'E-E-E-A-A-S-S-E." The Fox whispered emphatically. "I wholly swear it; why else am I risking me own life if it's all just a trick? The Fox began to cry. The tears streamed down his face... "I didn't mean for any of this to happen; I was a fool beyond a fool; p'ease, I beg of you, come with me; I have changed!"

Each block of cells was cramped and utterly detestable, "What do I do? What do I do?!" He then saw one of the Hounds possessed small jingling keys attached to his belt. Whyles eagerly bided for the large group to split up and devised to have the prisoners make as much noise possible to distract the guard so he could be able to pickpocket the key off him. Whyles passed on his plan to the prisoners, and so they obliged. The plan was set into action. Whyles gave the word; he made his move and darted for the key while the prisoners distracted the key bearer, whose back was turned, "SHUDDYDUP IN DER!!!!" The guard snarled as he went about smacking the wires with his whip. Brilliantly, and without any cue from Whyles, little bunny Clarence threw a rotten apple core, which struck the guard in the eye. Whyles saw his chance. In a flash of nimble agility, he lurched silently forth and ripped the dangling bunch without a sound... Success! The Fox snagged the key and rolled back into the bushes.

'OOO THREEEW THAAT AT MEEE.WHICH OOONE OF YER SCUUURVY LOUTS???

"You'll all get it now... ALLL OOOFF YEEEEE!!!" Adelia, now set in a kind of smug satisfaction that they most certainly get anything further from these devils, chuckled to herself. 'SEEERVEEES YEEE RIGHT YEE BLAGGARD!!"

"WHIICH UN OF YEE BLOWSEEEEES SAID 'AAAT!?'" The guard scowled.

The prisoners cheered but were muted once again by the guard, who was quite confused by their outburst of cheers. The Fox felt great pride in himself almost to his mind; he felt redeemable.

But it was not over yet, he knew. He had possession of the keys, but the matter of freeing them all was still very troubling. Not quite knowing what to do, in a grossly reckless act, while the guard was off surveying the area and looking for help perhaps, Whyles jumped right in front of the cage complex as he fumbled with the assortment of random keys of all different shapes and sizes, unable to find the perfect match, the antsy Fox haphazardly resorted to jamming each little key into the lock trying to forcefully fit them in and unlock the cage, but without any such luck, that is until he wiggled the largest key into the colossal padlock, CLICK, the door swung open! The Riverfolk could not be any happier as they rushed out, thanking their hero! However, unbeknownst to the grateful prisoners, who were all too busy thanking the Fox to really notice anything at all, the gruff Hound swiftly turned, realizing the breakout, charged like a furious bull toward the horde.

"Loook out behind you!" They announced; the mongrel viciously lunged at the startled Fox; his attacker seized ahold of Whyles, throttling the very life out of him, feeling his lungs collapsing and his ribs cracking. In a fierce struggle, Whyles retaliated, using his sharp claws to scratch at the Hound's arms, desperately trying to fend off his attacker. Whyles managed to squeeze out a muffled command to the onlookers to break for it and meet him up the road. "RUUUUN GET OUTTA HERE! HURRY HURRY BEFORE THEY CATCH YOU!!!" Whyles cried as the

shackled prisoners fled the tussle as fast as they could, which wasn't so fast, for they had no strength to carry on. They were withered and broken, and they hurtled onwards, tripping over themselves on the way to where Whyles directed them. The Fox bit hard on the Hound's arms, tasting the bitter blood in his mouth. He successfully escaped the hazardous restraint.

"Ye have the fight in ya? Well, this should be fun... for me!" The Hound laughed, licking his bleeding bite marks.

The Hound was violently snapping and biting; Whyles, writhing, tried to slip and slide like gliding on ice. Suddenly, Whyles was pinned to the ground by the embattled Hound, who kept on chomping and slashing at the poor Fox. With his frantic paws, Whyles tried to divert the gnawing mouth of the deranged Hound. The harrowing shindy was a horrible show; the petrified Fox blinded the Hound. Whyles had whipped a handful of clotted dirt at the Hound's eyes, but that did not seem to stop the Hound for very long; rather, he seemed to enjoy it. The Fox defended himself as well as he could with a long stick he somehow managed to grab ahold of as he was rolling in the dirt. He jammed the stick into the chomping maw of the feral Hound, keeping him at bay as long as possible, but to his dismay, the Hound's sharp fangs crushed it, snapping the stick in half! No longer could the weakly ox keep his resisting force. The Hound was overpowering the poor, overburdened Fox. In a grim second, he savagely ripped deep into the flesh of Whyles' right shoulder. Whyles severely mauled arm became paralyzed. In searing agony and with Whyles losing his breath, Whyles realized he may not survive another wound. He knew if he gave up, then surely Ambrodale would be doomed.

Steadfastly, he kicked out his legs from beneath the ravaging body of the rabid Hound. The surprised Hound, caught so unexpectedly by the little Fox, flew into the largest empty cage. Whyles, in a burst of anger, quickly crawled to the door, slamming it and locking it with the key in his waist pocket he so carefully guarded before the skirmish with the deranged Hound. As the Hound tried to rise within the cage, Whyles tossed the key, throwing it as far as he could. It landed a distance in the mucky swamp whose evil vapors seemed to surround the entire cluster of cages. The snarling Hound burned with seething acrimony. Entrapped now, having been outsmarted by the Fox, the Hound was licking the dripping blood from his muzzle as he kept trying to claw at Whyles. He went on dementedly, barking, frothing, howling! But to no effect.

Whyles, grasping his grisly wound, regarded the thrashing Hound and wondered if that would have been his own fate under different circumstances. He grimaced and right then bolted out of sight. As he ran, he heard a loud whistle penetrate the entire area. Whyles knew it was the trapped Hound blowing on the screeching whistle, alerting the rest to the sudden liberation of their captives. Whyles limped back to where a large company of prisoners gathered around. They were sullen and cheerless. They were all frightened and confused. Though beaten, bruised, and bloody, Whyles brought them together the best he could as they all followed in a dull wave of bodies. They turned to every pathway they thought sanctioned safety but were then to be redirected into the middle of the encampment, where they had begun. "Which way? which way!?"

No way is safe!!!!" They all cried. "What do we do???" When the dreadful sounds of the onrushing horde of merciless marauders answered the series of alarm trills, the group was in complete disarray as they frantically scampered in all directions. They were trying to hide, trying to plead, but in the very end, the freed captives were encircled by a massive pack of growling angry Hounds. All stood in dead quiet. Whyles stood in the middle, his tin pot in paw. As the Hounds started dashing to the captives, Whyles started batting them away, swinging his pot in all directions, but there were too many. The hostages feared for their lives as they all were frozen in fear. Then a wicked howl broke through the intense stillness as there came slow clapping which rent the stillness with its' unkind sharpness.

"Ah yes yeeees, a TRUUUULY mirandum shoooow! How very amuuuuuusing!!!" Kaliber cried out in mock applause of their failed collective effort. Whyles scuttled back into the masses and crouched beneath the captives, trying to blend in, hoping to hide from the Wolf. Whyles knew so very well that the punishment for treason would be severe. Kaliber knew instantly that Whyles must have been the leader and called out to the Fox. "Ooooooh, Whyles, my dear friend, come on out! You can't hide from me! I'll give you a chance to come out if you are so bold; come then... on a count of three!" Kaliber, mockingly again, started to count. He held his long fingers out while crying, "Unus!" Nothing happened. "Duo!" A still silence prevailed. Kaliber screeched, "I'm not one to wait, FOX!! FACE MEEEE!. Tres!" Kaliber was now positively out of his mind. Collecting himself in his ire, Kaliber said in a pitying tone, "How very sad... but, very well.. you've had your chance for an honorable explanation, now it's time to pay DEARLY!" Kaliber pointed at one of his hulking goons. "Fetch!" He ordered.

The growling Hound rushed in, nipping and snapping his way through the crowd to find the Fox. Whyles was found curled and trembling beneath the lumbering. The Hound dragged poor Whyles by his ragged tail. The Fox frantically clawed at the dirt as he pleaded and cried for mercy, "Please have mercy on me, Lord. I onla..."

"Only what!!!?" Kaliber snapped.

The captives couldn't help but watch. "Ah, Whyles, you certainly are a brave one! Oh, how very disappointing. I sincerely thought more of you but very well.

Come NOW; we have FAAAAR TOO MUCH to discuss…" Kaliber sneered, patting the Fox on his head. Then, he harshly gripped him by his yellow jacket and forcefully pulled Whyles up toward him. The Fox stared at the appalled and shocked prisoners before him.

"You were with them? All of this time!?" One of the prisoners cried out in a flush of resentment as they, too, were being escorted back to their confines.

"Im sooray, I- I- I tried…" the Fox weakly bleated in response.

"And you failed horribly! Now it's time for gravis repercussions." Snickered Kaliber, blindfolding the Fox, as he could not see, but he could hear all the madness of Hounds calling him names and swearing to "burn him alive!!!" And to hear Kaliber wickedly call out, "ALL IN GOOD TIME!!!!" He shivered, and he had every right to, for he foresaw this twisted end, and at this exact moment of the shaming, Whyles was derogatorily marched before all to see, to be mocked, jeered at.. As the Hounds witnessed Whyle's downfall, they threw all sorts of rubbish at him. How Whyles now wished he hadn't tried to do what he did. He deeply regretted that he did not run away when he had the perfect chance to escape all of the madness now before him. He heard the sounds of clanking and angry threats arising somewhere before him.

When the blindfold was finally yanked off, Whyles, disoriented and unsure of his surroundings, scanned the area. To his horror, he found himself in the center of a dimly lit dungeon. Amidst the shadows, he glimpsed a spectral figure of Clovis Kaine. Kaine seemed to hover in a corner, his fiery eyes and infernal chest glowing ominously as smoke swirled around his imposing form. "Unforgivable!" the apparition bellowed repeatedly.

However, Clovis was invisible to Kaliber, who stormed into the chamber with a golden chalice in hand, sipping from it as he passed right through the ghostly figure. As Kaliber moved through the vision, Whyles felt a chilling draft, and Clovis Kaine abruptly vanished as if swept away by the wind. Whyles was left wondering if Clovis had been a mere figment of his troubled mind, though the echoes of the ghost's furious cries lingered in the air.

Then, like a spotlight, many objects had grabbed the Fox's attention and to his greatest fear, torture devices of all menacing kinds displayed like glorified prizes; he was terrified of them all, as Kaliber proudly pointed and sadistically boasted each one, fingering the many whips hanging on the wall. "They are my TRICAE!

Do you like them, my dear friend? I sincerely hoped you wouldn't have to meet them, but oh, well, it's much too late!!! Now, I'm very afraid if you don't talk… well, these certainly will! Are not they marvelous!?!"

Whyles eyes widened with terror, and they pleaded with the Wolf to spare him. The Wolf smiled heinously, stretching and leering over him, and he spilled the drink all over the Fox. "Oooooooh, my dear Whyles, it utterly pains me to see you grovel if only… if only you had OBEYED, then nothing like this would ever happen! Sadly, I must expel any little inkling you have to ever BETRAY MEE AND DISOBEY MY TRUST AGAIN by ANY means! Understood? The Wolf snarled, squeezing the chin of the poor, frantic Fox; Whyles pleaded with his master to forgive him, assuring him it would never happen again. Kaliber said with a deriding solace, "Dear Whyles, did I misspeak that? What fun would it be if I just let you go without any consequence from your WICKED TREACHERY? How veeeeeery shameful, but how I truly blame myself for your despicable defiance! Oh, my poor aching heart is breaking!!! Kaliber mewled, "I thought you would understand MY MAAAAAANY SACRIFICES I MADE FOR YOOOU!!!! MY OOOOOOWN REPUTATION ON THE LIIIIINE!!! Where did I go wrong RAISING you?! But it was my mistake to trust any lowly servant! But this treachery shall never happen again!" Kaliber cackled, choosing his preferred torture utensil. "Ah so so sooooo many to choooooose which one which one…" I know I'll let the dice decide!" curling his lips, he commanded one of his goons who had escorted him in to gag him just before Whyles could utter any justifiable excuses for his bold betrayal.

"I've heard enough of your blubbering! You had it coming; I TRIED protego you from all this!!!!! YOU HAD TO MEDDLE AND BE THE HEROOOOOOO!!! My dear fool, how I pity you; THERE ARE NOOOOOOO HEROOOOOOS IN THIS saevus WOOOORLD ONLY WINNERS AND LOOOOOOSERS, MIIIIIIGHTY RULERS AND THE INDIGNANT DESTITUTE SWIIIIINES!!! I SHALLL NOOOOT LOSE NOOOO NOT AGAIN!!!! You

SHALL SUFFER FOR SUCH A MINDLESS SCHEME!" And so the Fox was gagged by the order. Kaliber had then grabbed ahold of the Fox and promptly tied the trembling Fox onto two stakes planted on the floor, Whyles's arms tortuous outstretched on these poles, blood dripping from his wrist in which the rope sliced; Whyles retrained, waited for the cruel punishment. He watched Kaliber, who stood next to the many other tools, his face rippling the vilest and crooked expression, a warped, bitter expression of pure madness. Kaliber taunted the poor Fox. "Soooo, you think you are sooooo clever, do you?!!! Do you think you can trick me?!" Kaliber asked, knowing whyles could not respond, for he was gagged, and in a maniacal cry, he wailed, "WELLL YOOOOOOUR NOOOOOOT!!!! I AM NOT ONE TO BE FOOOOLED!" The

fuming Wolf with quick, choppy breaths as his face reddened in a sudden frenzied surge of aggravation as he ripped poor Whyles's face with his shaking claw, leaving a horrible bloody gash; Whyles burst into tears in his extreme pain. Kaliber had exploded like a volcano into an abhorrent sadist ignited by the act of betrayal and deception, an action he knew all too well and deeply loathed. "Bonum bonum!!! Feeeeeel the pain I feeeeeeel!!! You WORTHLESS wretch, RESPECT ME, DAMN YOOOOOU! FEEEEEEAR THE COVETON WRAITH!!!! I AM YOOOOOUR MAAAAASTERRRRR," Kaliber cackled in a twisted scowl.

Kaliber then tore the back of his yellow jacket, exposing the Fox's bare back. With a malevolent grin, he rolled the dice, savoring their outcome before slipping them back into his pocket. He selected the most fearsome of whips from among the assortment, its menacing presence unmistakable. "AHHHHH, SOOO GLOOOOOORIOUS!" The Wolf exulted, brandishing the cruel cat-o'-nine-tails. The lashes were long and cruel, almost resembling fangs, and with every crack as Kaliber practiced, the whip seemed to hiss, eager for the taste of flesh.

Kaliber directed the whip at the Fox's exposed back, swinging it with ruthless abandon. He bellowed in a wild, incoherent frenzy, his voice a cacophony of barbaric rage. Each lash seemed to embody his frenzied state, striking out at his own tormented memories with a savage, hypnotic fervor.

Like a hysteric barbarian, viciously lashing out at his memories in a bellicose hypnotic state. The striking lashes venomously warbled.

Crack! Crack!

Feed us

With your sweet taste of fears and tears.

Snap! Snap!

Plead for mercy.

We hear your mournful cries, Your trembling lies.

Bleed! Bleed!

Whyles could only think, 'Why do I even care for them?' Tears brimmed in the Fox's eyes as the lashes fell, each cut a piece of his soul cleaved away, pooling beneath him.

With each corrective cutting blow, Kaliber's fury twisted into a warped fantasy. In his mind, he wasn't striking Whyles but at the Bourchiers—the ones who had sneered at his hunger, mocked his missteps, and cast him away.

"Damnate vos, Bourchiers!" he snarled, spittle flying as streaks of blood spattered across his twisted muzzle.

For Whyles, though, the pain was all too real. Every lash felt as though a piece of his very soul was being torn away.

'I'm nothing but a husk.' Whyles thought, emptied of spirit.

Kaliber took a moment's rest to ease his frazzled nerves. He wiped off the putrid blend of sweat and gore, dabbing the stains on his smeared jacket with his handkerchief. The depraved Wolf, his bowler hat slanted and veins bulging, stood tense like a scarecrow above the draped Fox, ready to strike again. 'But I can't let him win,' Whyles silently vowed, drawing upon the flicker of hope that still lingered deep within him.

As Kaliber prepared to deliver the next blow, he began to recite his riddles with a cruel edge, each line punctuated by the lash of his whip:

"I promise you safety, but lead you astray, My path is a web where your trust is my prey. What am I, who trades truth for deceit,

Bringing you to ruin with every deceitful feat?"

(Crack!)

"I wear many faces and speak with a smile,

Yet my words are falsehoods, my actions beguile. I offer a hand, but it's always a snare,

What am I, who makes trust rare?"

(Crack!)

"A friend in the daylight, a foe in the dark, I plot, and I scheme, leaving behind a mark.

What am I, whose loyalty is a fleeting dream, Always ready to shatter the trust that might seem?" (Crack!)

"A smile upon my lips, a dagger in my hand, My loyalty is but a lie, a treacherous stand.

I offer you warmth, then leave you to chill, What am I, whose deceit is the deadliest thrill?" (Crack!)

Kaliber fell silent, a devilish glare and smirk locked upon the grisly discipline that had been sculpted into Whyles's searing back—a sight that was far from pretty.

"My beautiful artwork, how truuuuly MAGNIFICENT!!! I really do outdo myself!" Kaliber profoundly admitted. The Wolf proudly marked the broken Fox, who was hardly breathing. Thick, scarlet blood oozed like a leaking foist, and the gruesome, clotted lacerations were deep and raw, like clumps of uncooked pastries crisscrossed on one another. Patting Whyles on the head once again, Kaliber clenched his jaw, showing fangs that jutted out like a beaver's teeth as he snarled, "Always remember Whyles, I am your MASTER; you are nothing without me; if I didn't care about you, I would toss you to the Hounds for FOOOOOOOD… I am not your enemy; I am a great ally but ever dare to try to betray me again. Weeeeeeelll, I guess you will have to wait and seeeeeee! I wouldn't wanna spoil any fuuuuun! Just know this! You owe me your life and service and, most of all, GRATITUDE… after all, whooooo saved you?

When I found you half dead?" Kaliber asked, ungagging Whyles, urging him to speak his mind because he felt the Fox had something to say. In a murmur, the Fox complied, avoiding any eye contact.

"What do you have planned for them?"

"I beg your pardon!?" The Wolf cackled, cupping his ears and leaning forward. The Fox muttered to himself.

"SPEAK UP!" Kaliber roared, kneeling in front of the helpless Fox, grabbing him by his chin and forcefully pulling his heartrending face towards him to where their eyes met.

Whyles could not help but weep. In a soul-stirring reply, he cried aloud, "WHAT DO YOU HAVE PLANNED FOR THEM? P'EASE TELL MEEE." Kaliber laughed in his face.

"Enough with your mortifying sentiments! It's all to simply appalling for me to think you actually care about those dull-witted sluggards! Tell me, Friiiiieeeend, why do you seek their paltry approbation sooooo desperately? Perhaps you secretly wish to be adopted by them? It would most certainly seem that way! Am I wrong?!

"I d-d-dunt mean to offund b-b-but if I d-d-d do-o-o speak troo' I am vury afraid uf yer reaction ye will have... I dare not say. M-m-m-m mouth is sealed."

"Come tell me NOW. I desire to know. I DEMAAAAND to know. I COMMAND IT!!!!" Whined Kaliber dramatically, like a stage actor wanning for an encore.

Whyles did not say a peep. To the Fox's unresponsive slant, the snarling Wolf, in a blaze of unrelentingly winding fury, backhand slapped Whyles across his bleeding face, leaving a perfect imprint of the Coveton signet ring. The shock and power of the strike caused the already debilitated Fox to spout up more blood.

"I suggest you start talking, or I may just lose my temper again, and we wouldn't want that now?! I'd really hate to resort to any other forceful means... If I lose my temper, you lose something faaaaar woooorse! Do I make myself Cleeeearrrrr?!! Now, pleeeease, I implore you to tell meeee. If you do, I solemnly swear by my RIGHTEOUS Coveton code I will not come to harm you, and furthermore-"

"Promise?" The Fox groaned, distrustful of Kaliber.

"Deeeear dear beloved SNOOOOOOPY friend, why a Coveton never eveeeeer saaaay anything they don't mean… it's distastefully undignifying!"

"Wit' all due respuc, it is me job ta be snoopin like!!! Is it not?"

"Aaaaaah yes, of course, how right you are! I do apologize for such a brazen comment of mine. How foolish of me, but please understand you can never be too cautious!"

"Well, it ju-ju-just t-t-th-at I- I- I fe-fe-fe-els whuts ta wurd?" "Special, fortasse?" Kaliber simpered as he clicked his tongue. "Y-y-y-yes th-th-ats i-i-it!

"There, there, it is all over now…you see, that wasn't difficult in the slightest; it's actually quite understandable!"

"Wh-Why-y-y is t-t-th-th-at?"

You see, you have been brainwashed by them, that's all, but thankfully, I am here to set your confusion aside! ALL YOU HAVE TO DO IS OBEY OBEY OBEY and learn your place! The receiving benefits are GRAAAAAND! Now that you are fully cooperative, then yes, you should deserve to know what the future holds… It's genuinely an ingeniously brilliant, nay MAGNIFICENT idea I have concocted!" Kaliber declared and cleared his throat, and began his history and scheme rather theatrically.

"Since that very tragic unforgettable day of my deplorable expulsion of the Coveton heir, MY GIVEN BIRTH RIIIIIGHT, I must add, MY DESTINY SNATCHED AWAAAAY! Taken by

my knave Bourchier relatives that stormed our gates when I, but a mere young lad, witnessed such chaos, soon forcing us, the Covetons, to surrender our rightful domain, stripping us of any power and claiming it for themselves as my family who was left alive after the bombardment pathetically gambled everything we had! All our divérsis speciébus treasures, our lives, and our heritage are lost to them! We were imprisoned, my former shambling family shamefully duressed to live out the rest of our miserable lives as inferior subjects! By the time of my formal parting from AltaRotha, my vision was already set in motion! I vowed to claim the power I long before was wrongfully deprived of and in the name of all Covetons alike!!! TO RESTORE OUR COVETON EXALTED preeminence is not only my ambitious vision but an ensuing reality! My right. Firstly, we needed to establish my foothold, and so that pesky and grotesquely rotund swiiiiiiine!"

"Y-y-y o-o-o-u-u you m-m- me- I mean Th-th- the Hor- Hor-kers?!"

"YES, YES, WHATEVER! Whoever they were, they were in MY way. I had no choice but to EXTERMINATE the whole lot of them. It's simply called conquer and expand!! OH hoooow, am I a true virtuoso!" Little did the Wolf know as he went about exulting that the Horkurs were not completely killed off, that Whyles perfectly knew. "And now it all comes down to this: capturing this little settlement for ourselves is all toooooo peeeeerfect! My reason for committing such a questionable method as to lure the unsuspected and incarcerate them was not of ill intention but rather, in fact, shall I say, a crucially cautious procedure of bargaining, just in case they refuse what my request is, of claiming their little valley as my own."

"What if they refuse? What then!?" The shivering Fox asked, afraid of Kaliber's solution.

Engrossed by his scheme, the Wolf expected that said question and was thrilled by it; raising one of his eyebrows, Kaliber's face sickly contorted into a deranged beaming sneer so broad it exposed his inflamed gums, a truly chilling expression. He went unblinking as his crazed, filled, leering eyes sadistically bulged, his broad shoulder stiffened and jutted forwards, and his wrinkling nose flared. He tented his long twiddling fingers and gnashed his pearlescent teeth, cocking his head side to side, the rigid joints of his slender neck cracked. In a gritty voice, he amusingly growled.

"If that incident does sooooo happens to be the dreadful case, sadly, I will have no other choice but to DISPENSE duteous order and simply eradicate the captives until they submit to my most generous proposition! But from what you have seen and said, I do not suppose they will ever let that happen to their loved ones… or… would they? I mean, I'm sure they wouldn't mind if yes, just maybe a couple-"

"You-You-ou-ou wouldn't da- are! You- you are b-b-b-b- bluffing!" Whyles blatantly opposed Kaliber's extreme elucidation. "I-I-is there n-n-n-n o- no no oo otha wa-wa-way?!"

"WOULDN'T IIIIII!!!???? DON'T GET TRIVIAL WITH ME, CRETIN! Or have YOU

FORGOTTEN WHOM YOU ARE SPEAKING TO!!? Must I remind you the bloody scars on your back are just a trifle of what might have been, do you hear me? A TRIFLE!!!" Kaliber scornfully declared, digging his two fingers into the open wounds of the Fox who cried in agonizing pain.

"Im S-s-s —sorry s-s- sorry. Y-y-y yes, I know m-m-m my place n-n-now," The Fox cried aloud. Kaliber erupted into an all-out erratic burst of maniacal cachinnate over the Fox's cry. The abrupt surge of the Wolf's disturbing earsplitting cacophony echoed in the chamber like an eerie choir in a dead quiet church...his distorted face then narrowed into a blithe lour.

"Besides, it is as written in my covenant they so willingly scrawled; I have it in print and at my disposal for proof if need be! But in lighter news, you have my utmost gratitude, Mr. Whyles--"

"Wh-Wh-wh- why-y-y is t- t—th- th-at?" The Fox asked timidly.

"You are most certainly tooooooo naively mooooooodest! It's all thanks to you. We have the striking supremacy required. Have you not scouted and spied on such a peeeeeerfect settlement of our future bailiwick? I surely would have peeeeeriiiiished in such harsh and utterly destructive tribulation! I have you to thank for giving me not only hope but also my own salvation. And so by such courage, you are rightfully spared from a gruesome execution, for now, that is, but ever attempt any other tricks then you shall pay dearly, but presently you have served me well, fear me not Whyles, from this moment I have forgiven you and overlooked your betrayal because I do know now that such an unthinkable act is merely an act of desperation! For I, too, betrayed my own kin seeking appraisal, an easy but effective fix with some punitive! Am I wrong?! NO, I AM NEVER WRONG! Besides, there are many more things to come that will require your craft." The Wolf went on explaining his loathful plan.

"Certainly, there will be great risks involved, and sacrifices must be made in order to keep virtuous command... but most importantly, when the hard laborem has ended, the light will shine above the ruination and with the crumbles of past the Coveton Empire shall prosper once again!! Those who dare to oppose my rule will be crushed. Then I shall finally earn the mighty place I rightfully deserve among my revered patriarchs!! I will have the last laugh when I triumphantly march my way back To AltaRotha and avenge my family! My retribution is at hand!! All will perish! All will fear my Coveton wrath!! And it all starts here in this pitiful village! My future illustrious empire finally begins!!" Kaliber vociferated, acting on his instinctual, insane comportment.

"Oh, that's right, before I forget, that pesky owl that used to spy and overhear our plans, you remember him, don't yooooooouuuuu?" Kaliber asked with a hideous leer that froze Whyles' palpitating heart; an iceberg impaled it. His mid raced, digging way back to old fading memories of such an owl, a close acquaintance of Wally and company, but what was his name? Darn it all. Why couldn't he recall it? Then it rang out, 'OL BEN!'

"Ye- ye yeees, I do, very much so, a funny little fulla; why, what about him?"

Kaliber's monstrous smirk stretched like putty. His ghastly leer went unblinking as if he could read the Fox's every scrambled thought, scanning and manipulating them with sharpened precision and carving them up and served on a platter in slices.

"Nothing at all, really. I just want to pass along the good news that he shall no longer trouble us! Noooow, im awfully afraid I cannot stay any longer, you see now, with that accursed storm finally lifted, it was a downright hindrance; oooh, how I utterly despised the looooong, grueling wait. The mortification of patience for my upcoming glory was all tooooo tiresome, but now, now that it's over, I think it is the best time to convoke my force and claim my KINGDOM while they are still distracted! Have you anything you'd like me to say on your behalf, Whyles?"

Whyles said not a word; he was utterly speechless; he was crushed, devastated.

"Very well, I'll be most delighted to send them your regards; I wonder what they will think of you when you are discovered to be their undoing, especially that Wally friend of yours's oooooo, I cannot wait, Ciao!" Kaliber then stormed off, commanding one of his Hounds to keep close watch over the imprisoned Fox.

After his counsel with Whyles, as Kaliber strolled into his quarter, a strange fog blanketed the ground ankle high. He found none other than Clovis Kaine eagerly awaiting Kaliber's return in lighted only by the monster's inflamed chest, and in his paw, the gigantic fiend hovering over the misty rolling beneath the bare spot where he floated, gripped what seemed to be a contract of his own written in ancient glyphs. If followed at the very bottom of the lengthy document, signed in perfect flowing cursive, was Kaliber's own signature. The Wolf smiled up upon viewing the pact. A drawn keen look of satirical amusement.

"Surprised?" Kaine growled in disgust. "YOU thought maybe I had forgotten? I think by the look in your eyes, you may be surprised by our word of the day, perhaps?"

"I am never one to be surprised!" Kaliber trailed off into a slight whimper.

"YOU SHOULD BE! Have YOU forgotten what's due?" Kaine snapped, bellowing like wind in stormy sail about to be pulled back in a rage.

"How can I forget? As you well know, I've been veeeeeery busy. In fact, maybe I've had my fill! But for this matter! Perhaps we can discuss this later?" Kaliber cheekily replied, cooly, deflecting any chary accusations on his part.

"It would be most unwise to make me upset. After all, you awakened me from my ancient bond, scalding your offering in that, my blazing pit. Awoken by your pitiful entreaties of groveling despair and offering certain pledges."

"I fully assure you, Kaine, everything you want shall come-"

"It's not what I want as much as it is OWED! AND WHEN WILL I BE ABLE TO COLLECT? Had you not promised as you did, this would not have been a concern, but your time is coming up. I diligently granted your wishes for power and domination! Are you not yet satisfied?" He glowered, "YOU hold exactly what was promised, what was asked for...don't you recognize your own desires come to life before you? Oh Lord, KAALLLEEEEEBYYYYAAAHHH!" At this pronouncement, Clovis shook the room with an echoing laugh that first ripped the air with the pounding of drums, wavered in the air with a startling shriek, and yielded itself to a protracted moan of pity.

"YOU FOOL! So puffed with your own sunken PRIIIIDE!! This destruction you call your life is waving before you! Did you think I could be bested in this game? You sniveling roach! You thought you did all this, didn't you? You offered, I accepted! Worthless trash! Do you know how many times a degree like yours has come in pieces to my hole? Now, what will you do? Do YOU have a plan of your own, NOW? Or are you satisfied with your pledge as it stands?" Clovis's eyes raged in a dark red fire. His chest heaved, exposing his cavernous interior. He was nothing Kaliber had ever known could exist. Kaliber drew his eyes away for a moment, drew a breath, and met Clovis's gaze.

He wailed, "THIS HAS NOTHING TO DO WITH SATISFACTION; THIS IS WHOLLY ABOUT SEEKING RETRIBUTION!!"

"If you don't hold your end of our bargain, your agony will be beyond mine." Hissing the last few words, Kaine extended his corpselike paw with long, chipped, blackened fingernails and waved it around the room; there was an orb of colors emanating within Kaine's rugged palm, unfurling as a flowing curtain became a holographic exhibition frightfully depicting an otherworldly chthonic dimension of infernal perdition. The shrouded panorama was eternally eclipsed, lighted by fiery colossal volcanoes ceaselessly erupting, causing the ground to tremor, only occupied by hordes of screeching gooey ghouls, their pellucid and slimy bodies dripping off like rancid tallow and plopped down in jiggly sludges. These foul entities aimlessly wandered across the lava-soaked terrain that scorched their dragging feet, without peace or memory.

Forever knowing their sin was their only comforts and to eternally mourn for an intangible absolution. Shattered structures, rattly stacked high by rotting bones, gelatinous hummocks pasted by decaying carnage, and grated peels of raw flesh.

Levitating spiked cages, whipping hurricanes made of ash dancing in circles around a widening gruesome gulf of boiling blood.

"Welcome to the ABYSS!"

"I AM NOT AFRAID OF ANY OF THIS!!!! These are just fatuous illusions, tawdry parlor tricks! I am not a lowly beggar; you, Kaine, have seemed to stretch to the truth of the matter! In fact, as I recall, you offered your service without me begging!?"

"Oh Kalibah, I see your pitiful denial right through your arbitrary senses. You can't hide or lie to me; I see and know allllll!"

You most certainly are brave to underestimate me, and my rightful AUTHORITY MUST I KINDLY REMIND, I am a Coveton?"

"Aye, but of course, you are, which is more of the reason to be most wooooooried. Be a naysayer if you so do choose young Coveton; it makes no difference, whether it be past, present, or, in your special case, FUTURE; you must reap what you sow; no one can ever cheat or evade such a harvest, not even those who are remarkably distinguished must all atone, I have come to expect that through eons of my deals, but eventually you shall come to learn what true fear is Lord

Kaliber, you should be very afraid of what is to certainty come, be warned of your most dishonorable and greedy deeds they shall determine where you are placed hereafter." And with this, Kaine swiped at the image as it evaporated and absorbed into his palm, the orb of light conjured into a mystic amulet. Dangling the strange object flickering small glints within its golden shell as if it was a heartbeat, in front of Kaliber's most dazed face. "What is that?" Utterly astonished, Kaliber stared with rapturous desire and wonder-lust at the glimmering amulet as if it was calling out to him. Hearing these strange whispers piecing inside his throbbing head, most of all, he was attracted by small jewels embedded in the glowing runes intersection into three rings, all of them different and misaligned as they were intertwined and looping in an unformed and scrambled symbol crafted in the middle of the pendant needing to be solved correctly, in order to see it whole. "You shall see whence completed!"

With twists and jiggles, Clovis started to solve the intricate puzzle with ease, pulling some glowing runes away, extending out from the rings with spindly shanks, rotating the inner bands till they clicked into place, then proceeded to recenter the runes, pushing them in left to right order, until the runes once jumbled and disordered locked into the correct position and translated into a mortifying phrase, " Final Judgment" the symbol that before could hardly be discernable was finally decoded, and the final form was revealed the embossed icon turned out to be of that of a blazing skull. Its bare soul-sucking eyes bewitched the Wolf as if drawing onto his every breath and every lingering memory as if it had all been temporarily erased; the Wolf couldn't think, he couldn't speak properly, all he thought was revenge, the foreboding skull solely focused him! Like a record, all he heard was earsplitting echoes! Disdained echoes of curses and regrettable wishes come true. All he felt was baneful acquiescence. Yet it was all so enticingly pleasing!

"This is a most exquisite treasure I present to you..."

As if all time froze dead, the supernatural medallion compelled his true twisted motivation. He could not resist its enchantment; its toxic abnormality warped his mangled thoughts into sheer irresistible malevolence. Evoking such brooding knowledge, unlocking and exposing his true chaotic desires once repressed, now rejuvenated, it was all too warmly comforting. Anything he so wished could most certainly come to fruition; these vagary manifestations seemed to conform to its nocent bidding.

Its unabating seduction tugged his aching heart as it was racing. His head was throbbing as if shot right through his skull point-blank, a compulsive caprice slivered through his twinging veins. He felt immortal. He felt all-knowing. He felt unstoppable.

"GIVE IT TO ME!" Kaliber demanded, lunging towards the amulet like someone parched with an unquenchable thirst. Clovis closely observed Kaliber's altered reaction, foreseeing the Wolf's outburst; Kaine immediately pulled it away from the grasp of the adjuring Wolf, and Clovis wagged one of his filthy fingers. "Wait a moment! If I may and SHOULD, I was trying to give proper instructions of its utility!"

"I don't care what you have to say, give it here!!! Whatever a Coveton wants, they GET!!!! By my name alone, I demand you give it too!!!!" Kaliber's voice thundered, his cane slamming against the ground with a sharp crack. His eyes blazed with fury, his presence suffocating the room like a storm pressing down.

"Do not rush what I urgently must forewarn; it may cost more than you ever accorded if blatantly ignored! Treat it well. It remembers it remembers everything…it-"

"You dare refuse my behest!? I don't care about the cost; a Coveton's worth is PRICELESS! GIVE IT HERE, NOOOOOW!"

"Have it your way then! Let us first see if it accepts your nominal worth!" "GET ON WITH IT!"

Clovis clasped Kaliber's wrist, guiding the transfixed Wolf's paw, and hung it over the medallion. Kaliber's paw slowly descended. In its descent, one of Kaliber's fingers stroked the medallion, pricking his tips on the razor-edged ridge; it chilled to the touch like a frostbitten serenade of excruciating throes; it felt as if it was draining his vitality. He felt numb and stiff.

The blood started drizzling onto the etched markings that magically absorbed the droplets. Infused with the necessary essence, the stained amulet started sizzling. As if progressively awakening from a dormant state, the skull's blank eyes, flooded by the blood streaming from the grooves, shone a red luster. As if struck by a bolt of lightning, Kaliber snapped back into reality, sending him reeling; after he steadied himself, the Wolf stomped to where Clovis loomed over and snatched the gleaming amulet from Clovis's open paw.

"It's mine! It's all mine!!! It chose me! Magnifico!" "So it has!"

In a fit of rhapsodizing pride, he began to flout at Clovis Kaine, who had a sudden growth spurt and grew twice his size. His giant shadow shrouded the room, glaring down at the haughty Wolf with sharp, deadly daggers.

"Are you so eagerly shallow for power that you overlook its psychic hold and choose not to even question it's tempting call? It shall now forever be attached to you for better or worse; whatever your heart truly shows, it shall provide.

"I am in control, FOOOOL, nothing else!! You are my servant, my famulus! I don't owe you ANYTHING, you cretin!!!! I am the sole leader; I need no charity!!!!! Never did I ask for it!!!! You leach!"

"Listen, young Master Coveton! What you wanted, what you desired, I granted with pleasure! Wanted a bloodthirsty gang to take the lead!? I gave! You desired a kingdom to take over? It is awaiting your family to please so they can welcome you back! Wanted your own way!? I Allowed, I acquiesced! I broke the natural physics for your requests; anything you had craved, I pulled it out from my hand of tricks!!!!"

And with a series of thunderous claps, sparks flickered with the sounds of firecrackers!

"And all with a cost, a simple deal that we shook on, and you have everything you want!!! Nothing is EVER FREE, COVETON!!! The sooner you learn it, the better! I expect what I am guaranteed!!!! Or there will be DEADLY consequences beyond your control and beyond what frightens you most! BEWARE Coveton, you can never fool oneself without a price!" Suddenly, two humongous tenebrous bat wings sprouted from Kaine's back.

"Because of your blinded pursuit of selfish, destructive pleasures, you will ultimately drown in your own sorrow and regret. The heavy burden of your guilt, stemming from a single, inconceivable transgression, will drag you down to a tragic end. When that woeful day arrives, you will truly understand misery, and you will have no one to blame but yourself. In the end, you will be powerless, worthless, and alone. Take heed, take heed! When that fateful day comes, I shall come for you!"

"Ha! Do not DARE to threaten me; I am all that's mighty! I, a Coveton by royal birth, does not fear anything, especially fraudulent ultimatum, and don't ever oblivisci! You swine! " The Wolf guffawed at the fiend's heed, and like a wild eruption, the Wolf's spittle sprayed from his lips onto Kaine's red torn jacket; little did the cackling Coveton notice the golden medallion in which when the words of Clovis was spoken the engraved symbols shone red luster as if it had transcribed every word or…. Curse? Uttered.

"As ye wish ye ungrateful knave as ye wish! But do take care! Your enemies will eventually have your number! When it starts to rain blood, you shall see young Coveton what you have wished for! And when you finally realize such a mistake."

"A Coveton makes NOOOOOOOO Mistakes!" Kaliber hissed, a clear attestation of his impulsive petulance.

"Very well," he rasped, his voice dripping with venomous disdain, "believe what you will—such delusion is its own fatal mistake. But when that final bell tolls, I shall not heed its call!" He gestured with a long, bony claw toward the haughty Coveton.

In that moment, a ghastly transformation overtook Clovis. The right half of his face began to twist and writhe as the flesh tore away in horrific ribbons, exposing a nightmarish decay beneath. His pale, withered skin clung to the bones, while a swarm of repulsive insects scuttled across his exposed flesh, feasting with an unsettling, relentless hunger. Where his right eye should have been, only a hollow socket remained, and from this dark pit, a bloated, wriggling mealworm slithered, leaving a vile trail of ooze that dripped mournfully down his ruined face.

"This," he intoned with a chilling finality, "is the true face of an unredeemable curse. Look close!" Clovis thrust his mutilated visage mere inches from Kaliber's pristine and smug countenance, a horrifying contrast that seemed to taunt the very essence of cleanliness and pride.

"Fortune is never an ally lest it be a vicious anathema of its very own accord." His gossamer wings curled around his form, enveloping him in a shroud of shimmering light that pulsed with an unnatural fervor. From within, a spectral glow bled through—an insidious, flickering flame that seemed to throb with the very heart of some forsaken inferno. The air grew thick and oppressive, as if burdened by the weight of the darkness itself, and the shadows that once clung to the room now recoiled, as though they feared to witness the transformation. A deep silence fell, broken only by the crackling of the fire that burned within Clovis. Then, with a sound like the final, tortured breath of a dying wretch, the monstrous form was consumed by the blaze—a searing burst of light that cleaved the very air, its intensity... blinding, its heat... suffocating. In an instant, the creature was no more, vanishing into the fiery sphere as though it had never existed. Only the faintest echoes of its torment lingered in the void, fading like a nightmare that would never fully depart.

Staring at the special pendant that hung heavy around his straining neck seemed to start to hunch in Kaliber's back from its weight. Its dark, gleaming beauty entranced him; Kaliber suddenly started to flail like a lunatic, screaming aloud as fizzy froth cascaded from his mouth.

Yet shortly after his extreme outburst, Kaliber met with his rallied battalion of goons who were restlessly awaiting his final orders outside of the encampment. They cheered when they saw the confident Wolf swaggering forth; his chest pushed out, his chin proudly lifted. Seeing all of his loyal subjects bow before him and those who didn't, the Wolf struck a blow to the ground to make them grovel. With zealous cheers they chanted his exalted name aloud: "Hail Lord Kaliber!"

The Coveton's banners raised high, everyone clustered around the luminary Wolf for his sermon; clearing his throat, he began.

"Listen and listen well, my scaber mutts! The glorious day of our triumphant debut has come aaaaaaat laaaaaast! And what a magnificent debut it shall be! No longer shall we linger in destitution! Forced to endure such horrendous strains of sheer survival in the foul mud and slimy pits, praying for a miracle! Finally, our prayers have been answered! No longer shall we suffer from starvation! No longer shall we be ashamed of our aberration! Embrace it, use it, and make those who scoff and at us pay dearly!

We are strong, we are fearsome, and we are UNSTOPPABLE! Be proud! Be Ruthless! Be BOLD! WE ARE DESTINED for greatness! WE ARE PUGILES! We shall dance to the banters of victory. I promise all the splendor for all those loyal and obedient! NOW is OUR CHANCE!!!! Now IS OUR OOOONLYYYYYY CHANCE!!!! The final judgment is ours for the taking! Those who are weak and frail shall perish from our bloody maws. They have no purpose!"

The gung-hoed Hounds clamored in a celebratory and frenzied fever; Kaliber calmed the combative situation down as he hushed their arousing tumult. "Round all the prisoners, and let us be off!" With a wave of Kaliber's wrists shooing them off, they diverted into a barking pack, and as quick as they left, they came back in a rushing swarm like a flock of crows to a crop field. They ushered back the weary captives held for wicked sort of surety. The prisoners were shackled and shuffled in organized rows as they intently listened to whatever Kaliber had planned, fearing the absolute worst of what would become of them and their precious, unsuspecting home village.

"Onwards to glory and prosperity!" Kaliber declared, aiming his cane, wavering it to the onlookers. With the final words yowled, fueled by seething hate, blinded from his self-pity grievance and obscene iniquity, the arrogant Coveton instantly received tumultuous plaudits in which, in return, he took deep courtly bows.

The Hounds, led by Kaliber in front, jumped into the cockpit of his red auroplane and took to the skies with cackles spiraling above. His legion below all saluted him as he went gliding by; the ragged prisoners in the back who slogged behind were whipped to follow faster, they all trudged their way towards the direction of Ambrodale to witness its dismal subjugation.

Chapter Ten

Invasion of Innocence

Game of Chance, or the fall of Ambrodale

Marked on this fateful, chilly October 10th, Kaliber the wicked, the cruel, the pompous, marched forward with his band of goons. They dragged their weary prisoners behind them, trudging toward peacefully sleeping Ambrodale. Off to invade. Off to prove his self-worth. Off to reclaim his lost respect and title. Off to build his empire. Hearing the rumbling commotion beckoning from the other side of their ramshackle homes that they had managed to rebuild after being obliterated by the storm not so long ago. Yet, it was poorly reconstructed. The amalgamation of a grave sonance. A symphony of chaos, menacing laughter, cracking whips, miserable mewls, and distressed pleas was marching ever forward.

As the heinous sounds drew closer to Ambrodale, its humbled occupants huddled outside in wonder of who or what was coming!

"Look to the sky! What is that?!" Several of them announced in alarm. They were all pointing to where they saw a mysterious flying object. It looked like a smoky dragon soaring above and in towards them. It made a horrendous rattling buzz that could drown the hum of fields of honeybees who flew through the great and vast meadows when summer arrived. Gazing up, and to their shock, they saw the red auroplane hovering over them. Just then, as the plane started to land in the middle of where the crowd formed, the legion of ragged Hounds halted in front of Crestwick Bridge, blocking the only exit as they reshuffled the fumbled, gaunt prisoners; pushing them forward so they could be in clear sight. Their sorrowful faces became overjoyed whence they saw their loved ones watching back at them; as the rejoicing reunion proceeded, it abruptly ceased as some of the sprightlier tried to escape the Hounds' tearing clutches by scurrying forward and rejoin their community. Still, it was to no avail, for the Hounds who held their chains yanked them back hard as they squealed and yowled like lambs to the slaughter.

With open arms and ridged composure, the imperious Wolf slowly sauntered to the crowd, a broad, crooked crocodile smile plastered on his deranged and domineeringly sly face.

"Ah, what a marvelous entrance and welcoming party this is! How very proper! Salutatio and good health to all! For those who have the shameful displeasure of not knowing who I am, my name is Lord Kaliber Coveton the 7th, and how very nice it is to see you all as chipper and laughably dumbstruck as I expected! I feel so refreshed!" Kaliber said in a peremptory bearing.

Seeing the many neighborly faces, their friends and family, who were shackled and barred in little cages, shouted, "Let them go!" They all rallied, mustering up their courage, creating quite a disruption. They charged forward, waving their first, demanding an explanation. The Hounds rushed in, confronting the masses of the opposition, biting and clawing at them to stand down.

"Settle, settle down; everything will be adequately explained, all in due time, of course, but only if you do exactly what I say and request; if you do, then we'll get along so cheekily! There will not be a problem, but if you don't, then there's no doubt of your future…troubles? Yes, let's start there. Most of you are confused about why these strangers are here and your loved ones are, let's say, locked up, but just know this, you are the presence of royalty! You all should be very thankful that I am here, to civilize you, poor simpletons! I certainly do hope we come to an agreement, and dare I say, I fear that things will turn ugly for these helpless imbeciles you ..love uhh.. mm if we ah..do not?.Yes..? We wouldn't want to do or risk anything lamentable occurring here. Perhaps a specific grudge or two would persuade you not to intervene. There's only one way to find out! Kaliber started to grind his teeth and continued:

"You will see what happens to your friends and family if you refuse what I request!"

Many of them did not believe what the Wolf had bluntly declared, their naïve cynicism called him on his word. They continued to stare rather blankly, as if dumbstruck, at his continuing pronouncements.

"Ah, so be it! If I must prove this is no joking matter, then I shall! How pitiful! I surely thought you would know better, but I guess not!"

Kaliber scoffed. "You drove me to this!"

With a snap of Kaliber's fingers, one of the brutish Hounds hoisted one of the smaller animals and suspended the quivering creature over his unbarred jaws as if he were ready to devour the poor soul.

"Now, we can choose the easy way or the hard way?! What will you choose? Tick-tock!"

The watchers, shocked with horror, cried out for forgiveness: "W-w-w wait. We want no trouble. Please, we'll do anything you say! Just don't hurt us. What do you want?!"

"Ah yes, how very smart! I knew you would see it MY way. Well, well first and foremost, I'd like you to bring who you call Wally since he's obviously the brightest of your savages, and make sure to clarify that it's most certainly a matter of life or DEATH!"

One of the Riverfolk rushed over to the Hare's cottage, frantically banging and ringing his doorbell. "Please, please be home!" He beseeched. The door gently swung open. The Hare's head popped up from the side and kindly hushed the frantic neighbor, explaining that Miriam was still asleep and did not want her to be in distress. "But it's a matter of life and death!! They got them; they have all of them!"

"Please slow, slow down. Now, who's got who?" The Hare asked, trying to calm his visitor down.

"The many who went missing got captured by some roughies. They are here now; the leader demands to speak to you urgently. He says he knows you! Please, there is no time to waste. You must come! There's no time to explain further!"

Just then, Miriam, overhearing the panic when she shouldn't have, could not help but barge into conversation… "Is my sister there!? I must go!" Wally refused her request, saying she was too sickly to be outdoors. "Wallis Tunnelly, nothing is gonna step in between me and my sister, not even you! And be golly, if you dare, tink' I'll be on the sidelines this time, you are dead wrong! She's the onla un I have when Mumsie strictly ordered us to never separate and to allaways take care of each other. We made a solemn promise, and a Quaddling, sick or not, never breaks promises!" Miriam retaliated.

"Yes, I understand-" Wally gave a deep sigh.

"Understand? You don't remotely understand! I'm coming whether you like it or not!" Miriam's stubbornness spoke true to her utmost devotion to her unbreakable bond of sisterhood. Wally could say no more. "Show us the way then!" Wally remarked; with a hopping, a jumping and a stumbling here and there, they traveled with haste.

Sampson lumbered from his dark cave. Seeing the scampering escort, he yawned a great big yawn and bellowed, "What's with all this hubbub? It woke me up!"

"That's what we're going to find out!" Wally waved him over as Sampson joined the company.

Seeing the large mass ahead, Wally took a lead, jostling through the distressed crowd and up in front of the assembly; he was met with a familiar cackling. Kaliber and his goons approached him.

"Ah yes, how excellens! However, you're a tad bit later than I hoped. Any later, I was afraid I would have to carry out such a messy ordeal! I thought for sure you left your loved ones for dead!" Declared the Wolf. Then with a twisted grin, he glared at Wally, who met Kaliber with an uneasy stare. Wally then saw the mass of weary prisoners chained behind Kaliber. "Ahhhh, Wally, how nice it is to see you again!"

Wally had no recollection of who the Wolf was. Agitated by the Hare's unsubtle forgetfulness, Kaliber reminded him of their conclave many months back, once more jogging Wally's memory.

"What is all this, Kaliber? What have you done?" Wally asked, horrified; what he saw made him sick.

"Progress! Conquest! Domination! The exact reason we Coveton's are superior to the naïve dullards we are forced to converse with! "

"Kaliber, you simply can't do this!" The Hare rebutted.

"Oh, but you see, I can! If you recall correctly, we made a deal! Did we not?!

The Hare looked baffled. "I don't remember any such deal! Nor did we ever agree to-"

"Come, don't be daft! Your signature is written here on this contract. If it must be proven, so be it! According to this, I own everything here, even you uncouth savages! It's all here in print!" Kaliber then pulled out the contract and unraveled it for everyone to see. He began to read it out loud.

"It is hereby written and shall be duly recorded that the residents of Ambrodale, hereby represented by Mr. Wallace "Wally" Tunnelly, that the rights to the future development of the said property, The Village of Ambrodale, SHALL BE GRANTED IN PERPETUITY!" Kaliber snarled. "Furthermore..." Kaliber now assumed an erudite tone. "Compensation for said development shall be repaid promptly and on demand without prior notice. Compensation is to consist of such constituencies as laborers or designated workforce, site amenities including but not limited to freshwater sources, raw materials, existing building ownership, products of service..."

"Wait." Wally said, "I feel sick."

"As such, an agreement has been signed by yours truly, Wally." Kaliber's laugh rang out, a cacophony of scorn, echoed by Sampson and that absurd babbling brought by Booney the Frog Kaliber's composure faltered. "I... I feel something. I mean, I pity your soft-hearted simpletons. How, pray tell, have you managed to exist in such a state of retrograde docility?" His laughter turned to a throaty chuckle, then faltered into an almost hysterical growl as if on the verge of an explosion of sheer hatred.

"As you see, it clearly states I, Kaliber, own everything you see and everyone you love!! But that's not all, no, no, no! Here's a marvelous surprise! You had a very special friend among your miserable kindred who's a traitor; he turned you allllll into meeee, and I think we all know who this certain someone is!? Yes? Your friend Mr. Whyles was working for me all this time. He didn't care for any of you, not one bit; it was all just an ACT! In all honesty, it was completely his idea in the first place! A pure genius, if I say so myself!!, his idea to nab your friends and capture your precious home when he first set his eyes on it!"

"No, that cannot be true! He was my dear friend and would never do such a thing!" Wally defended the Fox as he continued stammering. "Now, he may be strange, but by no means would he ever do such a horrible deed!"

"Oh, he very well did believe it or not, I don't care! You call him a dear friend, but how well and how long did you really know him? I really wonder, tsk… I'd hate to break you out of your shell, but the hard, cold fact is he lied to you. He lied to ALL OF THEM." The Wolf howled in mock anger as it pointed at the fearful crowd. "He nabbed your friends, your trust, and now you're LAND! Poor, poor Wally, too trusting, too puuuuuure for your own good! So blissfully content in your own self-assurance! Too welcoming, you welcomed your demise right in with open arms without even a question or concern! Looking through the foggy lens as you presumptively assume everything you see and everything you hear is all upright and charitable, as you protect yourself with this false sense of farfetched security that nothing bad will ever happen, the world will never crash and burn… you're wrong… You are dead wrong; I am proof of that! But fear not; I have come to teach you what you do not know or freely choose not to!

This will all go the hard way if need be! HOW COULD YOU, YOU FOOOLL!" Kaliber shrieked, breaking the silence into a pitch of terror.

"How could you! It's all your fault! You're responsible for all of this!" Screamed the eldest within the crowd.

The Hare's once true friends were nowhere to be found as the massive crowd swarmed in against the poor, shuddering Hare with disgusted glares that pierced him. The extremely nauseating feeling of guilt and shame choked him and overwhelmed him.

"I didn't know! I didn't know!" He cried aloud, but alas, it garnered no sympathy from his friends. Rather, it only garnered Kaliber's malicious amusement.

"Settle, settle, Dear ones...Wally surely cannot be entirely blamed for this change! You all had a wonderful part to play and did fantastically! Bravo, bravo!" The Wolf started to clap, but he was puzzled when he realized he was clapping alone before them.

"And if you ever want to see your friends breathing, I suggest you do exactly what I demand! Otherwise, we might have to dissect this poor Frog FIRST!"

With a snap of his fingers, one Hound rushed over with a small cage in his paw covered with a sheet. "What's under sheet numerus unus? Let us see, Voilà! Kaliber unveiled the cage, and inside of the rusty cage was Booney. He was stretched out on his back, each limb tied to the cage bar. He was withered, beaten, semi-conscious, and forlorn. The pummeled Frog hardly breathed; his formerly lustrous and shiny skin was like dried-out leather. His body seemed to crackle as he gasped for breath.

Wally called out for him, but there was no reply, no movement, just dead silence; Booney was never silent in his whole jumpy life until now!

"What have you done to him?" Wally cried, not believing what he saw. Was this all just a nightmare? Was everyone having the same dream all at once!? At any second, any second, I shall wake up in my warm bed bright and early with the trickling sound of Bromby river and whistling kettle, the smell of sweet grass and glazed treats, and the sight of all my smiling friends! Oh please, let it be so!" The Hare desperately tried to convince himself as he kept pinching his arm until it turned purple. Still, with a last hard pinch, this hope and expectation vanished, abruptly replaced by dread, disgust, and despair whence he finally realized this horrible display, this verily tumultuous shrift, was not at all a conjectural dream hooked on the Hare's vivid imagination. An appalling reality dawned, bringing out the welling of bitter, acrid tears forthwith; what was indeed happening here and now made the poor Hare almost wretch. never had he ever seen nor read of such a devilishly abominable exhibition of amoral and insensate misuse of power and influence..

"I have fully broken his will! Snapped it like a twig!"

"This is wrong, all wrong! Have you no sympathy? No compassion? No feeling at all? Is this all a sick joke? This crucible seems to delight you?? Why?" Wally blurted out aghast.

"No, no, nooooo, this is no joke! A Coveton never jokes when there's proper metier to be had … it is Right! You don't understand, but how could you? You are all inferior to the likes of true nobility! A Coveton doesn't need sympathy, compassion, or any feeling for any lower CLASS, caste, OR CREED! All we need is STRICT OBEDIENCE! We dispense justice thoroughly with no remorse for the guilty! We, the Covetons, have our honor at stake if we don't live up to our own expectations! We would rather be executed like this silly stupid Froggie will be within moments. Do you all understand what I AM SAYING TO YOOOOU! But that's beyond the point, RIIIIGHHTT??" He managed a pseudo-sickly-sweet voice and whined, "Won't you think of the poor sweet children!? You wouldn't want to make them cry, would you?!" He snarled as a row of blubbering children were dragged in front, roughly smacking each one on the top of their heads and forcefully pinching their cheeks.

"And how could I ever forget this babbling, kooky ninny? She talks and talks and rambles on and on. I HATED IT, EVERY EVERY CONFOUNDED MINUTE OF IT. SHEEEEEERE

LUNIANCY!!!! Her inane prattling gave me such a splitting headache. I look forward to cutting that beak of hers right off! You there, DUCKIE!" Kaliber pointed at Miriam with a sinister sneer.

Kaliber snapped, "I bet on anything you sure miss your sister; she awfully missed you, and my deepest apologies," he bowed, growling. "For such an abrupt separation, you can thank Wally and your incapable Fox friend for that! It would be a very happy reunion if you agreed to my offer! I might just roast her if you dare defy me!"

"Why you MONSTAAAAA! You… you betta let me sista go... or ill'…CURSE YOUR BONES AS LONG AS LONG AS YOU LIVE!! On the count of t'ree."

Wally watched in disbelief. Was this actually Miriam?

"Or you'll what, DUCKIIEEE MA'AM???" Howled Kaliber. Miriam began counting:

"One!" she squawked, winding up her webbed feet, flapping her wings ready to charge, and in a bluster of feathers, she went bolting toward the hysterically laughing Kaliber. Now quite amused by her hopeless courage, Kaliber quickly extended his arm. With a quick twist of the brass knob, he unsheathed his long, engraved saber from his cane and pointed it directly toward Miriam, who stopped dead in her tracks. "Come on and try me!" He hissed, lunging forward while thrusting his sword. "No? Anyone else care to try!? Wally-bunny? How about you?? I must warn you I am a masterful swordsman... and crave a good fight today!"

The Riverfolk, unable to defend themselves from this escalating crisis, fell back into a dispirited, stuporous silence, "That's what I thought!" The Wolf added.

"Come... come, what's with all these gloomy faces!? You should all be pleased that I am here! I shall bring this little unprepossessing village prosperity and rules, which it desperately needs!

Order is essential, and a fair ruler like me can provide it! We shall build a grand EMPIRE... TOGETHER, All I ask is for your service, and at the very end, this little frontier shall be the greatest envy of the wooooorld!"

'What world?" Many had begun to ask themselves.

"We don't want to be a part of any empire! This is our home!" Kaliber heard them shout. "Well, that's unfortunate, a shame, but YOU don't get to decide! I DO! Besides, this isn't your

home any longer. This is MY home! And you all so happen to take far too much space...it is time to get hard at work and earn your place here!"

Kaliber was not met with the thrilled remarks that he was expecting but with dull-witted, forlorn mumbles and blank stares. "I DEMAND smiling faces NOW! If, OF COURSE, you don't want your friends to perish!" The Wolf snapped his fingers again, and the Hounds snarled at their captives.

The community forced their collective smile.

"Ah yes, that's the spirit! I'll tell you what: I'm feeling quite generous and quite sorry for all of you. It's such a pathetic lot, so I'll give you a proposition! Let us play a game of Bluffers Roll! And why, if you win, we will all simply pack up and leave! You will never hear from us again, and you can all go about living your miserable lives, living in this dirt. Rest assured, I swear, A Coveton never breaks their sworn oath. You keep your land, and you will free your people! But if I win, I will keep and acquire EVERYTHING. Do I make myself clear?"

Wally agreed to his offer forthwith.

"I must warn you the chances of you winning are extremely slim to none at all! Why, I'm the best there is! Are you still up for this challenge?"

"Well, what other choice do we have!?"

"Veeerry perspicacious, aren't we? None whatsoever!"

"Then yes, let us play your game! With luck, it will turn out well."

"Ah, how very noble indeed, foolish, but still noble! I am awfully afraid luck isn't on your side!"

After hearing this smug comment, the befuddled Hare gulped hard as if swallowing shards of broken glass.

"Are you sure you would like to proceed? There is no hope for you to win, and there will be great risk involved!"

With a questioning smirk, Wally had no choice but to play. Everything depended on this match, so they shook and made the deal. Everything was up for grabs, determined by the ministrations of one rolling die.

"Ah yes, how splendid! Let the game commence! Ahhhhhh, I must confess, for a simpleminded delusional peon, you do have admirable courage for someone who is about to lose everything.

You still show decency; I'm wholly impressed!!"

The match was set; drinks were passed, and the table arranged with two ornate dice boxes, their open lids serving as screens to shield the rolls within. The dice were placed in the center of the table; Kaliber was gleaming with palpable rapture. He was overcome with the feeling of power and authority. Soon, everything his heart desired was to come true in an instant! His most outstanding cabal was about to be directly played out, and unknown to the viewers, a dirty trick was tucked up in his iniquitous sleeve. He was absolutely dying to ply it; he was not going to lose this match. Everything was at stake for both sides, the weary Riverfolk for their home and sanctuary and for Lord Kaliber Marcellus Coveton the Seventh, for his lost pride. Everything was on the table; everything was up for grabs. A shifty intelligence would rule as it always did. Everyone but, of course, the young Lord Coveton thought it would be a fair game. After all, wasn't the young noble honorable, with honest and upright intentions? His wounded heart had never healed; rather festered within him. Sadly, his false pride was furthest from the actual truth. The Riverfolk didn't realize after Kaliber's public charade, that this was just his cruel jest; the gleeful Wolf had the exact dice. The loaded game would shuttle Kaliber to his immanent victory. He would do everything and anything within his most flagitious power to claim what was lost, no matter the cost for anyone else. After all, chicanery was his fundamentally fixed disposition! To gain was the reality, to lose was another's destiny, no matter the literal nor esoteric price.

After Kaliber went over the rules again and again upon Wally's request, the Hare was quite confused with the directions, asking for clarification as Kaliber explained it multiple times. The spoken rules went circuitously in a word scramble, requiring the sense of legalese that Wally was unaware he had lacked his entire lifetime. Such concerns were not even a worthy entertainment (as he might have come to know of from his inherited library). Wally was growing frustrated and confused as the rules spewed out of Kaliber's mind, then muzzle, over and over again, Wally let a frustrated yelp escape his quiet demeanor. Kaliber secretly enjoyed the Hare's apparent stupidity. The Wolf relished the idea of an easy win which cost him little in actual labor. "NOW REMEMBER, winner takes all!"

The match then began with a hollow-sounding roll-off upon the game board.

"Six," Wally announced, hoping for a farfetched chance of somehow gaining the upper hand. "Ah, marvelous! Ten! I go first!" Kaliber mockingly declared.

The first round went smoothly for Kaliber. The three rolls were exactly perfect; there was no huff or puff for him. "SEVENTEEN EXACT! How mirabilis! I win this round!" Kaliber was ecstatic. Unsure of Kaliber's roll and entirely puzzled by the impassive semblance of the flinty Wolf, Wally called the bluff. Still, to the unnerved Hare's dismay, he was shown the board, and all three dice added to seventeen.

"Do try harder! Everything is at stake for you, after all!" The Wolf gloated. The discomfited Hare slumped back and shivered, slipping momentarily beneath the high table.

The next round, Wally, was quite nervous as he had never lied in his life, nor gambled. He was honest, too honest; he greatly valued honesty and strictly lived by it. Unluckily for him, this game was not made for the honest! Bluffer's roll is a game for when an agreement cannot be made rather be played instead. A game of raw will where fear of losing could cause the opponent to act rashly. Typically as it went, any involved party in it for themselves would try to best the other with only false maneuvers and blatant intimidation. Whoever could lie with every breath might be highly rewarded with grand possessions.

The Hare then rolled for the second round, accompanied by a disheartening frown that fully attracted Kaliber's exuberance. "Triple ones," Wally groaned, trying to hold back the tears. Kaliber cackled in his face. "Give up now! You have no chance! I am a Coveton! We are all that's mighty, and we never lose! It's hopeless!" The Wolf went on intimidating Wally.

The third and final round proceeded, the momentous finale to such a heart-rending match. The gathering crown bleated furiously as the Hare with agitated demeanor, played to win for his own. All the while, Wally made insincere supplications to the Wolf, who, as an exemplar custodian for thralldom, mocked such nugatory entreaties. "Don't count on your ludicrous groveling to gain any clemency from me."

If the Hare were to lose, he could never live it down, nor would any in his predicament. The coming presage of servitude or death was far too demoralizing for the Hare to logically comprehend. His nerves were shattered and, even more so, his heart, which had always been full of merriment and palpable cheer. Wally, now breaking and submerged in fear and distress he tried hard to conceal. Everything was at stake for everyone; these looming barrages penetrated and caused a great distraction to the poor Hare's concentration with parlous queries and utterly irresolute prospects of losing all that he loved. Wally asked for a quick intermission, giving a most practical reason "so he could play with a clear mind," but in great vehemence, the supercilious Wolf, starched as his skintight spiffy habiliment, promptly denied his request. With a stark bearing and a snarky retort, he mocked, "If you call time, you automatically forfeit! I'm terribly sorry, but that's how the game is played, at least for the most dignified! Or are you saying you are not highly principled, and cannot continue/ It is as I thought?" The tension was skyrocketing into a dangerous misunderstanding between the players. Wally felt scorching inner heat and gulped hard like a skiff crashing onto jagged rocks and sinking or a large tree falling in a clear forest with a deafening thud. To his credit, he suppressed his dolorous deportment rather inconspicuously. Though playing his very best, he wasn't up to par with the Wolf. Giving credit where credit is due, Wally did not back down. He wholly knew there would be no possible way he would gain the upper hand. He still proved his steadfast and hardy constitution. Eventually, by the perfectly ignominious game's end, such courage too ended, poor Wally uncomfortably maintained his sense of dignity. A parlous sense of hopelessness and dire possibilities did not shake him. This attempt to remain brave was not squandered, even as the Wolf loudly and laughingly predicted the Hare's final roll was not to be in Wally's favor. The shattering pronouncement produced a great mortification within which flooded Wally with an insane regret at his gullibility. Wally believed that he was solely accountable for Ambrodale's subjection. The defeating emotion was bolstered by Kaliber's malicious imputation, conveyed to Wally in the heat of battle and before the Hare's aghast community: "If only I knew what that rotter Fox was up to! I shoulda known, it's all me fault… what is to come of us now?" He cried to himself, publicly admitting his defeat.

The game was now over, the rounds were tallied, and the gloating Wolf appeared unfazed by this tremendous outcome in his favor. Kaliber could not resist proudly announcing his victory over all, incredulous or not to hear!

"I told you! You had no chance! Glory to the Covetons! I win! Everything is MINE! EVERYTHING FOR THE TAKING! Let it be known from heron that I, Kaliber the seventh, have proved not only my worth but my rightful prestige for all to fear and OBEY!" He boasted with an overstretched sinister smile. "What absolute fun it SHALL BE indeed!"

How could I have been so blind? Wally's heart thundered within his chest, each beat like a drum of impending doom, as the dreadful weight of his own folly pressed upon him with suffocating force. Whyles had never belonged—this much was certain—but Wally, in his foolish naivety, had looked past that. He had wanted to believe, had so desperately clung to the idea that the Fox, with his sly charm and quicksilver ways, might yet find his place among them. And in that hunger for belonging, Wally had let him in. Now, as the ruin of their efforts lay bare before him, the price of that misplaced trust was clear—Booney, locked in his cage, gasping for breath; Miriam, shrunken in fear, her spirit crushed beneath the weight of betrayal. Wally could not conceive of what else foul may occur as the Wolf's grip tightened upon them all.

The rattling of shackles in the distance only heightened his misery, a cold reminder of what he had allowed to happen. He had, in his folly, trusted Whyles. Trusted him as one might a fellow soul, a kindred spirit. How could he have not seen the cold calculating nature that lay hidden behind the Fox's eyes? How could he have missed it? Wally had been blind to it, too eager to hope, too desperate to believe. And now, as he gazed upon the consequences of his foolishness, the truth could no longer be ignored.

He had let Whyles in. He had believed in him, even when the signs screamed otherwise. And now, in the dim light of reality, he saw it all too clearly. The ox had used him, used them all. And Wally had been a fool to let it happen. A fool to trust him.

A sharp, gnawing pain twisted in Wally's gut—like swallowing thorns—ripping through his thoughts with every passing second. He had failed them. His friends, his family, were paying the price for his trusting heart. And the Fox, with his trickery and lies, had led them all to this dark place. The bile of guilt rose in Wally's throat, thick and bitter, choking him with every breath.

"I let him in," Wally whispered bitterly, as though the words could purify him, cleanse him from the stain of his mistake. "I let him in... and now look at this."

The shackles clinked again in the distance, the sound a cruel echo of his failure. The Riverfolk's impending servitude was the ugly consequence of his blind trust. He had been too eager to see the good in everyone, to hope for change, even when he should have known better. Whyles had not changed. He had never changed.

The anger that flared within Wally now was not only aimed at Whyles, but at himself. Why had he been so eager to trust? So eager to believe that the Fox could be one of them, could be different? Had he truly been so desperate for connection, so thirsty for friendship, that he had ignored the truth staring him in the face?

With a sharp exhale, Wally clenched his fists, the weight of his own folly like an anchor around his heart. He should have known better. He did know better. But now, all that was left was this bitter, searing realization. And the thorns of his failure sank deeper with every thought.

He had let Whyles in. And in doing so, he had betrayed them all.

Chapter Eleven

Kaliber's Reign

Sunny skies and cheerful days were now a thing of the past in murky Ambrodale. The beautifully clear vistas sweeping across the acres of countryside with green hills and fragrant gardens now stank with oil and its views obscured by smog. While in the dawning Coveton Age, and with the accursed arrival of the marauding Hounds and Lord Kaliber himself, so too did the disease and macabre scenery of Gorse End proliferate. The poor Riverfolk felt the grip of the Age's toxic tendrils, as the many creatures desperately, and in vain, tried to preserve the natural beauty of their home. They first were coerced to "embrace the new change, change is always beneficial!" This was the slogan. Beastly ordinances perfectly displaced on giant placards formally named the dictums of Kaliber, ending in grueling hours of labor for all.

1. YOU shall not question Kaliber or his men in any way. We know what we do.

2. ALL are required to pay for ANY and ALL services rendered unto you. This ensures the availability of services in the future.

3. IF any questions are asked, we shall provide ALL answers.

4. ANY event or occurrence of suspicious nature or intent must be reported, NO EXCEPTIONS. We will handle it.

5. HOARDING or self-supplying of necessities is NOT permitted.

6. PUBLIC assembly without a permit or express permission will not be tolerated. NO EXCEPTIONS!

7. TAXATION payments are a public matter regarding payments. Private arrangements may be requested, and ALL taxes must be paid in full! NO EXCEPTIONS!

8. INCARCERATIONS: Long-term and temporary is the sole discretion of the court led by Lord Kaliber and or his appointees.

9. ALL natural, manufactured, or otherwise resources must be used, collected, or distributed with the approval of Lord Kaliber or his designated appointee(s). NO permits are issued to conduct private industry of any kind... refer to the binding terms of the Laws of Taxation delivered to each domicile.

10. JUSTICE, its maintenance, and provisions for such is the express right of the COURT OF LORD KALIBER. This is for your protection. There are NO EXCEPTIONS.

11. CURFEWS shall be imposed liberally when required. There are NO EXCEPTIONS.

12. NO dealings with any outlying groups shall be conducted. Penalties for such are irrevocable and capital in nature. THIS LAW IS CONSIDERED OF A CARDINAL NATURE And finally... in bold red letters...

13. WORKING AND PRODUCING MEMBERS OF OUR SOCIETY ARE THE BACKBONE OF OUR SUCCESS. ALL MEMBERS OF OUR

SOCIETY SHALL BE DULY EMPLOYED IN THE MANNER PRESCRIBED BY THE LAWS OF KALIBER. THIS LAW IS OF THE HIGHEST MAGNITUDE. IT IS DECLARED A CAPITAL OFFENSE TO VIOLATE THIS REQUIREMENT. ABSOLUTELY NO EXCEPTIONS FOR ANY REASON SHALL BE TOLERATED.

The sign ended with the Coveton seal burned into the placards. There were also two stained handprints of different sizes in dripping red. There were no names below them. Just titles. The more considerable read Court Minister, the other read Director of Violations.

Brutally enforced by Kaliber and his staunch goons to build his perfect empire, the Riverfolk endlessly indentured, were less concerned for the past beauty of their homes and disdainful of their own well-being. These new changes were not even remotely complimentary to their former happiness, nor were they sanitary in the least. The rules were all-dominating, and all of it was humiliating to be endlessly a part of.

A lingering memory of everything cheerful and bright was now replaced with a terrifyingly unfamiliar way of living. Living meant surviving, not joy and laughter, where good food and drink were always plentiful and shared with respect and with pleasing company. Work, though necessary, was never too important to get in the way of all things wonderfully enjoyable. Yet such blissful moments had been snatched by enforced toil and emotional mortification. "A life with no enjoying is a life not the worth living," so they sermonized, but without a proper platform to speak from, such voices could not be heard over the cracks of whips and the haunting wails and moans from the abused ones, feeble and timid.

A once serene little valley, where peace was deeply cherished and any notion of barbarity was considered a wholly profane misdeed, had now been violently transformed. The tranquility had given way to a chaotic escalation of nefarious exploits, all brought on by none other than the young Lord Coveton and his ragtag rabble.

The children were savagely torn from their families, rigidly indoctrinated, and ruthlessly bound to serve as Lord Kaliber's personal servants, or "Kallabees" as he trenchantly coined them.

Under the threat of merciless punishment. If any child failed to obey the Wolf's capricious demands, and if a refusal was ever made, it would certainly provoke Kaliber's infamous cruelty—a cruelty in which the surly Wolf took great joy. He delighted in the cries for mercy and the sight of blood streaming from the guilty. Not only would the child be severely punished for the smallest protest, but their already disenfranchised family, stripped of any rights, and would be broken into total submission as well.

From sunrise to sundown, the grinding work seemed infinite, with no breaks and no excuses. If anyone were to be seen slacking, Kaliber vaunted an irredeemable malice, as the family themselves were to be shamelessly branded as useless freeloaders in dire need of disposal. With no trial, they were immediately sentenced and be publicly executed by hanging and to be left to rot as food for the swarms of pests smothering their lifeless bodies. From sunrise, the community once was proud of what they constructed and protected for so long, now it all was being tearfully dismantled with each demolished timber wall falling. From sundown, by the iron thumb of Kaliber's peremptory vision, they were to woefully rebuild what was scavenged from the destruction. Homes were replaced with militia and supply depots, and the evacuees bereft of their residences would shuffle in migratory waves to fend for themselves in search of a new home.

The twilight sky hung heavy above the moor, draped in a shroud of mournful gray, as the skeletal trees swayed like sentinels watching over the laborers toiling beneath their twisted branches. Among them was Miriam D. Quaddling, her once-vibrant spirit now dimmed by the relentless grip of illness and overwork. In the deep trenches, where the cold earth met the chill of despair, she fought against the encroaching shadows that sought to claim her.

As Miriam dug with trembling wings, the biting wind howled around her, a cruel reminder of her fragile state. Each strike of the shovel resonated with a hollow echo, much like the hollow laughter that had once filled her home. The stones of the unfinished manor loomed overhead, mocking her with their steadfastness while she crumbled under the weight of her burden. The air felt thick with despair, heavy like a funeral shroud, and the chill seeped into her bones, robbing her of warmth and will.

Then it happened. The unusual drowsiness that had lurked at the edges of her consciousness surged forward, engulfing her like a dark tide. The world blurred into a swirling vortex, where flames of hellish fire danced tauntingly in her mind, promising both torment and relief. Each breath became a battle; her lungs wheezed in protest as she succumbed to the creeping chill of death, the icy fingers of the reaper wrapping around her fragile form.

From the depths of her despair, she felt the presence of the grim specter, not cloaked in black with a scythe but manifesting as a bitter gale that swept through the trenches, chilling her to the core. The warmth of life drained away, replaced by the stark cold of inevitability. With a final, feeble attempt to rise, Miriam collapsed, shaking and gasping onto the unforgiving earth.

"What's this? Napping on the job? Get up, you slacka!" Barked the Hound, overseer of this grim task, as he struck her with a crack of his whip that echoed like a death knell.

"I c-c-can't do anym-more, please! I need m-medicine!" She cried, her voice a mere whisper against the harsh wind.

"We don't get any! Get up, slacka!" The Hound's voice dripped with disdain, echoing in the hollow of her despair.

With another crack of the whip, Miriam forced herself to stand, using her shovel for support. But her legs betrayed her, quaking beneath the weight of her agony, and she tumbled back to the cold, unyielding ground. The Hounds summoned a stretcher, and she was hoisted onto it, the world spinning around her as her strength ebbed away.

"Bah! She's useless! Put her with the rest of 'em, the mound!" One of the Hounds spat, dismissing her like discarded refuse.

As they carried her away, Wally, sweat-soaked and weary from stacking stone upon stone for the unbuilt Coveton Manor, glanced up and dropped the heavy block he was lifting. Panic surged through him as he rushed to her side. "Miriam! Miriam! What's happening!? Where are you taking her?" He demanded, his heart racing in fear.

"None of your business, runt!" The Hound growled, pushing Wally to the ground, but the Hare persisted, desperately clinging to her wing.

In her fading consciousness, Miriam pulled Wally closer, her breath shallow. "Do not worry, Wally. The light feels so good on such cold days as these…"

Tears welled in Wally's eyes, threatening to spill over as he choked back a sob. "You go on ahead, my dear friend. May the sun forever keep you warm…"

"One more thing, Wallay. Please don't think I'll of Mr. Whyles. He is just as innocent as us, just scared and confused like all of us."

"Bless your heart, Miriam…" Wally whispered, his voice trembling with grief as he watched them carry her away, a flicker of warmth extinguished in the encroaching darkness. The cold wind howled around him, carrying away the last remnants of Miriam D. Quaddling, leaving only silence in her wake—a sorrowful testament to the sacrifice of one who had given everything yet found only the chill of despair in return. Wally stared after her, his heart heavy, the weight of his sorrow pressing down as hard as the stones he stacked for the manor. But there was no time for grief—not here.

It is very dismal news to report that the dreadful toils forced upon the humble creatures were anything but merry. One such job was given to Sampson. Sampson, a broad-shouldered Moose with sweeping antlers, trudged through the village, the weight of his duty evident in every step. His debt ledger, hanging from his side, seemed to pull him down, each name within it feeling like a heavy chain around his neck.

His task was grim, and today's name was Milla, a widow whose husband had been taken by Kaliber's Hounds just weeks before. The thought of confronting her filled him with dread. Arriving at Milla's small burrow, Sampson felt a deep, uneasy twist in his stomach. The thought of confronting her, who had already lost so much, seemed terribly cruel.

He tapped gently with his hoof on the entrance to the burrow. It creaked open, revealing Milla, a stout mole with a tired face etched in sorrow. Her eyes, once bright, were now shadowed by fatigue and grief. Behind her, three young moles peered out from the dim interior, their wide, fearful eyes watching Sampson. The smallest one clung to Milla's side, trembling.

"Milla…" Sampson began, his deep voice heavy with remorse. He lowered his head, his antlers casting long, mournful shadows. "I'm here on behalf of Kaliber."

Milla's ears drooped, and her gaze fell to the ground. Her voice was barely more than a whisper, strained with emotion. "I know why you're here, Sampson. I don't have it."

Sampson's breath caught in his throat. He glanced inside the modest burrow. The shelves that once held provisions were bare, and the storage areas were empty. The weight of the loss was palpable. "I… I'm sorry, but Kaliber expects something else by the end of the week. I don't have a choice," Sampson said, struggling to keep his voice steady.

Milla's lower lip trembled, and tears welled up in her eyes. She drew her young ones closer, trying to shield them from the harsh reality of their situation. "I have nothing left, Sampson," she said softly. "The last of our food was taken. Our belongings were sold to survive. There's nothing left but my children and me."

Sampson stood there, feeling like a failure in a play he had no control over. His large, powerful frame felt oddly frail in the face of her suffering. He wanted to turn away, to throw the ledger into the wind and escape this cruel task, but his duty held him fast. "Please," Milla begged, her voice breaking. "They've already taken so much from us. Can't you see? We have nothing left."

Sampson's gaze dropped to the dirt. He was aware of the cruelty in his role, and the sight of Milla and her young ones, so vulnerable and desperate, was more than he could bear. "I can give you a few more days," he managed to say, his voice thick with emotion. "But after that... I don't know what will happen."

Milla nodded slowly, tears streaming down her face. Her young ones clung to her, oblivious to the gravity of their predicament. As Sampson turned to leave, the burden of Kaliber's expectations weighed heavily on him.

Suddenly, the oppressive silence was broken by the sound of heavy footsteps. Kaliber appeared, his dark eyes flashing with irritation. He looked at Sampson with barely concealed contempt. "Sampson," Kaliber said, his voice cold and cutting. "Have you collected what was required?"

Sampson's voice faltered as he replied, "There was nothing to collect. Milla has nothing left." Kaliber's face twisted with anger. Without a word, he drew his wickedly sharp blade from his cane. His eyes gleamed with a cruel determination as he approached Sampson. The Moose stood frozen, unable to move, his antlers casting long, mournful shadows on the ground.

Kaliber raised the blade, and with a swift, brutal motion, he cut through the base of Sampson's antlers. The Moose gasped in pain as the antlers were severed with a harsh, grinding sound.

Blood trickled from the raw stubs, and Sampson staggered, clutching at his head where the once- proud antlers had been. Kaliber held up the severed antlers triumphantly, a dark smile spreading across his face. "These will serve as a reminder of what happens when one fails to meet my expectations," he declared coldly.

Sampson fell to his knees, his head throbbing with pain, his spirit crushed. The once-ma.j.estic antlers, now a brutal trophy, were a stark reminder of his failure and Kaliber's ruthless power. As Kaliber and his enforcers departed, the village seemed to mourn with Sampson, a silent witness to the harsh cruelty of a tyrant and the shattered dignity of a loyal servant.

In another part of Ambrodale, the once-thriving area of blooming berry patches, which had attracted the community with its vibrant colors, was now a washed-out wasteland of weeds. The scene was filled with the droning sounds of work as a line of weary villagers, ragged and broken, stood before a group of Hounds wielding crude tools and construction equipment.

"Next!" one of the Hounds barked. A timid otter slinked forward and was handed a double-sided axe.

"What do I do with this?" The Otter asked nervously. "You get to work!" The Hound snapped back. "Sector 8!"

The Otter, struggling to manage the heavy axe, dropped it, accidentally cleaving off the Hound's big toe. The Hound shrieked in pain, and a supervisor quickly arrived, brandishing a whip. The whip's cruel cracks drowned out the otter's terrified pleas.

The sight of the bloodied axe and the sobbing otter prompted Wally, who had been observing from the back of the line, to step forward. He stood bravely between the frothing Hound and the blubbering otter. "You expect us tiny folk to do all the hard lifting while you and your Lord sit and reap the benefits?" Wally declared, his voice rising with indignation.

"Quiet, you!" The Hound snapped.

"We are not your puppets to manipulate and abuse at your liking. If we are to work, we shall work for what is right for all of us." Wally's impromptu speech sparked a deafening cheer from his companions.

"Yer got a death wish?!" The Hound growled. His voice laced with menace.

Just then, Kaliber arrived on the scene, his dark eyes flashing with irritation. "Well, if it isn't Mr. Wallis! How delightful. I'll take it from here, lads!"

Kaliber pulled Wally from the crowd and drew a line in the dirt. "You see this line here?" he said, his tone dripping with menace. "If you were ever to cross this against my wishes, I would cut you down instantly. My Hounds will shred you to pieces at my command. However, if you were to draw a line before me, insisting that I do not cross it, your line would be broken before the span of a single breath. You don't hold power as you think you do. Can't you feel these hands tightening around your throat? That single breath of yours would be your last!"

Wally stared defiantly. "What does that mean, exactly?"

"Obey, Obey, OBEY! Disobey, and you will be nothing more than this twig." Kaliber picked up a twig, snapped it in half, and threw the pieces at Wally's face. "Broken! Intellige?" Kaliber chortled.

"You are a monster!" Wally retorted.

"A monster? Nonsense! I'm an innovator, the sole proprietor of progress here and now. It's mine for the taking!"

"Progress? Death is what you bring to us; my friends are dying from what you call progress!"

"If they are not fit enough for change, they are better off dying! Besides, it is for the right cause!"

"What cause, might I ask, may that be?"

"Reformation. Turning this savage land into a prosperous one! A land worth occupying my empire!"

The confrontation between Wally and Kaliber left a charged silence hanging over the scene, the weight of Kaliber's harsh words and Wally's defiant responses stood palpably hanging in the air. Kaliber's face twisted with dark satisfaction, his gaze lingering on Wally with a mixture of disdain and unspoken threats. The Hounds, now subdued by their master's presence, fell silent, their cruel glee giving way to an uneasy tension.

With each step Kaliber took away from the site, his mind churned with a tempest of rage and frustration. The thought of Wally's defiance, the tears of the Otter, and the relentless grip of his failures gnawed at him. The relentless pressure of his own ambitions and the unforgiving weight of his actions drove him toward a restless sleep.

In the depths of his troubled slumber, Kaliber's thoughts twisted and warped into a vivid, haunting dream. In the dimly lit corridors of Coveton Castle, Kaliber wandered, his footsteps echoing with an eerie cadence that reverberated through the empty halls. The castle exuded an oppressive atmosphere as if it were a living entity writhing in its own agony. Shadows moved with malevolent intent, coiling around the ancient stones like the serpentine grasp of an ancient, undying despair. Each room, each corridor, bore the weight of untold sorrows and unspoken secrets, embodying the profound madness that had taken root within its decaying walls.

He approached the grand doors of the ballroom, once a portal to opulence, now sagged and battered. The intricate carvings adorning the doors were marred with deep gouges and cracks as if something had clawed at them in desperation. With a push, the corroded doors fell inward, their broken hinges groaning under the strain, revealing a scene that made Kaliber's blood run cold.

Tyrus stood in the center of the ballroom, a mocking smile stretching across his lips as he danced with Lucrecia. Her ethereal beauty glowed in the dim light, her movements graceful and ghostly, as if she were a specter gliding through the gloom. Tyrus held her close, his grip possessive, his gaze locked with hers in a way that twisted something deep within Kaliber.

A surge of rage exploded within him, hotter and more intense than anything he had ever felt. His vision blurred with red as he let out a roar, rushing forward with wild fury. His paws tore at the drapes, and he flung the ornate furniture at the swinging chandelier above. With a deafening crash, the chandelier plummeted to the floor. Everything felt like an affront, a blasphemy in the face of this betrayal. He grabbed a vase from a nearby pedestal and hurled it across the room, shattering an elegant stained-glass window. Shards of colored glass rained down, scattering across the floor like fragments of his fractured sanity.

But Tyrus remained calm, his grip on Lucrecia unyielding, his smile never wavering. When Kaliber hurled a heavy candelabrum across the room, Tyrus released Lucrecia and drew his sword, the blade glinting menacingly in the dim light.

"So, it's come to this, Kaliber?" Tyrus' voice was a cold taunt seething with disdain.

Kaliber's rage reached its zenith. He unsheathed his cane sword with a sharp hiss, the elegant weapon an extension of his fury. He lunged at Tyrus, their blades clashing with a thunderous ring that echoed through the ballroom. The fight was a ravening dance of steel—Kaliber's strikes wild and desperate, while Tyrus parried with unnerving calm, every movement deliberate and precise.

Tyrus struck with a brutal motion. The edge, blinding Kaliber, cleaved across the young Coveton's lip, the sharp steel carving a deep and cruel gash. A burst of crimson erupted from the wound, staining the pristine marble floor in a stark, shocking contrast.

Kaliber reeled, his body rocked by the searing pain, a guttural howl of anguish and disbelief escaping his lips. The cut burned with a vicious intensity, the blood trailing down his chin, marking him with a vivid emblem of his downfall. The wound, already beginning to form a scar, would etch itself permanently into his flesh—a grim and bitter mark of his utter inadequacy.

The family's cries echoed through the room, disembodied voices mingling with the sound of clashing swords. Kaliber's heart pounded louder, the weight of those voices pressing down on him, fueling his rage and despair.

No matter how fiercely he fought, Tyrus seemed untouchable. Always a step ahead, he skirted around the green-eyed Coveton with adroitness, a sharp and glaring revelation of Kaliber's deficiency. Finally, with a swift, calculated strike, Tyrus disarmed Kaliber, sending his cane sword skidding across the marble floor. Kaliber stumbled back, his breath ragged and his mind spinning with the realization of his defeat. Tyrus's smile widened, his sword now pointed with an air of finality at Kaliber's throat, but the mockery in his eyes cut deepest.

"You're always so predictable," he sneered, his voice a cold, venomous whisper. "She never loved you."

Kaliber could bear it no longer. With a guttural cry, he turned and fled, the remnants of his pride crumbling behind him. He bolted through the hallways, knocking over relic suits of armor, tearing down tapestries, ripping the elegant wallpaper and leaving a trail of destruction in his wake. The castle itself seemed to scream in agony, the wails of the family now a deafening cacophony.

Reaching the end of the corridor, Kaliber burst into the courtyard, where the family's old biplane lay in wait. His paws trembling, he clambered into the cockpit, the controls familiar yet foreign. Without a second thought, he started the engine, the roar of the plane drowning out the ghostly wails that pursued him.

As the plane lifted off, the screeching castle shrank below him, a dark and twisted monument to his failures. The wind slashed through his fur as he soared into the night sky, but no matter how high he climbed, the shadows of Coveton Castle clung to him, their Hadean tendrils tightening with each pulse. These tendrils writhed and coiled, growing thicker and stronger, latching onto him like a living noose. The higher he flew, the more monstrous the castle's presence became, its tendrils dragging him back into an abyss from which there would be no escape.

Back in the dim reality of his private chamber, Kaliber lay sprawled across his lavish bed, the silken sheets twisted around him in a chaotic tangle. His face was contorted in a grimace, his brows furrowed as he wrestled with the remnants of his nightmare. His breaths came in shallow, uneven gasps, each exhale tinged with a faint whimper that betrayed the torment simmering beneath his calm exterior.

Around his neck, the jeweled medallion—the gift from Clovis—gleamed with a malevolent light, its dark surface pulsing with a sickly glow that ebbed and flowed in time with Kaliber's ragged breathing. The twisted metal seemed almost alive, drawing strength from the fears and fury that plagued his subconscious. The medallion flared intermittently, casting an unsettling light that seeped into the very walls of the chamber as if it were feeding on Kaliber's anguish.

It throbbed with a life of its own, the glow spreading out in tendrils, wrapping Kaliber in an invisible grip, tightening with each pulse. Despite the feverish glow of the medallion, Kaliber remained lost in his slumber, powerless to escape the grip of the cursed artifact that clung to him with an insidious hunger.

A Founding Death

Accompanied by several Hounds, Kaliber strolled to the center of Ambrodale and gazed at the massive Miracle Tree rooted in front of him. A crowd of river folk surrounds them, terrifyingly anxious about Kaliber's intentions while staring at their sacred emblem. An emblem that brought mystical curative to those ailing.

"Ah yes, this is the most perfect spot for which I have something incredibly important to build. All that stands in the way is that blasted tree! I wish for it to be chopped down.

The crowd burst into anger and rushed toward the tree, forming a massive blockade, chaining themselves around its base and peacefully repelling Kaliber's insidious scheme as they tried to prevent Kaliber and his goons from marching any closer.

"What's this? Do I see insubordination? Kaliber growled

"We will not allow you to cut it down. This is sacred! This is our guardian! If you cut it down, it will bring catastrophe to us all!" They cried in unison, holding their paws together. Unwilling to fall victim to manipulation.

"How utterly ridiculous! This is nothing more than a hunk of wood that is in my way! Now, I command all of you to move aside or face the deadly consequences. The Riverfolk didn't budge an inch and started to chant.

"Father Tree binds us. Father Tree protects us!" They protested in unison.

"I've heard enough of this drivvel! Chop this tree to oblivion, boys!" Kaliber declared. The Hounds grabbed their axes and started flailing them wildly.

In a scene of heart-rending disarray, the crowd's shrieks of terror rang out, mingling with the grim echoes of their panic. Those who dared cling to the Miracle Tree in a futile bid for survival, met a merciless fate. Their bodies, bloodied and broken, lay strewn around the once-hallowed trunk, now marred by the brutal onslaught. The Hounds' coats streaked with gore, encircled the tree with grim efficiency. With cold, relentless purpose, they commenced their hacking, the ancient bark surrendering to the relentless assault.

Sharp is the axe that cuts, with cruel bite, Against the bark, where once the stars did light, A sacred oak, where ancient whispers sang, Now falls to earth, its final dirge has begun.

Its leaves of green to withered brown doth turn, The blue flame fades, no more to brightly burn, A shriek from deep within, a voice forlorn,

As if the earth herself doth deeply mourn. O'er roots entwined in soil of ages past, The life that held now slips away too fast, The forest still, save for that sorrowed cry, As eldritch glow doth dim, and softly die.

The wind doth weep, the sky with tears doth weep, For now, the sacred tree doth fall to sleep,

In silent rest, beneath the moon's cold gaze, Where once it stood, in ancient, holy days. No more the song, no more the light so true,

The axe hath felled what time alone coulds't rue, A relic gone, its spirit fled afar,

Yet in the earth, its echoes still do scar.

Though bright in the sky, the sun did little to lift the pall of sorrow that lay heavy upon the forest. Once a ma.j.estic sentinel that stood tall among the woodland, the great Father Tree was now reduced to a splintered stump. The Hounds, those ruthless agents of destruction, had done their work, leaving only a memory of what had been. The air was thick with the scent of fresh-cut wood, mingled with a strange, lingering sadness, as though the forest itself mourned its loss.

Kaliber, the Wolf, prowled cautiously around the remains of the Father Tree. His yellow eyes, sharp and cunning, surveyed the scene with a mixture of curiosity and something darker—a hunger that went beyond mere sustenance.

The Hounds had taken their leave, and the forest was quiet, save for the occasional rustle of leaves underfoot. Kaliber approached the stump, his nose twitching as he caught an unfamiliar scent. It was not the scent of the wood or the earth but something otherworldly, something that drew him closer with an irresistible allure.

A small object lay there, nestled within the heart of the stump, where the roots of the Father Tree had once held fast to the soil. It shone with a faint, blue light, pulsing softly as though it were a living thing. Kaliber's breath quickened, and his eyes narrowed as he crept closer. The gem—if it was a gem—seemed to whisper to him, its light promising secrets, power, and more.

His heart pounded with greed as he reached out with one paw and touched it. The moment his paw made contact, a shiver ran through him, and the blue light flared as if in recognition of his presence. The forest seemed to hold its breath.

Kaliber's lips curled into a sinister smile, baring his sharp fangs. This was no ordinary stone; it was a prize beyond measure, something that could elevate him above the other creatures of the wood, something that would make him feared and revered. This odd gem was the very heart of Ambrodale. The Wolf, driven by the greed that had long festered within him, seized the gem with his paw, feeling its strange energy course through him as he pulled it from its resting place. As he did so, the blue light dimmed slightly, as if in protest, and for a fleeting moment, a deep, mournful sound—like the last sigh of the Father Tree—echoed through the forest. But Kaliber paid it no mind. His thoughts were consumed by visions of power, dominion over the forest, and the riches that would surely come to him now that he possessed such a treasure.

He turned, the gem still clutched between his fingers, and with one last glance at the stump, he strutted away. The blue light, though dimmed, continued to glow faintly, casting eerie shadows, his fate forever intertwined with the power of the stolen gem.

∽

The Great Hunger Plight

Food became incredibly scarce, almost impossible to grow with all the overpopulating masses and the continuous demand. There was hardly any food anywhere, in fact. All the farms they delicately cared for had been ravaged by the sickeningly unbreathable air. Whatever had remained was taken by the Hounds and brought to Kaliber.

The confiscated food was served as the entrees, waiting to be cooked by the sudoral children, or "Frylings," as Kaliber nicknamed them, who were shackled to the searing stoves and regularly scalded themselves owing to their inexperience. As Kaliber and his goons feasted, getting fatter and fatter, amassing twice his average size, the corpulent Coveton assigned Adelia Quaddling as his personal tailor, tasked with resizing and readjusting his taut attire. With food not properly allocated, the skeletal Riverfolk groveled for any measly scraps they could attain by entertaining the Lord in humiliating performances. If Kaliber were indeed amused, he would gift the performers flavored crumbs of sustenance.

So, the starving creatures of Ambrodale had nothing to eat, which devolved into a detestable famine. Thus began the food stockpiling.

Unfortunately, such endeavors never worked in the Riverfolk's favor; whenever the Hounds came for routine inspections, concealed produce could be detected by their keen senses of smell. The prosecutor who confessed to praying for a pardon explained that they had received strange and poorly penned letters. Inevitably, they would be charged with violating the most wretched sin of hoarding and "a betrayal of our mutual and high public trust." Elated and fetching a royal bearing, Kaliber took great and perverse pleasure in his work, methodically stoking their shame to a fevered pitch, relishing every moment of their degradation. Kaliber impetuously queried, "How could you do this to us?

We share and share alike; if you go hungry, we all must!" Thus, this proclamation was an obvious falsehood considering the blatant fact that these banned harvests were instantly confiscated and brought to the only table that was allowed to boast such prerequisites for survival. At Kaliber's grand table, his mangy Hounds gathered around as they feasted upon the steaming food served by the manacled children.

These children were the front-line victims of the frenzied gorging among the rabbling lot. Living on whatever meager scraps were left, if any, even as those scraps hit the cold floor. Finally, having appeased their monstrous appetites, such were truculently gifted. Such was the law, but this uncontrollable problem of food peddling escalated into a more untenable issue. Kaliber declared a serious mandate to stamp out these despicable reprobates; these convicts and freeloaders were branded with the mark of "G," forever marking them as Glutters! The hot iron left its mark on their bodies, a reminder of their outcast status within a community that once thrived on camaraderie and generosity. This branding divided the once harmonious community, where generous tidings were once exchanged. Now, the Riverfolk's interactions had soured into a living opportunistic avarice, with mistrust and resentment lurking behind every exchange. The formerly esteemed aspects of their festive lives had crumbled into a shambling disarray of perpetual misgivings and misunderstandings.

A most cherished motto, 'What yours is mine, and what's mine is yours!' drastically morphed into: 'What's mine is mine, and I hide it from all.'

Even with the Glutters' ostracization, they were not detered from secretly hoarding food—until Kaliber's wrath descended upon their homes with merciless fury. His Hounds tore through Ambrodale, sparking terror as they targeted the dwellings of the Glutters. Flames surged from thatched roofs, licking hungrily at the night sky. Their orange tongues writhed like feral beasts, devouring everything in their path. The acrid stench of burning wood filled the air, mingling with the anguished cries of families trapped within, their screams cutting through the roaring inferno in a haunting symphony of despair.

As the inferno consumed the village, flickering shadows danced across the stricken faces of onlookers. Mothers clutched their children close, shielding them from the horrifying spectacle, while fathers stood paralyzed—grief and fury warring within their hearts. Each crackling flame drove home the enormity of their loss—not merely their homes, but the fragile threads of security, hope, and community that once bound them together.

Kaliber stood apart, silhouetted against the hellish glow, his eyes gleaming with sadistic satisfaction. "Let this serve as a warning to all who defy me!" he bellowed, his voice cutting through the roar of the fire and the mournful wails. His enforcers prowled the edges of the flames, forcing back anyone who dared to approach in an attempt to save those trapped inside.

The fire swallowed their homes whole, leaving only ash and smoke in its wake, along with bittersweet memories of laughter and warmth that now felt like distant echoes. Inside the burning structures, the heart-wrenching screams of the Glutters faded one by one, a chilling reminder of Kaliber's unforgiving rule.

As charred beams collapsed, hope crumbled with them, reduced to embers swirling in the oppressive night air. The glow of the blaze cast harsh light on the cold dread creeping into the hearts of the Riverfolk. The unity that once defined Ambrodale dissolved into mistrust and fear, while Kaliber's laughter, cruel and mocking, rang through the chaos like a twisted celebration of their suffering.

When the flames had devoured the last remnants of life, Kaliber raised his voice once more. "Hear me!" he thundered. "From this day forward, any food discovered must be surrendered immediately! Those who conceal it will face public execution at the highest gallows! But to those who report such treachery, you will be richly rewarded for your loyalty and courage." His decree fell upon the people like a crushing weight, extinguishing the last vestiges of camaraderie that had once been the lifeblood of Ambrodale.

Under the pall of his rule, desperation replaced kindness, and betrayal became a means of survival. Roving gangs of Kaliber's mongrel enforcers scoured every corner of the village, their relentless training rendering them ruthless and efficient. They destroyed lives without hesitation, striking down violators and their families in daylight or under cover of darkness. The once- vibrant Ambrodale was reduced to a place of pervasive dread, where no sanctuary remained, and the warmth of compassion gave way to the chilling reality of forced surrender.

Day and night, Kaliber and his Hounds continued their brutal campaign, ransacking homes and razing them to the ground at the slightest suspicion of hidden stores. The infernal cycle ground on, turning Ambrodale into a smoldering shadow of its former self—a bleak monument to Kaliber's tyranny.

But yet there was still hope! Wally was a collector of things and knew how to stock, wrap, and preserve things. He felt his parcels this time might be the power of life itself. Carefully collecting, organizing perishables and durables, and packing them in a manner that looked innocuous, he distributed these packs from his home. The packages looked like the abhorrent stacks of books that the Hounds so hated. They were marked as such. They were covered in a layer of pine bark shreds and undetectable as to make Wally himself chuckle in delight as he disguised flour, apples, cornmeal, etc., though Wally never laughed loudly. Wally knew the gravity before him. The Hare knew precisely how to avoid detection. He moved beyond his own protection and became the deliverer to those who knew how to visit him at his door. Each night, visitors would appear empty-handed, be asked for the password, and leave with boxes of books.

"What ya doin' stupid bunny? YOUR BOOKS ARE MORE USELESS THAN YOURSELFY. "The Hound bands would ripple with laughter. Wally had also learned how to chuckle with them. 'YOU know, lads, have to get rid of things. Books, yes, useless, but the paper, the paper, sooo many uses!"

Grumbling followed, but Wally was too insignificant to bring down. He would hand the parcels to a tearful set of eyes and cover the soft sobs with his own laughter. "Yes, yes, take these. Fun pictures to keep you going in these hard times," he'd whisper, his voice light yet warm. His laughter always trailed off into a frozen grimace once he returned inside. "Yes, keep you going," his words faltered in the quiet of his empty room, the warmth evaporating as the cold reality crept in. "Keep us going..." Wally's words hung in the air, empty, as if he himself were waiting for someone else to answer.

But there was no one, only the silence. And Wally, unaware of the eyes that had been watching him. Kaliber's loyalists, scavengers who lurked in the shadows of the alleys and between the market stalls, had taken careful note of Wally's activities. They approached him, feigning desperation, seeking his kindness, only to betray him the moment his door closed behind them. With parcels clutched tight, they scurried like rats through the night toward the den of Kaliber. There, the Wolf awaited, knowing full well what they carried. Inside his darkened chambers, Kaliber lounged on his throne of weathered oak, eyes glinting with curiosity as the parcels were placed before him. His claws slowly tapped the armrest, a steady beat echoing through the tense room.

"Where have you uncovered these parcels?" He asked, though the cruel grin on his face betrayed that he already knew. His voice was laced with sarcasm, the question more of a game than a real inquiry. He leaned forward, eyes narrowing, eager to relish in the fear that radiated from his informants.

They fidgeted before him, the weight of his gaze pressing down on them as they stumbled over their words. "F-from the rabbit, s-sire. Wally... Wally," one finally confessed, too afraid to meet Kaliber's gaze.

"That silly little rabbit thinks he can bend the rules, does he?" Kaliber chuckled, low and dangerous, leaning back once more. The malevolent glee spread across his face as his tail swayed lazily behind him. "We shall soon see who'll be laughing."

The Wolf stood abruptly, his towering figure casting long shadows across the room as the flickering firelight danced on the walls. He paced, slow and deliberate, his steps echoing off the stone floor as the tension in the room thickened. His thoughts twisted with dark delight, savoring the prospect of Wally's impending downfall.

"Prepare the gallows," Kaliber ordered, his voice cold and final, sending a chill through the room. "I want Wally strung up by sunrise. Let's see how he likes facing the consequences of his little games."

His minions exchanged uneasy glances, but none dared question the order. They scurried off, eager to escape the Wolf's presence, as Kaliber turned to the window, peering out into the night. His grin widened as he imagined the sight of Wally, helpless and dangling from the noose, the smugness wiped from his face, the rabbit's laughter silenced forever. "His arrogance will cost him dearly," Kaliber muttered to himself, the wicked smile lingering on his lips.

But in the cold night, beyond the reach of Kaliber's twisted grin, Wally was still unaware of the doom gathering around him.

A Missing Convict

Locked away in an isolated cell, Whyles, beaten and bloodied, curled in his filth in the grimy corner, dispirited. The cell was bare, too bare, stripped of any hygienic necessities. The only real luxury was a bed made of clumps of hay. Maggots and fleas made their home in the tangled tufts of Whyles's scrubby fur. Throughout his spindly body, little bite marks could be seen. No doubt, he was his little pest's feast!

Locked in that desolate cell for what seemed an eternity, Whyles found himself imprisoned not just by stone, but by an ever-echoing cacophony of voices. These spectral murmurs taunted him with relentless scrutiny, their insidious whispers ceaselessly pricking at the frail fabric of his sanity. Madness, that pernicious blossom, had taken root within him, feeding on the haunting visions of his treachery—the ruin he had wrought upon those he once cherished. His pleas and prayers were futile against these grotesque phantoms of death and decay, which danced before him with a cruel jest. From the ashes of bygone joys arose a monstrous specter, a demon birthed of avarice, a fiend whose very shadow cast a pall over Whyles's fragile composure, which now lay shattered amidst a ceaseless psychic onslaught.

In his fogged and fevered sight, Whyles perceived a shadowy figure—another Fox, but with eyes aglow like burning coals—emerge from the wreckage of his fractured mind, seeping through the cold iron bars and pointing accusatorily at him.

"Do you know me?" Whyles inquired, his voice trembling as if he were lost in a shifting dreamscape.

"No…" hissed the Shadow, "YOU… know… ME!"

The Shadow's insistence jolted Whyles awake, pulling him from the abyss of his reverie. The spectral form sank beneath his trembling feet.

"I know you," Whyles stammered. "But I can't see you… is this some new game?" "The game ended long ago. The very fact that you know me means you know yourself."

Whyles, accustomed to the labyrinthine twists of thought, found himself ensnared by the shadow's enigmatic statements. The Shadow materialized behind him; its frosty paw gave a chilling grip upon his shoulder.

"Oh, I see now. I know you so well that I need only glimpse a mere shadow. Yet, I doubt that I-"

"Silence! Your pitiful pelt of spent troubles!" the Shadow interrupted with derision. "You see me as you! And YOU forged me from your own misery. A life so wretched and pitiful. Were you to peer within, these embers for eyes would behold nothing but your own reflection. Filthy, worthless, a rotter born of decay, lies, and neglect!"

"STOP... STOP IT! YOU ARE NOTHING LIKE ME!" Whyles shrieked, his voice rising in desperation.

"Think... yeees... good."

"Useless fool, unable to offer anything beyond licking the boots of—"
"NOOOO!" Whyles cried out as an icy grip seemed to close around his throat.

Before him, the visage of a solitary, abandoned cub—his past or perhaps his future?—loomed uncertainly. Was it a memory or a mere dream?

Two fiery eyes glared down upon him as the Shadow crawled across the ceiling, its head spinning in a disorienting whirl, a dizzying blur of malevolence.

"Yeeeeeesssss..." Whyles shuddered. "Yeeesss... yeeessss," came the profound reply. "Yes. Yes... that's it."

"What is it?" Whyles asked, his voice a whisper. Had he grown inured to the accusations, or had something shifted in his surroundings?

"Yes, Whyles dearie, the letter. Your writing—better than you thought. You impress me, lad. Who knew?" The shadow's tone was tinged with mockery, a happy trill echoing in the gloom. "Though I cannot fully grasp your writing and reading, you are skilled, my dear."

"Writing... reading... ah, yes." In his confusion, Whyles had forgotten—whose eyes were those? The red eyes that now met his were Miriam's.

"I almost forgot," he muttered to himself, a touch of sheepishness creeping into his voice. "I almost... forgot..."

The Shadow faded, leaving only a stain upon the cell wall. Whyles scratched his ears, then began to dust himself off, noting the grotesque infestation that clung to him.

"It's odd..." he murmured, trailing off into the darkness, his memory slipping away once more.

A sliver of sunlight, strange and irregular, cast its pallid beam across the far corner of his cell, while the distant sound of bells began to ring. 'Hmm." He muttered. "I don't remember there being a bit of sun in this place." He continued brushing himself off as he rose and walked toward the diminishing shaft on the wall.

"I really, really, really… I almost forgot…"

A Hound approached the rusty cell bars, and one of them was holding a bowl of food, which, in truer terms, was a rotten slop that reeked of putrid sewage.

"Wull, Wull if it ain't ta sly, ungrateful, double-crossing Fox! Yer must be 'ungray! Comes an' gets yer grub!" The Hound ordered. Whyles turned and faced the Hound.

"I ain't much fer eatin'! Don't t'ink I'll eva be!"

"We wouldn't want yer starving! Lord Kalibah still got plans for ye! Busides, now with da food shortage ye sud be eatin' whutcha ya grubby paws can get 'fore it runs out!"

Upon hearing the grave news of Ambrodale's food shortage, Whyles scuttled toward the Hound, inquiring about it.

"Oh yuh, it's getting real bad out here! Take me 'urd; it's safer here than out there! So, eat up!"

The Hound slowly handed the bowl to Whyles but intentionally dropped it as the food splattered all over the dirt.

"Oops! Oh wull, ye don't mind! After all, ye is a tinsy wurm, ain'tcha?

The Hound laughed and strutted away while the hunched, twitchy Fox frantically paced back and forth. Suddenly, the dismal cloud hanging over his mind subsided, and courage sprouted as an answer to his desperate orison.

"I dare say I must fix what I wronged! T'ese folk are good folk, and if'n it means me death, I will gladly accept it, for rightful froodum! Now, how will 'eva break free? T'ink, Whyles, t'ink!" Whyles knocked his head with his fist, and then, like a bolt of lightning, there came an idea. He rushed toward the clumps of hay and dived in headfirst, burying himself within it.

Minutes passed as Whyles kept quiet in haystack, his mouth involuntarily stuffed with strands of hay. During Whyles's artful act of stealth, a Hound guard came to check up on the Fox, just as Whyles planned. To the Hound's surprise, the cell was empty, and the Fox vanished without a trace.

The Hound unlocked the door and started investigating the cell. Tensions were high. Whyles looked through the stack, waiting for the perfect opportunity to strike. At long last, the opportunity did reveal itself, and Whyles seized it. Just as the Hound's back was turned toward the hay, Whyles gloriously leaped out of his hiding spot armed with his tin pot hat and pounced on the unsuspecting Hound. The Fox wrapped his arms around the neck of the struggling Hound while simultaneously clubbing the Hound's head with his tin pot. As quickly as the struggle

began, it ended, and Whyles was the victor, leaving the Hound sprawled beneath him unconscious. Whyles brushed himself off and caught his breath. Whyles quickly retrieved the cell key and stuffed it in his raincoat's pocket. He tiptoed out of the cell, locking it behind him, and continued to slink down a dimly lit hallway.

The hallway was filled with supplies packed in large crates. As Whyles crept further, he noticed a group of Hound guards having a conversation. Wanting to avoid detection, he slid behind one of the large crates and listened in.

"Aye, it's true Kalibah is gonna start raiding dem homes and take whatever foods they gots!" One of the Hounds chimed in.

"Oh no, I must warn them before they start the raids. But how?" Whyles asked himself. "Pen! Paper!" Whyles thought! "I'll deliver the warnings!"

Whyles kept watching the group until they eventually dispersed, and he continued to trek toward the exit until he spotted Kaliber's secondary office. The Fox cautiously slinked to the door. His paws grasped the brass, ornate knob and turned it.

"Locked!"

The Fox, using his long fingernail, started to jiggle the lock. Then, with a 'pop', the door was unlocked. Whyles darted into the office, closing the door behind him. He rummaged through Kaliber's desk, finding a quill, a bottle of ink, and a stack of paper. Quietly dipping the quill into the ink, Whyles started to question his task.

"What to say… What to say!?" Whyles thought, tapping the pen on his head. Then it hit him, and the Fox hastily scribbled letter after messy, illegible letter warning the villagers of the impending raids.

Whyles, long accustomed to Kaliber's wicked machinations, had foreseen the doom that would inevitably befall the innocent villagers. He recognized his own inadequacy in reaching out to others. The others had always seemed inclined to regard him as a useless and perhaps even foolish figure. Yet, despite these unfortunate misjudgments of his character, they would prove to be profoundly mistaken about the small hero who had learned to place himself last in the lineup of the virtuous. Something within him, a lingering sympathy for those who labored earnestly amidst the chaos, compelled him to set aside his own concerns and dedicate himself entirely to a cause greater than himself.

Jolted by some unknown force, Whyles continued jotting the letters, these squiggles, these w. o.

r. d. s, they called them, burst out with maddening, artistic strokes. THE WORDS that Wally so lovingly preserved. He felt its power and attraction; this attention to the WORDS was so evident in the silent hours Whyles stared alone into the darkness of Wally's writing cupboard, where books and pictures of the past danced before his bleary eyes.

These words could be MADE. MADE to talk to folk. When Wally read, the Quaddling's shmaltzy phrased devotions to Wally in letters…Whyles was amazed!

These squiggles could talk about nice things, not only rough commands and censures. Kindnesses, admiration, maybe recipes for those too-softy berry muffins he hated. But. The WORDS, they could make a body SPEAK!

Then, one of those nights alone after the Quaddlings' lessons to help him along with his writing, he heard it—a sad old cry of a neighbor whose devoted wife had gone mysteriously missing.

Whyles knew what was starting long before then, but to hear that mourning and then …then… the tiny cry of a motherless lad.

Whyles redoubled his efforts. 'THE WORDS… they're good. Veery 'eery good.' He almost said out loud in that moment of realization alone. At last, the final test was here as he continued to write his squiggles.

Whyles had grown bold to defy his past limited knowledge. His apparent stupidity he now disregarded; by now, he had learned to use it. He did not like but also did not confront the inevitable pushings, rushings, and beatings he received at the cruel claws of his oppressors. The thought of the brutal punishment, if caught, didn't sway Whyles to back down. His deliveries would have to be made, even if it meant the death of him.

'Make it they will'. That became his reminder.

"I have one more idea. Here's hoping it works," Whyles said, jumping back into the present.

Whyles placed the several notes he had just written in his pocket and started jotting down another letter.

"Dearest Kaliber, how we miss you in Coveton Manor. We were wrong to bunnish thee frum our estate; 'p'ease come back among our family in a jiffy. Ye brought us everlasting joy. We await your return with open arms. With kind and hopeful regards, the Coveton family." Whyles read the letter back to himself, trying to contain his enthusiasm.

"Sounds perfec' ta' me!" Whyles boasted quite proud of his plan. Sadly, his forged Coveton letter contained numerous spelling and grammatical errors, which he was unaware of, considering his lack of refinement in writing skills.

Whyles caught sight of Kaliber's silhouette as he twisted the doorknob. With a swift, anxious movement, he rolled beneath the desk and fell silent. From his hiding place, Whyles shuddered as the door creaked open with a mournful sound. Kaliber entered, moving with an unsettling silence. Whyles could only see the Wolf's foreboding figure as he advanced slowly, his presence more sensed than heard. The Wolf's imposing form loomed against the dim light, casting a formidable silhouette and filling the room with a sense of dread that seemed to weigh heavily on the air.

Kaliber's breathing was steady and cold, a harsh and unyielding rhythm. He began to whistle a low, haunting melody, its discordant notes slicing through the stillness of the room. The tune was eerie and unsettling. Each note was a spectral echo that seemed to cut through Whyles' composure. It was as though the melody were a ghostly presence, weaving through the silence and embedding itself deep within Whyles' very soul. The haunting strains of the whistle clung to his senses, each wavering note intensifying his terror and making each moment beneath the desk feel like an age of torment. Whyles felt as though the melody was closing in on him, tightening its grip around his heart and leaving him breathless in its wake.

He approached the desk with careful steps, his keen eyes scanning the room with a predatory sharpness. Each rustle of paper above Whyles felt like a thunderclap in the suffocating quiet, a reminder of the danger that was so near.

A sudden knock at the door sliced through the tense silence.

"Come in," Kaliber's voice was smooth but edged with irritation, carrying an undercurrent of menace. The door swung open, and a Hound rushed in, clearly flustered.

"We have a situation!"

Kaliber's growl was a deep, resonant sound filled with suppressed rage. "What situation?" He demanded, his voice holding a note of impatient menace.

"There is no time to explain. It seems your rabbit chum is causing some trouble."

Kaliber's expression darkened, and his growl grew fiercer. "Bring me to that troublesome rabbit," he commanded, his voice carrying an ominous finality. "I've had enough of his antics!"

As the Hound hurried out and Kaliber followed, Whyles released his held breath. Emerging from his hiding place, he hurriedly placed the forged letter and quill back on the desk. In his frantic state, he knocked over the ink bottle, its dark contents spreading across the desk and staining his paws. Desperate to contain the mess, he used his coat to mop up the ink before fleeing the office, his paws marked with the evidence of his narrow escape and forgery.

Once he escaped the compound, he trekked his way to Ambrodale, fretting the approach of the hordes on their rounds that might've spotted his tiny, rat-like frame.

"Words you can't smell. Make it, they will. Make it they must!" He muttered as he continued sneaking past the many patrols that passed his way. Gliding with precision, he hopped into bushes and slid behind structures so that he could not be detected. Once the paths were clear, he pressed on, driven by his commitment to make his deliveries on time. The familiar sound of the rippling river in the distance brought a fleeting sense of relief. He had always found solace in its gleaming waters, a beacon of life and purity. But as he drew closer, his heart sank.

The river, once a silken ribbon of silver, now lay before him a darkened and lifeless stream. Its once lustrous surface, now thick with a foul and oily film, seemed to mock the memory of its former glory. The water, robbed of its clarity, emitted a stench of rot so pungent that it stung his senses, lingering in the air like a curse. His eyes widened in disbelief and sorrow as he beheld the fish that once darted through the crystal depths. They seemed rare now as the few visible floundered pitifully in the sludge, their scales dulled and their movements feeble, as though suffocating beneath the weight of the foul water. Some broke through the thick surface, gasping in vain for the air denied them before surrendering to the poison that had claimed their world.

The river, now a slick floating graveyard, carried their lifeless forms in clusters, drifting aimlessly toward a fate no longer their own.

It tore at his soul—a most dreadful reminder of what had been lost. Where once the river stood as a symbol of life and purity, it now served as a monument to decay and death, an emblem of something that had once been cherished, now despoiled beyond recognition.

He surveyed the Creswick Bridge, its looming form guarded by Kaliber's sentries. From within the cover of the thicket, he drew forth his fife and played a gentle, lulling tune. The melody floated through the still night air, casting a soporific spell upon the Hounds. Their ears, once pricked with vigilance, slowly drooped as weariness overtook them. With a yawn, one after another, they succumbed to slumber, their heavy breaths lost within the soft breeze.

With naught but the moonlight to guide his way, the Fox slunk across the bridge on silent paws, his heart beating in rhythm with the quiet night. Each letter—folded and weighted with urgency—was tucked safely in the pockets of his coat, the ink barely visible in the soft light.

Whyles knew the importance of the task at hand: each letter was a warning, a plea for those who read it to act, to be prepared for what was coming.

The first homes loomed ahead, quiet and still; their doors shut tight against the world. Whyles moved like a shadow, his body pressed close to the stone walls, his every step calculated. He paused, listening intently as the distant sounds of a patrol echoed in the streets. The Hounds were near, their heavy paws and sharp eyes sweeping the village in search of trouble.

He froze. His breath slowed, barely a whisper against the night. After a long moment, the patrol passed, the Hounds' distracted chatter fading into the distance. Whyles let out a quiet breath, then dropped to all fours and dashed to the first home. With the swiftness of a whisper, he slid the first warning letter beneath the threshold, his paw brushing the cold wood before he retreated back into the shadows.

"Words you cannot smell," he muttered under his breath, a sly grin playing at his lips. The Hounds would never find these letters, no matter how hard they sniffed. For now, the warning would remain hidden, waiting to be read when the time came.

The air around him was thick, the faint scent of rot and decay seeping from the corners of the village. It wasn't the sweet aroma of freshly baked pies or morning bread, but the stench of death, lingering in the spaces between the homes. Corpses hung from long poles along the main street, swaying gently in the night breeze like grotesque lanterns. Their twisted, lifeless forms were stark against the darkness, reminders of the price of defying Kaliber's cruel dominance.

The smell was overwhelming, clinging to the very air Whyles breathed, but he pushed it aside. There was no time to dwell on it.

He moved to the next home, keeping low. The stillness of the village surrounded him, but he knew he couldn't stay in one place for long. Slipping another letter under a door, he barely paused to glance over his shoulder before darting to the next. The air, thick with the scent of death, carried no signs of life—just the quiet rustle of leaves and the faint murmur of far-off footsteps.

At each home, he delivered his letters with practiced speed, gliding silently from one door to the next. He wasn't certain how long the Hounds would be distracted, but he trusted that they hadn't yet caught wind of his trail. The letters, one by one, slid beneath the doors of the Riverfolk's homes. The warnings would remain hidden, tucked away until the first sign of danger arose.

Winding his way through the village, his pace suddenly faltered. There, at the heart of Ambrodale, where Father Tree once stood tall and proud, was a sight so monstrous it seized him with horror. The great tree, the village's symbol of unity and strength, had been felled. In its place stood a towering statue—Kaliber's grotesque effigy, crudely carved from the very wood of the sacred tree. The twisted figure, bedecked with gaudy trinkets and adorned with parcels of dried fruit and berries at its base, seemed to leer down at Whyles with a sardonic grin. The ruby eyes, gleaming in the moonlight, burned with a malevolent fire that sent a chill through him.

The rubies—they had once adorned Miriam Quaddling's Sunday bonnet, a cherished heirloom passed down through generations. Whyles could still picture Miriam and Wally laughing in the meadows, the sunlight catching the gleam of the rubies as they strolled together. Now, those same gems glinted cruelly from the hollow sockets of Kaliber's statue, mocking the joy that had once been.

A surge of nausea gripped him, but he forced it back. There was no time for weakness. His mission remained—he had to keep going. The letters had to be delivered.

Whyles continued his task, slipping under doorways with renewed urgency. His paws light on the cobblestones, slipping from one threshold to the next, unnoticed and undetected. He was only one Fox, but with each letter, he was making a stand against Kaliber's tyranny. The letters may be small, but they were a defiance of Kaliber's twisted intentions.

With each door he passed, the weight of the village's suffering pressed harder against him, but he didn't stop. Not yet. The Hounds might catch wind of him soon, but for now, he had the cover of night and the silence of the village streets. Each letter was a spark—small but necessary.

For days, Whyles remained hidden in the oppressive shadows of Ambrodale, skulking through the village's desolate backstreets and forgotten alleyways, always avoiding the relentless patrols. He could do nothing but watch as Kaliber's cruelty tore through the village like a disease— villagers dragged from their homes in the dead of night, their cries echoing through the empty streets, hollow and filled with terror. The crack of the whip was a constant sound, a sickening rhythm that cut through the quiet, followed by the tortured screams that clawed at his soul, dragging him deeper into despair. Each cry was like a stone thrown into his heart; each sound was a reminder of his own helplessness. The more he watched, the more it felt like the village was dying, its spirit being crushed under Kaliber's heel.

Whyles' paws trembled as he lingered in the shadows, paralyzed by the bitter knowledge that no matter how desperately he wished to act, he was small, powerless, and too late. His paws curled inward, aching to strike, to do something—but what chance might a little Fox like him have against Kaliber? He wasn't a hero. He was nothing, a fragile creature dwarfed by the Wolf's towering cruelty. The letters he had sent in secret had only stoked Kaliber's fury, sparking new waves of torment as innocents were dragged away, interrogated, and punished for the origins of words they had never written.

His chest tightened with shame. His paws twitched with the urge to lash out, to silence the tyrant, but it was pointless. He knew it. He cursed himself for not standing up sooner—for not being braver before the storm had grown too wild for even the largest of acts to matter, it seemed.

Tonight, though, something was different. Something stirred within him as he hid in the mill, tucked away in the heart of Ambrodale near the square. From the shadows of the mill's loft, he could see the gathering crowd below, the torches casting long, flickering shadows across the square, and the gallows standing like a looming nightmare in the center.

And there, at the gallows, stood Wally, his fur pale in the flickering light, a noose tightening around his neck. Whyles' heart clenched as he watched his friend stand there, trembling but defiant. The Hare's head was held high despite the terror in his eyes.

Kaliber, standing at the foot of the gallows, addressed the crowd with a sneer. "This Hare thought he could defy me, smuggling food as I wouldn't know. Let this be a final lesson to all of you." His words were cold, cruel, each one sharp and cutting.

Whyles' paws gripped the wooden beams beneath him, his heart pounding. Every instinct in him screamed to leap down, to stop this madness, but he held still. What good would it do? Kaliber's guards were everywhere. One small act of defiance would only make Wally's fate worse.

Adelia's voice broke through the tension, rising above the murmurs of the crowd. "He risked his life for us all—Let him free!"

Kaliber's gaze flicked to her, icy and unforgiving. "Then perhaps you'd like to join him," he growled, the words dripping with venom.

Whyles' stomach turned, his paws shaking as he prepared to act—but he hesitated. What could he do? What could anyone do?

Then, a sound broke the air, and Whyles' ears perked. He had heard the rough bellows, the atonal clankings, and belchings. It sounded like nothing he had ever heard in Ambrodale.

"T'ems Horkahs...t'ems Horkahs!" Whyles whispered, his heart racing, his spyglass pressed to his eye.

A brigade of Horkurs were marching toward Ambrodale.

It was apparent to the shaking Fox from where he crouched. They were ready for battle. "Oh my, what a glorious sight to see!" Whyles exclaimed, thrilled by the prospect tha reinforcements had arrived to free Ambrodale. He could hardly believe it. The ancient warrior tribe was coming. Whyles surely believed that the Horkurs would prevail in the upcoming clash.

Kaliber's attention snapped toward the sound, his face hardening as the first echo of the Horkur march grew louder. The Vuggahorn blared again, shaking the air. The crowd around the gallows hesitated, confusion rippling through them, and Kaliber snarled in frustration.

Wally, standing tall despite the noose tightening, suddenly spoke, his voice cutting through the tension, unwavering and clear: "If this is how it ends, then let it be known—I fought for what was right. And no matter how this ends, they'll remember me... and they'll remember Ambrodale."

Whyles barely noticed the shift in the atmosphere. His paws itched with anticipation, a mixture of hope and exhilaration rushing through him. The Horkurs were coming. The fight for Ambrodale was about to commence.

Battle of Bromby River

The tension in the air was thick, a suffocating weight pressing down on everyone. The murmur of the crowd at the gallows grew distant, swallowed by the oppressive silence of the night. Then, like a crack of thunder, the stillness shattered, broken by the unmistakable blare of a war horn.

Kaliber, his gaze still fixed on Wally at the gallows, froze. The sound was unlike any other—a call to battle, a summons that resonated deep within Ambrodale. Without a moment's hesitation, he motioned sharply for his guards to follow and strode toward Crestwick Bridge, his steps purposeful.

With practiced urgency, Kaliber drew a spyglass from his side and pressed it to his eye. His sharp gaze swept across the distant horizon, scanning for the source of the sound. His heart quickened as he saw it—an immense brigade of Horkurs marching toward Ambrodale. Their footsteps rumbled like distant thunder, their presence undeniable.

At the head of the horde, leading with grim determination, was Cap'm

Thistleworts.

The Horkurs were a fearsome sight: massive, heavily armed, their misshapen faces painted in vibrant tribal warpaint, each design marking their rank. The air was filled with the pounding of drums, synchronized and rhythmic, while war horns blared, signaling the imminent clash.

Kaliber's lips twisted into a wicked grin, the prospect of bloodshed sending a thrill through him. His fickle thirst for violence would soon be sated.

"What der yer see, me Lord?" a Hound asked, his voice edged with curiosity.

"A bunch of crude invaders," Kaliber sneered, his eyes narrowing in contempt. "Fetch me my hunting rifle, cito. Let's send these pigs squealing home. It's time for battle."

"As ye wish, me Lord!" The Hound scampered away, eager to spread the word. News of the approaching force quickly spread, and the Hounds began to prepare for the confrontation.

Kaliber turned his attention to two others. "You two, roll out the cannon. It's about high time we put it to use." The Hounds nodded sharply and hurried off.

"Gather the Riverfolk," Kaliber barked. "Round. them up for assembly."

The Riverfolk shuffled together, forming a large, uneasy crowd as they were herded toward Kaliber and his Hounds.

"I requested all of you because, as you can hear, our beautiful residence is under threat! Raise your axes and follow me into battle; defend our home from the swine that dare defile it!"

"We are not warriors! We don't know how to fight!" The crowd cried. With a heave and a ho, the Hounds hauled an enormous cannon and placed it in position. The two Hounds manned the cannon and loaded its first shot.

"It's up to all of us to stomp out these wretched invaders! Loyalty will be rewarded. Cowardice will be treated as treason! Make no mistake, they want to slaughter each and every one of you! Fight for your home, for your family, for your survival!" Kaliber proclaimed.

The returning Hound handed Kaliber the long-barreled hunting rifle, and the Wolf pointed the hefty gun toward the Horkur brigade.

"They're savages ready to destroy all of us! Protect those you cherish from the wicked who commit harm! Battle awaits! Are we to sit idly by and let them pillage our land? Primus ferire, fortiter ferire!

Kaliber's overzealous, resplendent speech placed a fanaticism on the Hounds as they chanted and hollered. Still, the same reaction could not be said for the Riverfolk as they shared the same blank expression as Kaliber's speech, which had little effect on them.

"If you aren't willing to protect the Homeland, then you shall die for it! Get these sniveling cowards upfront, boys. They shall make a wonderful shield for us!" Kaliber commanded.

With this insidious command, the Riverfolk started to flee, but they were flanked on all sides by the snarling Hounds, who trapped them in place and started to push them toward the bridge. The Riverfolk were now stuck between the two armies used as a divisive living shield. Kaliber jolted to the cannon behind the shield of residents and checked to see if it was loaded.

"Now, when I give the word, fire without hesitation!" The Wolf responded and strutted back behind the shield of residents. Cap'm Thistleworts, seeing the innocent lives thrust in the middle of the impending battle, raised his hoof, signaling his army of swine to halt, and so they did.

Droplets of rain began trickling from the sky, and not a second later, the clear night morphed into a thunderous storm. The wind blew hard. The night sky lit up with a series of flashes conjured by lightning. The pelting rain made the two armies standing across from one another appear as shadowed specters.

Cap'm Thistleworts hailed the Wolf as he pointed his jagged spear at Kaliber. The Wolf crouched behind a young opossum who was stricken with fear. Kaliber aimed through the rifle's sights, which was propped up by the Opossum's shoulder.

"Whut's dis? A great commanda' such as yursulf nee' ta' hide behind the hupless masses? Whure's yur pride? Dis is between us. Leave t'em o'tt'a it.

"I have plenty of pride, you swine! Where is your so-called pride? You clearly have the advantage!"

"Whut may thoot be?"

Kaliber, glaring at Cap'm brashly, declared. "You do have the advantage; yes, we do outnumber you. Yes, I am a well-bred individual who strives to be perfect. Yes, people follow me out of fear of my censure. But YOU, who look like a shambling pile of filth. YOU who wreak of stale rot.

YOU who speak from the gurglings of the mud pits you bathe in. YOU have their respect. Why, that's hardly fair, my amice! I must confess that is quite a glorious trait to possess."

"Aye, like any good commanda', I ruspet my band, unlike yer who think he's so high and moighty! I tulls yar whut, uf'n we duel ta' loser must go home!"

"You must be daft! There is no chance you can ever claim victory over me! I am the greatest of all swordsmen!

"I'll take me chunces! Whut say yur?"

"If you are looking for a quick death, then so be it; you have one. "

Kaliber passed his rifle to a Hound and stepped forth at Crestwick bridge, with a woosh, Kaliber unsheathed his elegant sword from his cane. The Wolf started showing off his quick strikes and parries with similar flawless motions as a graceful dancer.

"Come and face your doom, you heathen!" Kaliber stood firm, pointing his blade at his rival.

Cap'm Thistleworts clamored his way up to the bridge until he was six feet away from the Wolf. A solo war drum started beating in rhythmic and rapid repetition. The two foes began circling one another, waiting for the other to strike first. Kaliber lunged in with several slashes at the grizzled Boar, but these slashes were deflected by Cap'm Thistleworts's sturdy spear. In response, Cap'm too tried sticking the Wolf with the spear's edge, thrusting in rapid succession; all of them dodged by Kaliber's agility as he effortlessly skirted around each oncoming jab, all the while humming a childhood ditty, he learned at Coveton castle.

The blocking and striking continued as Kaliber's nimble feet kept him safe from barraging jabs from the spear. Cap'm Thistleworts could fend off Kaliber's ruthless flurry of swipes and stabs, that is, until Kaliber successfully sliced Cap'm Thistleworts. In a state of shock, Cap'm Thistleworts noticed a sharp pain, and with this pain, he saw a thin gash on his belly that started streaming blood. Cap'm Thistleworts plopped on one knee and leered at Kaliber, who held the tip of his blade to Thistleworts's slobbery triple chin.

"First blood! It appears I once again am the victory before I shall end your miserable life. Do you have any last words?"

There was a moment of awkward silence, but the mysterious sound of a fife playing in the distance soon broke it. The music fluttered in the air and seemed to have attracted the Riverfolk, as in an instant, they rushed back, toppling the unsuspecting Hounds to the ground. They were freed from their captivity by a mysterious savior.

"Seize them, you fools. Don't let them escape!" Kaliber shouted as he watched the Riverfolk flee in anger.

Just as Kaliber was distracted, Cap'm Thistleworts, though wounded, was quick to disarm Kaliber and pin him to the ground.

"Yer wanna know my last wurds? Attack boayz!" The gruff Boar announced. The Horkurs charged into the mishap with this command as they snorted a battle cry.

"Fire!" Kaliber screamed as he kicked Cap'm Thistleworts off, regained his sword, and retreated behind the cannon. The curs lit the cannon's fuse, and the large lead ball flew out with a deafening boom crashing into the charging horde of Horkurs, knocking them down as if they were bowling pins. The Hounds regrouped with Kaliber at the cannon, watching the result of the cannon blast.

Through the dense smoke, they saw the snorting Horkurs advancing, fewer in number than before the blast but still a large mass of foes. The two Hounds started to reload the cannon, shoving a cannonball into the barrel. Kaliber grabbed his rifle and took aim at one of the many Horkurs. Having a clear line of sight, Kaliber fired his gun, and with an agonizing squeal, the Horkur dropped dead.

"What are you buffoons standing here for!? Charge!" Kaliber declared while reloading his black powder rifle. The Hounds advanced with dreadful swiftness and dived into the wave of Horkurs, and with their dive, chaos commenced. The frenzied Hounds bit and clawed the Horkurs, sinking their fangs into their flabby flesh.

In return, the Horkurs impaled the Hounds with their tusks, all the while clubbing them with their clubs, chopping them with their stone axes. One after another, Hounds and Horkurs fell dead in the slick mud with each exchange of deadly blows.

Cap'm Thistleworts, alongside his most esteemed warrior, Bilmey Toags, bypassed the central conflict and focused their attention on the artillery. Anyone who dared to spring to protect the artillery was immediately trampled to death by the mighty charge of the two Horkurs. After another devastating shot out of the cannon and three deadly shots from Kaliber's rifle, Bilmey tackled the two cannoneers and skewered them as he tore their abdomens wide open with his massive tusks. Unfortunately, just as Bilmey hooted in celebration, stamping in place, the Boar felt an intensely burning tingle and fell to the ground, wounded.

Disoriented, he lost all sense of time and feeling. Bilmey grasped his hip, and he looked at his hoof in disgust; it was drenched in blood. Kaliber stood above the bleeding Boar with a sinister smile glued on his face; his rifle was still smoking.

Bilmey Toags had been shot!

Currently weakened by the mighty shot, Bilmey writhed on the muddy ground. His breath was short and choppy. The taste of mud and gravel submerged in his mouth. The blood gushed from his hip; Bilmey could only watch Kaliber raise his rifle like a club as the Wolf wound up a final strike. The descent of the rifle's stock was intervened By Cap'm Thistleworts' fierce rush as he bulldozed Kaliber into the dirt, continuing to trounce him. Issuing from his massive snout, slobber ran all over the Wolf, which ruined his fancy attire. Amid Cap'm Thistleworts' tirade, Kaliber's heart raced, and his blood froze over.

"Please… Please have mercy; you clearly have the victory you deserve! Just please spare me, oh Mighty One!" Kaliber pleaded to Cap'm Thistleworts. Kaliber's fingers inched toward a large rock unnoticed By Cap'm Thistleworts.

"Tulls me why I shud dew t'at?" Inquired the old Boar.

"It would make you the most honorable adversary I have ever faced! What a magnificent skill you possess. Oh, merciful me! I yield, I yield! You certainly can't murder someone who begs for clemency!" Kaliber spawned tears. His talent for deception had always served him well, and in times when most needed, he'd spin a role so exaggerated and pathetic that not even the most ruthless of thugs could finish the Wolf off. If not for his deception, he would have surely perished long ago; from the numerous plays he had attended before his banishment, one can only guess he had picked up a knack for gaudy theatrics.

"Aye... but be wary ye aun yur crew ain't welcome in t'ese purts! Leave now, aun nevah retun!" Cap'm Thistleworts commanded as he shook Kaliber's collar.

With a twinkle in his eye, Kaliber's tearful face stretched with a vile smirk, having now obtained the large, jagged rock. The faded frown confused Cap'm Thistleworts, and just before he concluded his scattered thoughts, Kaliber struck the Horkur down with all his might, cracking his head right open, a gruesome sight, similar to the cracking of a gooey soft-boiled egg with a spoon. Cap'm Thistleworts laid on the ground, helpless. The side of his head was splotched with blood that kept squirting out, streaming down his lumpy face. Kaliber proved himself to be as proficient a thespian as he was at swordsmanship, if not better.

"You simpleton! To think I'd ever be bested by a hideous lout is to not think at all! Ah, the cleverness of me!" Kaliber boasted, striking the Boar again and again with the rock.

"Cow- Cow- Coward." Cap'm Thistleworts whimpered.

"Speak up! I can't hear you!" The depraved Wolf shouted, twisting the Boar's ear. The Boar's blood spattered across Kaliber's face.

In a quick act of desperation, Cap'm Thistleworts threw a clump of dirt at Kaliber, which rendered him momentarily blind. This provided the old Boar with ample time to rescue Bilmey and retreat with the others who already lost morale and began fleeing once the Hounds gained battle superiority.

Kaliber wiped his eyes frenetically, and once his eyes were free from the debris, he watched the Horkurs' sloshy withdraw. In a silent rage, he grabbed his rifle, loaded it, and while taking aim at the wounded Cap'm Thistleworts carrying Bilmey, he pulled the trigger. The expectation of downing the plodding Boar at long range with a single bullet was ill-fated, as the projectile misfired and exploded in his paws. Kaliber threw the rifle on the ground.

"Kill those savages at once before they escape!" Commanded the Wolf, throwing an frenetic tantrum.

The Hounds led by Captain Silas pursued Cap'm Thistlesworts, who was crossing the bridge, they were far behind the rest of the Horkurs, and the Hounds were catching up. Kusnus Utag and Gredd Chusser looked behind and descried their leader in dire danger and with fleet hooves, both raced past Cap'm and met the swarm of Hounds, staving them off. They had safeguarded their leader while giving the time needed for Cap'm Thistleworts's proper retreat. Cap'm Thistleworts turned around watching the valiant Horkurs make their last stand, as the cataclysmic billow of the ravenous Hounds smashed upon the boulderlike Boars.

"Kusnus! Gredd! Get chur arse back to da tempull!"

"Yur go on aheed boush! Weez gunna take care of dis rabble!" Gredd Chusser proclaimed.

"S'a been a rul honoor ta' serve yur, Cap'm! May we feast in Yollgikkos tugether!" Kusnus Utag added.

"Yus me boys, may wraith be yur guide to Yollgikkos! May Ivarg greet yur at the gates! Cap'm saluted and continued to retreat.

Kusnus Utag and Gredd Chusser stood tall, their gigantic forms engulfed by the mass of attacking Hounds. Both possessed titanic power, their movements reflecting their formidable strength as they fought with unwavering resilience. Together, they walloped the tide of clawing beasts with their clubs and tusks. Each swing and thrust was delivered with fierce precision, cleaving through the ranks of Hounds with brutal efficiency. Despite their valiant efforts, for every Hound that fell, another surged forward to take its place, driven by an insatiable hunger for blood.

Kusnus, a true warrior of Herculean strength, roared as he wielded his club and tusks with relentless vigor. Beside him, Gredd, equally mighty, moved with fierce determination, his powerful strikes and unyielding defense against the whirlwind of claws and teeth. The once- ma.j.estic bridge had become a grim stage of slaughter, with Hound claws lashing through the air in a relentless whirlpool of savagery. Each vicious swipe and gnashing bite served as a cruel reminder of the Horkurs' mortality. The air was thick with the smokey scent of blood and the thunderous roar of combat. Each clash, a desperate stand against the encroaching darkness.

As the battle raged on, Gredd's strength began to wane under the ceaseless assault. His form, once resilient, grew weaker as the Hounds pressed their advantage. Despite his valiant efforts, he fell amidst the carnage, his sacrifice marked by the relentless fury of the enemy. With his dying breath, he whispered, "For Ivarg," a final homage to their shared dream of Yollgikkos.

Kusnus, though fighting until the end, found himself increasingly overwhelmed. His club and tusks, symbols of his unyielding spirit, struggled to fend off the ceaseless tide of beasts. With each passing moment, the Hounds' savage assault pushed him closer to defeat. His final breaths were a poignant mix of fierce defiance and profound sorrow as he, too, declared, "For Ivarg."

The Hounds celebrated stomping over the Horkurs corpses, their sacrifice, marked by the relentless onslaught and their valiant stand as the final bastion, became a poignant reminder of their courage and commitment. Their deeds would be echoed in the halls of Yollgikkos, their bravery etched into the annals of history. Thus, the ancient bridge, now forever stained by the blood of heroes, bore silent witness to their final, sacrificial stand—a tribute to their courage and the enduring spirit of their kin.

The battle had ended, and the land was now covered in the bloody aftermath. The fresh corpses of Hounds and Horkurs alike were set aside, and the remaining Hounds licked their battle wounds. In his gleaming moment of victory, Kaliber sauntered over to the corpses of Kusnus and Gredd.

"Step aside! Step aside!" Kaliber bellowed, shoving the clustered Hounds away from the fallen Horkurs.

"Give me an axe!" the Wolf commanded a Hound, and a moment later, he was handed one. Kaliber bent down, grabbed hold of Kusnus's head, and, with a clean swipe of the axe and a disgusting crunch, severed the Horkur's head from the body. He held the Boar's head high.

"You savages! Take a close gander and see what your future holds! We will find your hiding place, and when we do, every one of you will be on a pike!" Kaliber shouted, catching the attention of Cap'm Thistleworts and his band of Boars.

"Yur shul pay dearly!" Cap'm Thistleworts retorted across Bromby River.

"Oooooooh, will I now? Ha, don't make promises you can't keep!" Kaliber laughed. With a dismissive flick, he kicked the severed head like a soccer ball, sending it soaring into the distance.

Chapter Twelve
Fox Hunt

After the Horkurs were dealt with, the next afternoon brought a raucous feast. Kaliber and his ragtag pack were gathered around a lavish spread of roasted Boar, dripping with rich, creamy sauce and accompanied by an array of sumptuous side dishes. The Kallabees had outdone themselves. Kaliber rose from his seat, brandishing a knife with a cut of meat held high.

"I cannot express how utterly superbus I am in all of you! We have crushed those swine menaces! They shall no longer be a burden!" Kaliber took a large bite and started chewing; his pleased face morphed into disgust as he realized the meat he was chewing was charred to a crisp and inedible, to say the least; he immediately spat it out, pointing to one of the Kallabees which so happened to be little bunny, Clarence.

"You dare serve me burnt trash! This is utter garbage! Poison me, shall you!?" The Wolf screamed, grabbing Clarence by his ears and lifting him high. He grabbed a whip and cracked it at the quivering Bunny. Such an act was a common occurrence during these meals, and so if any taste was inadequate to Kaliber's standards, the Kallabees would be brutally punished by a hard whip. The Wolf sat back down, disgruntled, but he was still eager for what was yet to come. In a twisted form of a dinner show, the crude bunch was thoroughly entertained by stage performers forced to engage the young Coveton with physical toiling gags on stage.

"Sophos! Sophos! Plas, Plas!" Kaliber cackled as he watched the mayhem unfold before him. The stage was a grotesque display of slapstick violence, where entertainers battered each other with increasing brutality, putting themselves in grave danger for his fleeting amusement. Each grotesque stunt seemed more desperate and painful than the last, their suffering eliciting a dark pleasure from Kaliber. As the performers twisted and contorted, their cries and thuds echoing through the room, Kaliber, wiping tears of cruel laughter from his eyes, dug into his pocket. With a dismissive flick, he tossed a few worthless trinkets onto the stage. The performers, desperate and frantic, scrambled over each other to grab the meaningless rewards, their injuries forgotten in the face of their desperation.

Kaliber took slow sips of his wine, his gaze fixed on the pitiful struggle below. The sight of their agony and desperation was a perverse source of fascination for him, and he watched with cold detachment as the performers fought for scraps, their suffering a mere spectacle for his amusement.

Captain Silas scuttled toward the Wolf and whispered in his ear. Upon the last word uttered by Silas, the Wolf spat out the wine, and with the end of his celebratory mood came the great vehement reaction. He clenched the Captain around his neck and began choking him.

"Escaped?! You jest, don't you! Please, for your sake, tell me you are!" The Wolf inquired calmly, wiping his green coat and, with a hint of nerves, erratically dabbing his face with a handkerchief.

"I'm afraid not; the Fox slipped away!"

"You dare spoil my celebration with news like this. Are you mad?" Kaliber pounded on the table.

"Tell me, do you seek mortem? Death?" Kaliber snarled, squeezing Silas's throat harder; the Hound struggled to breathe. The performers, seeing the unhinged Wolf's implosion, fled the scene. The rowdy table became dead still with the exchange of awkward stares.

"He just up well and vanished! We can't find him anywhere!" Another Hound said, who came bounding from the distance.

"Well, you better find him, or heads will roll! Curse you all, mangy mutts! Spread out and find him, and he shall suffer the consequences! Just as I praised you all for a job well done, you disappointed me and made me look a fool!" Kaliber unclenched Silas's throat. The Hound dropped to his knees and started to kiss Kaliber's feet.

"Oh, merciful Lord, thank yer for sparing me. I will not let ye down. I shall gather up everyone immediately," Captain Silas said, catching his breath. He then started to round up all the Hounds and thus began the search for Whyles.

In the quaint, cobblestone streets of Ambrodale, the tranquility was pierced by the raucous cries of the Riverfolk, whose relentless pursuit of Whyles the Fox had cast a pall of urgency over the town.

Kaliber, the sinister Wolf with a vendetta, bellowed his frustrations into the night sky. His menacing growl reverberated off of the surrounding houses.

"Agarrrh, that lowly Fox shall rue the day he slipped free! I shall cut his ears off when he's back in my grasp!" His fury was palpable as he swung his clawed paws, sending the hapless Riverfolk scattering like leaves before a thrashing gale.

Despite their valiant efforts, each lead seemed a cruel jest, ending with nothing but a dead end. The Riverfolk, their faces etched with frustration, tried to appease the enraged Wolf.

"We will find him!" they cried, their voices trembling with determination and fear.

Meanwhile, Whyles, the crafty Fox, darted through the winding pathways, his heart racing with every footfall. The frantic scurrying of the Riverfolk had forced him into a desperate gambit. In a fleeting, panicked glance, he spotted a cottage, its laundry flapping wildly on the line like frantic signals in the dark. With no time to spare, Whyles darted behind the cottage, his breath coming in ragged gasps, the weight of the moment pressing down on him with almost tangible force.

His eyes, sharp as ever, scanned the array of garments fluttering in the evening breeze. In vexation, he threw several pieces of clothing onto the ground, creating a disheveled heap of fabric. His paws rifled through the mess with increasing desperation until, at last, he spotted a potential savior: a royal violet-colored scarf, resplendent in its elegance.

With no time to savor its opulence, Whyles seized the scarf and hastily pulled it up to obscure his face. Grabbing a ragged broom, Whyles transformed into a convincing yet unlikely sweeper amidst the chaos. The Fox's quick thinking and the soft rustling of the scarf against his fur were his only allies as he prepared to blend into the bustling streets of Ambrodale, hoping the Riverfolk's sharp eyes would be fooled by his hastily adopted guise. Hastily and sloppily scuttling across the cobbles, Whyles sincerely tried to blend quickly into the mass of folks going before him in all directions; somehow, despite Whyles's inherent lifelong nervousness while dodging Kaliber, it worked.

As the mob's relentless pursuit continued, Whyles maneuvered through the streets with cautious confidence, his heart pounding with every step. The Fox's mind raced, plotting his next move while keeping a watchful eye on his would-be captors. The last glimmers of daylight faded, casting the streets of Ambrodale into a soft, dimming light. The first stars began to twinkle faintly in the sky, the air growing cooler with the coming night. In the murky twilight hours, shrouded in a purple scarf that fluttered like the wings of a ghostly moth, Whyles skulked through the shadowy lanes toward Wally's humble cottage. His steps were heavy with an earnestness, newly adopted to his nature.

The cottage, nestled at the edge of a thick wood, exuded a warmth that contrasted sharply with the chilling air. Yet, that warmth was not to be offered to Whyles, whose heart pounded against his chest as he knocked gently on the door.

From within, the soft flicker of a candle illuminated Wally. His brow furrowed as he unlatched the door, his eyes narrowing as he took in the sight of the Fox before him.

` "Wally," Whyles whispered, his voice quaking with urgency, "Kaliber doesn't know where the Horkahs temple is. It's the onla place left where yer be safe. Ye need ta come wit' me—now.

T'ere's no time ta waste."

"Another part of your tricks, 'ay? Get me to leave and throw a sack over me." Wally's gaze hardened, his lips curling into a bitter smile. "Whyles, you expect me to believe you've turned against your Master, Kaliber? You, who have thrived in his shadow? A snake does not shed its fangs."

"I swear to you, Wally," Whyles implored, his voice hoarse with sincerity, "I have changed. My actions, though unseen, have been against Kaliber. I no longer wish to serve him. I only wish to see ye and t'ose ye love safe. Give me a chance!"

"Haven't I given you enough?" Whyles was quiet.

Wally's heart was unmoved, the scars of betrayal too deep, too fresh. He shook his head slowly. "You speak of change, but words are wind, Whyles. I cannot trust you."

"But... but..."

I'd like you to leave," Wally said, dejected. He slowly began to close the door, but just before it shut, Whyles wedged his foot in the doorway.

Desperation clawed at Whyles's throat. His eyes, once gleaming with the slyness of a Fox, now shone with the earnestness of a soul unmasked. "At least tell me where Miriam is. I have something important to tell her that might change everything." He produced a small, smooth pebble from within his scarf, glistening faintly in the dim light. "She gave me this once. When hope and trust were still a currency between us."

Wally's expression softened for a fleeting moment at the sight of the pebble, but a profound sadness quickly replaced it. He turned his gaze away, pointing a trembling paw towards a distant mound, barely visible in the growing darkness.

"There." Wally said, his voice a whisper of sorrow, "'neath that mound. That's where you will find Miriam."

Whyles's breath caught in his throat. "What do you mean?" He asked, though dread already gnawed at his heart, not wanting to know the answer because he was terrified of the response.

"Ye mean?"

"Indeed, I do... Miriam perished." Wally replied, his voice breaking, "Kaliber's wrath took her, just as it will take us all. To think she ever believed in you! To think her last thoughts were wasted on hope for one as treacherous as you."

Whyles staggered, the world spinning around him as the weight of Wally's words bore down upon him. He opened his mouth to speak, to explain, but no words came, only a choking silence.

Before he could gather his wits, a chilling howl pierced the night, followed by the thunder of hands on the earth. Kaliber's Hounds had found them.

With grim efficiency, the Hounds seized Whyles and Wally, dragging them away from the cottage. The Fox's purple scarf fluttered uselessly in the wind as they were hauled to Kaliber's dungeon; the door slammed shut with a finality that echoed in the darkness, sealing their fates.

Chapter Thirteen

Stand Brave, Mr. Whyles

Whyles and Wally sat in opposite corners of the dim, musty cell, the silence between them thick with unspoken tension. His pride wounded, Wally had turned his back on Whyles, his rigid posture and stubborn silence speaking volumes. Whyles, the Fox, felt the icy barrier of discontent that had risen between them though he remained silent. The space separating them felt like an ever-widening chasm, filled with unvoiced grievances and bitter reproach.

"How could you betray us, Whyles?" Wally's voice was low, trembling with barely contained fury. "You had us all fooled with your lies and pretenses. We opened our hearts to you, and you made fools of us! The deaths of those good folk are on your shoulders."

Whyles sighed deeply, the sound thick with remorse. "I had no choice, Wally. If I hadn't complied with Kaliber's demands, he would have skinned me alive."

"That's no excuse!" Wally snapped, his voice rising. "You chose to betray us. You chose to serve him."

Whyles's face twisted with pain. "It wasn't a choice, Wally. It was survival. But there's still hope. We can free Ambrodale from Kaliber's grip. You need to trust me! Challenge him to a game he can't refuse—a game of chance."

Wally's gaze hardened. "Like Miriam? You expect me to trust you after that?"

Regret clouded Whyles's eyes. He pulled out the pebble Miriam had given him and stared at it. "I wronged her, and I'm deeply sorry. But I'm not beyond redemption, Wally. I'm trying to make amends. Who do you think sent those letters warning you about the food raids?"

"You mean…?"

"Yes, I did! With a little help from those silly Ducks. I've changed, Wally. You have to believe me—for the sake of Ambrodale, p'ease!"

Wally remained defiant. "And what can you possibly offer now?"

"Once the coast is clear," Whyles said, his voice soft but firm, "ye need to make a break for it. Head to the Horkurs Temple. T'er the only ones Kaliber fears, and he doesn't know where t'ey are. I'll create a distraction to cover yer escape."

Wally's eyes searched Whyles's face, torn between bitterness and hope. "And why should I believe you now?"

"Because," Whyles said earnestly, "I'm offering you a chance to correct me mistakes. To fight for what's right and free Ambrodale. It's not too late for redemption, Wally. Trust me, just this once."

The torchlight flickered, casting long shadows that bridged the gap of mistrust between them. Wally's gaze softened slightly, though doubt still lingered. "I think ye should have this. She'd want you to have it," Whyles said, placing Miriam's pebble next to Wally. The Hare picked it up and gripped it with mournful memories.

Whyles continued his eyes a mix of relief and sorrow. "I won't fail you.

The Fox and Hare sat in the dank, dark cell, the weight of their past choices and the faint glimmer of hope for redemption hanging heavily in the air, a silent testament to their struggle and the uncertain future that lay ahead. Whyles paced back and forth, his feet scraping on the ground so fast and hard that they left tracks in the stone. His sharp ears twitched with each creak and groan of the dungeon.

Wally, the Hare, sat huddled in a corner, his long ears drooping as despair weighed heavily on him. "Whyles, just forget it! We'll never get out of here." Wally muttered, his voice trembling.

"These walls are too thick, and there's too many Hounds." "That's it!" Whyles said, snapping his fingers.

"What is it?"

"Ah, my dear Wally, it is not the walls that shall keep us nor the Hounds that shall doom us. It is our own minds that hold the key to our escape."

Wally blinked, unsure of what his companion was suggesting. "What do you mean?"

Whyles leaned in close, his voice dropping to a conspiratorial whisper. "Just follow me lead." With a sly wink, Whyles straightened up and took a deep breath.

Before Wally could concede, Whyles lunged at him with a wild growl. The Hare, catching on to the plan, uttered a shrill scream and recoiled in mock terror. Whyles, not one to do things halfway, began to jump and thrash about, his once-cunning eyes now wide with feigned madness. He howled, squealed, and spoke in nonsensical gibberish, his tail whipping in the air.

"By the whiskers of the moon! They've trapped the stars in a jar, and the moon's made of buttah!" Whyles raved, his voice a crescendo of lunacy. "The Hares are plotting! The Hares! They'll rise and prance on our tombstones!"

Wally, playing his part to perfection, cowered in a corner, his paws covering his eyes as he wailed, "Help! Help! He's gone mad! The Fox is mad!"

The commotion quickly drew the Hounds' attention, who rushed to the cell with growls and snarls, their heavy paws clattering on the stone floor. They barked and snapped, trying to make sense of the chaos within the cell. One Hound unlocked the door and rushed in, barking orders at the others to hold the prisoners down.

Whyles, seeing his moment, redoubled his antics, flinging himself about the cell in a whirlwind of fur and noise. The Hounds struggled to contain him, their confusion mounting as the Fox's feigned madness seemed to reach new heights.

"Run, Wally! Run while you can!" Whyles screeched, his voice breaking into a series of high- pitched yelps as he twisted free from the Hounds' grasp. The momentary distraction was all Wally needed. With a swift, silent skip, the Hare darted past the distracted Hounds, slipping through the open door and into the dimly lit corridor beyond.

As Wally fled, his heart pounding in his chest, he could still hear Whyles's voice echoing down the stone hall, now a blend of manic laughter and wild howls. The Hounds, too preoccupied with subduing the Fox, did not notice the Hare's escape until it was too late.

Wally paused only once to glance back, a pang of guilt tugging at him for leaving Whyles behind. But then he remembered the Fox's final words, and with renewed determination, he bounded away, disappearing into the night.

Back in the cell, Whyles allowed himself a small, satisfied grin as the Hounds finally managed to pin him down. "A fine performance, if I do say so meself," he murmured under his breath, the madness gone from his eyes, replaced by a glint of triumph. "Run free, Wally. Run free."

"That's enough of this! Take him to Kaliber's chamber—Kaliber will deal with this madness!" commanded one of the Hounds. Dragged by his tail, Whyles clawed desperately at the stone floor, splitting his claws.

In the opulent, dimly lit chamber of the esteemed Kaliber, Whyles the Fox sat with unease. The room was a testament to grandeur, adorned with richly embroidered tapestries and furniture of the most sumptuous mahogany. Ornate candelabras flickered with soft, golden light, casting dancing shadows upon the walls. The air was thick with the scent of jasmine and polished wood, but despite the luxurious surroundings, Whyles was anything but at ease.

He paced restlessly across the plush carpet, the soft rustle of his fur barely audible. His sharp eyes, ever watchful, roved over the chamber's lavish appointments, but the grand mantelpiece held his attention.

There, mounted with a degree of solemnity that bordered on the macabre, were the prized antlers of Sampson, and at the center of the antler, the blue gem Kaliber had stolen from Father Tree.

Uncertain if Sampson was another victim of Kaliber's wrath, he fell deeper into despair.

As Whyles waited, the chamber grew colder, the warmth of the candles offering scant comfort against the chill of his mounting dread. The sense of impending doom was palpable, and he could not shake the feeling that the antlers were not merely a trophy but a harbinger of the trials yet to come.

With a deep breath, Whyles turned away from the mantelpiece, his anxiety giving way to a steely resolve. He knew he must remain vigilant and resourceful if he was to navigate the treacherous waters of Kaliber's world. As the moments ticked by with agonizing slowness, Whyles braced himself for whatever lay ahead, the grandeur of the chamber doing little to assuage his fears.

Kaliber Marcellus Coveton entered his chamber, his gait burdened and cumbersome, as though the weight of his sins clung to him with a grim tenacity, far surpassing the mere heft of his own body. The door, groaning on its ancient hinges, seemed to lament the sins it had borne witness to, mirroring the oppressive gravity that dragged him forward. As he shuffled into the dimly lit room, the flickering corridor light cast grotesque, writhing shadows upon the walls, while the medallion around his neck exuded an almost sentient malice, its weight warping his form into a hunched and distorted shape.

To Whyles, confined and observing, Kaliber appeared as a grotesque parody of his former self. The once-ma.j.estic Wolf now bore a monstrous hunch, his posture a repulsive caricature of its former elegance. His back arched in agonizing defiance of its natural curve, contorting in all the wrong places, shoulders sagging under the medallion's cruel grip. His fur, once regal, was now a patchwork of sickly, mottled stains—green and yellow blemishing its former richness. A creeping fatness now marred his once impeccable, noble appearance.

The transformation was jarring and pitiable. The Wolf who had once exuded grace and nobility was now a defiled figure, a living and breathing or rather wheezing nightmare to his excesses and corruption. Each step he took was a laborious struggle against the crushing weight of his unbridled overindulgence and the medallion's dark influence. The stark contrast between his former grandeur and his current deformed state served as a chilling reminder of the price he paid for his boundless ambition and moral decay.

"YOU? Oh, you?" Kaliber grimaced. It looked more like a twitch to Whyles.

"YOU, YOU, YOU! Well, worse foes are there than you." His voice trailed off uncharacteristically, slurring into an odd, muddled tone.

'Whyles, do you know that someone is sending out the most unusual letters about OUR plan." Kaliber declared, his words as thick as the drool sloshing from the corner of his drooped mouth. Whyles gulped involuntarily as his heart jumped. 'He has gone mad,' Whyles thought as he swallowed hard against his mounting disgust.

Kaliber looked deep into Whyles' own eyes. "Aaand at this time, of all things, my family seems to want me back. Can you believe that? Do you know all I have done these years has been an effort to rejoin them?" Whyles saw in horror that the pupils of Kaliber's eyes danced spasmodically as he glared at Whyles. The Fox braced himself. 'He knows...he knows..my doom has arrived.' Whyles felt himself sink.

Kaliber continued, 'And Whyles, they want me back veeery veeery badly. Can you imagine this?" Whyles drew in a slow breath.

"How badly do you think it might be that I return to them all?"

Whyles was silent. "HOW BADLY EXACTLY?" The wasting frame of Kaliber quaked. "I don't know" replied Whyles firmly, betraying an exasperation. 'Get this over with, old dog.' Whyles caught himself thinking.

Kaliber started to hiss his words. "Sooo badly, Dear Whyles, that this scrawled PILE OF NONSENSE HAS NOT OUR FAMILY SEAL UPON IT!"

Whyles felt a blast of emotion erupt inside him: 'The seal...the seal...' as if Whyles was trying to reconstruct his writing of the letter in his mind.

"The seal.. oh yes, the seal," Whyles sighed audibly.

"YES, THE BLASTED SEAL. DID YOU THINK I was so easy to FOOL? TWISTED

SERPENT!" Whyles could feel his own emotion of fear turn to courage. "And you, Dear Whyles, bear the ink of this failed transmission on your ragged little mitts... YOU SWINE!" Kaliber roared, gripping the Fox's paw tightly, his eyes narrowing at the sight of the ink stains.

Whyles started to laugh as one who had never known terror.

"AND NOW YOU LAUGH AT THIS TRANSGRESSION. OF MY FAITH IN YOU! Impudent

WOOORM! You swine!"

'Swine... yes, swine. let us hope.' The smile on Whyles' snout had made him seem threatening for once to Kaliber. He recoiled involuntarily.

Kaliber spoke softly now directly to Whyles. He mockingly hissed. "I was done with you the day I found you, except to mock your stupidity!" Kaliber's face yielded a frightening harlequin demeanor. "Because Dear Whyles. Stupid you are ... such you have always been…"

On scoffed Kaliber. Whyles no longer heard anything. Save one last command from the haggard Wolf.

Kaliber's grip on Whyles' paws tightened, his blistered knuckles reddening with rage. He reached for a heavy iron paperweight on the table. His eyes blazed with fury as he slammed Whyles' paws down, pressing them against the cold, unforgiving surface of the table. With a swift, brutal motion, Kaliber brought the paperweight down. The awful crunch of shattering bones echoed through the chamber, and Kaliber's smile grew wider, savoring the horrid sound.

Instead of a cry, as Kaliber yearned to hear, a deep, unsettling chuckle emerged from Whyles.

Whyles' eyes met Kaliber's with a cold, detached gleam. 'Is this supposed to break me?' The thought flitted through his mind. His laugh continued, almost mechanical, as if the pain was a distant sensation, one he could no longer truly feel.

The raw and mocking laughter echoed through the chamber, filling Kaliber with a new level of fury. He slammed the paperweight down again, harder this time, as if trying to silence the laughter by sheer force. But Whyles only laughed louder, his eyes shining with a wild, defiant light.

Kaliber's face contorted with anger, veins throbbing in his temples as he stared at the laughing Fox before him. "YOU DARE MOCK ME?!" he roared, his voice trembling with a blend of rage and disbelief. But Whyles only continued to laugh, the sound more defiant and unsettling with each passing second.

A Hound burst into the room, frantic. "Lord Kaliber, the rasbit is gones!"

"Gone?! Not this again!" Kaliber snarled, his frustration mounting. He turned his piercing gaze toward Whyles.

"You know where he's headed, don't you? Perhaps to the Horkurs temple?" "My lips are sealed," Whyles replied, his voice steady.

"You will give me the location of that rabble!"

Whyles remained quiet, peering at Kaliber with a look of amusement. Kaliber's eyes narrowed. "Do you seek death, my friend? Are you afraid of it?"

Whyles smirked. " I'm not... not anymore." He chuckled, his tone dark with satisfaction. "We shall see!" Kaliber's voice boomed, his expression darkening.

"GUARDS REMOVE HIM FROM MY SIGHT! DO WHAT YOU WILL TO HIM BUT

MAKE IT PAINFUUUL!" A bellicose laugh attended the command.

The laugh shook Whyles. As the Hound dragged the Fox away, he heard the Wolf saying, "You have no hope of ever seeing the light of day again, worthless one!"

Whyles began to laugh aloud. "Ignorant Kaliber, we shall see who really is to lose it all."

As the guards pulled him down the cold, stone corridors, Whyles whispered a verse, more to himself than to the guards:

"In the heart of darkness, where shadows dwell, Stands a Fox who knows the tolling bell.

Whyles, the name that echoes near, A Fox of courage, without fear."

The guards tightened their grip, but Whyles continued, his voice steady, defiant: "No chains could bind his spirit wild,

No threat could tame the forest's child.

And as the darkness closed its grip, He held within his heart a quip."

He paused, letting the words hang in the damp air, a testament to his resolve. The guards sneered, but Whyles felt the truth in his words, felt the strength they gave him as they dragged him toward whatever torment awaited. His final thoughts lingered on the last lines, his eyes glinting with a wildfire that not even Kaliber's wrath could extinguish:

"A Fox unbroken, wild and free, For in my laugh, there lies the key."

Whyles' laughter echoed once more, filling the cold corridors with a sound that sent shivers down the spines of those who heard it, a reminder that not all could be broken—not by Kaliber, nor by the world itself.

Chapter Fourteen

The Final Match

The dawn, bereft of sunlight, cast a serene twilight over the world, poised delicately on the brink of night. The sky, a deep, inky blue, slowly receded from the blackness of midnight. The horizon hinted at a coming change, yet the light was still absent, consuming the landscape in darkness.

Wally, his heart pounding with both excitement and trepidation, led the Horkurs through the village's winding streets. Each step echoed with the hope of deliverance and the promise of restored peace.

As they neared the village square, the imposing figure of Kaliber awaited them. He stood amid the cobblestones, surrounded by the grim facade of the nearly completed Coveton Manor, looming behind him like a dark sentinel.

"Ah, so the little hero has returned. How delightful!" Kaliber sneered, his voice ragged, each word a strained effort.

Kaliber's arrogance was perceptible as he toyed with the luxurious fur draped over his shoulders. The tail of Whyles twisted into a grotesque scarf, hung limply, its once-vibrant hues now muted by the pallor of Kaliber's triumph. Kaliber's fingers glided over the fur with deliberate mockery, casting sidelong glances at Wally with a sinister smile.

"Such a shame about your dear friend." He mused, his voice dripping with false sympathy. Each caress of the tail was a calculated taunt designed to heighten Wally's tension. The soft, silken strands served as a brutal reminder of loss. Kaliber, digging his cane into the dirt, hobbled

closer to Wally, his breath cold against Wally's cheek as he continued his malicious game.

"Tell me, how does it feel to have lost everything?" He sneered, tightening his grip on the fur as if to choke the spirit from Wally. The words hung heavy in the air, and Wally's paws clenched into fists at his sides, his cheeks flushing with anger. Kaliber's enjoyment was unmistakable, reveling in Wally's mounting rage, a predator savoring its prey.

Further compounding his repulsiveness, Kaliber's visage was further marred by his constant, involuntary drooling, which he dabbed at with his ornate belcher handkerchief, only for it to return moments later. His hunched body, a ghastly mockery of any attempt at dignity, accentuated his grotesque form and twitched sporadically, a constant reminder of the incurable itch that plagued him, gnawing at his skin with relentless irritation and momentarily alleviated by his scratching fits.

"Kaliber, we're here to end this tyranny. We've come to reclaim what is rightfully ours. Ambrodale shall be freed today!" The Horkurs are ready for battle, but enough blood has already been spilled. Instead, I propose a game of chance. Wally declared, his voice resonating with fierce resolve. Kaliber's eyes gleamed with malicious amusement. A smirk tugged at the corner of his mouth, distorted by his deformity

"Another game of Bluffers Roll, is it? You really are a fool, Hare. I've already bested you once." The Wolf croaked, his voice a blend of curiosity and contempt.

Wally shook his head, a slight smile curled on his lips. "Not quite. How about a game of Rummy? A classic woodland game!"

"Bah! Your pathetic proposal is beneath me," Kaliber sneered, his eyes narrowing.

Wally stood firmly, his gaze unwavering. "But you haven't heard the conditions. If you win, you retain control of Ambrodale without a single complaint. If I win, the deed is ours, and Ambrodale is free. It's a fair chance, and it might even entertain you."

Kaliber's smirk faltered, replaced by a thoughtful frown. He glanced at the eager faces of the Riverfolk and then at Wally and the armed Horkurs, who stood resolute despite the gravity of the situation. The challenge intrigued him, a test of his cunning rather than brute force. Kaliber's grin widened, the prospect of yet another victory feeding his arrogance.

"Rummy, you say? Very well!" Kaliber said, his voice tinged with mockery. "I shall indulge you. But know this—my victory is all but assured."

"We shall see!" Wally replied, his voice steady.

With a resounding clap, Kaliber summoned a grand table. The Hounds bore forth a lavishly ornate box, which clattered down with a most satisfying thud. With a flourish, Kaliber lifted the lid, unveiling a deck of cards that seemed imbued with mischief. These were no ordinary cards; some bore marks that whispered of victory, while others betrayed the player with the promise of loss, expertly shuffled to ensure the favor of their cunning master, Kaliber.

Before the game began, Kaliber leaned back in his chair, a sly grin creeping across his face, picking up the deck that had been lying on the table. "A little demonstration, if you don't mind," he said, his fingers already moving with unsettling speed. Without waiting for approval, he began manipulating the cards, each flick and twist of his hands revealing his unnerving expertise. He fanned the cards in a wide arc, then snapped them back together, shuffling so fast the deck blurred. In an instant, he spread the cards across the table, only to gather them up with a deft flick of his wrist, barely breaking eye contact. Kaliber's fingers danced over the deck, lifting a single card—the queen of hearts—and spinning it in the air before it disappeared as if swallowed by the shadows.

With a sudden snap, the queen reappeared, now nestled between the fingers of a startled onlooker. "A quick hand is often misjudged," Kaliber remarked, his voice smooth and teasing. His fingers never stopped moving, splitting the deck, making cards jump from one hand to the other, seemingly bending to his will.

He flipped the cards in a fan once more, but this time, as he closed them, the cards vanished completely. "Misdirection," he said, grinning. "The heart of every gamble."

With a fluid motion, he reached behind his back and revealed the deck, whole and untouched. Setting the cards back down, the Wolf's smirk widened as the audience shifted uncomfortably, unsure of what they'd just witnessed.

The Riverfolk clustered around the players with a mixture of hope and anxiety, their breaths collectively held as Kaliber shuffled the deck with unsettling calm. Every flick of his claws seemed to tighten the knot of dread in their chests, yet they watched, unable to look away.

On the other side, the Horkurs stood at the ready, bracing themselves for any underhanded tricks. Their sharp eyes darted between Kaliber's hands and the menacing Hounds nearby, knowing well that anything could tip the scales.

Kaliber, with a slight, smug adjustment of the fox tail scarf draped over his shoulders, finally dealt the cards. His movements were slow and deliberate, the corners of his lips curling into a knowing grin. Wally's cards slid across the table— marked with subtle scratches that only Kaliber could detect. They were losing cards, handed over with a flourish as if fate itself had already been decided.

"Let's see what fortune has in store for you, Hare," Kaliber murmured, his eyes glinting with malice.

The game began, and Kaliber, with a sharp smile, laid his cards down with steady hands. "Look at this, Hare!" He jeered. "I told you I was the best. You haven't a prayer!"

Wally's eyes narrowed. "I guess you haven't seen the last of our surprises!" He shot back, smirking.

As Wally drew the cards, he could feel the weight of his friends' gazes and Whyles' voice urging him forward. Every breath felt heavy, a reminder of the stakes and the trust placed in him. 'I can't let them down.' He thought, gripping the top of the deck tightly. 'Not after everything we've been through.'

Kaliber won the first few rounds with buttery ease, his hand filled with winning cards, while Wally struggled with the losing ones he had been dealt. The Riverfolk watched nervously, their hopes fading as they saw their champion faltering. Kaliber's smug satisfaction grew with each round, his taunts becoming more frequent and biting.

Wally's paws trembled as he drew his cards, his heart sinking with each betraying hand. The taunts from Kaliber pierced his resolve, making him question whether they could win. He fought to maintain his composure, even as the Riverfolk's anxiety grew palpable. Each round that slipped away made his hope seem like a distant memory. Yet, in his mind, he recalled Whyles' bravery and the sacrifices of his friends. It was their spirit that kept him fighting.

But Booney the Frog, ever observant, was ready. His Grumpappy had been a Carny, and he knew all the secret tricks. It was clear that Kaliber was rigging the game, distracting the audience with his tawdry talent. But Booney wasn't impressed, nor was he about to let Kaliber get away with it.

With every flush of a winning set, Kaliber's confidence grew as he taunted Wally.

"I am the finest at any game!" He declared, his voice echoing with derision. "You're all outmatched. I've played and won every game thrown at me. You're nothing."

Wally, despite his best efforts, found himself on the losing end. His frustration grew as Kaliber's winning streak continued, the cards always falling against him. With every flip of the card, its betrayal cut deeper than Lord Coveton's mocking. 'There has to be a way,' he thought, clenching his fists and focusing harder than ever.

As Kaliber's winning streak persisted, Booney spotted an opportunity for an intervention. One of Kaliber's Hounds accidentally spilled a pitcher of ale, causing a minor commotion. Ever the opportunist, Booney hopped to a nearby cart laden with colorful streamers, fireworks, and other festive commodities remnants from the inauguration of Kaliber's ascendancy.

"O'ley whompers! Behold these banners!" Booney exclaimed, his voice brimming with an overblown excitement. "Are they not simply splendidibibble? And these cherry crackers, skybangers, and fire whizzies—why, they're most delightful! The speckled Frog grinned mischievously as he twirled the streamers, then set off the first firework. It whizzed into the heavens with a resounding boom, bursting into a magnificent cascade of red and gold. One after another, the others followed in a dazzling chain of explosions, each more vivid than the last.

Fiery blues and greens twisted into spirals while shimmering purples and silvers blossomed like celestial flowers. Soon, the sky was ablaze with fantastical glory, the fireworks painting the darkness with a living tapestry of alluring light and color.

The Riverfolk, intrigued by Booney's sudden enthusiasm and the unexpected, mesmerizing fireworks explosion, gathered around the cart, their attention diverted from the game.

Momentarily distracted by the commotion, Kaliber and the others failed to notice Booney's swift movements. With the crowd's attention shifted, Booney deftly swapped the marked deck with a fair one he always carried for solitaire. The switch was seamless, unnoticed by Kaliber, who was too engrossed in his apparent victory to notice the change.

As the game continued, Wally's luck began to turn. The new deck dealt him with better cards, and slowly but surely, he started winning rounds. The Riverfolk's spirits lifted as they saw their champion fighting back against Kaliber's seemingly unassailable lead. Kaliber's face twisted in frustration.

"This can't be happening." The Wolf muttered, his voice cracking with anger. "I never lose…"

But lose he did. With a final, decisive move, Wally laid down a winning combination, sealing Kaliber's defeat. The square erupted in cheers, the Riverfolk celebrating their unexpected victory.

As the final card was laid down and Kaliber's defeat was sealed, a wave of relief washed over Wally. He looked out at the cheering Riverfolk, their faces alight with joy and disbelief. Wally raised his paws, a smile breaking through his exhaustion. "We did it," he said softly, his voice barely audible above the cheers. He turned to the crowd, "Ambrodale is free!"

Kaliber, however, was seized in a tempest of wrath. A volcano in the throes of eruption, he struck the table with such ferocity that the cards flew asunder. "You cheated!" He bellowed, twisted by both his deformity and uncontrollable fury. "This cannot be!"

Wally stood tall, meeting Kaliber's enraged glare with calm resolve. "A fair game, Kaliber, just as you agreed. Now, leave Ambrodale, as you promised."

Kaliber's face contorted with rage, his fingers clawing at his neck as the unbearable itch consumed him. With a furious roar, Kaliber overturned the table. His tantrum grew more violent. His face twisted in fury and pain as he kicked over chairs, threw down his bowler hat, stomped on it, and shouted incoherently. His arrogance and his refusal to accept defeat made for a strikingly dramatic and pitiable spectacle.

The Riverfolk watched, stunned by the sight of their once-feared oppressor reduced to a howling mess. Booney danced on the cart, throwing streamers into the air with jubilant abandon, his spirit ever so thankful for the teachings of his Grumpappy.

Wally, though exhausted, felt a wave of relief and triumph wash over him. The battle had been fought not with swords but with wits, courage, and a little clever trickery. As Kaliber continued his ranting and raving, the Horkurs and Riverfolk embraced in celebration, their voices rising in a triumphant chorus. The game was over, and Ambrodale was free at last. Or so they thought.

The first rays of sunlight crept over the hills, bathing the landscape in a soft, golden hue. The darkness retreated as the light spread, illuminating the dewy grass and casting long, stretching shadows that danced with the morning breeze. The hills began to glow with warmth, their contours softened by the gentle light. As the sun continued its ascent, the sky transformed into a canvas of pastel colors—pale pinks, soft oranges, and hints of lavender—heralding the arrival of a new day. The world seemed to awaken under this tender embrace of dawn, with every blade of grass and every leaf glistening as if touched by a brush dipped in liquid gold.

I lost!? No, that's impossible! I, Kaliber Marcellus Coveton the Seventh, never lose. I am the best there is—perfection itself! How could you insignificant little pests have defeated me?!" Stunned, Kaliber's gaze fixed on the sun, his disbelief reflected in its golden light. Bewildered, he snickered in a raging fury. Kaliber's decisive loss shocked him into a paralyzed stupor.

Kaliber picked up one of the cards on the ground and closely examined it; he shrieked in a raging tantrum as he checked the others.

"These aren't my cards! I only play with my deck! Where is it?"

"Looking for these?" Booney chirped in, fanning himself with Kaliber's marked cards standing on a stump.

"You sniveling thief!" Kaliber wailed, and the creatures shuddered by the high-pitched screech.

"How dare you ingrates trick me! Such insolence shall not be tolerated. I'll bring you all down groveling for misericordia you don't deserve!" Kaliber scowled and shrieked in belligerence, railing against the realization of his loss. Before any action could be taken, a strange stirring surrounded him and his gang. Animal by animal. Rodent by scuttling rodent. Insect by buzzing insect. Bird by flying bird came out from their hiding and stared at Kaliber.

"Give us the deed! The deed is ours!" they chanted in unison, their voices rising in eager anticipation.

Kaliber cocked his head, a slow, condescending smile creeping across his face. "Deed? What deed?" he asked, hissing with mock innocence. "I haven't the slightest idea what nonsense you're on about."

"We won, Kaliber! We beat you! Why it is only fair!" Wally commented as the leader.

"Fair, what's fair? You ninnies switched the deck!" Replied Kaliber snobbishly, having no such word for it.

"Give us the deed, Kaliber! If I do recall, that was the gamble, and you lost!"

Kaliber sighed deeply, rolling his eyes in a grand, exaggerated motion. "Ah, yes, the deal," he mused, his voice light and careless, as though discussing the weather. "Very well. Let it not be said that I, Kaliber, am a poor sport."

With deliberate slowness, he reached into his worn green jacket, making a grand show of it, fumbling around inside.

The crowd held their breath, eyes fixed on him as though they could will the deed into their possession.

Finally, after what felt like an eternity, Kaliber produced a battered, crumpled piece of paper, holding it up between his thumb and forefinger.

"There it is," he said, waving it lazily before them. "The precious deed. Just what you've all been waiting for."

The crowd stirred, excitement bubbling up as they leaned forward, eager to snatch it from his grasp. But Kaliber, ever the showman, held the document just out of reach, his lips twisting into a sly grin.

"Ah, but wait," he continued, his voice slow, teasing. Before I part with it... you all still want this, don't you? Of course, you do." His smirk widened, relishing their impatience.

"Enough!" Wally shouted. "Stop stalling and hand it over, Kaliber!"

Kaliber's grin widened, his eyes gleaming with malicious delight. "Oh, Wally, always so serious. Very well, I shall honor my word." He moved as though to hand the deed over, only to stop just short, a finger raised in mock consideration.

"Or... could it be," he said, his voice soft but filled with cruel amusement, "that I've made a mistake?"

The crowd murmured in confusion, their excitement quickly turning into frustration. Kaliber folded the paper once, then twice, before tucking it back into his jacket with an exaggerated sigh.

"My sincerest apologies," he said, shaking his head in mock regret. "It appears this isn't the deed at all."

The group erupted into angry shouts, but Kaliber's expression never wavered. He raised a paw to silence them, his face twisted.

"Ah, what a pity," he said, his voice thick with mockery. The sound of sloshing drool slurring his words.

"No deed, no victory. What can I say? Perhaps this is a lesson for all of you— never make deals with a Wolf."

With a final mocking bow, Kaliber turned on his heel, his pack of Hounds snickering as they followed him, tails high, leaving the group staring after them in helpless anger.

"Begone, Kaliber! Leave Ambrodale!" Wally's voice rang out, commanding and resolute. "You and your ruffians shall trouble us no longer!"

Kaliber halted mid-shamble; his pride stung as he turned slowly to face the rebellion. His eyes narrowed in disdain. "Pardon?"

"You heard me!" Wally stood tall, flanked by the Riverfolk.

"We want you and your gang out of our valley! You've turned it into a morbid wasteland!"

Kaliber's lips curled into a sneer as he polished his signet ring with a deliberate, condescending air.

"Oh, Wally, such grand ambitions from such a little Hare. Do you think this valley was ever yours? I've merely given it the refinement it always lacked. And as for leaving, let's say it would take more than your pitiful whining to make that happen. I must admit you halfwits are courageous but pathetically weak!"

The skies above darkened, echoing with distant thunder, and the ground beneath them seemed to tremble and shift. The creatures of the countryside, united in their fury, began to chant, their voices merging into a single, overwhelming force.

"Leave, Kaliber! Leave!" They cried, the chant starting as a low murmur and swelling into a deafening roar. Kaliber clutched his ears, attempting to drown out the noise. The Hounds, once ferocious, now cowered in fear, their bravado evaporating in the face of the uprising.

"You have poisoned our waters!" the creatures shouted. "Cut down our sacred tree! Shattered our peace with your greed!"

His eyes wild with rage, Kaliber bellowed over the noise, "No, no, no! How dare you disrespect me? I am perfection! I am your righteous ruler!"

"You're nothing but a cold-hearted murderer!" Wally's voice cut through the chaos, unwavering and clear.

Kaliber's fury boiled over. "Curse you all! Filthy savages! I own everything! I am your master!" "You own nothing!" Wally shouted back, defiant.

"SILENCE!" Kaliber shrieked, his voice cracking with madness.

"JUSTICE!" Wally countered, his voice a beacon of hope amidst the tumult. As the words left his mouth, Wally turned slightly to rally his friends—but it was the opening Kaliber needed. With a wicked glint in his eye, the Wolf raised his cane and struck Wally hard across the back. Wally cried out in pain, staggering forward from the blow, and collapsed from the sudden, vicious strike.

Before Kaliber could strike again, Sampson, antlerless but still formidable, rushed forward and pulled the injured Hare to safety, shielding him with his massive frame.

Just then, Cap'm Thistleworts charged forward, his club in hoof, with a thunderous roar. He swung his club with all his might, intercepting Kaliber and knocking him off balance.

Kaliber stumbled back, his hunched back and twisted form contorting awkwardly as he was taken aback by the sudden attack. A cruel smile spread across his deformed face as he quickly recovered. As Cap'm advanced, Kaliber deftly drew the sword concealed within his cane and lunged at him with a vicious thrust.

Cap'm swung his club to deflect the blow, but Kaliber's sword was too quick. The blade sliced across Cap'm's side, drawing blood. Cap'm grunted in pain; his movements momentarily slowed as he felt the sting of the wound

"You think you can best me, you swine?!" Kaliber snarled, his hunched back and deformed features radiating malice. "I am the superior! I am all that's mighty!"

With a determined growl, Cap'm ignored the pain and swung his club again, this time with a force that sent shockwaves through the air. Kaliber barely blocked the blow, but the impact was enough to send him staggering back.

Bloodied but undeterred, Cap'm stood his ground, eyes locked on the Wolf. Sensing the tide turning against him, Kaliber feigned another attack before swiftly darting to the side, aiming to wound Cap'm further. But Cap'm was ready this time. He anticipated Kaliber's move and struck Kaliber's arm with a mighty swing, causing the Wolf to drop his sword with a pained yelp.

Enraged, Kaliber whistled sharply, signaling his Hounds. Seeing Cap'm wounded, the vicious pack pounced on the ol' Boar with savage fury. They bit and clawed at him, their sharp teeth sinking into his flesh as they tried to bring him down. Cap'm fought back fiercely, swinging his club and throwing off as many Hounds as he could, but their numbers were overwhelming.

Seeing Cap'm in danger, the Horkurs, led by Bilmey, charged forward with a battle cry. They crashed into the Hounds with unbridled fury, tearing them away from Cap'm and engaging them in a fierce battle. Booney, quick and nimble, hurled stones at the Hounds. Others joined in throwing stones at their oppressors.

Midst of the revolt, Kaliber, clutching his wounded arm, retreated behind his minions, his bravado dissolving as the tide turned against him. "You shall all rue this day!" He spat with a sneer, his eyes aglow with vengeful fury. Yet, as his words fell from his lips, an inescapable spell of dizziness overcame him. Kaliber's sneer faltered, his vision dissolving into a haze. He swayed unsteadily, grasping at the ether, before collapsing to his knees. His medallion, aglow with an ominous crimson hue, began to buzz and ooze blood, each droplet hissing as it met his flesh.

Kaliber's gaze fell upon a murky puddle, and he froze, his heart sinking as his distorted reflection morphed into Clovis Kaine's malevolent countenance, the demon's eyes ablaze with an inferno of damnation. A chilling bolt coursed down his spine, paralyzing him as his breath caught in his throat. A queasy churn in his stomach mirrored the chaos around him, and each gasp a strangled plea for merciful deliverance. He shivered uncontrollably, the initial paralysis giving way to violent tremors, as if the very essence of fear had seeped into his brittle bones. The air grew thick with the stench of sulfur, and dark forms began to stir around him, alive with sinister malevolence.

The choking sensation coiled tighter, a constrictor of dread with the remorseless grip of a noose that tightened with every frantic heartbeat. Panic enveloped him, a suffocating shroud woven from the threads of his deepest nightmares, ensnaring him in a wretched reverie of his own design. As his chest splintered in agonizing protest, echoes of lost souls surrounded him— hauntingly familiar, clawing at his sanity. Shadows writhed and danced, their insidious murmurs slithering into the recesses of his disintegrating mind—a vessel for their infestation—cruel reminders of the horrors he had wrought, reverberating endlessly in the cavernous depths of his despair, a relentless symphony of dread that threatened to consume him whole.

"Creatures of Amberwood, what say you? Must you be ruled by a ruthless blaggard! Stand fellow animals. Stand for your friends, for your families, for those who had lost their lives under his murderous reign!"

Wally, now resolute and back on his feet, casted a profound sympathetic look towards Adelia. The creatures, with eyes aglow and expressions set with grim resolve, directed their steely gaze toward the Wolf and his infamous band.

"Begone Kaliber Begone!" They all continued chanting.

"Murderer, murderer, murderer!" Their voices rose in a relentless chorus that made the once- prideful Wolf tremble. The masses, who had once served and sacrificed for Kaliber's brutal pleasure, now surged forward, emboldened by the anger born of his barbaric treatment. Kaliber scrambled backward on the ground, his confidence shattered, his eyes wide with panic. His paws clawed at the dirt, leaving frantic streaks as he dragged himself away from his approaching adversaries. His once-proud attire was now caked with mud, and his legs, usually so surefooted, kicked out desperately behind him as he scooted back, his bottom scraping against the rough terrain. Each retreating motion was fueled by fear and disbelief, his face twisted in sheer terror as he realized that the power he once wielded had slipped through his fingers. As the Riverfolk closed in, Kaliber leaped to his feet and bolted, running as fast as he could with the enraged creatures hot on his heels.

The swarm of bees surged ahead of any other ferocious creature, their stings delivering sharp, searing pain that caused the Hounds and Kaliber to yelp in agony. Every inch of their bodies soon turned red and swollen, covered in welts and angry marks. Meanwhile, birds circled above, swooping down to peck and nip at their heads with vicious precision. The creatures behind them surged like a tidal wave, wave after relentless wave, all crying, "MURDERER!" As they chased the fleeing Wolf and his Hounds.

Desperately, Kaliber and his gang tried to swat away the stinging and pecking onslaught, but they were overwhelmed by the sheer number of attackers. Kaliber finally reached his plane, his paws trembling as he hurriedly turned on the ignition, casting frantic glances at the wrathful creatures closing in on him. The aircraft began to take off, but Kaliber didn't wait for his trailing gang, who were still struggling to catch up.

In a panicked frenzy, the Hounds leaped onto the moving aircraft, clinging to the wings and forming a precarious, wriggling pyramid. The sudden weight was too much for the small, single- cockpit plane. It wobbled and wavered in the air, dipping low and then jerking upward in an unsteady, erratic flight. The retreating plane slowly disappeared over the hills, its unbalanced flight marked by wild dips and sways. Even as the plane vanished from sight, the Hounds' yelps, wails, and cries echoed across the landscape.

"IT'S NOT OVER!" Kaliber shrieked, his voice carrying a final, desperate proclamation.

Once the plane and its cruel master were gone, the creatures erupted in celebration throughout Ambrodale. The tyranny of Kaliber had ended, and the Riverfolk, fueled by their newfound freedom, gathered around the wooden statue of Kaliber. With chants of victory and the sound of hammers against wood, they set about toppling the monument that had stood as a symbol of his oppressive reign. Cheers erupted as the statue crashed to the ground and splintered into pieces, and the Riverfolk danced triumphantly around the debris, their joy unbridled.

The following nights were filled with festive parties and exuberant revelry. Every corner of the village came alive with music and laughter as creatures of all kinds danced merrily in the streets, their spirits lifted by the end of a dark era.

Yet, amidst the collective cheer, Wally felt a deep sorrow. He wandered away from the jubilant crowds and made his way to the mound where the dead were buried. There, he found a group of mourners, including Adelia, with her feathers ruffled in grief. The weight of loss hung heavily between them.

"Adelia," Wally said softly as he approached her. "I thought you might be here."

Adelia, her gaze fixed on the earth that covered her sister, Miriam, nodded. "It's just so hard to believe she's gone. She was always so full of life."

Wally stood beside her, his heart aching in solidarity. "Miriam fought bravely for all of us. We owe it to her to carry her spirit forward."

Adelia glanced at him, her eyes shimmering with unshed tears. "I keep thinking about the laughter we shared and our plans. It feels so empty without her."

"We'll remember her," Wally assured, placing a comforting paw on her shoulder. "Every time we spread cheer, every moment we find strength, she'll be with us."

They stood in silence, mourning Miriam together, the sounds of distant celebration fading into the background. In that moment of shared grief, they found solace in their connection, a reminder that they were not alone, even amidst sorrow.

The burial mound lay cloaked in shadow, the moon casting a pale glow over the somber scene. With careful paws, Wally placed Miriam's speckled pebble atop the burial mound. The silence of the night seemed to deepen the gravity of the moment.

"That was her favorite pubble!" Adelia's voice trembled through the stillness, her eyes wide with the sting of sorrow. "I thought she had lost it ages ago. Wherever did you find it?"

Wally's face, illuminated only by the moon's soft light, was marked by a deep, poignant sadness.

"A friend found it," he murmured, his voice calm and laden with the weight of his grief. After a moment, he added softly, "The pebble should stay here. It belongs with her now, where it can rest in peace with the rest of her memories."

After spending some time in quiet reflection with Adelia, Wally felt a pull to return to the revelry. As he walked back to the festive scene, he noticed the distant echoes of laughter and music, but his mind was still weighed down by thoughts of Whyles and the sacrifices made. When he finally reached home, he noticed something unusual at his front door. There was a letter lying on the ground, wedged underneath it. He picked it up and unfolded it, revealing a clumsily written note filled with heartfelt admiration: "If folk were only like you, spreading cheer and strength, the world would be a better place."

As he read the letter, Wally's heart sank with a mixture of warmth and sadness. The words, though poorly written, carried a familiar tone. He suspected the letter might have been penned by Whyles, whose voice and spirit seemed to resonate with the message. It was a small, poignant reminder of the Fox's enduring presence and the kindness he had tried to show.

With a sigh, Wally folded the letter and tucked it into his pocket. As he stepped outside again, he gazed up at the night sky, where a strange sight caught his eye— a cloud slowly drifting by, taking the form of a fox with twinkling eyes. The apparition seemed to watch over him briefly before fading away with a gentle breeze.

Wally took a deep breath, reflecting on the true nature of sacrifice and loyalty. "The truest of creatures are those who sacrifice for others to remain," he whispered, his voice soft but resolute. "And those loyal never leave your side nor let go... for a friend is always a friend."

In that moment, Wally realized that though Miriam and Whyles were gone, their spirits would always live on in the laughter and love that filled Ambrodale, a testament to the bonds they had forged and the joy they had shared.

As the night wore on, the stars above twinkled with quiet brilliance, a reminder that even in the darkest of times, light would eventually emerge. With renewed purpose, Wally headed back to join his friends.

As he stepped into the heart of Ambrodale, Wally was enveloped in a rapturous tornado of joy and laughter. Creatures swirled around him, their faces aglow with happiness, the weight of the previous days seemingly lifted. But Wally's heart, though heavy, began to feel lighter, touched by the warmth of their celebration.

Amid the jubilant celebration, Wally spotted Booney the Frog, now decked out in an extravagant suit of shimmering blues and golds, laughing and chatting with everyone. Sampson, with his exuberant energy, was leading a dance that had everyone clapping and stomping in unison.

Booney caught sight of Wally and hopped over, his expression a mix of excitement and a touch of disdain.

"Wally! You finally made it back to the fun. Can you believe it? Kaliber's statue is down, and we're having a blast. As for Whyles—well, I guess he's out of the picture. Never cared much for him anyway. T'a less we t'ink about him, tha' better."

Wally managed a weary smile, feeling a bit of warmth from Booney's enthusiasm despite the speckled Frog's cavalier attitude. "It's been a somber day, but yes, we're celebrating." Booney's eyes twinkled with mischief. "Miriam will surely be missed. As for Whyles, well, he neva munt much ta' me. If'n you askin' me that no good Fox had it comin', soona t'an later! What's important now is that we keep moving forward and enjoy ourselves!

Sampson joined the conversation with a grin. "Booney's right. Let's not let the past weigh us down. We've earned this moment. A party for the ages is what we need!"

The night's festivities reached their zenith as the Riverfolk continued to celebrate their freedom. In a final act of triumph, they gathered around the now-toppled wooden statue of Kaliber. With cheers and laughter, they smashed the remnants of the statue, turning it into kindling and tossing the splinters into a bonfire. The blaze danced with the same fervor as the villagers, consuming the last vestiges of Kaliber's rule and lighting up the night sky with a warm, flickering glow.

As the night deepened, the laughter and music grew louder, echoing through the village like a vibrant heartbeat. In the eyes of his friends, Wally saw not just the celebration of their freedom but a shared commitment to carry on the legacies of those they had lost.

They were all intertwined in this tapestry of life, love, and loss, each thread vibrant with stories yet to be told. With that thought, Wally twirled with a smile, the letter in his pocket and the warmth of his friends surrounding him. The festivities carried on, a testament to resilience and the enduring light of friendship, a promise that they would always remember and always celebrate.

RiverFolk Revel

Where moonlight casts its silver lace, The Riverfolk, in boundless bliss, Awake the night with merry grace.

With laughter's sound and music's call, On flutes and lutes, their voices soothe. In bonds of kin, they stand tall,

Their hearts aglow, their spirits bright. From ancient lore and tales of yore,

Their songs take flight on evening's breath. With every note, their spirits swept,

With boundless joy, they seek the best. The feast of joy, a pure delight,

Unites their souls in harmony.

The stars alight, their hearts shine-free, For in the stillness of the night,

Their legacy shall ever gleam. A beacon of the purest light,

To guide the weary through their dream.

Epilogue:
A Dawning Age

The time had, alas, finally arrived, much to the sorrow of all. Cap'm Thistleworts, once a mighty force to be reckoned with, had succumbed to the ravages of time, his age advancing far too swiftly for his liking. Despite his obstinate will, the Cap'm could no longer command his clan of Horkurs with the vigor of his youth. Though his spirit remained fiery and undaunted, his body betrayed him—his strength waning, his once sharp faculties dulled by the inevitable march of years. His hearing, once keen, had dulled; his memory, once sharp, flickered like a dying flame; his vision, once clear, had dimmed, and his once tireless mind wearied with each passing day.

Yet, despite such undeniable truths, the Cap'm refused to relinquish his hard-won mantle without a fight. He would not simply step down; he demanded an open challenge to any Boar bold enough to test their mettle against his formidable strength. Only one who could best him in this arena of brute force would be deemed worthy to succeed him.

The dirt ring was set, and a line of eager, brawny Horkurs stood ready, each impatient for their chance to dethrone the old Cap'm. As the Vuggahorn sounded, the first contender entered the ring, the crowd buzzing with anticipation. Cap'm Thistleworts, remembering the days of his own youth and brashness, braced himself for the coming clash.

The two Boars charged at one another, their grunts echoing through the air as they collided with a resounding boom. They locked their brawny arms, each trying to force the other off balance and out of the earthen ring. The struggle was fierce, the wear and tear of battle evident on their straining bodies. But just as it seemed the younger Boar might gain the upper hand, the Cap'm, summoning the last of his reserves, executed a masterful hip throw, sending his opponent tumbling out of the ring. The crowd erupted in cheers as Cap'm Thistleworts emerged victorious, stamping in triumph.

One by one, the contenders stepped into the ring, and one by one, they were tossed out by the Cap'm's still-formidable strength. A massive line of defeated Horkurs Cap'm tossed them out to form, their dreams of leadership shattered by the indomitable Cap'm Thistleworts. The old Boar, amused by their futile efforts, taunted the vanquished with a brazen guffaw, praising his own might with every victory.

"Is there no one in this pitiful rabble who can best an old, blind Boar?" He bellowed, his voice dripping with disdain.

Finally, only one challenger remained: Bilmey Toags, the most promising of the Horkurs. Bilmey had been biding his time, watching as the Cap'm exhausted himself against the other contenders. Now, with the Cap'm visibly tired, Bilmey stepped forward.

"Aye, Bilmey," the Cap'm sneered, "ye've got a fine look about ye, but what makes ye think yer fit to lead this tribe? What makes ye special?"

"Ye are wise, Cap'm, but with that wisdom comes recklessness," Bilmey replied. "Yer bold, but yer old and bound to tire. I am Bilmey Toags, the one who shall gift ye yer retirement!"

"Bold words, Bilmey," the Cap'm growled. "But today ain't the day I give up me throne!"

"We shall see!" Bilmey grunted, stepping into the ring. The crowd hushed, all eyes on the two Boars as they prepared for the showdown. Bets were placed, teeth pulled from their maws as wagers. The tension was palpable as Bilmey and the Cap'm locked eyes, mimicking the other's every move. Then, with feline intensity, Bilmey sprang forward, but the Cap'm, with surprising agility, dodged the rush and tackled Bilmey to the ground, grappling him into a crushing headlock.

The struggle was surreal, the two Boars straining against one another with every ounce of their strength. But Bilmey, with his extreme power and girth, broke free of the Cap'm's grip— something no one had done before. Once again, they locked in combat, their battle-scarred bodies straining for dominance. They broke off briefly to regain their stamina, eyes locked in a deadly game of wills. But the Cap'm, his temper flaring, began to beat his chest and scream aloud, his rage fueling a final, desperate charge. Bilmey braced himself, planting his hooves firmly in the dirt, ready for the impact. The two Boars collided with the force of a train hitting a bull, the ground shaking beneath them. The Cap'm's rush was unmatched, but Bilmey, though nearly overwhelmed, managed to hold his ground. The two Horkurs strained against one another, their massive bodies teetering on the edge of the ring.

For a moment, it seemed the Cap'm might lose heart, the watching Horkurs unsure who would emerge victorious. The Cap'm, bewildered by the thought of being outmatched by the last challenger, fought on with a mix of pride and shame.

In a final, desperate bid for victory, the Cap'm resorted to a foul move, slashing Bilmey's right eye with his broken tusk. Blood poured from Bilmey's eye as he shrieked in pain, stumbling to his knees. "If ye want to be the leader of this clan, ye need the mark of a wun!" The Cap'm taunted, pummeling the blinded Bilmey.

But just when it seemed all was lost, Bilmey, fueled by the chaos and pain, found a surge of power within him. He broke free of the Cap'm's grasp, his strength astonishing the old Boar.

"Yer time is up, Cap'm. I am the one to lead the tribe now!" Bilmey proclaimed, lifting the Cap'm and hurling him out of the ring.

As the dust settled, Cap'm Thistleworts lay outside the ring, contemplating the match with a mix of bitterness and acceptance. Admitting his defeat, mortified by the outcome, the old Boar grudgingly handed over the cherished Vuggahorn to Bilmey Toags, the badge of leadership.

With a mighty and triumphant blast of the horn, the Horkurs rejoiced, welcoming their new leader, Bilmey Toags, who would usher their clan into a new age.

∽

Booney's Farewell

A cold and cloudy Sunday morning came, drizzling drops of rain pitter and pattered onto the wet, soft ground pat, pat, pattering. Leftover trickling's thrumming on roofs and the rhythmic drumming tapping, tapitty tapitty tap! The windows, all around the fire-lit, dark country homes spread. Booney's leaky log cottage was now empty, bare, and stripped of any silverware: pots and plates, kettles, and muffin tins for cakes and bakes. The cupboard, dull and unpolished, had nothing but dust, stringy cobwebs, and smudges from his past cooking disasters (while it was well-intentioned, his cooking left a lot to be desired. It was usually poorly rushed in preparation or caught ablaze from overcooking, and it contained questionable ingredients and seasonings.) Yet, many happy, merry memories lingered of warm Sunday meals with his friends as he often entertained them with his fiddle playing. The furniture, with its worn red velvet upholstery, recalled many late midnight musings alone and cordial afternoon teas with fine golden Darjeeling lightly steeped in his fine china. His furniture was now packed in the corner and carefully tied with rope and oilcloth for safekeeping. Quietly humming to himself, Booney stood ready in front of his yellow door. All packed now, he looked for any last remaining possessions that had not been already seen or taken. He strapped the giant oilcloth valise onto his now prostrated back, which was unbalanced by the jam-packed, unzipped backpack. His fishing pole stuck out, and even a grandfather clock (it was rather hard to believe and how he jammed it in only he had to know), as well as the rest of his cozy comforts. He had almost stumbled over several times due to his lank, feeble, shaking legs that looked like he was doing the jig! With hops and twirls, he rapidly spun in dizzying circles. Wobbling, teetering, and fumbling, he had to catch himself from falling while grabbing ahold of any stable object he could find just before he might tip.

Leaning on a rack, he mustered all the strength he could against the struggling odds and was once again back on his feet; awkwardly bent and squatted, he adjusted the heavy burden of the weight as he righted himself, little doohickeys, doodads, gadgets, and trinkets plopped, plop, plop, plop onto the red carpet floor, cracking and snapping upon the impact. Click, clack, crackle.

As anticipated, though having no free hands, he decided to leave them there in little broken heaps. Scanning a tattered map he tightly held, he opened his log door. Indeed, this renowned, quaint little valley became much too little and much too famous and drastically tedious for his own adventurous spirit likings.

After the story of Kaliber's defeat reached far and wide in a short time, Wally grew into a heroic legend, and his stature continued to grow! There was no reason for Boone to stay any longer. His time in Amberwood was indeed very well spent, but everything comes to an end eventually, he told himself. He could no longer hold back his yearning for a new thrill. Booney had 'new places

to travel.' And 'bright adventures to seek.' He proudly boasted in a false smile when approached by Sampson and Wally. They had come to see what all the commotion was about. He had, as he put it, "overstayed his welcome a bit too much to his liking."

Though Wally and Sampson tried to convince the stubborn speckled Frog to stay, alas, their reasons given for staying were futile compared to what plans Booney had already made in his mind.

"Dear friends, please do not heave in such gloom and sorrow," he said sympathetically now as he nibbled on a piece of a sweet apple fritter he pulled from his pocket.

"I do thank you for all your kind consideration for me to stay! But truth be said, there's an ongoing road calling me astray right before me! Where it leads, I will explore and follow. You see, me good friends, I'm not a one to let an adventure slip by... tis awaiting lands far, unknown to be in a search of, and I must seek them! With their dawning's beauty beckons!"

Booney started to cry, though trying to hold back the tears, he could not. For once, the first tear broke free and ran across; the rest followed in an unbroken, uncontrollable stream and seemed to spread to the others.

In an unbreakable bond of heartwarming and loving friendship, they were forever bonded, and in no possible way, none whatsoever, could it and would it be broken. Booney's watery eyes shuttered. His webbed hands turned cold and clammy from the nervousness of moving on.

"I will never, never, ever forget you, me friends, me companions, me family, and the many merry parties and festivals we have shared over the many, many, many nights. Nor forget the danger we 'as faced ta'gether!"

"Well, Boone, we sure will miss you!" Wally sadly professed he trembled with deep regret. With teary eyes, he did not want Boone, such a close and dear friend to whom he would call family, to leave. Even Sampson, who cried the most out of the three, admitted the same.

"Oh bother… I won't have anyone to teach to! Boone, you were my only student to teach and a fine one at thut…" Sampson proudly boasted, commending Booney but in a saddened moan. In his grievance, he wiped his snuffling, wet nose and cleared his misty eyes.

"You don't really have to leave, my dear friend; we still have plenty to do!" Wally exclaimed in sudden excitement, though Booney kindly denied the prospect. "Alas not, I'm afraid I turned over every nook and cranny here, tis time to turn over much more beyond what I can see!"

The trio of teary-eyed friends gathered in a circle. Embracing them, Sampson lifted both of them! Unperturbably, they locked arms around themselves. Booney and Wally were brought down with a strong squeeze of a hug. Slumping down, the ol' mumbling Moose once again gracelessly sat on the ground with a loud thud.

"Well, I should be off… Cheers, me, dear chaps! May ye have good, fine, fine, rich meals served on your plate and fine, fine red wine poured in your glasses, and shall ye never hunger!"

Booney wished them well and gave them both small trinkets from his pockets. "Something to remember me by."

"Even without this, how could we eva' forget such a stubborn Frog like yourself, Boone!?" Wally said with a doleful expression. The Frog grinned cheekily and began his new adventure, whistling a tune reminiscent of the one he sang on those lazy days on Bromby River; the lighthearted speckled Frog lifted his over-packed oilcloth knapsack valise behind his back.

His many belongings dangled loosely, clattering together in a merry jumble of jingles and jangles. Teetering for a moment, he finally marched on, slow but steady. A few of his rattling items slipped free, falling along the path and trailing behind the jostling Frog. As he followed the winding road ahead, he waved back, offering a warm, heartfelt smile to his heavy-hearted friends, who still wept, crestfallen, behind him. They remained close by his sod-roofed log, now abandoned yet blooming with the fragrant seasonal flowers and herbs Booney had so dearly loved.

The breaking golden light of the sun arose from the cloudy, murky sky above... Booney the speckled Frog was off for another of his unbelievable adventures... or maybe... two...

Traveling Song/ A Friend's Farewell

To the opening sky, I take my leave,

Where moon and twinkling stars weave,

The ground below, a path unsealed,

Across the desolate hill and fen revealed.

Oh, they pass me by, these shadowed lands,

Foot by foot, where my journey spans.

Trail by trail to Horizons Gold,

I voyage forth, my tale untold.

Alone again, I tread once more,

Seeking the hearth, the humble door.

O'er hill and vale, a sign I'll find.

Before the breaking of the morning's bind.

THE END

About the Author

Avi Albert is an author whose writing is deeply rooted in personal experience and an unwavering love for storytelling. Born with cerebral palsy, Avi faced a childhood often overshadowed by physical limitations and the isolation that came with being bedridden for extended periods. While other children were outside playing, Avi was confined to his room,- navigating a world that often made him feel invisible. Yet, within the confines of his imagination, a vast universe unfolded, full of adventure, wonder, and possibilities beyond the constraints of his body.

From an early age, Avi discovered the power of storytelling as a means of escape. What began as a simple pastime grew into a passion that would shape his life. In elementary school, he began sharing his stories with classmates and teachers, reading aloud and learning how to weave emotion and depth into his characters. These early moments of connection were transformative, helping Avi develop not just as a writer, but as a person who had something important to say. The stories that filled his notebooks weren't just fantasies—they were his voice, his way of engaging with the world beyond his physical limitations.

Avi's experiences with writing went far beyond the classroom. They were his lifeline to a world where he was not defined by his disability, but by the richness of his imagination and the stories he could create. Writing became his means of asserting himself, of connecting with people and

places that were otherwise out of reach. Over the years, Avi honed his craft, drawing on his unique perspective and experiences to create narratives that explore emotion, resilience, and the power of hope.

Today, Avi Albert crafts stories that transport readers into new worlds, offering them the same sense of escape, wonder, and belonging that storytelling provided him during his childhood.

Each word he writes is an invitation to step into a universe where anything is possible, and every character is a reflection of his journey. Through his stories, Avi hopes to inspire others who may feel marginalized or misunderstood, showing them that no matter the obstacles, there is always a way to find your voice and share your story with the world.

A Fox Song was conceived in 2014, during a time when Avi Albert was forced to leave high school due to illness. Struggling with long months spent bedridden and burdened by depression, he felt increasingly disconnected from the world around him, as it seemed to move on without him. Isolated and overwhelmed by emotions he couldn't yet understand, Avi turned to writing as a refuge.

The story of a fox tormented by his own conscience—plagued by paranoia and eccentricity—emerged from Avi's own emotional turmoil. This fox, grappling with guilt and self-doubt, reflected the chaos in Avi's mind during this dark period. As Avi poured himself into the fox's journey, the narrative became a powerful means of confronting the pain and confusion he struggled to articulate.

What began as a way to cope with the weight of his emotions evolved into a decade-long journey. For ten years, Avi worked tirelessly on A Fox Song, refining the story and imbuing it with layers of meaning and emotion. The process was not just about crafting a narrative—it was about healing, confronting his inner demons, and coming to terms with his own sense of self.

A Fox Song became more than just a story—it was a lifeline, an outlet for the pain Avi couldn't voice and a testament to his resilience. Over the course of a decade, the project grew from a personal expression into a fully realized narrative, giving Avi a way to process and understand the emotions that had once consumed him. The creation of the story not only marked a personal breakthrough but also solidified his passion for writing, something that would continue to shape his life for years to come

www.ingramcontent.com/pod-product-compliance
Lightning Source LLC
Chambersburg PA
CBHW070319030726
47505CB00004B/1027